THE SAILOR'S WIFE

THE
SAILOR'S WIFE

HELEN
BENEDICT

A NOVEL

Z

ZOLAND BOOKS
Cambridge, Massachusetts

First edition published in 2000 by
Zoland Books, Inc.
384 Huron Avenue
Cambridge, Massachusetts 02138

FIRST EDITION

Book Design by Boskydell Studio
Printed in the United States of America

06 05 04 03 02 01 00   8 7 6 5 4 3 2 1

This book is printed on acid-free paper, and its binding materials
have been chosen for strength and durability.

Library of Congress Cataloging-in-Publication Data
Benedict, Helen.
The sailor's wife : a novel / Helen Benedict.—1st ed.
p. cm.
ISBN 1-58195-024-1
1. Americans — Greece — Fiction. 2. Parents-in-law — Fiction.
3. Married women — Fiction. 4. Greece — Fiction. I. Title.

PS3552.E5397 S25 2000
813'.54—DC21   00-033444

To Emma, Simon, and Steve,
and to Nicola Sharp (1954–1982),
in memoriam

AUTHOR'S NOTE

Those who know Greece will recognize that Ifestia bears many similarities to the island of Lemnos. The mythological history of the island is indeed taken from that of Lemnos, as are much of the physical description and all of the place names. The island of Ifestia, nevertheless, is a fictional compilation of several different areas of Greece.

My accounts of events and experiences during the Second World War, the Civil War of 1945–1949 and the Colonel's Junta of 1967–1974 are based on historical sources and interviews. Janet Hart's *Women in Greek Society*, Anna Collard's *The Experience of Civil War in the Mountain Villages of Central Greece*, and C. M. Woodhouse's *The Struggle for Greece* were particularly useful.

I also want to thank those who gave so much of their time to help and encourage me with this book: Steve O'Connor, Bob Klitzman, Myra Goldberg, Joan Silber, Becky Stowe, and my silver friend, the lizard.

H. B., 2000

"I think only people who want to be free are human beings. Women don't want to be free. Well, is a woman a human being?

— NIKOS KAZANTZAKIS, *Zorba the Greek*

PROLOGUE

At night she dreams of supermarkets. Florida supermarkets. Aisles and aisles of boxes and cans. Things she had always taken for granted, not even particularly liked. Muzak. Tubs of cookies. Soda water. Colors like pale mint green and neon pink.

Every morning at dawn her mother-in-law awakens her by thumping on the ceiling with a stick. "Get up, lazy!" she shouts in Greek. Her mother-in-law speaks no English.

Here, nobody does.

It was in a supermarket that she met him. By the cornflakes. He backed around a corner, lost, holding a piece of paper and looking up at the aisle numbers in confusion, sleek in the dazzling white of his sailor's uniform.

She had never seen anyone so beautiful. When he turned to ask for help, she was unable to speak. She felt herself grow ungainly and plain in his presence, like a plant deprived of light.

Now at dawn three times a week, she gets up to load the donkey and lead him to market. Like most people on the island, her in-laws own no car, although it is 1975. Her job is to sell the herbs, melons, potatoes, and sesame seeds that her in-laws grow on their rocky patch of land. If she sells well, she is allowed goat's milk and bread at bedtime. If she sells badly, the family will fast.

While she is at market she must on no account look at the soldiers. The island of Ifestia is overrun with them, hordes of teenaged boys barracked in every hotel and spare room in the place. Greece and Turkey have been bickering over Ifestia for centuries, so the Greeks keep it packed with soldiers. Just in case.

If Joyce is caught raising her eyes to a soldier or to any strange man, her mother-in-law says, she will be beaten and turned penniless out on the street.

In the supermarket, he came up to her in the aisle, slim and graceful in that lithe, unconscious way of young men. A cluster of black curls fell over his forehead. He looked at her with great wide eyes, a golden amber ringed with dark lashes. His face was delicate, cheekbones sharp, lips a bitten red. His skin was browned from the sea, but smooth, smooth as syrup.

"'Scuse me," he said, his voice low and uncertain. "I no speak English."

Joyce thrust her breasts forward. She couldn't help it. They weren't much but they were there. She also tossed back her long, blond American hair, bleached to a frosty platinum only last week. She even had time to wonder whether she had put on her shimmering pink lipstick.

"Let me help," she said, reaching out her polished fingernails to take his piece of paper. Back in Florida, Joyce was the kind of girl who polished her nails and bleached her hair. She read true romance magazines, too, and spent long hours dreaming about a love that would rise and swell like the crescendo of an orchestra. None of it prepared her for this.

Her fingernails are broken off now. The palms of her hands stained and callused.

*   *   *

"It says oatmeal. You want oatmeal?"

The boy shrugged. He obviously had no idea what she was saying. She led him to the right spot in the aisle. "Instant or regular?"

"Yes," he said, and laughed. His teeth were white but crooked, his only flaw. He was taller than she by a head and a half. His hips, snug in his uniform, looked taut and promising, his shoulders broad. She slipped off her denim jacket, worn only for the air-conditioning, and tossed it into her shopping cart. Underneath she had on a skimpy yellow shirt and a miniskirt. On her feet were thin white sandals, showing off her pink toenails.

He looked her over. His gaze was like a caress.

Joyce was still a virgin. Eighteen and still intact. When she felt him look at her like that, she knew, with a certainty she had never felt before, that she did not want to be a virgin any longer.

Now he is her husband and he is hundreds of miles away over the sea.

PART ONE

I

festia sat in the middle of the North Aegean, isolated like a raft in a bay. The western half of the island, where Joyce lived, was the unlucky half: dry and treeless, rocky, its earth the color of sand, its scrub silvery and timid against the solid blue of the sky. Few tourists visited Ifestia, for it lacked the drama of the islands Lesbos and Thasos nearby, and it was constantly overrun by bored, restive soldiers.

The island was also poor. The peasants of Ifestia had to struggle like peasants everywhere, but on the western side they were helped by neither fertile soil nor natural ponds. Their goats were more suited to the land than they. Joyce's mother-in-law had worked so hard all her life that she'd never had the leisure to learn to read. Both she and her husband told time by the sun. They looked like shriveled prunes, but their muscles were as dense and knotted as wood.

In 1975, by the time Joyce had spent two years getting used to life on the island, more soldiers than ever came and drove away the few remaining tourists she liked to seek in town for company. They drove away the Germans, who shouted commands and never said thank you; the English, who drank too much and burned themselves a lobster red in the sun; the rare Americans, who gawked at Joyce when she spoke and begged her to find them bargains in the market. And they brought instead playfulness and lust and dark, quick eyes waiting to catch her like nets. They brought young male bodies, gleaming hair, laughter, carelessness — everything she had relinquished.

Joyce stood in the marketplace one summer morning, selling the week's produce from her in-law's farm. She had grown thinner during her time in Greece, her once soft limbs now sinewy and hard. Her family in Florida would barely recognize her. Her skin, unprotected by lotions, had deepened to a honey brown. Her hair, long since grown out of its bleach, was tied back in a dark golden knot. Her green eyes looked paler than they used to against her new complexion; sage in the sunlight, olive in the shadows, giving her narrow face a look of feline secretiveness. Her lips, unadorned by cosmetics, were thin and delicate. But her legs glinted with long, blond hairs, and her hands and feet were scraped and cracked and seamed with dirt. Her dress — her mother-in-law never let her wear trousers — was a shapeless pink, faded and stained. On her left hand, her wedding ring had grown dull with neglect.

She was selling eggs and the oil and seeds from her in-law's precious sesame plants. She also sold spinach, dark and crisp. Basil, lentils, and beetroot that ran red as a wound. Beans, pungent marjoram, globes of perky garlic. Little red potatoes, sweet as plums. She sold from a rickety stall in the small market square, and she had learned to drive a hard bargain.

"For you, *Kyria* Fakinou, I will throw in an extra egg, but only if you buy my garlic here. It is the sweetest in the market, watered by my mother-in-law's own sweat and tears. Yes, and my eggs are three centimeters bigger than any others — you bring a measuring tape and see!"

The townspeople liked to buy from Joyce. They found her American malapropisms amusing as she wrangled with them in Greek. They liked to gaze at her hair, which she often forgot to hide under a scarf, as a proper young woman should. The old teased her about being a rich *Amerikeedah* who had come to live like a peasant. The young matched their wits against hers to see if they could outdo this upstart Yank. Joyce relished all this. It made her laugh with triumph, with pride. With affection.

She sold from dawn until almost noon. Then, when the market was emptied, the sun high and strong, and her voice raw from calling out her wares, she strapped the wicker baskets onto her donkey and headed home for the remainder of the day's chores.

"Hey, little mama, you go home already?"

It was one of the soldiers. They taunted her every day in pidgin English or saucy Greek. She turned her back on him and steered the donkey out of the market square, frowning. Her only protections were Greek curses, her married status, and spitting. Yet sometimes she longed to kick the donkey away, undo her hair, and dance into the soldiers' arms. Nikos, her husband, had been away this time for seven months, the last time for almost five. He had deflowered her, given her a taste for it, kissed her, and fled. Left her gasping like a fish on a bank. In between he wrote her long, steamy letters in broken English that made her toss in the night, her fingers between her legs, hoping her in-laws on the other side of the wall could not hear her panting.

"Come with me, baby. I lick you all over."

The men hissed in her ear.

The vegetables sold badly that morning — there was too much competition at that time of year — and as Joyce walked the donkey home, she worried about her in-laws' reaction. They lived hand to mouth, every bad market day a strain, every quirk of weather a potential tragedy. She had learned this on only her fifth night in the house. Lying wet and sweating in Nikos's arms, her thighs streaked with semen, she had been awoken by the shouts of his mother. A windstorm had risen from the sea and swept all the sesame seed capsules off the plants just a day before the harvest. Her father-in-law lit a kerosene lamp and plunged out into the storm, his wife shouting at Nikos and Joyce to join him. They ran from plant to plant in the darkness and rain, scrabbling at the ground for the capsules, praying they had not burst open and scattered their precious contents to the wind. But it was useless. The most valuable crop of the year, destroyed in an hour.

That had been before Joyce knew Greek, when she and Nikos could barely speak to one another, only touch.

The first time Nikos had left was only six days after he had brought her home. "I back soon," he'd promised, then disappeared for five months. He was a merchant marine, working for Greece's great glory, its shipping magnates. The ships went tramping, as the Greeks called it, all over the world. Instead of following set routes like other shipping companies, they took one-time trips anywhere that paid. "I go only Spain," Nikos had assured Joyce. "I come home and bring back much money." His mother, Dimitra, had laughed approvingly and rubbed her fingers together. No one had told Joyce that was how it would always be.

For weeks after Nikos had left that first time, Joyce lay in her bed each night, aching with exhaustion and loneliness. After she'd overcome her fear of bats, she would leave her wooden shutters open so that she could see the night sky through her window; and the boundaries of her life, of the room around her, the bed beneath her would seem no more solid than the ceiling of the Milky Way. Where am I? she would find herself wondering. How did I get here? Who knows me? She had felt herself floating loose, drifting on the edge of a void, tethered only by the thin, tenuous strand of Nikos's love.

Joyce led the donkey, a tired old male called Phoebus, through the dusty fields to her in-laws' house. They lived above Kastron, the main port on the western coast, up a hill of treeless volcanic rock. As she left behind the cluster of whitewashed stone houses, their walls blinding in the sun, their umber roofs dulled in its glare, the heat seemed only to increase. It breathed down on her, cooking the pale yellow dust beneath her feet as it cooked her hair, her flesh, her thoughts. Around her, the grass was scrubby but fragrant with herbs: oregano, oleander, sage, mint, thyme. The only sounds were the clop of the donkey's feet, the rasping of cicadas, and the creak and rustle of the baskets on Phoebus's back. His hooves scuffed up the dry earth, making Joyce cough.

Joyce was dizzy from lack of food. It was August and the people of the village were fasting for the Assumption of the Blessed Virgin. They could eat nothing that symbolized Jesus Christ, so could have no product from the olive, upon which they usually depended. No fish, either, no lamb, no sheep's cheese, no wine. For nearly two weeks she and her in-laws had lived on watermelon, potatoes, and bean soup; not enough, for Joyce at least, to sustain her constant labor. At the end of the fast, however, Petros, her father-in-law, had promised, they would catch a boat to the neighboring island of Lesbos, hitch-hike to the mountaintop, and feast for three days.

Joyce tethered Phoebus to his post and stumbled through the back door of the squat stone house, scattering the chickens and hideous guinea fowl that ran at her feet. Inside the white-plastered walls, the shade soothed her like satin. She threw herself on the Turkish pillows piled in a corner. As her sweat dried she felt the dust form a gritty seal over her skin.

"Any good today, little one?" Dimitra said, entering the house. She, too, in her blue sack of a dress and bare feet, looked layered in dust. She was carrying a huge earthenware jug from the well. They had no running water.

"No good, Mama, I'm sorry," Joyce replied. She handed over the meager purse of drachmas. "Alexis was there with his crops — he had three times as much as ours. He cut the prices. And people aren't buying much because of the fast."

Dimitra frowned but said nothing. She heaved the jug up on the rough wooden shelf that served as a kitchen counter. Although Dimitra was sixty-four, the sun and work had made her look eighty. The skin on her heavy, square face was as cracked as dry earth, caving in at the mouth, where she had lost several of her bottom teeth. Her once wide almond eyes were dim and hooded. Her hair was now a steel gray, braided and circled about her head like a crown. But her back was upright, her heavy bosom proud. She was as strong as any man.

"And the eggs?"

"The eggs I sold. And the potatoes. The money is there. Can I wash, Mama? I feel dizzy with the heat."

"Go wash. No soap on your feet!"

Dimitra said this to her every day, barking it in her gruff, rasping voice. Soap on the feet makes a young girl infertile, she told Joyce over and over. Joyce laughed to herself as she splashed water on her legs at the outside pump. How am I going to get pregnant with Nikos across the sea? What does Dimitra expect, immaculate conception?

In the supermarket, Nikos had followed her as she filled her shopping cart. He had mimed questions to her, compliments. "*Amerikeedah* pretty," he'd kept saying, the only phrase she had understood. But his teasing eyes, his strong, tanned limbs — she understood those. He paid for his oatmeal and followed her outside to her car, where he stood clutching his shopping bag and looking bewildered.

"Are you lost?" she said hopefully.

He frowned. "I walk here. Far." He lifted his shoulders in a shrug.

She invited him home "My mama and papa will help you," she said, figuring those were universal words.

"Mama good, yes?" he replied and went with her without protest, as if he had planned it all along.

Her parents welcomed him with surprised curiosity, while

she explained that he seemed to have wandered away from his shipmates. They were used to seeing sailors in Miami, although they had never had one to the house before — the sailors usually stayed around the bars and clubs in South Beach. Nevertheless, they took pity on him and invited him to a barbecue out in the yard. Her father flipped patties, her mother served drinks. Joyce's two elder brothers, meaty and blond, snickered uneasily at Nikos and refused to take their eyes off the living room television.

"Where did you say you're from?" Joyce's mother asked eventually, her smile oozing like her hamburger.

"*Ehlenekoss.*" He patted his chest. "*Amerikeedah,*" and he pointed to her.

"What in God's name is the man saying?" Joyce's mother murmured.

"He's Greek, Mom, I told you. I think his ship came in yesterday."

"Ah yes, Greek." The mother looked at him calculatingly. "*Moussaka!*" she pronounced with triumph.

Nikos nodded and flashed his crooked white teeth.

After the meal, Joyce offered to drive him back to the ship. As soon as they climbed out of her car, he took her hand and kissed each finger as solemnly as if he were at prayer. "You are so beautiful," he said, a phrase he knew from pop songs. He said it to each finger, looking at her seriously with his amber eyes.

Joyce's heart squeezed until it hurt. He was so alive compared to everyone she knew, so exotic.

She moved to him, tilting up her face, opening her eyes as wide as she could. "You are beautiful, too."

11

Every Sunday, Dimitra took Joyce to church, the Greek Orthodox in Kastron. She went on weekdays as well, particularly when she needed a favor from the Virgin or her name saint, but she allowed Joyce no other time to leave her work. In most local homes the mother was the one who kept up communion with the saints. The daughter-in-law scrubbed the floors.

"Don't forget your scarf!" Dimitra called to Joyce from the courtyard. "We must pray for a good harvest. Hurry!"

"I'm coming, Mama." Joyce tied her church scarf, a triangle of rough white cotton, over her hair, and ran outside.

"I don't know why you bother to primp," her mother-in-law grumbled. "Father Poulianos does not care what you look like. Come, and keep your eyes off the soldiers." She hooked her elbow through Joyce's arm, giving her an affectionate squeeze, and propelled her down the hill.

Joyce had hated Dimitra at first. After Nikos had left, with a kiss and a promise, her mother-in-law had begun to work her mercilessly and Joyce had hated her. The moment they'd met, Dimitra had pinched Joyce's bicep as if she were buying a chicken. Then she had plunged her gnarled hand quickly down Joyce's shirt and squeezed her breast. Joyce had leapt back, horrified. The old woman had cackled and said something Joyce could not then understand.

Now she knew. "Too flabby," Dimitra had said to her son. "No good for work. Make her have children."

Since then, however, Joyce had learned that she was lucky in Dimitra. Most of the young brides in Ifestia suffered much more than she did at the hands of their husbands' mothers. Beaten by them, humiliated daily, ordered about like servants. In some of the mountain villages, Joyce had heard, a new bride was forced to spend the first night in her mother-in-law's bed, not her husband's, to show who really owned her. And it was not uncommon to see young wives in Kastron with black eyes and bruised cheeks, received just as often from their mothers-in-law as from their husbands. The people of Ifestia were not gentle. The old had lived through war and starvation, and the whole country had just emerged from seven years of dictatorship. Ifestians had no patience with mild encouragement or compliments, no time for the coddling of newcomers. Dimitra was a lamb compared to most.

When they reached the church, a simple rectangle of white-washed stone, topped by a dome and a bell, Dimitra hustled Joyce inside and up to the *gynekeion*, the women's section upstairs. There, they greeted the other women, exchanged news, and chatted between their prayers. There was little reverential about the church of Kastron. People thought nothing of milling about and talking, even during Mass, of comparing the sexual prowess of their goats or the marriageability of their daughters while the priest chanted, ignored, at his altar. Joyce had often thought that the church was more like a teeming marketplace than a house of worship.

Joyce had learned all about church on her second day in Greece. She had come down from Nikos's room early that morning wearing cutoff jeans and a sleeveless shirt — standard dress in Florida's heat — and Dimitra had let out a yelp at the sight of her as if she'd been stung. Picking up a long-sleeved shirt off a chair, she had thrust it at Joyce, knocking at her bare arms and legs in disgust. Dimitra always moved this way, Joyce was soon to discover — abruptly, forcefully, often thumping and bruising her, but never quite meaning to. Then she had shouted something Joyce could not understand, gesturing with disdain at her skimpy Florida clothes. Knowing her now, Joyce suspected she had said, "You dress like a Yankee whore. I won't have a tourist slut in my house."

Hastily, although somewhat amused, Joyce had climbed the ladder back up to the bedroom, pulled on a skirt and Dimitra's shirt, and presented herself again. She did, after all, want to make a good impression. She wanted to fit in, be accepted, even to be loved. She had no interest at that point in rebellion. With an approving grunt, Dimitra had pushed her out of the house, almost making her fall, and led her in grim silence along the dusty path to town, leaving Nikos asleep and satiated in his bed.

The first time Joyce had seen the village priest, Father Poulianos, she'd thought he looked like a painting of God. He was draped head to foot in a black robe, an imperious pillbox hat on his head, and his gray-streaked beard hung in a great bush down to the middle of his chest. He was an enormous man, and liked to stand at his full height, watching his flock with mocking gray eyes. As Joyce approached, she had glanced curiously into his face, but Dimitra had put a hand on the back of her head and pushed it down violently. Shocked, Joyce stared at her feet, not daring to raise her eyes. She knew so little, she realized, about how to behave.

Muttering something to the priest, her mother-in-law kissed his hand, then pulled Joyce into the dim, candlelit interior of the church.

Inside, Joyce looked about her, amazed. The contrast between the ancient, crumbling village outside and the rich glitter within the church astounded her. Even by her second day in

Ifestia, she had grasped how poor it was. Her in-laws lived with a simplicity Joyce thought had ended hundreds of years before. No electricity, no running water. No indoor toilet. No stove. Yet the church was opulent to the point of vulgarity.

Impatiently, Dimitra pushed her up to the row of icons separating the sanctuary from the nave, her hand again firmly on the back of Joyce's head. Christ was first, a tall, gilded painting of an emaciated Jew with cartoon eyes. Then came the Holy Virgin, her teardrop face dark and mournful. Joyce stared. The Virgin's dress was smothered in silver and gold. She was surrounded by elaborate carving, inlaid with mother-of-pearl, enamel, even jewels — it was clear the Virgin was more precious to the villagers than even her Son. At her feet were a cluster of flickering candles, dripping like lava to a glowing mound of molten wax beneath. A crowd of *tamata*, votive offerings, were hung on the wood around her: slivers of tin and silver cut into the shapes of tiny feet or arms, hearts or heads, of men crying in prison and children crushed in car crashes. The Virgin's hands, folded gracefully together over her protruding belly, were barely visible, washed away by a thousand kisses.

Grabbing the hair at the back of Joyce's head, Dimitra had pushed her face up to the icon of Christ, making loud kissing noises. Too bewildered to resist, Joyce closed her eyes in disgust and kissed first Christ's feet, then the Virgin's painted fingers.

What she had been too afraid to say, what she had not even known how to say, was that she was Jewish.

It wasn't until her mother-in-law had made Joyce kiss the icons of Saint Dimitrios, other local saints, and several angels that she'd led her to the *gynekeion* upstairs. There Joyce had stood, staring down at the men, shocked and ashamed of herself.

Now the church was a refuge for her. It was always cool inside. It always smelled of incense and old women. It was the one place she was allowed to rest.

During the first year or so her prayers had gone like this: "Dear God, I'm so sorry. I know I'm in the wrong place. My parents would scream. But I am being good. Keep Nikos safe."

Now her prayers went like this: "Bring Nikos back, O Lord. Help me stay a wife."

When Joyce had first met Nikos in Miami, he had been on a week's shore leave and had come to see her every day. The first time, the morning after he had kissed each of her fingers, he'd knocked on the door, a huge bouquet in his hands, and presented it not to her but to her mother. The woman was shocked. She stood in the doorway, round and sunburnt, her black hair showing gray at the roots, blinking in bewilderment. "Thank you," she finally managed to say, shouting at him as if he were deaf, and clumped off to the kitchen.

"Why the hell is he giving them to me?" she muttered to Joyce. "It isn't my pants he wants to get into." She rammed the flowers into a vase and waved Nikos away, as though he were a bothersome dog.

After that, Nikos bought a Greek-English phrase book. He began to lavish clumsy praises on their shabby clapboard house. The tiny yard, the clattery garbage disposal, the plastic deck chairs, stained and shredding. He learned to compliment the tent dresses Joyce's mother wore, decorated with giant flowers in turquoise or orange. "Pretty!" he would say. "Flowers pretty!" She would stare at him, then down at herself, and laugh. "He's shameless!" she once said to Joyce. But then she blushed.

With her father, Nikos was more reserved. He would shake his hand, hold a chair for him; fall silent whenever he spoke, his face serious and respectful. Joyce sensed that had Nikos been able to speak more English, he would have brought up politics with her father, or tried to draw him out about the shoe store where he was manager. It would have gotten him nowhere. Her father engaged in conversation as little as possible. He preferred to stare in grim concentration at the television.

With her elder brothers, Ben and Joey, Nikos was playful. He brought them beer and drank them into a sodden daze, arm-wrestled with them both and let them win. One night he made them dance the *Hasapiko*, a serious dance of stately grace performed by three men. Slowly, Nikos tried to get her brothers to follow his steps, one under each arm. While he moved with the ease of a panther, his face lifted, patient, they stumbled beside him, tripping, hiccuping, embarrassed. Joyce sat on the kitchen table, choked with laughter.

The more Nikos shone in Joyce's eyes, the more paralyzed her family seemed to her. Her mother leathery from too much sun, dumpy around the middle, face bloated and eyes narrow with disappointments. Her father silent and inexplicably sad, a paunchy shadow slipping in and out of the house. Her brothers, stubble-haired jocks who had done nothing but ignore or torment Joyce her entire childhood. The cold silence of their lives. The blanks where passion should have been.

They began to look gray to her. Dull and gray, like a washed-out photograph beside a shock of bright balloons.

At night, in the hot, silky air, Nikos and Joyce would go to the beach and lie down on the sand. She was ready to give herself to him then and there, disregarding every story she had heard about sailors and their diseases. Joyce was eighteen and she wanted everything. She wanted the exotic world embodied in Nikos's knowing eyes. The ancient history evoked by his strange, guttural language. The secrets promised by his uniform. All her life she had felt stifled, smothered by a family too passive and defeated to know ambition or adventure. So she opened herself to Nikos. Eagerly. Shamelessly. Bravely.

But Nikos insisted on taking it slow. Each night he would prop himself on an elbow, kiss her lingeringly, and expose only one part of her flesh. On Saturday he lifted her skirt up one leg, as if to reveal a dangerous surprise, sliding his hands along her thigh, brushing her hip. On Sunday he unbuttoned her flimsy summer shirt and pushed back only the left side to gaze at her breast, puckered at him longingly. On Monday the other breast, his lips running over it until she moaned. On Tuesday a hip, a hint of ribs. On Wednesday the taut plane of her young belly, the navel curling like a dimple.

Each night he kissed her, caressed her, made her pant for him. And each night he stopped too soon, until she could think of nothing but him.

Their talk was mostly sign language. He was good at it, funny, graceful, his fingers weaving words out of the air, but all they did was exchange vows of love and name objects. He would point to a star and ask her for the word in English, then say it in Greek — *astro* — making her repeat it and laughing at her pronunciation. He would compare her to flowers, the moon, the pale silver of its reflection upon a wave. These compliments meant nothing to Joyce. It was Nikos's own beauty that filled her eyes. She could watch him for hours, forgetting even to reply to him in her wonder that anyone this exotic could want her. His skin was so smooth that her fingertips felt rough and inadequate when she touched him. His cheekbones were high and sharp, the lines of his face sensual and delicate. His glossy black curls smelled of soap and the sea. When she gazed into his eyes they flickered gold, amber, and green, the whites bright, the lashes dramatically dark. He moved with sinuous languor, the muscles under his skin rippling like contented animals. His beauty consumed her, made all around her, like her family, fade to insignificance. She wanted his body, his world, his mystery.

And so he worked her into such a fever that when, on Friday night, seven days after they had met, he asked her to marry him, she gasped yes, and felt a bird fly free from her chest.

He left the day after he proposed, forced away by his ship's schedule. But by pointing to the days on a calendar, he made it clear that he would be back in a month, during which time Joyce could arrange the wedding.

She cried when his ship pulled out. He had filled her with hope and the promise of escape, only to leave her bereft. Doubt, and a great chasm of loneliness, yawned within her.

Then came an endless month of counting the days, of watching the hours creep by, of seeing all around her with new impatience and distaste. A month of inwardly saying good-bye to all she had known and all she had been. A month of desperately pretending that she was sure he'd come back.

Her parents laughed at her, saying Nikos would never be seen or heard of again. "He may be a knockout, honey, but you know what sailors are," her mother said in the kitchen one morning. She lit a cigarette and narrowed her eyes behind the smoke, leaning her heavy elbows on the Formica table. "Forget him. Think of it as a summer fling and move on. Anyway, he's a goy. Catholic or something."

"What do you care?" Joyce said with a pout. "You've never even been to temple since Joey's bar mitzvah."

"So? I care." Her mother waved her cigarette for emphasis, the smoke curling around her sun-cooked face like a cowl, the flesh under her arm swaying. "You should care, too. You need to find someone like us. Not some foreigner who can't even speak English."

Joyce leaned against the counter, scowling. "Like us? What's that supposed to mean?"

Her mother shifted her weight on the kitchen chair. She coughed, a deep phlegmy hack, and tapped some ash into the cereal bowl in front of her. "You know, *us*. American, Jewish. Nice, normal folk." She sighed, almost as if she were losing faith in her own words. "You know, ordinary."

Joyce gazed at her mother, the body round and fleshy underneath an orange muumuu, the eyes defensive slits in her swollen face. Her mother: brusque, critical, willing to dispense affection only in begrudging spurts, as if it were an expensive medicine. Was she ordinary? Joyce had gone through a period when she was younger of trying to find a word that would describe her mother and father. She had looked for the word in television sitcoms, in books, and in the complaints of her friends, searching for something that would help her categorize her parents, talk about them — that would help her know them. *Warm, happy, loving* — these words she'd had to discard. There was nothing warm about the isolating silence that seemed to smother her father and embitter her mother. Yet nor did *cold* or *cruel* fit. Nobody locked her in closets, beat her, slid hands up her skirts. Even *strict* or *unfair*, the favorite words of her friends, didn't apply. Her parents never dragged her off to synagogue, made her go to Sunday school or work for hours every night at her books or music; nor did they set unreasonable curfews or force her to spend her weekends doing hateful chores. But when she read portraits of citizens in the local paper whom she considered ordinary — the kind who joined the PTA or raised funds to open a Jewish preschool — she found nothing there to fit her parents, either. They never went out, they never voted, they never socialized. They seemed unaware of their community. Only she and her brothers ventured into the world, participated in the expected rituals of American suburbanites: baseball and football, dates and school dances on her brothers' parts; shopping and primping and waiting long hours by the telephone on hers. Her father's life, as far as she had ever been able to see, was to work all day and then come home to sit in front of the television. Her mother talked to the neighbors, but spent most of her time reading advertising circulars and searching for bargains, while cigarette butts, potato chips, and empty Coca-Cola cans piled up in front of her. Once, when Joyce had brought a fourth-grade friend home after school, the girl had hung around the kitchen staring at Joyce's immobile mother for several minutes, watching in fascination as she worked her way through a family-size sack of Doritos and a packet of cigarettes, ignoring the children. "Come on," Joyce had said impatiently. "Let's go upstairs." "No," the girl had whispered in reply. "Your mother's too weird. I wanna go home."

Joyce had never been able to find the right word for her family. But *ordinary* certainly did not fit.

While she waited for Nikos, she took to going to the library, where she would take out travel books about Greece. She read about the Acropolis and the oracle at Delphi. She studied dozens of photographs of eyeless statues and contorted black figures on the sides of vases. Everything new and unfamiliar she absorbed hungrily, haphazardly, understanding little of what she read. Then, tired, her mind would wander, slipping into dreams of Nikos's lips, his teasing hands. Of the worlds he could open for her and within her.

Her father grew irritated. "Snap out of it," he barked at her one morning. "Now you've graduated high school you should be looking for a job like your brothers."

Joey worked in a garage. Ben was a pizza delivery boy. Joyce watched them, their arms like slabs of meat, their faces alternately cruel and uncertain, their minds shifting dully between football and money, their girlfriends sullen and shy. I don't want to be like them, like any of them, she thought. I want to make more of my life. I want adventure. Excitement. I want danger.

"He'll never show up," her brothers jeered when they heard her boast to friends that she was engaged. "He's a fag anyhow. Couldn't keep his hands off of us, the greasy perv."

Joyce eyed them with contempt. Her dead family. What did they know?

When Nikos astonished them all by reappearing a month later with a ring and a new, shiny suit, Joyce turned to her mother in triumph. "See? I told you he was serious. You never trust my judgment in anything."

"You're too young to get married," her mother said, her smoke-coarsened voice rough and bitter. "Look at me, stuck here with your father. Don't make my mistakes."

I'm not going to, Joyce thought. So she married Nikos at City Hall, a high school friend the witness, and rented a room in a cheap motel to serve as their honeymoon suite.

Joyce still liked to remember their wedding night, when Nikos finally undressed her completely. He made her enjoy displaying herself, for she had grown to feel safe, not exposed in his love. He laid her out on the bed and arranged her limbs as if she were a doll, while she felt her passion rising. Then he stripped off his own clothes, revealing himself in all his beauty, his shoulders broad, his waist tapered, his chest as smooth and soft as the inside of her own legs. He lowered himself over her, starting at her feet, brushing his lips up her knees, her thighs. Opening her slowly, he licked her with a delicacy that made her cry out — she had never been touched so reverently before, only groped by clumsy, ragged-nailed boys. Finally, when she was panting his name over and over, he slowly pushed into her. My virgin, my bride, he moaned in a Greek even she could understand.

It hurt, of course. It hurt and she bled, making her instinctive defenses clamp down. He stopped, waited for her to relax, kissed her lips, held himself above her on his arms. But then could contain himself no longer and thrust into her, adding his cries to hers, although his were of pleasure.

Thinking over that night afterwards, Joyce always brushed the memory of the pain aside. It had only been part of the necessary suffering, she had decided, only a part of earning love. Nothing compared to the glory of joining herself to him, body and soul. After all, she had been groomed to succumb. Her romance magazines. Her girlfriends' plotting. The sinister chatter on television. The seething fantasies of her supermarket novels. They had taught her that suffering, submission, patience, and self-sacrifice were a woman's way of winning the redemption of love.

The next time, she had been afraid. Nikos sensed this, so he went back to their earlier slow caresses, to his leisurely arousal of her lust. He got her used to opening her legs for him, letting him lick her, allowing him to stroke her gently until she became so wild and feverish that she lost her fear.

And then the real lovemaking had begun, the lovemaking that still made her writhe, alone in bed, with longing.

The morning after their wedding night, Joyce and Nikos had flown to Athens, insulated from their future in a metal tube in the sky. They left without saying good-bye. The City Hall ceremony, the shabby motel, the airport — and that was it; life with her family was over. All Joyce had managed to sneak out of the house was her baby-sitting money and an old canvas suitcase filled with summer clothes. The thought had occurred to her that if she'd insisted, tried a bit harder, she might have persuaded her parents to let her marry Nikos, to throw a proper wedding and say a real good-bye. But she had pushed the thought away. This was love, not a lesson in duty. She looked out of the window as the plane took off, the land shrinking beneath her, and felt her body lift in excitement. Her old life, her old self, fell away from her like sand brushed off a knee. She felt elated, terrified. Free.

On the plane Nikos had stroked Joyce's then-soft hands and tried to teach her some Greek. *Neh* for yes. *Ochi* for no. Mother and husband. Please and thank you. When people nod they mean no, not yes. You must call my mother *Pethera*, mother-in-law; my father *Petheros*. The only warning he gave her of what to expect came after he searched his Berlitz phrase book for a long time, gave up on it, and said "Mama, Papa, no dollars." He had not been able to find the word for poor.

Joyce gazed at him, only half-listening, steeped in wonder.

This beautiful man was her husband? She felt reckless with gratitude and love. Ready to do anything he asked.

After the plane had come a long, hot train ride to Thessaloniki, and at last a series of rattling buses and slow, chugging ferries to the island. Joyce looked about at the bundled peasants, the goats and chickens, the golden dust and pale olive trees, and thought it all thrilling. She had never gone anywhere, had never expected to. Nobody in her family traveled. Travel was for people who didn't like home, who didn't like America, her father had once said. She had never felt so defiant. She wrote her parents a postcard.

Dear Mom and Dad: We're in Greece and it's beautiful. Nikos is treating me like a princess. Marriage suits me! I've never been so happy.

Once they reached the house, Joyce slipped into a daze she would not emerge from for weeks. She was so disoriented by the unfamiliarity of everything she saw and did, by the new faces around her, the strange language, that she lost her footing and her judgment. She found it hard to measure distances in the clear, hard light. She kept stumbling and almost falling to her knees. They arrived in the summer, and the heat was so dry compared to Florida's that she felt constantly, unslakably thirsty. Nikos added to her confusion by making love to her all morning, all night, sometimes dragging her up to their room in the middle of the day when his parents were working outside. She was sore and weary and dizzy with lovemaking, but never quite satiated. He teased her, taunted her, held off her orgasms until she would do anything he wanted. He made her so delirious that she was unable to grasp what she had lost, where she had come. Who she was.

Twice, in the midst of her disorientation, she persuaded him to take her to the telephone office in Kastron so that she could call home; like many of the villagers, her in-laws owned no phone. She had to borrow the money off Dimitra to do it, money her mother-in-law could ill afford, for Nikos had taken all her cash and handed it to his parents. "You my wife," was all he'd said by way of explanation. The first time she called, her father yelled at her until she hung up. The second time her mother said, "I just hope you're happy after the stupid thing you did."

"I am, no thanks to you!" Joyce yelled back. And slammed down the phone.

After that she'd written an angry postcard.

Dear Mom and Everybody: I'm doing great. Greece is much prettier than Florida, and there's more to do. You should have let me and Nikos have a real wedding, you wouldn't have been sorry. You never did trust me enough. I'm happier than I've ever been in my life. Here's my new address.

They had never answered. She wrote again and again. They still would not answer. She thought of calling them once more, but her hurt and fury at their continued silence stopped her hand. They had her address — if they wanted her to telephone them, let them ask her. Until then, all she would do was write.

Joyce would not admit to herself how much it hurt that her family had cut her off like this. Once she'd ventured a complaint to Dimitra and Dimitra had said, "A daughter belongs to the husband's family after she is married. Her parents have no obligation to her anymore." Joyce had stared at her. Was that what her own parents felt? That they had washed their hands of her?

"You belong to us," Dimitra had said.

After church on Sundays, Dimitra allowed herself a rare few hours to socialize. Meeting up with the other old women of town, most of whom had been widowed by war and were in permanent black, she visited their houses to gossip and lick spoonfuls of a sweet white paste called *mastic*, plunged into glasses of cool water. Joyce was supposed to stay in church and pray for Nikos's safety and for the Virgin to give her children, but secretly she walked through the town instead. The shops were closed, the cobbled lanes quiet. There was nothing really to do. Yet the chance to walk unfettered by her in-laws, her donkey, or her marketing baskets — the chance to walk as she would at home — was too precious to sacrifice.

Even so, these were the times Joyce missed Nikos the most. All week she worked so hard that she had little time to think of her loneliness. Her thoughts were taken up with the tasks at hand, with village matters and the gossip that filled her and Dimitra's lives. But on Sundays, as she was wandering the streets, an emptiness would seep into her like a cold fluid. It was not that she missed Florida. There she would only be battling with her mother, or raging unnoticed in her house. Drifting along the beach, the vacuousness of her family surrounding her like a cloud of ether. Anyway, she told herself, her family had given her up, proven that they'd never cared. But here, slipping through town, surrounded by dessicated peasants and black-clad widows, she longed afresh for her husband's company. His youth, his intoxicating body, the sensuous promise of his gaze, the safety and pride she felt holding his hand in the street. She liked working the land, selling in the market. She liked the life of the village and the sense of belonging it gave her. But at times she felt as abandoned as if she had been shipwrecked.

This Sunday she walked for a while before she saw anybody to talk to. Stratis Farmakides, the village butcher, was seated as usual in a plastic chair in front of his closed shop, his thick body sprawled in aggressive relaxation. He was holding a fat, hand-rolled cigarette between his thumb and forefinger and watching with relish as two dogs wrestled over a hunk of gristle. The headless carcass of a skinned goat hung upside-down from an iron hook beside him, dripping blood into a bucket. Flies swarmed around it and Stratis, although the butcher seemed unconcerned. Given to profanity and sweat, his belly hard and his neck as wide as his jaw, Stratis never went to church. "I have the souls of too many slaughtered animals on my conscience," he had once explained to Joyce with a wink. So he spent his Sundays lolling about and dreaming of his future.

Joyce approached him, as she knew he expected. He was planning to move to Chicago and get rich, so he insisted on practicing his nonexistent English with her whenever possible.

"Plgety noming, si?" he said to her as she strolled up to him.

"Excuse me?" Joyce stopped in front of him.

"I am saying it is a pretty morning in your language." Stratis said, retreating to Greek. "What's the matter, you don't understand me?" He brushed a fly from his nose.

"Oh, I see. I was confused because *si* is not English," she replied with tact.

"Ah yes, I get all mixed up with Italian I know from the war. My head is filled with pieces of knowledge, stuffed with it like a sausage." Stratis sighed and removed the cigarette from his mouth, leaving a piece of paper clinging to his lip. Balding and dark, his head looked like a large, polished bone. "But this will do me no good in Chicago unless I speak better. I have the ear of a tree stump when it comes to languages. I need your help. When are you coming to give me lessons, little American?"

He had been asking her this for months, but Joyce knew better than to accept. Respectable housewives did not sequester themselves with single men, as Stratis knew perfectly well. And it was more than likely that he would pounce on her among the lamb chops.

"I'll start now," she said mischievously, and added in English, "Good-bye."

"What is that?"

"It means *andheeo*, Mr. Farmakides." And she left him mouthing the word as she turned up the hill.

Joyce walked on, heading towards her friend Marina's house. She nodded politely to acquaintances, old women and housewives, ignoring their disapproving glares. She knew young women should not be out alone, but she had learned to use the fact that she was American as an excuse for an occasional rebellious act. Sometimes being a foreigner was useful. Nevertheless, children, barefooted, scuff-kneed, many in rags, ran up and stared at her. Soldiers tried to catch her eye. Every step seemed a test.

Kastron was a modest port and market town that straggled up the foothills of Ifestia's westernmost mountain. It had barely changed since its stone houses had been built during the Ottoman Empire, the four centuries of Turkish rule that still made Greeks spit with hatred, and much of the town, now between two and five hundred years old, was slowly crumbling into a dusty heap of stones. The walls of the houses were rough, jutting, and splashed unevenly with whitewash. The narrow streets were so haphazardly cobbled that they were more like the rubble of a building site than roads. The town, Joyce often thought, looked as creviced and broken as most of its inhabitants.

The seafront belonged mostly to the fishermen, who gathered there each evening to mend their nets as the orange sun slipped quickly into the sea. Gulls and pelicans patrolled the harbor, on the lookout for unguarded catch. The smell of seaweed and fish pervaded the air, mingling with the sweet fragrance of the wind. Fishing boats rocked listlessly off the shore. As much as Joyce loved it there, however, she could not safely walk the seafront alone because it was a favorite haunt of soldiers, who went to drink at the tavernas and watch the women's skirts blow against their legs. She dreaded the gauntlet of the soldiers' hungry eyes.

Instead, she climbed higher up the mountain, where the

town was wholly residential. Here the streets were so tiny that two men abreast could touch a wall on either side. Alleyways snaked behind houses, providing secret entrances to court-yards and homes. The stony lanes dipped in the middle to a gutter, down which trickled soap suds and whitewash, spiced on occasion with the odors of ammonia and excrement. Scrawny dogs ran past, sniffing their mysterious trails, ignor-ing the cats who yawned and licked the dust off their hot, mangy fur.

Joyce turned up a narrow lane to her favorite part of Kastron. Here the houses were piled so close together that it was hard to tell where a particular house began and another ended. One person's terrace might be somebody else's roof. Walls turned into staircases. And all were built of stone so ancient and thickly whitewashed that the houses had grown smooth and rounded, like melted sugar. Magenta flowers and pine green vines trailed over walls and cascaded out of the pots people had arranged along outside steps, and the roof of each house was capped by overlapping waves of burnt orange pantiles. To Joyce, walking these streets was like weaving through a vast, bleached honeycomb. The town here looked not so much like something people had toiled for generations to build as some-thing that had grown spontaneously out of the ground. It made her feel protected, sheltered. Cupped by history, as a stamen is cupped by a tulip.

She drifted around a corner, feeling lazy and a little tired, and found herself facing a clump of soldiers sitting at an out-door *kaphenio*. Normally she never looked at the soldiers, not only because of Dimitra's warnings but because she knew it would invite trouble. But in her surprise at seeing them in this unlikely part of town, she found herself staring directly at them. They wore an expression on their faces that she had learned to fear: the intent, predatory glare of young men on the prowl. She turned on her heels to leave, but it was too late. They had caught her look and considered it an invitation.

Shouting with laughter and obviously tipsy, four of them leapt to their feet.

"Check out the tits!"

It was only the new soldiers who behaved like this. The ones who had been stationed here awhile knew her now, had learned to keep their advances to comments in the marketplace and to the flirtation that spun her into secret dreams. She had spat on their shoes, insulted them in Greek. Her mother-in-law had threatened them and they had finally accepted that although Joyce looked like a tourist slut, she was really respectable and married. But every few weeks a new batch of soldiers arrived in town and they had to prove their *mangas,* their unconquerable Greek machismo, by hunting down women.

"Hey, beautiful!" the soldiers shouted and tumbled into the street.

Joyce walked rapidly in the opposite direction, trying to keep calm, but the four boys staggered after her, taunting. "Nice ass! Swing it for us, baby!"

Willing herself not to run, she quickened her pace, her skin tightening. Perhaps if she remained unflustered they would give up. They usually did. But their steps came closer. She could hear them panting behind her.

Suddenly two of them materialized out of an alley and jumped in front of her, grinning. She stopped, shocked, and swiveled, but the two other boys were right behind her. "Leave me alone!" she hissed in Greek, furious at their audacity. They hesitated and blinked, surprised. "My husband is from this island. He will kill you!"

The soldiers looked uneasy, but then one laughed. "She has no husband. She's a German slut. Look at her."

They stepped right up to her. One reached out and clasped her breast.

At his touch Joyce kicked out at him and spat, trying to shout, but one of the boys behind her clamped his hand over her mouth and pinned her arms to her sides. No soldier had gone this far before. She could not breathe. The boy's hand stank of tobacco and dirt. She gagged. They pressed in closer, surrounding her, reaching for her, grunting. One of them began to lift her skirt.

"Let go of my wife!"

The shout rang out. The soldiers jumped, releasing Joyce, and she ran. Broke through the wall of them and ran. She had no idea who had spoken but could not stop to look. She sprinted down the hill, stumbling over the uneven stones, the gutters, startling the dogs, until she reached the church. "Dimitra," she found herself sobbing. "Dimitra!"

At the church she stopped, suddenly aware that the streets were quiet again, the soldiers gone. Panting, she crouched to the ground so that she could pick up her skirt modestly and scrub her mouth with it. She could still taste the boy's fingers, as if he had plunged them into her mouth, not simply clamped them over her lips. They tasted of tobacco and salt, and of something bitter. She scrubbed and scrubbed until her lips ached. So much for feeling safe! Her eyes stung with rage.

"Are you all right?"

She jumped, looking up from her crouch in surprise. The words were in English. It took her a moment to realize this, they sounded so strange. Not even Greek-accented English.

"Did they hurt you?"

The young man standing above her was tall and blond like her, but there the resemblance ended. Under his lanky hair, which fell unevenly over his eyes, his face was long and angular, his nose sharp and peeling from the sun. His body was angular, too, flat and wide-shouldered as a plank. A faded T-shirt hung on him like a pillowcase from clothespins, and white cotton trousers dangled over his legs.

Joyce surreptitiously wiped her eyes on her skirt and stood up. "Were you the one who shouted?" she asked. She didn't even know which language she used.

"Yes, I hope you don't mind. It seemed the thing to say."

He was English, she realized. Not even American, but pure English. His voice was like ice tinkling on a hot day.

"Thank you," she said, still trembling. "God knows what you saved me from." She paused, trying to calm herself. "How come you speak Greek?" she managed to add.

"My mother's from here. She taught me."

The hair on his arms was bleached by the sun, Joyce noticed, a golden fuzz over brick red skin. His hands were long and delicate. Joyce looked down at her own. They had become farmer's hands, she realized, the knuckles already knotted with strain. She felt grimy and squat next to this man: a peasant.

"Why haven't I seen you here before?" she asked. Her voice was still shaking.

"I've only just arrived. I've not been here since I was sixteen." He peered into her face. "Are you sure you're all right? Those bastards!"

"Yes thanks. They probably wouldn't have really done anything. They'd get into too much trouble." She shrugged and looked away from him. Then glanced down the street, suddenly remembering her mother-in-law. She had not talked to a boy her own age alone for two years. If Dimitra caught her, God knows what might happen.

"I should go," she said quickly. "But thank you, thank you so much."

"Do you have to leave already?" He sounded disappointed. He didn't even bother to hide it. "You're the first person I've met here my age who isn't a soldier, let alone who speaks English. Can't I buy you a ginger beer or something, cool you down after all that running?"

Joyce smiled at the thought. Sitting in a *kaphenio* with a strange man for all to see! Heaven and earth would fall around her. Noticing the bewildered look on his face, she said, "I'm sorry. Thanks. I wish I could. But . . . well, it's hard to explain. I'm not allowed . . ."

"You mean you *are* married?" The young man's eyes dropped to her hand, where her wedding ring glowed its dull, possessive gold.

"Yes. It wasn't a story. I'm married to a merchant marine, Nikos Koliopoulos. He's away at sea right now."

"Oh. I see." The boy nodded. "Well, I don't know him, but . . . my name is Alex Gidding. Alexandros here. Pleased to meet you."

He held out his hand. She looked up and down the street. She looked behind her to make sure the priest was not there with his judgmental eyes. Only then did she reach out to slide her slim, rough hand into his.

Except for the soldiers just now, it was the first time she had touched a man in seven months. She had forgotten how thick men's hands could be. How their palms were broad enough to enfold her wrist. How their fingers could enclose and tighten like a huge, protective glove. The heat of Alex's touch penetrated her skin.

She pulled her hand away quickly, startled.

"Where do you live?" he said, and visibly colored. His eyes were a deep, faraway blue, the blue of the Aegean as it reaches the horizon. But his skin was so thin and light it lit up his emotions like a lamp.

"I can't tell you," she replied, shrugging apologetically. "You've got to understand . . . my mother-in-law. If she sees me talking to you, I'm — " She stopped, at a loss for words.

"Up a creek without a paddle?" He smiled uneasily and looked away, perhaps to hide his blush. His Adam's apple was delicate, vulnerable. Then he looked at her again. "How can you stand all the restrictions?"

None of the tourists she'd met had ever asked her this so bluntly. Yet she knew it was what they were all wondering — why she stayed, how she could bear it.

"I like it here," she replied defensively. Why was she even bothering to answer this stranger? "I'm waiting for my husband."

"How long has he been gone?"

But this was too much. She turned her head away.

"I better go," she said quietly.

There was a pause. They both stared down at their feet. The sun was high in the sky now, and most people were in bed to avoid the worst of the day's heat. The yellow dust throbbed around them, sucking the moisture out of air. Joyce closed her eyes, a sudden longing for that ginger beer clutching at her throat.

"My aunt owns the bakery," Alex said suddenly. "Perhaps when you are in town to do errands — "

"I can't," Joyce interrupted.

And she walked away.

I I I

When Joyce returned to the house, she found that Dimitra was not yet there, only Petros rising from his siesta. Joyce was pleased; she loved her moments alone with her father-in-law. Like her own father, he was taciturn, but not out of a willful refusal to join in on the world, only out of watchfulness. He liked to sit apart, to listen and to analyze, Joyce had discovered, and then to come out with pithy observations about the people around him. "Beware of silent rivers," he would say about a quiet woman. Or, after listening to a child blurt forth some insult, "Only from fools and children will you learn the truth." He often amused her with his remarks about the stinginess of neighbors, the corruption of politicians, or the foibles of his own wife. On the surface he seemed withdrawn and humble, as if he had decided that his lot in life was to be a workhorse and little more, but underneath he was surprisingly sharp and mischievous. And he was kind. Much kinder than her own father.

"*Koroulamou,*" he said, for they both called her "my little girl" now, "make me some coffee. My head is like wood today." He lowered his sparse frame onto a chair at the table and yawned, revealing his few teeth, discolored and crooked. "Where is your mother-in-law?"

"I thought she'd be home, *Petheros.* We must have missed

each other in town." Avoiding his eyes, Joyce opened the coffee tin and poured a few beans into the grinder, a polished brass cylinder that resembled a pepper mill. She turned the handle on top of it around and around; Petros liked his coffee ground fine as powder.

Petros glanced sharply at Joyce. He was small and skinny, shriveled as a dried mushroom, his gray hair cut in rough tufts. His brown eyes were sunk like pebbles in his sun-splotched skin, but they saw everything. He could tell that she had been distressed. His face softened but he asked nothing, as was his way.

"Tomorrow we go to Ayiassos for the feast," he said instead. "Forget all our troubles and drink to the Blessed Virgin, yes?"

Joyce nodded, touched at his effort to cheer her. She loved this festival. It was the only time she saw her in-laws become young again, reckless and joyful. And it was the only time all year that she was allowed to leave Ifestia.

Dimitra came in through the back door, fussing. She never entered through the same door she had exited, and would not let Petros or Joyce either because that allowed evil spirits to follow them and rest in the house.

"Where were you?" she said, knocking Joyce so that she staggered. "I told you to meet me at the church!"

"Sorry, Mama." Joyce rubbed her arm. "I forgot. I was too hot to wait. I am making *Petheros* some coffee. Do you want some?"

"No, no. We won't have enough for tomorrow with this extravagance." Dimitra peered into her face, just as Petros had. Then her eyes, too, softened. "You miss your husband today, little one? Come, put down the coffee." She pulled Joyce to her and sat on another of the wooden chairs. Taking Joyce in her broad lap, she cuddled her as if she were a child, not a woman, brushing away the hair that straggled over her eyes and clasping her head to her shoulder, rocking her. "We miss our Nikos, do we not, old man?"

Petros grunted and lit his pipe.

"I hoped and prayed he would come back for the festival," Dimitra continued, still rocking Joyce. "It is the time every good Greek must return to his family, make a pilgrimage to his home village. Why does Nikos not respect this? Widow Eskenazi, Mother Halaris — all the women I talked to today, all their grandchildren and children are coming home. But my son, my one and only son, he chooses to —"

"Dimitra, enough," Petros said quietly, smoke curling around his face. "You know he would come home if he could. Now let Joyce go. I want my coffee."

Dimitra pushed Joyce off her lap with a pat. Joyce spooned the ground coffee, sugar, and some water from the ceramic jug into the *briki,* a tiny brass saucepan the shape of a cup. Crouching to the hearth, where Petros had lit a small fire, she held the *briki* over the heat, stirring it until the coffee boiled to the brim.

Dimitra crossed her arms and scowled. "I will only say that it's lucky Nikos loves you so much, *pedhi mou.* Before he met you, he wrote to us so seldom we never knew whether he was alive or dead." She sighed, her great bosom heaving under her thick forearms. "I only wish he did not have to be away so long."

Nikos was gone for five months the first time he left, for six the second, then four and a half — in the first seventeen months of their marriage, he and Joyce had spent no more than six weeks together. Each time he'd left she had missed him afresh, feeling foreign and alone, terrified that she would hear of his ship having sunk or his body washed overboard. But gradually, as the weeks passed, she became used to living in his house without him, doing his work, filling his place. She convinced herself that his absences would only strengthen their love. Of all the women in the world, he had chosen her, had he not? Brought her home like a prize to show off to his family. Left her in their care, where she would be protected and safe, waiting for his return. She basked in this knowledge, feeling anointed, and accepted the affection of his parents as her due, once she was used to their roughness. She even came to relish the work of planting, weeding, selling their goods, everything she did suffused with the erotic status of a waiting wife. When, at night, she leaned against her window to look up at the star-clustered sky, loneliness knocking about inside her like a rudderless boat, she had only to think of Nikos's hands on her, of his lips murmuring words of passion, of the devotion he showed on his returns to feel that she was, at last, in the glorious romance she had always wanted.

When he did come home, the atmosphere in the house would turn festive. He would greet Joyce with a great shout of delight, pick her up and swing her around until she was dizzy, then hug and kiss his mother with almost equal affection. They would feast and drink, Dimitra having cooked for days in preparation, and Nikos would tell his sea stories while his parents hung on his every word, Joyce struggling to understand. He would bring them presents: squat, gawky figurines from Africa, bright cotton from India, nougat and pale sugared almonds from France. He would take Joyce around to show off to his friends, making her practice her clumsy Greek so that everybody laughed approvingly. "Is she not beautiful, my American?" he would say. "See her hair? It shines like the sun!"

Once he borrowed a fishing boat and rowed her out to visit a tiny island nearby for a swim and a picnic, his muscles swelling as he pulled at the oars. The island was nothing more than a beach and rocks, empty but for a few goats. They swam naked, made love while the goats watched, grew drunk and giggly on wine. Nikos clowned for her, caressed her, protected her tenderly from the sharp coral that ringed the beach. She ran her hands down his back, over his buttocks. Pressed her lips to his beautiful face, his glistening breastbone, and whispered to herself, "All for me."

Another time he took her horseback riding up a mountain, just the two of them alone with their ponies and the gulls. At the top they found a fifteenth-century monastery, its walls still upright and strong. "Let's go in," Joyce said, gesturing at the gate. "No," said Nikos. "Ghosts." Pale, he hurried them away, then glanced at Joyce sheepishly. They still had few words between them, Joyce's Greek being primitive, Nikos's English even worse, but the horror on his face was unmistakable. "All right, my love," she said gently. "Never mind." Later, when she found out that the monastery had been used as a prison and torture chamber by the Nazis, Nikos's superstition touched her even more. She liked that he shared the beliefs of the old; it made him so different from her parents, with their hard realism and willful ignorance of faith and history. She also liked that Nikos's fear made him vulnerable in her eyes. Vulnerable and tender, as only the fearful can be tender.

Each time Nikos came back, he would grow more passionate and extravagant in his lovemaking. He seemed to worship her body, her cleverness, crowing with pride each time she falteringly pronounced a word of Greek. Joyce would find herself floating on his adoration and on Dimitra's happiness, borne upwards as if on wings, dazzled, dazed, soaring in a way she never had back in Florida. When he was with her she needed no other company, wanting him all to herself, wanting his beautiful eyes to look into hers, his silken limbs to lift her, his melodious voice to speak to her of reckless lust and longing. And when he was away again, his letters, written with the help of his more literate shipmates, kept her desires alive and her senses enslaved.

So Joyce grew to love not only Nikos but his mother and father, his house, his village. His way of life. She had a place here. A place and a role that she had never had at home.

After Joyce and her in-laws had finished supper that night, their usual meal of potatoes and watermelon, they packed for the festival. At dawn the next morning they were to take a ferry to Lesbos, and find a ride up the mountain to the town of

Ayiassos. There they would sleep in the church, as always, refusing the hospitality of Petros's relatives. Dimitra insisted that in sleeping the church would make the Virgin appear in her dreams. Plus, she despised her husband's family. "When I sleep in the church, the Blessed Virgin smiles at me and hears my prayers," she told Petros every year. "When I sleep in the houses of your cursed brothers, I am plagued by dreams of crones and devils." So they packed sleeping rolls, which they had made by sewing together sheets stuffed with straw and rags; changes of clothes so that they would not stink; and money, money they had saved all year to spend on spit-roasted lamb and *kalamaria,* on succulent mutton and spicy sausages, on sweet rolls of *baklava* and, above all, on *retsina,* the local barrel wine that tasted of the volcanic rock upon which its grapes were grown, and the resin of the surrounding forest.

The next morning the three of them arose at dawn, before the heat made movement as hard as walking over sand, and Dimitra boiled the coffee. They spooned down yogurt and a little precious honey for strength — ambrosia, food of the gods — greeted the old widow who was to look after the house and animals while they were gone, and walked down to Kastron to catch the earliest ferry. They traveled peasant class, as Joyce liked to think of it, which meant sitting on the floor of the open deck with their own food and bedrolls, lemons in case they felt seasick, their own water, and nothing but a shit-stained toilet bowl for their use. But Joyce was happy. She had grown up on the ocean and loved the water still. The heart-torn cries of gulls and the salty wind on her lips.

Her first task was to help Dimitra and Petros settle. Once they were off their land and indulging in leisure, they became suddenly fussy, complaining about their comfort and infirmities as if they were not on their feet digging and plowing and planting and cooking from dawn to dusk all the other days of their lives. She folded their clothes and their bedrolls, nestled them by the railing so they could rest their backs, and left them to doze the hours away.

For herself, she was content to look around at other people. Today she was in luck, for a family of Gypsies was on the deck with them, and Joyce had always been fascinated by Gypsies. She watched them furtively. The father had a huge belly, drooping black whiskers, and thick legs encased in tight trousers. His wife sat beside him, her brightly woven skirt spread about her, her brown face smooth and still. Around them gathered five girls, black eyes peeking back at Joyce. One, a stunning teenager, returned her stare with arrogance. At first Joyce was taken mostly by their clothes, the most flamboyant she had ever seen. The girls and mother wore their long black hair under brightly colored scarves, along the edges of which shimmered tiny golden coins. Heavier coins dangled from their ears, and embroidery decorated their collars and the hems of their skirts. Even the father, in his elaborately embroidered waistcoat, cummerbund and collar and the billowing sleeves of his shirt, was gorgeous.

At first she admired only this, but later, as the long trip wore on and the sun climbed high and blinding in the sky, the father grunted a signal, and all the children and the mother huddled around his big belly like a pile of kittens, and slept. Joyce was astonished at this public display of intimacy. Her parents never even held hands in front of people. Her mother had hugged Joyce occasionally when she was a child but stopped as soon as Joyce reached puberty. Her father touched no one, not even his sons.

Joyce turned to look at her in-laws: two worn, sun-drained, peasants slumped in the corner of the deck. Dimitra's chin had sunk deep into her bosom, her silver mustache shadowing her crumpled mouth, her fat arms folded over her hillock of a belly. Her wrinkled face was shut down, mannish, whatever beauty she had once had drowned in hardship and willfulness. Petros looked frail beside her, a little old man in little old clothes. He, too, was asleep, his face grizzled, his battered cap shielding his brow from the sun. These are my parents now, Joyce told herself. Parents who have taken me in and grown to love me, who are not afraid to hold me when I cry, who touch me even if those touches sometimes leave bruises. Nevertheless, when she turned back to the Gypsies, her throat tightened with envy.

The trip was long, so eventually Joyce took to wandering the deck, stepping over the sleeping bodies of vacationing peasants and dodging the children who chased each other about, staring at her with provocative eyes. She leaned against the railing and looked down into the water, a brilliant aquamarine, clear enough to reveal the white sand beneath. The sun flashed off the waves, making her squint. Long ago, when she had been that other Joyce, she would have worn sunglasses. She had when she'd first arrived, but Nikos had said they made her look cheap. She looked up at the horizon. Already Ifestia was disappearing into the glare. Its mountain looked like a pile of yellow dust at this distance, as if sifted from some gigantic hand. Its coast was a rocky line, occasionally broken by a ribbon of white beach. The houses of Kastron sprinkled down to the sea, like a cluster of dry knuckle bones. For three whole days she would be away from that place. This meant so much to her, but it would be nothing to someone like that tourist boy she'd met, or the soldiers she saw every day. They could go wherever they wanted. They did not have to wait for festivals. The thought made her suddenly restless. It made her yearn, as she hadn't since she first came to Dimitra's house, for the chance to kick off her peasant skirts and run, far, far away, alone.

From Mytilene, the port of Lesbos, they hitched a ride to Ayiassos, a prosperous, tree-shaded town just under the crest of Mount Olymbos. The farmer who gave them a ride took Dimitra with him in the cab of his pickup, leaving Petros and Joyce

to bake in the back with some bedraggled chickens. Soon, however, they entered the valley, much more lush and wooded than
anything on Ifestia, and the shadows of the leaves crawled over
Joyce's bare arms and legs like cool, feathery insects. She
sighed with relief. She could not feel the thrill she used to before a party at home — here there were no boys to meet, no romances she was free to start or shun — but a dim, undefined
hope rose in her nonetheless. She knew that she would be exhausted by the end of the festival, stiff from sleeping on the
church floor and filthy from lack of bathing. But now it was all
ahead of her and she was happy. She would fill her veins with
wine and drown out her longing for Nikos, her doubts, and her
fierce, forbidden desires.

Nikos had last come home seven months earlier. He waltzed
into the house, his sailor's bag over his shoulder, a swagger to
his stride: the son and husband returned safely from his trials
at sea. "Mama, food!" he cried. "I'm starving. *Papas*, get me
some wine. I want to celebrate — I survived such storms! I
want to drink so much I piss resin tonight!" He turned to sweep
Joyce up in a hug, a passionate kiss. "My little wife," he
crowed. "How I have missed you."

She stared at him, laughing, yet disoriented. For the first time
she knew enough Greek to understand his every word, not
only the gist of what he was saying. It made him different. It
made him strange.

Nikos had written to tell them he was coming, and for three
days Dimitra had been cooking for him. She had slaughtered
one of their few chickens, gutted and roasted it, made soup and
pastitsio and stuffed peppers. She had unwrapped the *feta*,
stuffed grape leaves with rice and soaked them in vinegar,
rolled out paper-thin layers of *filo* pastry to make *baklava*. She
had roasted sesame seeds, honey, nuts, ground them into deli-
cious confections. They never feasted like this unless Nikos
was home.

He had eaten it all with relish, making jokes in pidgin English to Joyce about how dreadful the food was in America. "Barbecue, remember?" he said, winking at her. "Mama, hamburgers?" He laughed again, kissing her cheek. He did not yet realize how much Greek she had learned since he had last been home.

Joyce looked about the room: at Petros, watching his son with delight, at Dimitra, hanging on his every word. All three of them looked strange to her.

After dinner that night, while Nikos regaled his parents with tales of his exploits at sea, Joyce rose quickly from the table to wash the dishes. She wanted to remove herself from the sight of him, catch hold of this new bewilderment, this sense of unfamiliarity, and control it. She went out to the pump, her basket filled with plates. The air was cold — winter in the northern Aegean is a season of rain and snow and unexpectedly icy winds. Squatting over the flat rock under the pump, she scrubbed the dishes, her fingers numbing, a doubt as icy as the water creeping into her chest. What was the matter with her? Each time Nikos had returned there had been an hour or so of awkwardness, shyness, of getting used to one another. Why did this time feel so much worse? Just because she could understand him now made him no different. He was still Nikos, her love! It was only that she had to adjust.

When Nikos climbed up to their bedroom that night, he was drunk. He sat beside her on the bed, his lithe young body listing like an old man's. He did not pull back the covers to look at her as he had done in the past. He hung his head over his knees. "I'm so tired," he moaned. "I've been working so hard. You have no idea how I have suffered. It's a hard, lonely life on the sea. Comfort me, my wife, it has been a long, lonesome time."

Joyce was indignant. "What about me?" she said in her perfect Greek. "What do you think it's like for me all alone here with your parents?"

He looked at her blearily, which only irritated her more. "What?" he said.

"You never think of me," she went on. "You never ask me how I've been. You leave me here alone for months at a time. You're gone so much I feel like I don't even know you anymore. Then you come back all sorry for yourself and get drunk! How can you be so selfish?"

He stared at her, as astonished as if a tree had spoken. "What?" he said again.

Exasperated, she began to hiss. "You never spend one minute thinking about anyone but yourself, do you? You're like a little boy!"

At that he stood up shakily, his cheeks darkening. "How dare you speak to me like that!" he shouted. And staggered out of the room.

Joyce would not go near Nikos the next morning. Their first quarrel, and she felt its bitterness like a scar across her face. She glared at him, waiting for his apology. For almost five months she had longed for his caresses, his lovemaking, and instead he'd come to her incapacitated and reeking of self-pity. She was outraged.

Dimitra was angered, too. "What are you doing here?" she barked at Nikos when she found him asleep on the Turkish pillows downstairs. "You leave poor little Joyce alone for half a year, and you don't even go to her bed when you return? What kind of husband are you?"

Nikos scowled. "She speaks to me with no respect, Mama. I come home from months at sea and find she has learned Greek only to treat me like a beggar." He spat and crossed his muscular arms. "A woman cannot talk to her husband so."

"She has waited for you." Dimitra spoke quietly, her voice

low and full of reprimand. "She has never looked at another man. You have nothing to complain of."

Joyce stood in the shadows of the room, listening.

"She tricked me!" Nikos exclaimed. "She listened to me, pretending not to understand, then she spoke to me as if I am a worm. You want me to be married to a woman who does not respect me?" He waved his arms at his mother angrily. "You never speak to *Papas* like that!"

Dimitra sighed. "She is a good girl," she said, "but it is true she was not brought up a Greek. She perhaps has not learned to honor her husband."

"Yes!" Nikos said, raising his handsome chin triumphantly. "You teach her that, Mama, it's your job. Tell her it is the Greek way, go on."

Dimitra sighed again. But she turned to Joyce like an old donkey, like a trained dog, and obeyed her son. "Yes, *pedhi mou*," she said, "what Nikos says is true. It is written in our customs, in the law. Husband is head of the household and we must show him respect."

Joyce could barely speak. Dimitra, turned against her! But Joyce had not grown up with two bullying brothers for nothing. "If he wants my respect, he must earn it," she said icily.

"You see!" Nikos spluttered. "You see how she speaks to me!"

Dimitra held her hands out to him pleadingly. "I will teach her," she said. "Leave it to me."

Then Dimitra did something Joyce would never understand. She went over to her, drew back her hand, and hit her hard across the ear, sending Joyce sprawling to the floor. For a moment Joyce could hear nothing, her head ringing, her mind numb with shock.

"*Mannamou*, do not hit my bride!" Nikos cried, as shocked as she was. He bent over her, his eyes filling. "My little Joyce," he moaned, lifting her to her feet. "Forgive us. It's our rough peasant ways." He sank to his knees, his arms about her thighs. "Forgive us, forgive me. I love you, my little Joyce, I love you."

Joyce gazed down at his curly head. She still had him, he was still hers. She shot a triumphant look at Dimitra.

"Come," Nikos said, rising to his feet. "Come, I will show you how I love you." And he carried her up to bed.

Joyce had it out with Dimitra that afternoon. The two women were squatting by the pump, rinsing the lunch dishes, their heads wrapped in thick woolen shawls against the cold. Petros and Nikos were already in their beds for siesta.

"You and my son, you've made up now?" Dimitra said. She chuckled, her wrinkled mouth pursing. "Your first quarrel. It is like a baptism."

"Yes, no thanks to you," Joyce replied sullenly.

"Oh, don't make such a fuss. A little fight, a little quarrel, this is nothing in a marriage."

"It's not that, it's you." Joyce glared at her. "If you hit me like that again, Mama, I'm leaving."

"And where will you go?" Dimitra said mockingly. She stood up and folded her arms across her bosom. "This is your home now. Nobody else wants you."

"That's not true!" Joyce rose to face her. "I have my own family. I'll go back to them."

"They have forgotten you. You told me yourself they have not written since you ran away with my son. They don't want you anymore."

"I don't care! I'll leave anyway. Nikos and I will find our own home somewhere far away."

"Then you have no sense of family! You are nothing but a pampered American!" Dimitra bellowed, unfolding her arms to jab her fingers at Joyce. "You think marriage is all love letters and rumpus in the bed? This is nothing, nothing! The first little fight with your mother-in-law and you want to run away! I thought you were wiser than that, I thought you understood. I thought you loved my son!"

"I do love him. But you hit me, Mama! You don't hit people you love!"

Dimitra laughed. Folded her arms and laughed. "You Americans! Where do you get such ideas? You are all babies." Then she stepped forward, her dark eyes serious again. "You cannot leave, you cannot! You are ours, you are mine!"

"I am not yours! I don't belong to anybody," Joyce retorted, one of the few things she had learned in America rising to her lips.

But to Dimitra these were empty words. "You are my daughter now," she said. "You are my family. . . . You must understand." And, to Joyce's astonishment, Dimitra began to sob. Joyce had never seen her cry. It had always seemed to her that this hard, tough woman had dried up inside like a spent fig tree.

"Mama, don't." Joyce stepped forward and folded Dimitra in her arms, a soft bundle of clothes and sorrow. "I love you, Mama."

So Joyce had stayed. For Nikos. For family. For Dimitra.

IV

The farmer dropped Joyce and her in-laws off at the edge of Ayiassos; the lanes were too narrow to penetrate with a car. Thanking him, they heaved their bedrolls onto their backs and made their way to the church to claim their customary corner. Now that the day was cooling into afternoon, the streets were streaming with people, the uneven cobblestones barely visible beneath their feet, and at first this disoriented Joyce. She had become used to silence and empty spaces, to entire days filled with no more sound than the clanking of sheep bells or the barking of a dog. So she stayed close to Dimitra and Petros, as much to protect herself as them, and stared, dazzled, at the waves of faces, and at the stalls along the streets, offering cheap ceramics, scarves, rugs, icons, and endless amounts of food.

The church was large, much larger than the one in Kastron, and already its shaded cloisters were crowded with bodies and sleeping rolls. Petros led them with confidence to his favorite spot behind a fountain, where the splash of water helped to drown out the murmurs and snores of the strangers around them at night. The spot was still free — it had belonged to Petros for over thirty years, and everyone knew not to challenge his customs — so they spread out their bedrolls and sat down for a rest. But Joyce did not want to rest. Her disorientation was quickly giving way to excitement. She wanted to go out and roam the streets, to buy things, to eat and drink. To find strangers and talk the day away.

At last Dimitra and Petros were ready. As this was the holiday of returning families, they first had to visit Sophocles, Petros's eldest brother, to feast with him and listen to his annual boasts. Joyce looked forward to this. The family was large, the food plentiful, Sophocles a great buffoon. She walked beside her in-laws, their arms linked affectionately, her heart lifting in pleasure.

Sophocles lived in a modern building of poured concrete on the edge of Ayiassos, bigger than any of the ancient stone houses of the village and clearly prestigious. The plastered walls were freshly whitened for the festival, the red tiles on his roof spanking new. The house itself was two stories high and equipped with carpets, an indoor toilet, even electricity. Yet it looked naked to Joyce without the cracks and moss of the older houses, smooth and characterless as a doctor's smile.

Sophocles was not only the most successful of his four brothers but much the largest. Rotund and perspiring, with a huge bald face and a ringing voice, he welcomed Petros and his little family with noisy cheer. "*Yassou*, my brother!" he shouted, opening his big arms to crush Petros against his mound of a belly. "Come share our egg!" he added with a proud laugh, referring with a wink to an old Greek saying of the poor, "Prepare an egg, there are nine of us." He waddled before them over his garish blue carpet to the back of the house, where a pretty courtyard sat under the shade of two plane trees and an arbor of grapevines. Mauve hibiscus hung down the white walls, mingling with the reds and yellows of the climbing impatiens that grew out of huge white urns in the corners. Deep red grapes dangled from the vines. A long wooden table stretched down the middle, laden with cheese, lamb, pastries, fruit, and wine. The smells of honeysuckle, jasmine, and coffee filled the air.

The courtyard was full of people. It was like a wedding, except that almost everyone was old. The men were in their nicest jackets and whitest shirts, their faces lean with work and furrowed by war. The women were stern in their loose dark dresses and sturdy shoes, like a regiment of irritated nurses. Joyce was greeted with a great clamor when she was noticed, pulled into the crowd by withered hands, patted and stroked like an amusing pet. "Look at her," an old man cried, "ripe as a pomegranate." His hand crept up her thigh.

"None of that, Granddad," she replied indulgently, and brushed him away.

Sophocles was a shopkeeper and "an American" as the Greeks call the emigrants who move to the United States to make money. After forty years in Brooklyn, first working in a grocery shop and then owning several of them, he had returned the most prosperous member of the family, and he was proud of it. Every year since, his relatives had been obliged to begin the festivities by gathering around him as he sat enthroned in a chair and listening to his boasts about the money he had made, his sons still in New York, and his daughters' generous dowries. The men sat on the benches alongside the table, or in chairs that had been arrayed about the courtyard, guffawing and nudging one another like restless children in church. The women remained on their feet, waiting to serve.

"My Christos is to start university next month," Sophocles announced solemnly, his cheeks so huge that his features looked like a tiny face superimposed on a gigantic egg. "He is to go to Columbia University, the most important college in America. A toast!" He raised his *ouzo* glass, his double chin trembling expectantly.

"Which son is that, the Greek or the Yankee?" a younger brother yelled out, going off into a high-pitched giggle. This was an old joke. Every year the brothers teased Sophocles about his "other" family, the American wife and children he insisted didn't exist. It always made him furious.

"Masturbator!" Sophocles shouted. "May your balls shrivel to the size of peanuts!"

"They'd still be twice as big as yours," the brother retorted. Sophocles struggled to his feet, his face purple, but Petros laid a calming hand on his arm. "Dance for us, brother," he said. "We will drink a toast to your son, then you dance for us."

"Yes, come on Sophocles," the others called, clearing a space for him in the center of the courtyard. "Dance, and later we will join you."

This was a favorite moment for Joyce. In both of her previous visits, Sophocles had executed a solitary *Zeibekiko* to celebrate his fortune, a dance that was meant to be graceful and dignified, but when he did it, looked more like a rhinoceros tiptoeing over broken glass.

As always, he allowed Petros to appease him, knocking back his *ouzo* and lumbering to the center of the courtyard. Someone brought out a *bouzouki*, a deep-bellied, mandolin-like instrument, and began the rhythmic, insistent music that induces men to dance. Slowly extending his stubby arms, Sophocles fixed his eyes on the ground before him and bent his knees.

"Saint Nicholas preserve us," his younger brother called out again. "Atlantis is sinking."

Ignoring him, Sophocles exercised a few wobbly steps to the left. He stopped, swayed a moment, then staggered to the right, his arms still outstretched. His legs stamped, his belly heaved, his cheeks trembled like puddings. He shut his eyes, his expression blissful, and plowed into the crowd. Amid whoops and shouts, the other men caught him, and soon they were all snaking about the courtyard, their arms over each other's necks.

Petros sat apart, watching his relatives with amusement. He smoked, ate a little, but said nothing. Joyce gazed at him affectionately. To her, Petros was the noblest man in the place.

A minute later Joyce found herself pushed off with the other women to serve, while the men continued to drink, dance, and cuddle one another. As she jostled to take a dish from her hostess, or to refill a jug with the sweet mountain water that is the pride of Greece, the other women — the grandmothers, the middle-aged aunts, the unmarried cousins — took turns looking pointedly at her belly and asking if any children were on the way. She dreaded this. It had happened the year before, too. No children still? And how long has Nikos been away this time? They looked at one another, their dark eyes pitying. It was clear what they were thinking: She was a failure as a wife. She could not keep her husband by her side. She had caught the most gorgeous nephew of the lot, and she was driving him away. She couldn't even prove herself a woman and produce a son. Yet Joyce knew that, with children, she would be here forever. Without them, she still had a choice.

"You might as well be a sailor's widow, your husband's gone so much," said one of Petros's sisters-in-law. "In our island it is the custom for a sailor's widow never to marry again, no matter how young. She cannot dance or look at a man again, either." The woman glanced at her mockingly. Joyce turned away. If she had been at home she would have fought back, said something biting. As it was, here, with no status, under the fragile protection of Petros and Dimitra, she did not dare.

It was Dimitra, however, who was the true outcast in this crowd. The brothers blamed her for using her land to lure Petros away from his native Lesbos, which everyone knew was the better island, and condemning him to scratch a living out of the obdurate rock that was Ifestia. They were inordinately proud of Lesbos and its splendid history, both ancient and modern. It was the birthplace of Sappho, the great poet, of Aesop and Arion, as well as of the more recent poet Odysseus Elytis. It was the site of prosperous *ouzo* distilleries and the proud holder of Greece's record rate of alcoholism. During the Second World War, while all the nearby islands were occupied by Italians or falling to the Germans, Greek Communists conquered Lesbos and declared it an independent republic. Later in the war, when inflation had made the drachma almost worthless, the same islanders who had been so avowedly Communist turned wily capitalist instead, offering the best exchange rate around and drawing money to the island like flies to a pork chop. Petros should have stayed at home with his cunning fellow islanders, his brothers believed, and married a woman from his own village, as they had. "A shoe from home is best, even if it's patched," they liked to say.

The brothers' wives felt much the same. They didn't like Dimitra's arrogance about her son, or that he was more beautiful than any of their children. And they found Dimitra's lack of submissiveness an affront. But they were also afraid of her. They suspected that she had the gift of the curse. A certain kind of power seemed to sit on her broad shoulders, her crumpled brow. Her black eyes could look right through a person — it was the blood of witches and heathens, they said, inherited from her Turkish mother. So the men welcomed her with careful courtesy and the women showed deference, though little warmth. For years Dimitra had been infuriated by all this, but in her old age she had come to enjoy it. She sat in the courtyard, accepting dishes from the younger women, and glared at her trembling in-laws with challenging arrogance.

"They've always hated me, the old crows," she whispered to Joyce. "I am as much a foreigner to them as you. You see why they give me bad dreams? They think they are better than us, *koroulamou.* But I cut them down to size." And she spat to ward off the evil eye.

After several hours of waiting on the men, fending off their groping hands and offers to teach her the myriad ways of love, Joyce was at last released. "Go," Dimitra said abruptly. "Get away from these shameless old rams. Go buy yourself something." She pressed a few drachmas into her daughter-in-law's hand. "Remember, we're meeting in your uncle Zotis's taverna tonight." And at last, as the sun lowered gently to the horizon, filling the air with a pink and golden light, she let Joyce leave.

*   *   *

At first Joyce followed the tourists. She did this whenever she could, sniffing out English speakers like a hungry dog. She only wanted to eavesdrop, to drink in their chatter, the dear, simple flow of their language. She found no Americans — Americans rarely came to this corner of Greece — but soon she heard English voices and followed them. They belonged to two girls, both of them in shockingly brief shorts and tiny T–shirts, underneath which they were clearly wearing no bras. No wonder the Greeks think tourist women are sluts, Joyce found herself thinking; she had not exposed as much as a knee in two years. She looked down at herself, at the faded blue dress made for her by Dimitra on her neighbor's treadle sewing machine, and suddenly felt hidden in a costume. A sheath of crisply ironed cotton, a shapeless sack like that of an old woman, hiding the body of a young girl yearning to dance.

The English girls were about her age and were talking animatedly, sharing a bottle of *retsina* and laughing at some joke she could not hear. Joyce followed them for some time but eventually grew discontented with merely listening. She could catch only the odd sentence anyway, not the flow of thei conversation. When they stopped at the edge of the street and pulled out a guidebook, she saw her opportunity.

"May I help you?" she said, stepping over to them.

The girls looked up. Their faces were hostile, and Joyce immediately realized that, to them, an American offering help must seem both condescending and ridiculous.

"No thanks. We can manage fine," said one, a slim, compact woman with curly hair and a large nose.

"No, I mean I live here," Joyce said quickly. "I know the" — she stopped, groping for the word like a foreigner — "ropes!"

The girls looked at one another in surprise. The second girl was plump and solid, her thick black hair curling slightly under her chin, her round face openly curious. "Oh good!" she said, and flashed a smile. Joyce was startled. She had forgotten how easily foreigners smile. Greeks hardly ever smile, and when they do, it is often in anger.

"Well," the plump girl continued, "can you recommend a good place for music tonight?"

"I'm eating with my family at Taverna Pelopi. They have music. *Santouri.* Would you like to come?"

"You're sure we wouldn't be intruding?"

"No, no. It's a matter of honor to have strangers at the table. My in-laws would love it."

The girls nodded eagerly. Their names were Sarah and Nicola, they told her, and they were from London. Sarah, the skinny one, was soon asking Joyce the usual questions about why she was in Greece, and Joyce answered with practiced ease, telling her story the way she always did to strangers, without revealing anything that mattered.

The three girls wandered the streets together, talking, for they still had hours before Joyce was to meet her in-laws for the evening feast. There was much to see, so the time passed quickly: The ancient streets and houses. The medieval monastery, its bell tower like the top of a white-iced wedding cake. The crowds of homecomers and tourists, most of them Greek, sweating and loud in their holiday mood. The girls browsed through the colorful stalls that lined the streets. Ivory pendants in the shape of bulls' horns to signify virility. Wooden icons of saints, angels, of the Virgin and Christ. Bracelets linked in the traditional pattern of the labyrinth, perfect symbol of human life. Everywhere was the tourist pottery, tiny imitations of classical Greek vases and bowls, decorated with the silhouettes of athletes, fish eyes, and Heracles. The girls could have bought an entire village made of glazed ceramic, small enough to fit on one hand. Joyce looked over all this, remembering when she had been unable to understand Nikos's scorn for it. Now it seemed like junk to her, too, a lie, a packaging of a Greece that had never existed, that had nothing to do with the harsh hierarchy that had put her at the bottom of the familial ladder, with the unyielding land, or with the brutal loneliness of a sailor's wife.

Joyce and the English girls soon finished the bottle of *retsina* and stopped to buy another, passing it among them. Joyce drank eagerly. Each sip seemed to bring her closer to her old self, to the careless, impulsive American she had been before meeting Nikos. "After the festival you should come stay with us in Kastron," she said to her new friends, the wine making her gushing and affectionate. "Take the ferry over and come see how we peasants live!"

She even dared, once or twice, to meet a man's eye.

The girls decided to buy some of the souvenirs. Nicola chose a strand of worry beads made of dark blue glass, each one painted with a white eye. Joyce explained that Greeks hang these beads around the necks of their children, donkeys, and dogs to ward off the evil eye of jealousy; Dimitra had told her that she'd hung them all over Nikos the minute he was born. Sarah bought some ivory bangles, which Joyce suspected were really plastic, but they looked nice against the tan of Sarah's thin arm. Joyce could afford almost none of this, but it didn't matter. At home she had loved buying things, but that seemed shameful now. Anyway, all Dimitra would allow her to wear was a cross around her neck — anything else she would have considered sluttish — and Joyce could not go that far. She might accompany Dimitra to church, she might even pray there and kiss an icon or two, but she could never wear a crucifix.

Just as Joyce turned away from the stall she saw the tourist boy who had saved her from the soldiers. He was standing in the street looking at her, his face reddening as it had before. She had forgotten how tall he was, tall and bony, towering over most of the island Greeks like the mast of a ship.

"Joyce?" he said. "I'm Alex, remember?" He stepped forward uncertainly.

Joyce found herself blushing, too, her embarrassment triggered by his. "Yes, of course I remember," she said hurriedly.

She turned to the English girls, who were looking at him with mild curiosity. "This is Nicola, Sarah." She gestured at them. "This is Alexandros. I mean Alex."

The three tourists greeted each other without much interest. None of them had come to Greece to meet other Brits.

"Here, want a swig?" Nicola said, holding out the new bottle of *retsina* to Alex. "We're getting into the mood of the festival."

He accepted the bottle and took a swallow, then handed it back. He was looking at Joyce so intently that she squirmed.

Suddenly a blast of Greek pop music assaulted them, and they looked up to see that they were standing under a large speaker suspended above the shop doorway. Clapping their hands over their ears, they moved away, laughing. Alex took the opportunity to bend down to Joyce. "Were you all right after that day I saw you?" he murmured in her ear.

She nodded and looked at him shyly. "Yes. Fine. Well, I was a little shaken up. Thanks again, I . . ."

"No, don't thank me any more. It's all right."

"Joyce?" Nicola's voice broke in. "Sarah and I want to go do something. We'll meet you at that taverna in a couple of hours, all right?"

"Oh." Joyce was disconcerted. She guessed that they thought they should leave her and Alex alone but could think of no way to explain the actual situation, so she had to agree. She hoped they would show up at the taverna. She wanted to talk English all night, to remember what it was like to be modern and carefree.

Alex, however, was visibly thrilled that the girls had gone. "Now I can get you that drink I promised," he said triumphantly. "That *retsina* tasted good. How about some more?"

Joyce looked about her again. She was so used to being watched. But this was the festival and her in-laws were elsewhere, lost in their own bottles of wine and frivolity. The sudden freedom almost lifted her off her feet.

"Yes!" she said, and laughed. "Yes."

They chose an outdoor taverna in the tourist-ridden section of the old bazaar, where Joyce could be the most sure of not running into anyone she knew — her relatives made of point of staying away from the crowds. It was set in the middle of the village square, a spread of little, candle-decked tables. The roof was the sky, now the luminous blue of dusk, the walls nothing but a row of flower boxes and the balmy evening breeze. A violin player serenaded couples at the tables, irritating the other tourists.

Alex ordered a jug of the local barrel wine and some *tzatziki*. Joyce was hungry, having eaten nothing but bread and olives on the boat — she had been too busy serving at Sophocles' house to eat — so she found herself scooping up the yogurt-and-cucumber dip greedily. The wine burned a happy hole in her stomach and rose instantly to her head. She felt as if she were hovering an inch above her chair.

"So," Alex said, "have you decided to answer my question?"

"What question?"

"Don't you remember? About why you're living here."

She looked away. Her face, narrow and smooth, was a little sharp when she turned, her jawline crisp, her nose long and thin. Having forgotten all her women's magazine advice, she had allowed her eyebrows to grow in, and they formed thick arches over her green eyes, adding a touch of fierceness to her feline looks. Her hair was loose today, in honor of the festivities, and hung straight and lank down to the tips of her small, pointed breasts.

Joyce looked away because she thought she didn't want to answer, but she had not reckoned on the wine or the intoxication of Alex's attention. Words rose to her lips like bubbles. She began her story with the supermarket, the way she always did when chatting to tourists. Her custom was to tell the tale as a romance, a myth she wove about herself as a protective web. But with Alex she found the web would not hold. So instead she spoke of the lengths of Nikos's trips and the life she led with Dimitra and Petros. She left out only how much she missed Nikos, her fingers in the night. The dreams triggered by soldiers. How hard it was to hold on.

Alex beckoned the waiter and ordered more wine. "How long did you say your husband's been away this time?" he asked, his eyebrows raised.

"Seven months." Joyce felt embarrassed.

"Seven months?" Alex's raw face was indignant. "How can he leave you for so long?"

Joyce looked down at the table. "He doesn't have any choice. They offer him these contracts he has to take if he wants to keep his job. He sends us money every month. A lot of Greek men live like that." She raised her eyes. "It's a tradition."

Alex looked dubious but refrained from pushing the point. Instead, he refilled their glasses. "If you married him when you were only eighteen, I suppose that means you never went to college, right?"

Joyce shrugged. "Yes. But I wouldn't have made it anyway. I was a terrible student." She laughed at Alex's expression: his blue eyes wide, his mouth pinched in disapproval. "Don't worry. I'm a complete screw-up, I know," she added, then looked away, suddenly serious. She didn't like how she sounded. She had never wanted to be stupid. She was growing sour, she realized, bitter like an old woman. "I like to read," she added quietly, wanting to redeem herself. "I've spent most of my nights learning to read Greek from kids' textbooks and newspapers."

At the word newspapers, Alex grew excited. "Isn't this an amazing time to be here?" he exclaimed, leaning towards her suddenly. "Everywhere I go I meet people who've just been released from prison for protesting the Junta. It's as if the whole country's having one big party."

Joyce smiled at his enthusiasm. "Yes," she said quietly.

"What? You sound doubtful. Isn't everybody in your village happy now the Colonels are gone?"

"Of course they are." She paused. "It's just that after every-thing they've been through, they find it hard to believe in any kind of government anymore. They don't trust anybody with power and they're scared of fanatics. Anyway, most people in my village wanted the socialists to win, not Karamanlis."

She told Alex about Markos Elytis, the schoolteacher who had lent her the books from which she'd learned to read Greek. The sole teacher of the village, responsible for all the children at once, whom he had to teach in one room, he had been a dedicated but impoverished man who had barely been able to hold on to his job under the Junta. Suspected of dissidence, he was constantly being watched, searched, bullied by the police. For years he had managed to talk himself out of whichever accusation had been leveled at him — that he was a Communist, an American sympathizer, a socialist, a corrupter of children's morals, an atheist — although not without cost to his nerves and pocket. But then one day he had made a fatal mistake: he had scolded a child for expressing fascist sentiments. The child had complained to his parents and the parents had denounced him as a Communist to the police. They had hauled him into the police station, beaten him, and confiscated his license. He and his family — his wife, his own children, even his widower father — had all had to leave Ifestia, their native island and the only home they had ever known.

"After that, no one in Kastron dared to say anything about politics in case the same thing happened to them," Joyce said quietly. "Even in our own house, when guests were over, we were afraid to speak freely."

"But what about now? Is it still like that now?"

Joyce put down her fork and leaned back in her chair. "Oh no, they're over that now that the Junta's gone. You can never keep a Greek down for long."

Joyce didn't know it, but she could not have spoken more seductively to Alex had she whispered of love or confessed her most secret desires. His obsession was politics, especially

Greek politics. Political science had been his subject at university, Greece his specialty. He wanted Joyce to tell him all about the politics in her island, her village, her family. And she could, for what else had she had to do every evening for two years but sit and listen to Petros and Dimitra talk about the many wars they'd survived, the rise of the Colonels' Junta, its seven years of dictatorship, and its fall?

Alex was fascinated by Greece. His mother's hot, dusty homeland, its silvery olive trees, immodest figs and thunder-dark cypresses; its people hard and passionate about money and freedom; its tales of heroism against the Germans and of political prisoners under the Junta. He had spent every summer in Greece since he was thirteen, and after he'd gone home the last time, having watched the dictatorship fall, his English friends had seemed empty and shallow, removed even from Vietnam, concerned much more with chasing sex and their own ambitions than with politics. He had found himself longing for the political arguments he'd had in tavernas under the balmy skies, drunk on *ouzo;* for the heroes he had met, released from prison at last and returned to wild welcomes in their villages; for the students he had come to know who had risked their lives demonstrating against the dictatorship. So he had returned, looking for purpose and adventure. For revolution and, perhaps, even a future.

But he had not reckoned on finding a damsel in distress. Or, he thought ironically, on falling, like one of Odysseus's unfortunate rivals, for a lonely Penelope.

Joyce was talking more than she had in years. Her throat was raw from all the words. She was being unguarded, foolish, laughing too loudly and telling too much. She and Nikos had owned no words between them, and once they had, the words had only caused trouble. With Alex she felt high on them. They bore her up like clouds, like wings, like puffs of air.

In her intoxication she wanted to invite him to the taverna. She wanted to keep her new friend by her side, to show him her Dimitra and Petros, the thought of whom filled her with a sudden, giddy love. But she was not sure this was wise. The English girls would be welcomed, this she knew, but a boy — even a tourist boy — was dangerous. Anyway, if she brought him in, publicly acknowledged him like that, she would make him safe. And secretly, so secretly she would not admit it even to herself, she did not want to make him safe.

"I've got to go," she said when he offered to refill another jug. "It's time for me to meet my family for the feast."

Alex said nothing but she could see on his face that he wanted to be invited. The face of this funny-looking boy hid nothing; it was as transparent as etched glass. Nikos's face, on the other hand, was a mask, a breathtaking mask. Is this always true of beautiful people, Joyce wondered, that one cannot read their faces?

But Alex was a gentleman, so he dropped no hints, only paid and stood. He walked around to her side of the table and held her chair as she got to her feet, as if she were delicate or infirm, not as strong as a farmboy. She giggled and staggered, the wine buckling her knees, and found his arm around her waist. She leaned against him, just for a moment, just enough to feel the sharp edge of his shoulder and the hardness of his body. Just enough to catch the tangy scent of his sweat.

For him, this moment was cardinal. Beneath her modest dress he felt the firmness of her waist, that she was lithe and shapely and strong. Her hair smelled of lavender and dust, her breath of pine-scented *retsina* and something indefinably sweet. Unable to stop himself, he pulled her to him, his long arms easily circling her waist, and pressed his lips to her forehead.

She staggered away, shaking her head, and led him unsteadily back to the street.

On the way to meet her in-laws, Joyce sobered up enough to realize that of course she could not invite Alex in. Just to step in the door with him would be a catastrophe. In 1975 women in Greece were still brought to court for adultery, which was a criminal offense; or simply beaten, with public approval, by their husbands. Joyce knew she would be turned out and worse if she were seen with Alex. She would be stranded and penniless, cut off forever from Nikos, forced to beg for help from her moribund family in Florida. And if she said no, your suspicions are wrong, Alex is just an acquaintance, no one would believe her.

"Alex," she said, and stopped to look up at him. "We better say good-bye here. I can't risk anyone I know seeing you."

"I understand," he replied, but his face was pained. He stepped close to her, the crowds parting to move around them, and put his hands lightly on her arms, those tough sinewy arms she had developed during her time in Greece. She shivered at his touch. "Are you cold?" he said.

She shook her head but could not make herself move out of his grasp. He stepped closer, just a little closer, and she began to tremble. It was as if something inside her were breaking.

Gently, he pulled her to him, then slowly, tentatively, embraced her again. A hug, nothing more, but she pressed herself to him, the top of her head against his collarbone, her nose buried in the sweet pungency of his sweat-stained shirt. His arms slid tighter around her back, pulling her to him until they were sealed together.

They stood like this for some time. Neither of them could bear to end it. Joyce told herself this was innocent, nothing more than a gesture of comfort. Alex buried his face in her hair.

"I have to see you again," he murmured at last. "I can't just let go of you like this."

Joyce shook her head against his chest. "Shh," she whispered, and with tremendous effort pushed herself away from him. It was like tearing wet skin from ice. Her trembling had not ceased, but her voice was calm.

"I've got to go, I'm late," she said, and ran down the street.

The taverna was cramped and smoky and packed with people sitting at long, cloth-covered tables. Even more of Petros's relatives had arrived, including a few girls Joyce's age, all married, several pregnant. The younger men were giddy, on leave from the army or the sea, and they shouted and laughed, raising their glasses in noisy toasts. Petros was telling a sly story to one of his elder brothers, his face creased in amusement. Dimitra beckoned Joyce over, squeezed her between herself and another old woman, and loaded up her plate with *rizi*, spinach, and lamb.

"You had a good time today?" she shouted over the racket.

Joyce said she had and gazed around the table. She was in a daze. She had so much looked forward to this, but now it was just a blur of noise and food. She could think only of Alex. She wanted to lead him away from town to a secret corner of the forest. To pull him down on the springy pine needles and open herself to him, as she had for Nikos. Love, her wifely vows, her belief in faithfulness — all these faded to insignificance compared to this sudden longing. She could not hear what people were saying to her, could not see anything but candle flames and red, shouting faces, mouths greasy with lamb fat. She surreptitiously sniffed her dress, her sleeve, to see if she could smell him on her. But she smelled nothing except the smoke of burning candles, the heavy scent of baked meat, and the cheap perfumes of the other women.

Eventually she remembered the English girls. She lifted her head to look over the crowd. She must have missed them by being so late. She felt a pang at having let them down and given up the chance for companionship, but soon let it go. The truth was, those girls made her feel old. No younger than she, better educated, they nevertheless seemed like children. She stared down at her work-scarred hands, the scuffed fingernails, the tough brown of her arms, and felt worlds away from those girls. Worlds away from what she once was.

But what was I once? she found herself wondering. A Jewish American girl from the Miami suburbs? Yes. Born in the postwar safety of 1955 and raised in the self-obsessed era of hair curlers and television sitcoms? True. But was that all?

Her mother had been a third-grade teacher until she'd had children; her father had stayed a sales manager all his life. They considered themselves middle class but were poor enough to cut coupons. Not poor by the standards of Dimitra and Petros, but poor compared to the American ideal. A dishwasher, a washing machine, a basketball hoop over the driveway — all these things they had and took for granted. Nevertheless, Joyce had grown up with a certain shabbiness. Furniture worn but never replaced. Toilet paper rough and thin, bought on sale or at discount stores. Clothes homemade from patterns and cheap, stiff cotton. Cars that always broke down.

Joyce shook her head. This was not what accounted for the distaste she felt about her old life. It was something else, something she could define only as an emptiness. A missing out. The affection she did not get when she ran to her mother for shelter. The conversation she was refused when she tried to talk to her father. The protection she expected from her brothers, which always turned into attacks. Even the turbulence of the sixties and seventies had passed her by. She'd been a teenager in the late sixties but too young to notice, a young woman in the early seventies but in Florida, on the wrong coast to count. Civil rights, Vietnam, hippies — she had watched it all in a black-and-white square in her pastel living room, then switched it off the screen and out of her mind as if it were nothing but a sitcom. She had existed in a void, she thought now, not quite part of her family or of her time. Belonging nowhere.

As children, Joyce and her brothers ran wild. Up and down the hot Florida streets on their bicycles, stopping to throw stones at the parrots in the trees or at each other. Most of their lives were spent in shorts or bathing suits, jumping through sprinklers, flirting on the beach. Joyce's brothers were experts at forming clubs whose sole purpose was to make girls and misfits feel excluded. They hid her dolls, broke her toys. Once, when she was twelve, Ben had tied her to a backyard tree and sprayed her with the hose, then had torn off her clothes and left her naked, her newly formed breasts and modest beginnings of pubic hair exposed for all to scrutinize. Later he returned with four other boys to taunt and touch. But she never screamed and she never told.

Her mother thought only of money and food. She made bitter comments about her children's lack of schooling and her sons' refusal to read but did little to remedy these things. She brought home books for Joyce, but they were carelessly chosen. Histories of trains mixed in with Tarzan tales. Harlequin romances jumbled up with *Jane Eyre* and Dickens. Joyce read lazily, picking the easy ones or reading them with half a mind. Sometimes a romance would catch her and whole days would disappear. Other times she pushed the books aside in favor of painting her toenails.

Day after day her mother sat out in the yard, growing fat and leathery in the sun. She worked out budgets, combed the newspapers for deals, a cigarette in her mouth and chips and Cokes piled in front of her. "There's a sale down at the A & P," she would say to Joyce. "Paper towels and Cheerios. Run down and get some, honeypie."

Her father watched his boys play ball from a deck chair, regarding Joyce with remote unease. He had no friends, grew more vague and gray every day, like a poster fading in the sun. Joyce visited him at work once in a while to buy a discount pair of shoes and saw that he bossed his salesmen adequately enough. But everything he said, every move he made, seemed deeply tired and sad, as if it were an effort even to breathe.

"What's wrong with Dad?" she once asked her mother.

"Nothing. He's just bored" was the only reply. "Maybe his circulation."

"He should go to a doctor."

"He did. They said he has a bad heart, but what do they know?" Her mother shrugged. "It's like that when you're old."

The whole family was stuck. No passion, no dreams, no ambitions. Passivity had sucked them dry, all of them, even her brothers. Turned them shallow. Indifferent. Stuck in their facile comfort, like lampposts in cement.

As for Joyce herself, she had tried to cling to some goals and fight against the paralysis of her family. For a while she'd thought about becoming an actress, but her plans had kept slipping, undisciplined, into fantasies of romance. With no one to scold or encourage her, she had ignored her homework, ridden her bike, barely graduated from high school. Avoided finding a job. Painted her nails.

And had waited, unknowingly, for someone to rescue her.

Joyce looked about the taverna. Not one of the women here had ever had the easy freedoms with which she'd grown up. Not one of them had ever had a choice about what to do with her life, about how to spend each hour of the day. Not one of them was free even now to walk the streets by herself, to hop a bike and go somewhere she had never seen. Joyce had grown up with that freedom, but what had she done with it? What had any of her family done with it? Poured it into bullying and football, into watching television and counting money and shopping for trinkets nobody needed. There they were, free from hunger, free from dictatorship, war, and the ancient shackles of Christianity, and they had wasted it all.

That's who I was, Joyce told herself harshly. Joyce Amelia Perlman, a suburban American girl whose freedom meant so little to me that I was ready to trade it all away for a kiss.

Dimitra was asleep on Joyce's arm, her heavy body making Joyce sweat in the smoky air. People had eaten enough and were now puffing on cigarettes and pipes, the powerful tobacco stinging Joyce's eyes. She yawned and reached for some water. Her head ached from all the wine she had drunk and she wanted only to lie down and sleep. Her desire for Alex was already sinking beneath self-reproach and the need for rest. She had been up since dawn, she had spent her siesta carousing, and it was now nearly two in the morning. She longed, suddenly, to be back in her regular life, free from dangerous yearnings. To be discussing prices with Petros, joking with Dimitra, planting vegetables. Waiting for Nikos.

"Hello, Joyce?"

The English girls were standing beside her, looking embarrassed. Their eyes glittered and they listed slightly, drunk like everybody else, but they still seemed shy. "Sorry we're so late," they said, giggling. "We got waylaid."

Joyce was delighted. Wide awake again, she stood, startling Dimitra into jerking upright with a bewildered glare. Joyce asked the people on her bench to squeeze up tighter and inserted the girls next to her. "I thought I'd missed you," she said. "I'm so glad you came."

She introduced Dimitra, Petros, his brothers and their wives. They welcomed the girls with clamorous cheer and plied them with food and drink.

"We can't," the girls protested in English. "We're full already."

"You must," Joyce whispered seriously, "or my family will be hurt."

Dimitra was staring at the girls in amusement. She leaned over to Joyce and whispered in Greek. "That girl with the big nose, she is like a scarecrow! The other is pretty, though. She looks like a good Greek girl."

"I think they're both pretty," Joyce replied, wanting to defend the scrawny like herself.

"The big-nose one looks like a Jew," Dimitra said and snorted derisively.

Joyce glanced at Dimitra, shocked. She had never heard her say anything like that before. Thank God the English girls couldn't understand Greek! Mortified, she frowned down at the table. She wanted so badly not to have to think ill of Dimitra. She hated it when disappointment or anger came between them, like the time when Dimitra had hit her. She wanted to have nothing terrible between her and Dimitra ever again, to have no guilt, no secrets, nothing but an honest, clear space — to make Dimitra as different from her own mother as possible. Yet her secrets were dividing her from Dimitra already. Her desires, her Judaism. And now, Alex.

The musicians arrived, blessedly saving Joyce from having to reply to Dimitra's remark. One played a clarinet, one a drum, one a violin, the last the *santouri* — a lap dulcimer, which the musician hit with tiny soft hammers. They started their thumping, rhythmic music, and as it escalated in speed and excitement, the men rose to push aside the tables and dance again. This time they were serious, each determined to show off the dancing style of his village or people. They stamped their feet and bent their knees with dignified grace, their heads high and their backs upright. Some held a scarf in one hand, held onto by a partner, in the heroic dance known as the *Tsamiko*. Others snapped their fingers as they turned and stepped in a slow circle. Sophocles stayed in his seat this time, too busy picking at the leftover food to look up. The women watched and clapped.

Nikos would love this, Joyce thought. He would love kicking his strong legs, turning his proud buttocks to the crowd, holding up his beautiful head, just as he did to embarrass my brothers. He would love the adoration.

"Don't the women get to dance?" It was Sarah asking, leaning over to shout in Joyce's ear.

Joyce shook her head. "Not usually. Sometimes. It's a men's thing, really."

"Everything here's a men's thing," Sarah pronounced. "It's fucking archaic."

That's not true, Joyce was about to protest. But then she fell silent.

V

The festival went on for two more days. Crowds ebbed and flowed, the number of tourists began to wane, but the hardy and the native endured. Petros, who usually drank no more than one or two *ouzos* a day, was catatonic with alcohol. Dimitra gave up drinking after the first night but was busy with her husband's relatives, examining with begrudging admiration the horses they traded and the blankets woven by the women. Joyce was left more to herself than she was all year. So she wandered in search of Alex.

She pretended not to be looking for him, of course, tricked herself into believing that she was merely trying to find other tourists to befriend, as she had in the past. But when she found them, she no longer wanted to lure them into conversation. Before in Ayiassos she had been like a seer, roaming the stony lanes in search of someone to hear her tales, trying to stop up her loneliness with stories poured out to strangers. She had no heart for this now. Instead, she wandered up and down, looking for Alex's tall figure above the crowd. The town was small. If he was still here she would find him. Or he would find her.

It took only one morning. She saw him first, which made it difficult. As a married woman she felt she could respond to him, but not seek him out. To receive his friendship could be innocent, to ask for it plainly corrupt.

She stood watching him, unobserved, for some time. He was talking to two young Greeks at an outdoor *kaphenio*, obviously about politics. The men were excited, leaning over their round metal table, waving their hands. Alex's face was alive and earnest, his eyes concentrated under his uneven blond hair, his nose glowing from sunburn. Dressed in loose cotton — a cream-colored shirt, floppy white trousers — he seemed surprisingly at ease. He looked happy, Joyce thought. He looked at home.

She stepped closer. "We British have no business interfering in Cyprus!" she heard him say. His Greek was elegant, that of an educated Athenian, she realized for the first time. Hers must sound rough to him, coarse, the way a New Yorker sounds down in Florida.

She didn't know what to do. She could not approach him here, in his male domain. Women did not go into *kaphenia* full of men, and they certainly did not walk right up to a man at a table. She looked around, perplexed. If she wandered away she would lose him, but she could hardly follow him all day, either. Finally she decided to duck into the shop beside her and while away some time until, with luck, he got up to leave.

The shop sold clothing, modern clothing, pretty, not like the sacks and unwieldy skirts Dimitra made her wear. Joyce was tempted to try something on. Picking up a pair of jeans and a light pink T-shirt, she asked for the changing room. Then she slipped them on and stood, staring into the mirror.

There she was, looking as sleek as a new gun. She gazed at her reflection, disconcerted. Tight jeans, sandals, skimpy shirt; a trim, saucy girl with a flip — well, a mop — of sun-bleached hair. She had never seen herself as so American — if she were chewing gum, she would look exactly like the metallic blondes who worked the cash-registers at her local Dunkin Donuts, minus the silvery eye-shadow. She looked daring, even dangerous.

The thought made her grin, and she kicked up a leg, free

from a skirt for the first time in years. She had accepted Dimitra's bulky clothes as a way of blending in, of looking Greek. But now these jeans made her want to leap in the air, run, turn somersaults. Shout insults. They made her feel uncorseted, as if she could cartwheel down the beach for miles.

Just then she heard men's voices on the street and rushed outside to look. Alex was shaking hands with his companions, bidding them farewell. Turning, he saw her instantly in the shop doorway.

"Joyce! I almost didn't recognize you," he stammered.

"I know." She shrugged, gesturing down at herself. "I was trying these on. I haven't worn pants in ages."

"You look great. But . . . it's so different." He was taken aback, she could see that. She had broken an image for him.

"I look like an American tourist, huh?"

"Well, you look . . . sophisticated."

She laughed. "You mean not like a peasant? I better go back inside and change before they make me pay for these."

"I'll buy them for you," he said quickly. "Wear them for today, while you're here. We'll get out of this crowd and hike up the mountain through the woods."

Oh God. Joyce wanted this so much she could not speak. A hike in jeans! It sounded so normal.

But of course she told him she could not accept such a gift, or such an invitation.

"Yes, you can," Alex insisted. "I bet you don't have to see your in-laws until tonight. I'm right, aren't I?"

She nodded. She was giving in already, she knew it. He did too.

He bought the jeans, she bought the shirt. It used up all her money but there was nothing else she wanted anyway. Then he bought olives, grapes, the wettest *feta* they could find, bread, water and wine, and they escaped.

They began by walking through a series of olive groves that lay like pale green pools outside the village. The trees were heavy with ripening olives at this time of year, their trunks dark and twisted against their silver-green leaves. Alex was so tall he had to duck under the branches, but they were both grateful for the shade. The sun was already high in the clear, merciless sky. He carried everything in his rucksack, including the wine he had wrapped in Joyce's dress, so her hands were unaccustomedly free. She swung them by her side as they climbed. Mount Olymbos was over three thousand feet high, and the ascent was steep and difficult. Joyce's new jeans were unbearably hot.

Soon the olives gave way to scrubby evergreen oaks and stunted pine trees, which emitted a sweet, spicy scent that clung to their skins like oil. They breathed hard as they climbed. The air was dense with resin and dust and the stillness of the forest.

For a time they said nothing, but the silence was not awkward. It was the silence of too much to say, of anticipation. Casually, Alex reached for Joyce's hand. But at his touch she pulled away.

"Thanks for coming," he said, disconcerted. "I know this is risky for you."

Joyce squinted at the ground. Layers of pine needles, rust and deep green, the earth a dusty red underneath. Her toes, scuffed and brown in her sandals. What the hell was she doing?

"It might be the only time I can do this," she said. "Ever."

"You can't be sure," Alex replied.

"But I've never taken off with anybody like this before, the whole time I've been here." She was speaking fast. She wanted him to know that she had been faithful, that she was a good wife.

"Joyce." Alex paused, breathing heavily. They were in the sun now, above the woods, on a goat trail that zigzagged up the scrub-covered mountain. His face was burning, his rough shirt already soaked with sweat. "Joyce, what are you worried about? That I don't respect you? I'm not Greek, at least not in that way. I don't think like that." He stopped, clenching his jaw. He did not want to go too fast, to frighten her. He had no idea what he was to her, except a moment's escape.

Joyce looked up at him, squinting against the sun. It was almost noon, the sky white with brightness. "I'm scared," she said quietly. "If anyone sees us . . ."

"I know." He took her hand. This time she did not pull away.

"We're safe here, look." He swept the view with his free hand. They were utterly alone, the wooded valley stretching far below them, Ayiassos out of sight behind the forest. Nothing was around them but fig and olive trees, scrub oaks and pines, the muted *tonk* of a goat's bell in the distance. Even the birds were gone, sheltering somewhere from the fierce sun.

"Let's go on, before we get burnt to a crisp." He turned, giving back her hand like a present. They walked single file up the narrow path.

At last they found an old stone wall to lean against and a spring, from which a tiny stream trickled down the mountainside. A twisted fig tree grew beside it, its splayed, heavy leaves providing just enough shade to protect them. Joyce plucked two early purple figs, tight bulbs of sweetness, peeled one, and handed it to Alex. A lizard lay on the wall, still as a rock.

They sat, side by side, eating the sticky figs languorously. Then poured water from the bottle into their mouths, letting it run over their chins to their chests. Joyce spilled some into her palm and splashed her brow with it. The water dripped to her breasts, making her flimsy new shirt cling to them like kisses.

"Are you hungry yet?" Alex asked to distract himself.

"No. I'm too hot. Let's wait."

He agreed, and they leaned back to contemplate the view. Below them, beyond the pale grass, the red dust, and the dark green of the valley, stretched a strip of white beach melting into the sea, and close behind that lay the coastline of Turkey. It all glittered like a mirage, stripes of misty, gradated color shimmering and wrinkling in the heat. The Turkish coast was tawny at this distance, the land beyond it a dim, ruddy brown. Even the Aegean was striated with color, turquoise nearby and farther out a deep, mesmerizing indigo. Joyce suddenly wished they had gone down instead of up. While she was acting so careless and American, she might as well go swimming.

"I wish I could live here," Alex said suddenly. "I love this." His voice was thick with emotion. "I love Greece."

Joyce turned away, smiling. She was touched but also cynical. He was in love with Greece the way a visitor would be. He wanted to live here because of the views, the colors, the brilliant, seductive light. And perhaps because of the debates he so enjoyed with other men in coffee shops. But these were not what made up a life, she knew that now too well. Life was made of the rocky land and its begrudging yields. Of the capricious weather and its capacity to create and destroy. Above all, life was made of other people and what they did to you.

"Yes, it's beautiful," was all she said. Then she relented and added, "But it's hard, living here."

Alex looked at her quickly. "How?" His voice had that eagerness again, the way it had at the taverna. Joyce's heart squeezed at the sound. No one, no one in her whole life had ever been this interested in what she had to say.

"Why is it hard?" he repeated.

"Well, it's hard for my in-laws," she replied, deflecting his real question. "All they have is this patch of dried-up land, a few goats and sheep and one cow. Just because my mother-in-law had the bad luck to be born on the western side of Ifestia. If they'd come from the other side, their life could have been completely different. Over there the land is fertile. Ponds and corn. It's real farmland. But we're trying to make a living out of a bunch of rocks."

"Can't your in-laws move?"

Joyce shook her head. "My father-in-law has spent his whole married life trying to save up money to buy land on the eastern side, but he's never been able to do it. My . . ." She hesitated, just for a beat. "My husband sends money, but each time Petros tries to invest it — to buy another cow or more sheep, or a machine to harvest the sesame — something goes wrong. The cow dies, the sheep gets sick, the gadget breaks. He thinks he's cursed."

She looked over at Alex, his hair straggling over his damp forehead, his eyes deep and dark in the feeble shade of the fig tree. "That's what I mean by hard. When you live on the edge like this, it takes only one little flip of bad luck to make everything hit bottom."

"How else is it hard?" Alex turned towards her, crouching on his knees like a supplicant. He was too absorbed in her words to be aware of his posture, but she noticed it.

She looked down at her lap, her thighs encased in the unfamiliar blue jeans, which were sticking to her now with a thick, cloying sweat. His question opened a great yearning in her. She wanted so much to tell him of how she had struggled to forget the freedom she had relinquished for . . . what? For love? For passion? For the chance to be needed? She wanted to confess how, even as she missed Nikos desperately, she longed for other men. But she was too ashamed.

"It's only the strictness, I guess," was all she said. "My in-laws love me. But they're rough and . . . you know how Greek women are restricted, Alex. You know."

Alex reached to take her hand but she pulled away. She was not asking for pity.

After a pause, he rearranged himself beside her. He was bursting with more questions but sensed her shifting mood and was wise enough to keep quiet. He pulled a bottle of Demestica from the rucksack and opened it, using the corkscrew on his penknife. Then he spread out a napkin, and on it arranged some slices of *feta* and cucumber, a cluster of olives, and a hunk of bread, and laid it all on Joyce's lap.

Rested now, and cooler, she found her appetite restored, and ate quickly, the buttery olives and salty tang of the cheese vivid and rewarding after the long climb. The wine clouded her mind instantly, numbing her anxieties, allowing her thoughts to drift lazily, butterflies in the wind.

After a stretch of silence while they ate, Joyce asked Alex to tell her about his family and his home. She wanted to distract him from her own tale, but she was also curious to know his origins and to find some explanation for his easy confidence. Joyce had no experience with the privileged. Alex's courtesy, his knowledge — she had no idea that these were the products of expensive schools and upper-class taste, of parents who had drummed such values into him with every word they uttered. She knew only that she found his manner restful and his attentiveness deeply flattering.

He complied, his voice low and relaxed. "Would you like to hear how my parents met? They've always loved to tell me the story," he said, settling his back against the wall. "It was in 1950, just after the civil war ended, when Greece was being pushed around by the Americans." He looked away from Joyce so as not to seem accusatory. "My father was fresh out of a postwar degree at Cambridge, about to embark on a career of teaching literature. He went to Thessaloniki for a holiday, on his way to hop the islands, and met my mother in a museum. They started talking over a painting. Apparently he was using the ancient Greek he'd learned at Cambridge, so he sounded like Chaucer, and she had her schoolgirl English, so she sounded about three years old. They began laughing about it, and soon they were meeting every day. She told him she was there to grab some culture and a last glimpse of the world before her parents took her back to Ifestia and married her off to some shopkeeper they'd picked out for her. My father stayed too, and the minute he got back to England, he wrote a letter of proposal. She broke off from the shopkeeper and accepted him, they wrote to each other for a few more months, then she took a ship to England, married him, and has stayed there ever since."

"Sounds almost as fast as my marriage," Joyce said. "How did she find the courage to do it?"

Alex looked at her curiously — that was exactly what he wanted to ask her. "Well, I think she did love him. But she also saw the chance to be sprung from a life like my aunt's, not to mention right-wing oppression, poverty, and a greasy old shopkeeper."

"Does she ever miss Ifestia? Does she miss the old ways?"

"No." Alex shifted, the ground under him suddenly feeling hard and stony. "She's never come back, even with me. She gives me letters to her relatives and sends me off to meet them, but she won't come here herself. She says she hates it."

My mother is the opposite of you, he wanted to add. She left the old for the new. You left the new for the old.

"I guess I can understand that," Joyce mused. "I feel like that about Florida. I don't want to go back there, either. Ever."

"Not even to see your family?"

Joyce spat an olive pit so far out they were both surprised. "Specially not to see my family. I couldn't stand to go back to them. They're like mud people."

"Mud people?" Alex laughed, delighted with her phrase.

"I mean . . . stick-in-the-muds. But no, that's the right way to describe them. They don't do anything, they don't say anything, they don't even think anything. They are mud people."

Alex looked at her, surprised. She can't mean it, he thought. Nobody is like that. "How are they mud people?" he asked quietly.

Joyce shrugged. "I feel necessary here" was all she would say. "My in-laws need me for my work. For their future. I never felt that at home." She looked over at him, unwilling to expose herself further, to admit that even with all the restrictions of her peasant life, the careless blows she received from Dimitra, the rare visits from Nikos, she had never felt so loved.

"Everything here seems more honest," she added. "Even its hardness is honest."

"Even its loneliness?"

Joyce darted a look at him. "Who said I'm lonely?" She pulled her knees to her chest protectively. "I'm too busy to be lonely. Anyway I do have friends, you know."

Alex looked down at the dry earth beneath them, cracked and caked and tired. "How could you not be lonely the way you live? I don't mean to pry . . . but it's obvious."

His voice was so kind, so reasonable, that Joyce's throat suddenly contracted. She turned away from him. Even worse than pity from him would be pity for herself.

He touched her shoulder lightly. "I didn't mean to upset you." She shook her head and rested it on her knees, her hair straggling over her legs. Her skin seemed to glow, her scent to reach out to him.

He leaned over, enfolding her crouched body in his arms. "I want you," he said huskily. "I want you so much it's killing me. Just tell me yes or no. I'll leave if you make me." He cradled her, rocking, rocking, his head reeling with wine and heat and his searing, wild lust.

Joyce tried. She tried to fight the onslaught of his sympathy, the words that pierced through to her own longings. But what chance did she have? She was an ordinary girl held prisoner by her fears and needs, by the peculiar circumstances into which lies and dreams had led her. For too long she had been burying her desires beneath her duties, playing the role of daughter-in-law and wife when, in reality, she wanted so much more. For too long she had been hiding, like the lizard behind her.

Their first kiss was fierce and greedy, as if they wanted to devour one another. Alex crushed her to him, tore off her shirt, pressed his head against her chest, his mouth over her breasts. No slow, deliberate teasing for him, but an impulsive hunger for her that he could not contain. He stopped only to lay down his shirt to protect her bare skin from the stones and ants beneath them.

"God, you are so beautiful," he moaned, then fell on her again, pushing off her jeans while she gasped beneath him. His body was heavy despite his thinness, much heavier than Nikos's, and she felt overwhelmed by it. But his desire only ignited hers, her months of pent-up lust, of soldier dreams and shame. He explored every inch of her, his mouth, his hands leaving nothing unworshipped. When he thrust into her, she cried out so loudly that her voice echoed against the mountain. She could not get enough. She asked for more and more. Until, raw and wet and slicked with sweat, they lay panting under the sky and realized that the day had slipped into dusk.

Only then was Joyce able to feel afraid. Not only of what she had done but of all the consequences. She had used no birth control. She must reek of sex but had no access to water. Her mouth was swollen and reddened. How would she hide all this?

"Oh God, this is terrible" was the first thing she said.

"Don't say that." Alex got up on his knees. His chest was flat and broad, a few blond hairs sprinkled over his breastbone. His penis glistened, already erect again. He reached for his trousers, suddenly shy, and covered himself. "I can't stop wanting you," he said sheepishly.

She smiled, but it was a wan smile. Putting one arm over her eyes to shield them from the dipping sun, she shook her head. "I'm serious, Alex. Look at me. How will I hide what we've been doing? Dimitra sees everything. She sniffs me, I swear it, when I come home from market. What have we done?"

She stood up and began to pull on her clothes. "Don't get dressed, not yet," Alex moaned, reaching for her again. But this time she stepped out of his grasp. He was not helping.

"I know!" he said suddenly. "We'll go swimming. That'll wash me off you." He grinned.

"Swimming!" She looked down the mountain pointedly. "We'll never make it down there. It must be almost five already." "We'll hitch. Come on." He stood, pulling on his loose Indian trousers and dusty shirt. "We're disguised as tourists, no one will recognize you. Don't worry. I'll look after you."

She could see no other solution. She would be late meeting Dimitra, but that was better than appearing sex-stained and swollen in these unfamiliar clothes.

Once they got back to Ayiassos, they caught a ride easily down to Polikhnitos, and from there to Vatera, a seven-kilometer-long beach. The festival traffic was plentiful, and people were in the mood to be generous. A vacationing shopkeeper picked them up, and Alex chatted in his easy Greek, explaining that he and his wife were on their honeymoon. Joyce looked down at her ring, its scratched gold gleaming like a reprimand. How easily he lies, she thought. How easily I have fallen into deception. Would it be like this from now on?

"Why have we come so far away?" Joyce asked when the farmer had dropped them off. "Why not Mytilene? It'll take us forever to get back."

"Joyce, do you have a bathing costume?" Alex asked in reply. She stared at him, then she understood. They would have to swim naked. They could not use the town beach.

"Come on," he said gently. "There are enough deserted places for us to be safe."

"Thank you," she whispered. "I'm sorry I've been so crabby."

"I know. It's all right."

He took her hand, and they walked down to the beach and along the powder-soft sand until they were alone. This time they walked as lovers, their hands still new in each other's fingers but their arms bumping familiarly.

It did not take long to find a deserted spot. Almost the whole island was celebrating, and the only people they could see were a Scandinavian family, bathing nude like themselves but so far away they could not tell if the children were boys or girls. Alex gently helped Joyce off with her clothes, lifting her shirt over her head as if she were breakable, undoing her jeans, crouching to slide them down her long legs. He could smell the scents of sweat and sex on her, salty and dense and unbearably enticing. He wanted to make love to her again, to lay her down and grasp her firm buttocks in his hands, feel her calves press against his shoulders, but he refrained. He could tell her mind was elsewhere.

They swam efficiently, strictly to wash, not to play. Alex would have loved to head out for a small rock he could see a few meters away, to frolic in the water with Joyce the way young people should, but this was more like a ritual cleansing than any kind of game. Joyce was keeping her eye on the sun, calculating the time. She looked at it constantly, the way other people would check a watch.

Their bodies dried quickly in the hot air. Joyce put on her dress, now wrinkled and stained with the oil that had leaked from the packet of olives. She folded up her jeans and T-shirt and looked around the beach, her brow furrowed.

"What are you looking for?" Alex asked, shouldering the rucksack.

"A place to leave these."

"Your clothes?" He was shocked. "You're going to just leave them here?"

"Yes." She shrugged. "I can't take them home."

"I'll take them." He held out his hands.

"What for, a souvenir?"

She sounded mocking, and Alex winced. "Well, I was thinking in case you ever wanted them again, actually."

"Again? Yeah, that's real likely." Joyce said this bitterly, and started walking up the beach.

Alex caught up with her. He took the clothes, which she relinquished carelessly, and stuffed them into his rucksack. He was hurt, unsure whether her hostility was worry or regret.

"There will be an again," he said, but it was more a question than a statement. "Tomorrow, for example. There's one day left."

Joyce could not speak. Her world had capsized. Couldn't he see that?

Alex had a mad impulse to ask her to run away with him, to never go back to her absent, careless husband and that hard-scrabble existence. But he figured she had committed an act of recklessness once already in her life, and had been paying for it ever since. He could not ask her to do it again. Not yet.

By the time Joyce ran into the taverna, hair stringy with sea salt, her dress dirty and crumpled, she was two hours late. It had taken her and Alex an hour to find a ride back up from the beach and when they had they'd found themselves stuck behind a herd of sheep for twenty minutes. Through it all, while Alex had chatted bravely to the driver, Joyce had remained silent. Tension had seized her neck, her temples had begun to throb. What would she say to Dimitra? What would she do if they found her out? She'd held Alex's hand in the back of the car, not even knowing how hard she was gripping it.

She'd hoped to be able to go back to the church and find her comb before seeing her in-laws, but that had turned out to be impossible. When they'd reached Ayiassos, all she'd had time to do was wave Alex good-bye, promise to meet him at the clothes shop the next morning, and run down the street. She had decided to tell Dimitra that she fell asleep in the sun and awoke sweating and rumpled and faint. She could think of no other excuse.

Dimitra shrieked when she saw her and rose from the table to make a great fuss. She stared at Joyce's flushed cheeks and swollen mouth, and fingered her hair, but said nothing more than "Thank God you are safe. I have been so worried."

"I'm all right, Mama. I fell asleep — all this wine every day! Then the shade moved and I lay in the sun for hours without knowing. I feel sick, I need water."

Dimitra poured her a big glass and watched Joyce swallow it. She made no remark about the crusts of salt clinging to the fine hairs of Joyce's arms, or the unmistakable sea smell coming from her skin — a smell that was not at all the same as sweat.

But Joyce was not lying about how she felt. Halfway through the meal, she put her head on the table and fell asleep.

Dimitra and Petros took Joyce back to the church early, supporting her while she staggered, half-feigning sun-stroke, half-relieved to give herself up to their care. They laid her on the bedroll, muttering between themselves, and both fell asleep troubled.

But the next morning Dimitra was ferocious. "Stand up!" she shouted at Joyce, who scrambled to her feet, still dazed with sleep. "Now I want the truth. Where were you yesterday?"

Joyce blinked, but she would not allow herself to be frightened. Usually she weathered Dimitra's storms meekly, preferring to acquiesce rather than risk turning their house into a battleground. This had never been difficult because she'd had nothing to hide and could be calm in her innocence. But now all that had changed. Now she was in the wrong, and the knowledge made her defiant.

"I told you," she answered sullenly.

Dimitra gasped but said nothing. She only stepped forward and raised her thick arm, her palm open, ready to slam into Joyce's face. Then Joyce did something she should have done the first time — she reached up, caught Dimitra's wrist, and stopped the blow. "I told you, don't ever hit me again!" she hissed. "I am not a dog!"

Dimitra staggered back as if she had been the one who was hit. Her arm turned limp in Joyce's grasp. Her eyes were fixed on the girl's face.

Joyce let go of her, triumphant.

And then it was Dimitra's turn to surprise Joyce. She dropped her arm to her side, and her sunken eyes filled slowly with tears. "You are right, my daughter," she said. "Blows are not the way."

She opened her plump arms and reached out to Joyce. "Forgive my suspicions, *koroulamou*," she moaned, her deep voice cracking. "Forgive your old mother-in-law. I only want not to lose you."

Dimitra was a woman who loved too violently because she had learned to love too late. She was a child of war, and as such her love — for her parents, for her sisters, for her fellow humans — had been beaten out of her or torn away. If she had been born with the ability to cry like other children, with a tenderness that could bend to love, she could not remember it. War had taught her that love makes you vulnerable, like the belly of a snake — it makes you worthless.

Dimitra was born in 1911, the last year that Ifestia belonged to the Turks. She grew up hearing stories of Turks enslaving Greek women and Greeks murdering Turkish men. Her Greek grandmother told her that when she was young she'd had to travel dressed as an old woman to protect herself from being snatched for a Turkish harem. Petros said that in Lesbos, his home, the Greeks and Turks got on well until 1923 and the Anatolian massacres, but not so on Ifestia. Perhaps it was their miserly soil, perhaps it was the blood of enemies mixing in their veins, but the Ifestians had never been a peaceful people.

"You Americans know nothing of war," Dimitra liked to say to Joyce as they milked the goats or pressed the sesame seeds into oil. "You drop your bombs on other people who are so far away they are like toys, while you stay safe and comfortable in front of your televisions. I know, I have heard from your uncle Sophocles. For us, little one, it was different."

By the time she was twelve, Dimitra had lived through three major wars and countless smaller ones. The Balkan Wars, which tore Ifestia and other dominions from the Turks. The First World War, which splintered the country between the king and Prime Minister Venizelos. The Anatolian campaign, which ended in massacre and humiliating defeat for the Greeks. The resulting Treaty of Lausanne in 1923, which ordered the exchange of religious minorites, forcing 390,000 Muslim Greeks to move to Turkey and a million and a half Christian Turks to Greece, every last one of them on both sides unwelcome and reviled. Endless battles between monarchists and democrats, Muslims and Christians, Greeks and Turks. Before she had even grown breasts Dimitra had become hardened and self-sufficient, as merciless as the soldiers who raped her mother and killed her uncles. She understood nothing about love until she became a mother herself.

All through her childhood, Dimitra and her playmates imitated war in the streets. They wanted to win for their fathers, kill the murderers of their uncles, the rapists of their mothers. So they reenacted what they saw, rehearsing for when it would be their turn. They split into gangs and threw sharpened stones at one another's faces, and snowballs packed with ice. They jabbed each other with wood they had splintered to cause maximum pain. War had not taught them to unite, it had taught them to battle. Dimitra put a boy's eye out. Her sisters drew blood from a two-year-old they had captured and tortured, just as they had seen the soldiers do to their parents.

Widows crowded the churches like flocks of crows. The wailing of mourners became as common a sound as the slap of sea on the Ifestian rocks.

As the eldest of a pack of girls, Dimitra was the family terror. A wild tomboy, she formed her four sisters into a gang, terrorized little boys, and fought mightily on the side of King Constantine. She got herself beaten and beaten again by other children for her monarchism, but to no effect. Her mother a Turk and her father a Greek, her parents were as torn by domestic strife as her country, too preoccupied with their own battles to pay much mind to disciplining their daughters. They scraped a living off their rocky land and tried to save for their daughters' dowries, cursing that they had no sons, but otherwise ignored the girls' behavior and education. Like their mother and her mother before her, not one of the girls grew up literate.

Dimitra's father died when she was eleven from wounds he had received in the Anatolian fiasco, and after that the family grew poorer than ever. The girls scandalized the village by foraging for food, stealing vegetables from people's gardens, fruit from their fields. Some of their neighbors helped, some refused — those Dimitra still would not speak to even now, fifty-three years later. She and her sisters did what they could to stay alive, but to the other villagers they were no better than a pack of Gypsies.

"I feel no shame about this, *koroulamou*," she had once said to Joyce. "I did no wrong, nor did my sisters. We were doing what we could to survive. Nikos, may the Lord watch over him, told me that in your country, in fat America, you throw away a quarter of the food you produce. A quarter! I look at you, my little one, sleek and smooth as a new kitten, and I see that you know nothing of what it means to struggle."

"We have hungry people, too," Joyce objected, but Dimitra would not listen.

By the time Dimitra was sixteen she had turned into a fiery warrior, her skin a dark olive, her eyes a flashing black, her limbs smooth and firm. She felt strong enough to kill any man, Greek or Turk, who even glimpsed her nakedness, let alone tried to rob her of her virginity. She had seen the soldiers burst into her house when her father was at war, throw up the skirts of her mother, and beat her about the face till she was too bloodied to fight back. She had heard the wives gossip about the grossness of their husbands, taking them at night without tenderness, without any care of whether the women wanted them. What use had she for such indignity? She was a leader! She had her gang of sisters, her own empire. When men turned their eyes on her, she spat. They thought her bewitched.

Then along came Petros, visiting from Lesbos, tiny but beautiful, like an elf. His face she could fit in one hand. He was quiet but full of surprising wit and, even better, he came from a prosperous family of shopkeepers. Here is a match for me, she decided. If he tries to take me against my will I can squash him like a fly. She was only sixteen, but she already knew how to dazzle him with flashing teeth and daring eyes. Her powerful shoulders and gleaming skin. Her breasts like the swelling of waves. Within a month he proposed, gasping like a fish in a net and, knowing his parents would be furious at the miserable scrap of land that was her only dowry, chose to stay with her family in Ifestia rather than return to his own.

"We built our home only a few meters away from my poor mother," Dimitra told Joyce. "The old lady was living in the past by then, fighting still with my father, shouting at the soldiers who came to attack her and pillage her town. 'The Turks pulled the hair out of women,' she told me in her ravings. 'They sliced open the belly of your pregnant aunt. Cut out the genitals of your uncle.' What all soldiers do, Turk or German, Italian or Greek, Anatolian or American. That is why, little Joyce, you must never look one in the eye."

Petros had turned out to be strong for an elf. He and Dimitra heaved their own stones, mixed their own mortar. The two of them worked like mules to make their home.

When Dimitra's mother died, they inherited a sliver of land and her dowry, four kilim pillows. And when all the sisters but Natalia married, they exchanged what money Petros had for their portions of land until they had the whole tiny farm. By 1936, when General Metaxas seized hold of the country, Dimitra and Petros were glad to be living in Ifestia, far away from Athens and its turmoil. Metaxas was locking up anyone who disagreed with him, barring unions, censoring the newspapers, terrorizing people with his secret police. But Petros and Dimitra hacked away at their reluctant soil, planted spinach and string beans, lentils and cauliflower, peas, beetroot, and their greatest pride, the sesame plants. While professors and school-teachers were being thrown in jail, they watched the sesame grow tall and majestic, some stalks as high as eight feet, their little bell-shaped flowers trembling on their stems, sweet-scented, pink, and delicate. While the country was beaten to its knees by Fascism, they plucked the sesame capsules from their stems and opened them to collect the seeds, thousands of tiny pearls — their oil, their gold.

"Looking back, the time of Metaxas seems like peace to me now," Dimitra often said. "It was the time we built up the garden and the crops you work for us, little one. You ask how I can speak kindly about a dictator? After the Nazis and the Italians, after the civil war, *koroulamou*, it is hard to hate a leader who at least wanted a united Greece."

Their life was good then, but for one matter. Dimitra was nearing thirty and still without a child. She could not conceive, largely because — this she did not tell Joyce — Petros had very little sex drive. He seemed happier alone with his sesame plants than in bed with a woman. Her powerful presence seemed to frighten him. She had to coax him for hours to get him erect, and when she did he gasped and gaped like a terrified child. She found it distasteful. "I was right to want to stay a virgin," she told herself. She found it a chore to have relations with her husband more than once a month.

But her childlessness was a great shame to her. Her in-laws, the relatives of Petros's snooty family, even her own sisters with children looked down on her, bossed her, whispered that she was being punished, cursed for her arrogance. Instead of their leader, she had become a nobody.

In 1941, when Dimitra was thirty and still not a mother, Germany invaded Greece and the Axis forces began a brutal occupation that lasted for three years. Greeks died of starvation by the thousands during that time, their imports blockaded by the war, their own food taken by enemy soldiers. Every region suffered, from Athens to the outermost islands. Food could no longer be shipped or carried from town to town. Villages became fortresses. Hungry and outraged, the women around Dimitra began working for the Resistance, doing what they could to help Greek and British soldiers escape the Nazis. Then one day Dimitra was called to the funeral of her three-month-old nephew, baby Kostas, dead from lack of milk. She stood by her wailing, emaciated sister, looking down at the infant, his head tiny and bony, his body shrunken like some hideous wax doll, and she decided to join, too.

Like many Greeks her age, Dimitra loved to talk about her days in the Resistance. In retrospect it was a time of romance and heroism, a time when Greece at least tried to overcome its factionalism to unite against a common enemy. Women broke free from their proscribed roles to take up arms, feed the hungry, and defy Nazi orders. Girls who had not been allowed to talk to men in the street were suddenly running guns. Women who could not read were risking their lives to disseminate anti-Fascist literature.

"We were starving," Dimitra liked to tell Joyce. "Those filthy Germans, Italians, too, they took all our food. Our corn, our sesame, our goats — everything was gone, everything we had worked so hard to grow. We had no coffee or tobacco, almost no milk or cheese. We lived on the few vegetables they did not steal and on the wild things we hunted and picked. Even fish was rare, for although we are surrounded by the sea, our boats had been taken by the soldiers.

"I will never forget, *koroulamou*, how the old people and the children began to shrivel up before our eyes, like grapes in the sun. Turn dark and die. My sisters and I, and some of the other women in the village, we made soup for the hungriest. We used beans and anything else we could get. Herbs from the fields, wild spinach and onions if we could find them, dandelions. Even snails. I can still see those children looking at us as we fed them, their eyes sunk into their skulls, no light in them, only despair." Dimitra would sigh over the peppers she was slicing as she talked, or the sheet she was washing, and shake her head. "But to feed the starving like this was a crime, *pedhi mou*, punishable by death. The Nazis caught my youngest sister, Natalia. She was barely sixteen. They raped her. They gave her dishwater to eat. They starved her to death."

Little Natalia. Her hair blonder than anyone else's — not unlike Joyce's. Her eyes the color of water in the shadow of a cliff. She used to run errands for her four big sisters. Meek and biddable, hopelessly dominated by them all, especially by Dimitra, she had been fetching and carrying for them ever since she was old enough to walk. She was only taking a pot of beans to old Widow Konstantinou because her sisters had told her to. She barely understood the war, who was on which side or why, but she had a strength none of them suspected. The Nazis beat her, starved her: Who gave you those beans, daughter of a whore? Who told you to feed the enemy? They called her words that her virgin ears had never heard. Yet she died without ever allowing her sisters' names to escape her lips.

"What kind of a man can rape a starving child?" Dimitra said to Joyce. "What kind of a human being can violate a body that is nothing but bones and scraps of hair? That has lost its strong young teeth and the life in its eyes? I saw her through the bars of her cage. She looked like a bag of bones."

Dimitra told all this to Joyce over and over, but Joyce never tired of listening. She had heard no such stories of survival and hardship from her parents at home. Her father had been too young to fight in the Second World War and had never been called up for Korea. Her brothers had been rejected for Vietnam, Ben flat-footed, Joey asthmatic. War had always been remote and foreign to Joyce, nothing but newspaper photographs or blurred images on television. Only the Holocaust had roused indignation in her house, and even that was a story from far away. Her family had been in America for more than a hundred years — the slaughter of Jews was a tragedy that had happened to other people's relatives, not her own. From her parents she had learned to see the postwar world as a bland, mild place, where nothing terrible happened to anybody who didn't deserve it. Where nothing much happened at all.

"Still, the girls in my village, even the children, we fought back the best we knew how," Dimitra kept telling her. "Some of us knitted socks and cooked food, which we smuggled to prisoners. Even for that the Nazis said they would kill us. But some of us did much more. Have you heard of Lela Karayanni? She was a mother of seven children when the Germans marched into Athens. She and her older children organized the escape of one hundred and fifty Greek and allied soldiers from those Nazis before they caught her. They shot her three years later, mother or not. Up against the wall along with seventy others. But the Nazis couldn't get us all. There were many others like her. Women who were as brave as any hero."

Yes, Dimitra loved to talk about the Resistance, but the civil war that followed on its heels was another matter. During the world war Greece had a common enemy. During the civil war, or the *andartiko,* as the Greeks called it, the enemy had been themselves. By the end of the struggle, which lasted from 1944 to 1949, with a short break in the middle, six hundred thousand Greeks had died at one another's hands, and one and a half million were homeless. Like most of her compatriots Dimitra said nothing to Joyce of this time. She was too ashamed.

It took until she was thirty-six and in the middle of the *andartiko* for Dimitra to bear a child. Twenty years of grunting in the dark, coaxing Petros to do what neither of them even liked. But at last there was Nikos, a son, and her womanhood was redeemed. Looking down into his precious newborn face, Dimitra learned that there was beauty in the midst of war and hope in the midst of terror. She also told herself that she would exact strict obedience from this boy of hers. She knew too well the heady excitement of defiance, the addictive thrill of flouting parental authority. She was determined to squelch it, stamp it out before one flicker of rebellion could catch light and burn her.

Of course this did not happen. When Dimitra made those plans she knew nothing yet of the heart-searing love a son ignites in his mother. As soon as she felt the small, powerful ring of his lips suckling her nipple, she was caught. Her hard, bossy heart melted into syrup. She lost all will to say no to him, she had no stomach for his anger. All he had to do was turn away and pout for her to give in, serve him, to wallow in her own need to indulge him at the expense of his soul.

So she pampered her long-awaited son, and he grew more stunning by the month. Some miracle had happened, she often thought; little Petros and his delicate, puny looks had combined somehow with her own thunderous complexion to produce the most beautiful boy in the village. Girls swooned over him, mothers eyed him with jealous spite. Dimitra had to make sure his entire life that he never went unprotected from the evil eye. She spat on him three times if someone complimented him. She draped him with talismans: amulets around his neck, down his back, over his bed, beads and herbs and paper saints sewn into the folds of his clothes. She sewed a blue glass eye to the back of every shirt he wore. Hung another by the door to ward off malevolent spirits. When he left for the sea, cruelly, indifferently, she felt her heart break the way no man, no parent, no war had ever broken it. A black loneliness caught at her like a great octopus. She had seen her mother raped, her sisters starved, but for the first time she wanted to die.

But then Nikos did something for her at last. He brought her a gift. He brought her a daughter, as if in exchange for himself.

Joyce had no idea of this, but it had been a struggle for Dimitra and Petros to take her in. She had no dowry, and families such as theirs depended on the dowries of their sons' brides. On the night Nikos came home, pulling with him this blond American stick of a girl — no warning, no wedding — Dimitra and Petros were in despair. How were they to feed a fourth mouth? What were they to do with this foreigner, who probably had sluttish ways and bad manners and would bring on them nothing but disgrace?

"Is she a virgin at least?" Dimitra asked Nikos that first night. "This tourist slut, was she a virgin for you?"

Nikos flashed his crooked white teeth. "Yes, Mama, yes. The last virgin in America!" He laughed when he said this, pleased with himself. "She's beautiful, is she not? She is a good girl, she loves me well. Keep her for me and she will make you proud."

"She's weak and skinny," Dimitra grumbled. "She probably can't even lift a bucket. I will end up waiting on her like a servant."

"Teach her to work! She'll learn." Nikos leaned forward and fixed his amber eyes on his mother. "Mama, don't indulge her like you do me. Don't be soft. Be strict with her. She is American, she knows no discipline. She doesn't know what hard work is, Mama, you understand? She can hardly cook! Teach her. Make her a good wife for me when I come back. When I am finished with this shipping job, I want to come home to a hardworking woman who will be a good mother to my children, not a lazy girl. I ask you this, *Mannamou*, do it for me. It is my future you will be making. I put it in your hands."

Dimitra listened to all this, amazed. She had no idea her son's mind ran so deep, that he thought about his future at all. He has entrusted me with his happiness, she whispered to herself, and she was filled with pride.

So she rained the blows on Joyce that she should have given her son. She tied a tight shell around her own heart and turned her face away from the sight of Joyce's loneliness. It is for my son, she told herself, for his future happiness. She worked Joyce like a servant, like a donkey . . . like a girl.

Joyce knew nothing of Nikos's instructions, of course. She resented Dimitra's hard rule, but it was better than the indifference she had felt from her own mother. She could tell that under the shoving, the barked orders, Dimitra was a lonely woman who ached for Nikos just as she did, that they had this together, and that a quiet love had grown out of it between them.

So when Dimitra opened her arms to Joyce in the church, Joyce's hesitation lasted no more than a second. She forgave Dimitra readily and stepped into her arms with relief. She was only twenty, and she still needed a mother.

Dimitra let go of her at last, pushing her away. "Petros," she said, poking him where he lay on his bedroll, having slept through the entire scene. "Petros!"

He opened his eyes and sat up, instantly alert.

"We are going home today. This place is causing mischief between us, the evil spirits are flying loose. Come, get up, roll up your bed. We are leaving now."

Petros didn't argue. He was worried about his cow — her milk was drying up, she was getting old. And he felt terrible from all the drinking, from the strain of making conversation with his sophisticated cousins and boastful elder brothers. He knew they all laughed at him and his domineering wife, too stupid to understand her. He would have much preferred to be at home, where she could scold him in peace.

"But I don't want to go yet!" Joyce blurted. Alex must be waiting for her already. She stopped herself, searching for words that would sound convincing. "You deserve this holiday, *Petheros*. Don't go back now. And Mama, you and I haven't even been shopping together yet."

But Dimitra was firm, and nothing Joyce could say would sway her. This was the way it always was.

VI

Once the festival was over, life in Kastron returned quickly to normal, despite the universal stomachaches and hangovers. There was too much to do to allow for sluggishness, so the very morning after they got back Dimitra dispatched Joyce to market. Joyce was glad. She was still reeling from her encounter with Alex, from her betrayals, so she needed to be kept busy. She could think of no other way to fill the hours that dragged on while she forced herself to forget him.

Forgetting him, of course, turned out to be impossible. The very act of trying to wipe him from her mind only implanted him there more firmly. It was as if her conscience and her memory were locked in battle. At the same time she was swearing to renounce him, she found herself wondering how she might see him again. At the very moment she was telling herself their encounter meant nothing, images of their lovemaking would flash through her — his lips on her breast, his first thrust into her — so vivid they made her moan aloud. She found herself obsessively imagining that Alex was watching her. Here she was being witty — would he admire her? There she was being kind — would he like that? She began to choose her clothes more carefully, to brush her hair till it shone, to dress for his invisible presence while still determining never to see him again.

Soon her mind was performing all the tricks of the unfaithful. What was one little indiscretion? she told herself. It will never happen again, no one will ever know. Time will pass and it will disappear into memory. Anyway, who was to say Nikos hadn't done the same? The last time he had come home, when he and Joyce had finally had language between them, he had sworn that he'd been faithful. "They bring whores onto our ships in port," he'd said, "but they are filthy women, my little Joyce. Filled with diseases. When I was single, yes I sometimes had a girlfriend. But now I have you to guard and honor. I will always be true to you." At the time she had chosen to believe him; now she couldn't understand her gullibility. But what did it matter? A few slipups would never be powerful enough to damage their marriage. Why should she be jealous of a prostitute? Why should he know about a one-time lover? In her unfaithfulness, Joyce had discovered a remarkably free-spirited tolerance.

Anyway, she would catch herself thinking, what the hell does he expect, leaving me alone like this?

Meanwhile, she had to concentrate on the market. In the summer, it was held three mornings a week in the village square, a small area paved with cracked, uneven cobblestones, shaded inadequately by four dusty plane trees. On one side of the square, fresh produce was sold. On the other, dry goods: heaps of nylon socks, bolts of brashly printed cotton, plastic shoes, ugly dresses, and notoriously unreliable kitchen utensils. Every market day at dawn, donkeys and mules, wagons and battered pickup trucks squeezed down the narrow lanes of the village to disgorge their loads onto the portable tables lined up in the middle of the square. Men with flat caps and little mustaches, their muscles like cords of rope, unloaded their goods, hoisted up tattered awnings, and proceeded to arrange their produce in tempting patterns. Fish were packed in ice and laid out in semicircular rays, a scaly mosaic. Olives, black and green, nestled glistening in wooden barrels. Cherries red as rubies glowed among tight, sweating clusters of maroon and emerald grapes. Eggplants lay between the lettuces like giant amethyst teardrops. Pomegranates were split open to reveal their sparkling garnet secrets. The spun gold of honey, snowy blocks of cheese, heaps of bright oranges . . . Soon the air was filled with the intoxicating scents of citrus, spearmint, bay leaves, and wine.

Then the marketing cries began.

"Melons as sweet as your mothers tits!"

"Oranges to bless your baby on!"

"Cherries picked this morning, tart as a kiss!"

As soon as Joyce arrived at the market, Phoebus clopping unwillingly beside her, she was greeted by her first and closest friend in the village, Marina Benaki, a baby on one hip and a basket on her arm. Marina was a tall, flaxen-haired young woman from the Peloponnese, with more education than most of the villagers and a fearless tongue. Pale-skinned but for a flush on her cheeks, she was strong as a statue. She carried herself erect, her hair down her back in a braid, her large frame languid and confident, and was quick to stifle insolence with one look from her penetrating green eyes. The old people of Kastron considered her brazen, the young exotic.

The two had become friends during Joyce's second year in Ifestia. "The peasants in this place are as suspicious as hogs in a slaughterhouse," Marina had said on their first meeting. "I might as well be as foreign as you for all the trust they give me." She had looked Joyce over appraisingly. "You speak good Greek for an American. I like Americans. My father is in your country, in the restaurant business. We will stick together and make all the old cows accept us, yes?"

With a rush of gratitude, Joyce shook hands with her. Up until then she'd had no such offer of friendship. "All right," she said laughing, "I agree." Now they saw one another almost every week, and even though Marina's baby had put something of a barrier between them, Marina was still the closest thing Joyce had to a best friend.

"So, did you get up to any mischief in Ayiassos?" Marina asked with a wink. "Any handsome strangers whisk you off for a night?" She laughed and lifted her baby up for a kiss, missing the blush that suffused Joyce's cheeks.

Joyce turned quickly away to unload her baskets from Phoebus. What would Marina think if she really knew about Alex? A sudden urge to confess coursed through her. To speak of the desire and restlessness he had awoken in her — what relief that would be! She longed for comfort, reassurance, for someone to tell her she'd done no serious wrong. But she wrestled the impulse down. In a place like Kastron, telling even Marina would be much too dangerous.

"I hear that Nikos did not come home for the festival," Marina said then. Settling her baby back on her hip, she eyed Joyce with concern. "That must have upset your mother-in-law. Was there a fuss?"

"Yes, some." Joyce laid out her vegetables on the table, avoiding Marina's eyes. She knew that her friend was really expressing sympathy over Nikos's absence. "He couldn't get leave," she made herself say. "He would lose too much money. Dimitra understands, but it hurts her, yes."

"It's terrible the way these shipping companies don't respect the family," Marina said tactfully. "They think of nothing but the drachma, the greedy *malachi*. They'd sell their mothers for soup if they could find a buyer."

Clicking her tongue in disapproval, she dropped onto an upturned basket with a groan. "God, he's heavy, my little Yiannis. It's like carrying a sack of flour all day, except this one wiggles." She stood the baby on her knees and watched him wobble on his fat, bandy legs while he squealed with delight. "Look how strong he is. Have you ever seen anything like it?

He's going to be a real bruiser when he grows up, God willing. Teach his *Papas* a lesson."

Joyce opened a burlap sack of onions and curled back the edges. Perhaps she would feel differently when she had a child, but baby adoration tired her dreadfully.

"Ah hah!" came a shout from across the marketplace. "It is my pretty English teacher returned to her stall!" Stratis the butcher swaggered across the square while Joyce and Marina glanced at each other, rolling their eyes. "Two lovely ladies, one the picture of a Virgin with her babe, the other shining like Lady Liberty. It is a sight to warm a man's heart before he goes back to chopping up pigs." Stratis leaned forward, his belly bulging, and grabbed the baby's pudgy cheeks between a bulbous thumb and forefinger. "My, what a juicy specimen!" he said, smacking his lips. "A touch of garlic, a sprinkle of oregano . . ."

"Stratis Farmakides, take your slaughterer's fingers off my Yiannis!" Marina cried, pulling the now wailing baby away from him.

Stratis chuckled. "Come see me without that dog of a husband of yours and I will make it up to you," he said with a wink. "Little American," he added, turning to Joyce. "I have something to try on you. Now don't break my heart like the last time, leaving me sitting there, a fool on the chair. Be kind, I have worked hard at this." Thrusting his hands in his pockets, he straddled the cobblestones as if readying himself for a blow. Then he pronounced slowly and loudly, "Chow ah ooo."

He beamed expectantly.

Joyce frowned. "*Ciao?* Is this more Italian?"

"No! Are you deaf?"

"How?"

"Yes! Ow!"

"How what?"

"Bah! This is no good, no good at all. I have a tongue like a mallet!" Stratis's polished head turned red as he pulled his thick hands out of his pockets to gesticulate furiously. "They should make one language only in the world, then all this bother would not be necessary. The Tower of Babel — it is all you women's fault!" And he stormed off, stamping and muttering.

"May he chop off his own balls one day, the dirty old goat," Marina said calmly, restoring her soothed baby to her lap. She yawned. "I can only stay a minute. I've come for some of your eggs but then I must get back. My mother-in law wants me to wash the sheets today."

"I'll give you the freshest," Joyce said, nestling her eggs in a bed of straw on her table. "I have to watch Widow Halaris," she added. "I caught her trying to steal some the other day."

"She has no money. Her son takes it all. Slip her an egg or two if you can afford it. I think he's starving her to death so he can get her dowry jewelry."

Joyce nodded. One of the things she liked best about village life was the undeclared sisterhood of its women. There was a tacit understanding among all but the most selfish that they must stick together, outfox the men and the laws that kept them penniless and subservient. Food was surreptitiously passed to the poor, old linens patched up and left lying at the bottom of baskets as if forgotten, dresses taken apart and remade for those who couldn't afford to buy. Even the odd coin bestowed in the guise of miscalculation — a secret currency of generosity that extended to all friends and relatives, except for sluts and husband stealers.

"Marina?" Joyce asked as she settled the last of her onions in an attractive coil. "When you had your Yiannis there, did things change a lot in your house?"

"Oh, yes. At least with my husband. He couldn't do enough for me. He even stayed away from the brothel for six whole weeks." She shook her head sarcastically. "The old cow didn't help much, though. Soon as I was up and about she put me back to washing the sheets, ironing, peeling the onions, all the worst work, never mind that I was nursing. I pray every night for the old bag to drop dead in her tracks."

Joyce laughed. Marina always spoke viciously about her mother-in-law, but Joyce had seen the two of them strolling along the seafront arm in arm. Marina was slow to confide, compared to Joyce's American friends, but when she did, she did it with shameless exaggeration.

"Why do you ask?" Marina said then, eyeing Joyce slyly. "You have some news to tell your friend?"

Joyce colored. "Not you too! It's all I hear. Babies, babies. I'm not a milk cow."

But her blush was not about that. It was her realization that her unfaithfulness was a betrayal not only of Nikos but of her family, of her friend, of their trust — of all that village life depended upon: the steadfastness of a wife.

Marina stood up, hoisted the baby back on her hip, and placed six eggs gently into the basket on her arm, dropping a few drachmas into Joyce's hand. "I must go. Come see me this Sunday evening, if *Kyria* Koliopoulou will let you. We'll take a stroll by the sea."

"I would like that." Joyce stroked the baby's head. "I'll bring you a treat when I come, little cherub," she said to him, and watched Marina saunter away, baby and braid swaying above her wide skirt.

Perhaps if I have a baby with Nikos I won't be so tempted to wander, Joyce thought. Perhaps it is time to fasten my anchor to this place before some new unforeseen wind rips me away.

For the rest of the morning, Joyce worked the market, bantering with the other housewives and sellers and fending off the soldiers who hovered about the women like bees. She always found it exhilarating to match wits with her rivals. It was a game for her, as exciting as gambling. At one point, noticing that Alexis, a rival farmer, had fewer eggs left to sell than she,

she took the risk of lowering her price and offering a whole basket at once. "A dozen for the price of nine!" she called out saucily.

"Don't bother. Her eggs are as old as Methuselah. Only good for bricking up the holes in your houses," he shouted back, but Joyce knew no one would believe him. She might have to put up with endless teasing about being a Yankee, but she knew that she had earned a reputation for good produce and honesty: solid, unassailable qualities in village life. As *Kyria* Mylona handed over the price for the basket, Joyce shot a triumphant look at Alexis.

"To pay you back for that sesame last week," she called to him, and winked.

Petros was the one who had taught Joyce how to sell. When she had been new and raw in the house, a dazed bride with the frightened eyes of a foal, he had taken her to market and made her stand by him at the stall and watch. Right away she'd been hooked. The heady smells of cheese and orange, of melons and anise. The vibrant colors of the fruit, glittering like heaps of jewels. The shouts and ribald laughter of the sellers, vying for customers. Soldiers strolling among them, their bodies young and strong, their lips pursed in lewd suggestion. Joyce had felt exhilarated, excited. She'd wanted, immediately, to be part of it all.

Once Joyce understood enough Greek, Petros gave her advice. "When you bargain, never stop talking," he told her. "Never give them time to think. Look worried, too, so they think you are losing money on the bargain. And, little one? Make them laugh. You are young and pretty — use it! Do not be ashamed." Petros winked at her and pinched her cheek. "Turn their heads, *koroulamou*, and they will buy from you blindly. They will not even see the drachmas fly out of their hands."

Joyce learned quickly. She studied numbers at night, picked up a few cheeky phrases that sounded so odd in her American

accent they made Dimitra cry with laughter, and soon was selling respectably enough for Petros to trust her alone. Naturally,
she made mistakes, but she clearly had a knack for it. Perhaps
all those years of watching her mother cut coupons and work
out budgets had rubbed off on her, Joyce thought. Perhaps
there was something she was good at after all.

Joyce had been working the market for five hours when the English girls showed up. She spotted them across the now empty-
ing square, wandering through the rubble of torn cabbage
leaves and newspaper, looking lost and beetlelike under their
huge backpacks, and trailed by three leering soldiers.

"Are you looking for me?" she called.

The girls ran over and hugged her as if they were old friends.
"We thought we'd never find you."

"You would have. All you need to say is *Amerikeedah* and
you'd be directed to me." She turned to the soldiers. "Get lost!"
she shouted at them in Greek, holding up her palm, her fingers
splayed, in the rudest Greek gesture she knew. "Leave my
guests alone!" They slunk off, affronted, and Sarah and Nicola
laughed. "Wait while I pack up," Joyce said then. "You're coming home with me."

Because the English girls wanted to buy Dimitra a present
before they arrived at her house, Joyce led them over to the
main shopping street, where a row of small shops displayed
their wares behind polished windows. "She loves Turkish delight," Joyce hinted. As she spoke, she glanced over at the bakery and remembered Alex's aunt. That was where he'd said to
find him when they had first met. Suddenly, she could not
speak.

"Okay, thanks," said Nicola, patting the donkey. "We'll be
right back."

The girls went into the sweet shop, leaving Joyce alone with
the terrible hope she had been battling all day. Perhaps Alex
had guessed what had happened while he waited for her so

uselessly. Perhaps he would come looking for her here. Stop it, she scolded herself. You promised not to do this. Quickly, she ducked behind Phoebus in case Alex appeared, buried her head in a basket, and stayed hiding in that ungainly position until the English girls returned.

"All right, we're ready," they said cheerily, waving their packages. Joyce hurried them away. And immediately felt a plunging disappointment that Alex had not found her after all.

The girls proved even more thoughtful than Joyce had expected, for they'd bought not only a big package of Turkish delight, a gelatinous confection smothered in powdered sugar, but wine and even scented soap: a fortune in goods for a family such as hers. She knew this would go over well with Dimitra, who never bought herself anything but accepted gifts with childish greed. Joyce, however, would get none of it, as was the daughter-in-law's lot.

When they reached the house that evening, after visiting the church and touring the town, Dimitra was indeed thrilled with her presents. She put the Turkish delight on a shelf over the hearth, where she admired it for days before she could bring herself to open it, and she wouldn't let go of the soap, which she clutched and sniffed at all night. Petros opened the wine for them, and the English girls drank most of it themselves, growing merry and loud. Dimitra and Joyce served them a simple meal of goat cheese, tomatoes, and potatoes fried in oil, followed by melon, but the girls seemed satisfied. They carried on a pointing, naming game with Dimitra, who flirted with them as if they were young men, cackling with laughter at things even Joyce could not understand. The game made her think of her early days with Nikos, lying under the stars while he compared her to the moon, dreaming of a freedom she had not yet understood.

That evening, as they sat at supper, a storm swept over Ifestia. They heard it first as a deep booming out at sea, like the distant shooting of cannons, but soon the skies were snapping with lightning, thunder exploding around them. It reminded Joyce of her fifth night in the house, when she and Nikos had been forced to scramble in the rain for sesame seeds, and an icy shock of reality hit her. If Nikos were to find out about Alex he would be devastated. It would dishonor him and his parents; it would alienate her from all of them forever. How could she even let herself hope that Alex would reappear? How could she delude herself with excuses and dreams? Joyce clenched her fists. I will never let them find out about him, she swore. I will never see Alex again. Never!

Worry about the sesame crop also plagued the house that night, but although the rain fell heavily, drumming on their tile roof in a steady, mesmerizing roar, the storm was not windy. Nevertheless, Petros slipped out with a lantern and stayed away for more than an hour. Joyce knew that he was searching through the downpour for capsules, that he would return soaked and shivering, his brow wrinkled in distress. If Joyce hadn't had guests, she would have helped him.

Storms had always been terrifying in that house. They meant destruction not only to the plants barely able to stand upright in the sandy soil but danger to Nikos at sea. Whenever there was a storm like this, Dimitra would light a candle and pray to her icon of Saint Nicholas, guardian of sailors and children, which she kept upstairs in her bedroom. "Nikos will be safe, God willing. I named him after his protector," she often said to Joyce, but that did not stop either of them from worrying. For two years Joyce had prayed with her. On her knees in front of the dark-eyed saint, crossing herself, promising him the best oil, the sweetest corn if he would only keep her husband safe from the hungry waves. Prostituting herself to a Christian painted face in order to protect him. Even now, with her love for Nikos wounded and vulnerable, she shuddered at the thought of him tossed on that voracious black sea.

Tonight, however, in consideration of the guests, Dimitra

clambered up the ladder to her bedroom and prayed to the saint alone.

The English girls thought the storm was fun. "What a relief," they kept saying. "All that heat. The air was so dusty I couldn't breathe." After Dimitra left, they suggested running out in the rain to shower in their clothes.

"My mother-in-law wouldn't approve," Joyce had to say, "It wouldn't look respectable."

Once Dimitra returned, visibly relieved at having sent up her prayer, she settled in again to enjoy the visitors. Unwrapping the blue scarf from her head and taking off her apron, she nestled into a chair to talk, looking as plump and contented as a nesting hen. She avoided talking to the girl whom she'd said looked Jewish, which only Joyce seemed to notice, but she teased Nicola, stroking her smooth arms and pinching her cheeks so often that Nicola became alarmed.

"Don't worry," Joyce said, laughing. "Greek women always feel each other up."

"But it hurts," Nicola said, rubbing her inflamed cheek. Then she laughed too.

While the English girls tried their best to entertain Dimitra, Joyce noticed them looking about the cottage, taking it in with the curiosity of alert tourists. A typical house of the island, it was squat and rectangular, built of thick, rough stone that had been whitewashed inside and out so many times the walls looked like scooped yogurt. The front door was narrow and the windows low, their wooden shutters folded open all summer long. A blue-striped curtain was draped over the open doorway, and beside it and each window Dimitra had hung a glass eye and a crucifix to ward off evil spirits.

The main part of the house consisted of only one room, but through an archway in the back was a small pantry that opened onto the courtyard, where chickens and guinea fowl scratched in the dry earth. Dimitra and Joyce did most of their cooking out here, over an open fire or in the white, igloo-shaped oven made of clay and brick. The well and the pump stood in the middle of the courtyard, beyond which were the outhouse and the animal pens.

The house itself was sparsely furnished. A rectangular table of thick planks, covered at times with homespun cloth; solid, hardwood chairs; the Turkish pillows from Dimitra's mother, arranged in a corner of the bare wooden floor. Across the low ceiling stretched two wooden beams, from which hung red peppers, strings of onions and garlic, and bunches of dried herbs, filling the room with the sweet and musty fragrances of oregano and thyme. In one corner of the room was a ladder leading to the second floor, which covered only half the ceiling, like a loft. There, Joyce's bedroom was divided from that of her in-laws by a thin wall and one modern concession, a closet.

The only decorations on the walls of the house were a cheap calendar marking the many Greek holy days of the year, a portrait of the Virgin painted on tin, and a few cracked and faded black-and-white photographs, which Petros had nailed to the wall. Above the fireplace, on a lace-covered wooden mantelpiece, sat an oil lamp, a fat beeswax candle in a glass box, and some of the souvenirs Nikos had brought home. Beside the hearth hung the family altar, a wooden frame containing icons of the Virgin and Saint Dimitrios, a candlestick, and two tin *tamata*, which Dimitra made Joyce polish every week.

When Joyce had first seen all this, it had not seemed real. It had seemed toylike and picturesque, a fairy-tale cottage. She had not known of its drawbacks — the rareness of privacy, the animals running in and out, the scorpions one had to search for before going to bed, the lack of electricity. Yet she had grown to love it. Only rarely now did she long for certain luxuries of her childhood home — a toilet down the hall, for example, or a stove that was inside the house and did not need to be stoked with coal. An electric light beside her bed. But what did all that matter? To her, thoughts of home were mostly of absences, inertia. Here, in her new life, every moment was filled. Every muscle she could move, every task she could perform, every word she could utter was accepted so eagerly that she felt she could never give enough.

At last Dimitra tired of the English visitors and took herself to bed, sending all three girls up the ladder to Joyce's room as if they were children. Joyce prepared to sleep on the floor, using one of the bedrolls she'd made for the festival, but the guests insisted on letting her have her own bed and taking the floor themselves. This was the first time Joyce had entertained overnight guests since she had come to Greece. She wanted to talk all night.

In the safety of darkness, after she had put out the kerosene lamp, the conversation soon turned personal. The girls pressed her for more of her story, for details about Nikos and how she coped with this strange, ancient life. "Do you really get on all right with your mother-in-law?" Sarah asked eventually, her voice skeptical. "She seems awfully bossy."

Joyce shifted in the dark, frowning. She didn't like to hear Dimitra criticized by strangers. "I don't mind," she answered. "She sounds meaner than she is."

"But do you have to work all the time? I mean, don't you ever have any time to yourself? To read or anything?"

"I read at night. I borrow books from the local school. But I like being busy. I like working the land, going to market . . ." Joyce trailed off. She was tired of talking about herself. Her old pleasure in telling her story, in entertaining her visitors with her polished romance, was tarnished now. She wanted instead to hear about the outside world, about lives other than her own. Thinking of Dimitra's unfortunate statement about Sarah, she ventured a remark.

"My mother-in-law asked me if you're Jewish," she said.

She sensed Sarah and Nicola look at one another in the dark. The room was blacker than normal, for storm clouds had hidden the moon and stars. Usually Joyce's bedroom was never quite dark, the dancing Greek sky keeping it alight all the night through.

"Yes we are," Sarah replied at last. "Why, does it matter?"

Joyce hesitated. She longed to tell these strangers the truth. It was one of the great pleasures of having strangers in one's house — the freedom to make them confessors. Harmless ears in which to pour complaints and secrets, in which to say all the forbidden things. But she had to weigh the possible consequences of her answer, as she had learned to do about all matters since she had moved to Ifestia. Secrets here were as hard to keep as honey in a sieve. They would ooze and leak sooner or later, no matter what. She had to remember this when it came to Alex.

"No, it's only that I am too," she said at last, just as the girls were drifting off to sleep. "But no one knows it here, so please don't say anything."

"Why can't you tell them? Are they so anti-Semitic?" Sarah said indignantly.

"It's not that, exactly." Joyce paused, thinking of Dimitra's ugly remarks in the taverna. "It's just that this family is Greek Orthodox and I was afraid they'd dissolve my marriage or kick me out or something if I told them. I didn't want to risk it. It's bad enough being American."

"But your in-laws were against the Nazis in the war, weren't they?" Nicola asked.

"Of course! My father-in-law fought them on the mainland and Dimitra joined the Resistance."

"They could still be anti-Semitic, though," Sarah commented. "Lots of people fought the Nazis but still hated Jews. Everybody resents an invader."

"But they hated Fascism," Joyce said quickly.

Sarah stirred on her sleeping bag, making a slithery noise that set Joyce's teeth on edge. "Maybe. Still, the Nazis massacred sixty-eight thousand Jews in Greece and they didn't do that without help. There may have been some Greeks who tried to hide Jews, but eighty-five percent of us still got slaughtered and a lot of people didn't care. They just looted our possessions instead." She paused and Joyce could feel the tension of the coming question. "Your husband knows you're Jewish, though, right?"

"No."

"Why not?" This time Sarah sounded astonished.

"When I first got here I didn't have the language to explain." Joyce knew how weak she sounded. "By the time I did it seemed too late."

"That's not right," Sarah said abruptly. Her voice was stern in the dark. "Sorry to put it so bluntly, but I think it's immoral to pretend you're not Jewish."

"Anyway," Nicola added more gently, "if you have to hide so much from the people you love, you can never be free. If you live your whole life pretending things, you just end up a slave to the people you're deceiving. You're giving them a power over you they don't even know they have."

"I know," Joyce spluttered, ready immediately to disassociate herself from anyone remotely like the type Nicola was describing. "I wouldn't dream of living like that," she added, and fell into the stunned silence of a person who had just caught herself in a barefaced lie.

Sarah and Nicola departed the next day to continue their travels, leaving Joyce feeling like a hostess whose party has ended too early. She wished they had stayed longer, for their conversation had made her deeply uneasy. She was filled with questions now about the Greek Sephardim and about how to recover herself from her deceptions. She wanted their advice. She wanted somehow to earn their forgiveness, even for matters they knew nothing about.

Once the guests were gone, the family returned to the urgent tasks of preparing for the coming harvest. Joyce was kept so busy that Petros had to go to market in her place. She hunted the courtyard and henhouse for eggs, scrabbling under heaps of stinking straw. She weeded the vegetable garden, pulling and yanking, her hands as hard as gloves. She heaved buckets of feed to the donkey and milked the cow and the goats, coaxing their teats until the muscles in her thumbs burned with pain. She boiled the laundry, pounded it against a rock, hung it to dry; ironed it with an old black iron, heated on coals, sweat pouring down her arms and chest until she was soaked. Like a son, she worked with Petros, hoeing, gathering the sesame seeds, fixing the roof. Like a daughter, she helped Dimitra cook, mend, and clean. The tasks were endless, ready to swallow her every minute, her every thought. Yet her body had adapted. She had learned to bend with the work, not fight it. Nothing like when she had first arrived.

For the initial month or so of her life with Dimitra and Petros, the work had been agony for Joyce. Dimitra was right — she had been weak and lazy. Her muscles were those of a pampered suburban girl. Biceps as stringy as bootstraps, back bony and frail, hands as soft as a duchess's. It had hurt terribly to callus those hands, to turn those muscles into cables strong enough to lift buckets of wet sheets, sacks of potatoes, to push the sulking Phoebus until he staggered. At the end of every day she had crept about the house, stiff and twisted with pain. Dimitra had laughed, cuffing her, but after a week began to massage her quietly and with great strength, using the oils and lavender water she kept in the pantry. Her strong hands kneaded Joyce's shoulders and arms, calves and thighs, back and buttocks with the casual indifference of a farmer grooming his horse. At times Joyce had to bite her lip as Dimitra's fingers dug deep into bruised muscle, but she was determined not to cry out, just as she hadn't cried out at her brothers' torments or her mother's needling remarks. She knew she had to battle Dimitra to keep her will alive. So she kept quiet. And gradually, more and more kindly, Dimitra had kneaded the pain away.

Now, Joyce was inured to physical labor. Her biceps bulged like a young man's when she lifted a bucket of water or a bale of straw. Her back was supple and strong, tight as Nikos's. Only her spirit felt weak. The English girls had left her with a cloying taste, like rotten melon: the taste of guilt vying with her longing for Alex, of remorse battling with lust. Why had she succumbed to Alex so readily? she wondered. And why was she now so possessed by thoughts of him? Was it merely the pent-up desire of a neglected wife, or was it something deeper, something rotten about her love for Nikos? This last thought frightened her so much that she pushed it quickly away. Yet it kept niggling at her, irritating her, like a mosquito bite that flares up each time it's touched.

Joyce worked doggedly in the hope that she could bury these disturbing thoughts in labor, just as she had always buried her loneliness, but she found the effort useless. She had to drag herself through her chores, her body automatically bending, pulling, lifting, while her worries banged about in her head like a trapped bat.

The work was somewhat alleviated by her intermittent conversations with Dimitra. Joyce's mother-in-law had never been one for talking much, except about her wartime experiences, but she did believe it her duty to instruct Joyce in the many customs of her village and the complicated rules and rituals of her beliefs. She had taught her that a puff of breath through pursed lips would deflect the evil eye of jealousy, and that, for the same reason, one should spit three times on any object or person who receives a compliment. Between Christmas and the Epiphany, when the *kalikantzari* — the hideous hobgoblins who live deep in the earth all year, eating snakes — were supposed to come, Dimitra told Joyce to distract them from poisoning her food by leaving a sieve on the doorstep. "They become fascinated by counting all the holes," she explained. "It keeps them from mischief all the night long." She also told Joyce to pray not only to

God and the Virgin but to her local and name-day saints for protection and help. "But I don't know my name-day saint," Joyce had said. "We don't do that in America." Dimitra had to run to Father Poulianos for advice. "Call her Justina," he declared. "It is the nearest thing I can find to her silly name." Saint Justina, it turned out, was a virgin martyr, a disciple of Saint Peter who was supposedly murdered by the emperor Nero. She was celebrated every October 7th. What Father Poulianos neglected to tell Dimitra was that the document recounting this history was a sixth-century forgery.

Above all, however, Dimitra was relentless on the subject of keeping Joyce respectable. "When I was young, a girl covered her hair as soon as she turned eleven, so as not to tempt men or the devil," she often said, eyeing Joyce's blond tresses disapprovingly. "I wish you would remember to wear your scarf to the market." And every day, over and over again, she warned Joyce that if she looked any man but Petros in the face — especially a soldier — he would take her by force. "The soldiers," she said ominously, "they are all rapists in their hearts. I know, I have lived with all kinds. Give a man a gun and he thinks he owns the world."

Joyce's part in these conversations was mostly just to listen and agree, but every now and then, when Dimitra was in the mood to be entertained or to feel superior, she would ask Joyce to describe America. Joyce found this nearly impossible. It was like trying to describe a nightclub to someone who had never left a convent. She always seemed to leave Dimitra with the impression that America was a chaotic, hedonistic place, where no one cared for family, for education, or for God. Dimitra told her constantly that she was lucky to have been rescued from such a hell.

"But we can do whatever we want there," Joyce said one day in defense, as they were slicing peppers and cucumbers to pickle in brine for the winter. "A girl like me, Mama, well, she can go anywhere, any time she wants."

"That's not what I hear," Dimitra retorted, brandishing her knife. "I hear the men over there are crazy with their guns. *Kyria* Douyatzi, you know the woman who has two sons in America? She says her eldest was held up at gunpoint and robbed! Like in the war! I cannot understand such people."

Joyce flushed. "That's exaggerated. People over here say those things because they're angry at America right now about Cyprus, but it's not really true."

"Tell me then" — Dimitra harrumphed — "what kind of freedom does an old woman like me have in your country?"

Joyce frowned as she considered her response. She remembered the old people's home down the road from her house in Miami, where her grandmother had been strapped to the bed whenever she'd turned obstreperous. The impatience with which she had seen supermarket cashiers treat the elderly as they fumbled for coins. On the other hand, there were the legions of old women on the Miami beaches, playing bridge, shopping, beholden to no one. Free to tan themselves all day long until they had metamorphosed into shriveled leather pouches.

"It all depends how much money you have," she finally said, "But it's freer than here. It is."

Dimitra laughed. "That's an American answer if I ever heard one!"

While Joyce was entertaining her English guests and working the farm, Alex was wandering the island in a pitiful state of distraction. It wasn't only his desire for Joyce that held him in thrall — although he longed to lay himself again along her naked body — it was her mystery, her knowledge, the strange contrast between her being married and trapped yet bold and free. She had dived headlong into this backwards life of hers without even looking first, an act of rashness he could never commit. Yet she seemed to have found something that he yearned to have himself. He wanted to rescue her but also to find meaning at her feet. To teach her, and to learn from her.

Alex had only tasted love three times. First, with his father's sister, a plump, blond twenty-six-year-old who apparently could think of no better revenge on her prudish big brother than to lure his son to bed. Alex was only seventeen at the time, and he had ejaculated all over her leg. Afterwards he had been filled with a blind, yearning need for her, which he could never differentiate from shame. Even now, at twenty-two, he could not think of her without squirming with humiliation.

Next, there had been the landlady of his small bed-sit in Brighton, where he had lived while at university. His only sexual experience having been with an older woman, he had never really learned to cope with girls his own age. So when his landlady, who was all but forty, came home drunk one night and propositioned him, he acquiesced with ready obedience. "It's only a one-nighter, mind you," she said blearily, her lipstick smearing his cheeks. "I don't approve of mixing with my customers. I just feel like a bit of a poke and tickle."

He gave her one, but she fell asleep before he found out whether it was any good.

At last, in his second year at university, he'd met a girl his own age and stayed with her for the rest of his undergraduate life. She was tall, leggy, intelligent, but insecure like most of the other students, and she and Alex latched onto each other as much for safety as from attraction. Her name was Lou, and by their second month of leaping into bed every few minutes, they decided to move in together. She had planned to come to Greece with him that summer, the summer of their graduation, but they had quarreled, she had fallen for a Frenchman, and gone off to Paris instead.

Now Alex found himself besotted. More than he had been with either his aunt or Lou. More than he had ever thought possible.

On the last day of the festival, Alex had waited for four hours in front of the clothes shop before he'd given up. At first he had told himself that Joyce's in-laws must have delayed her. Then that she'd had cold feet but would give in eventually and come. It was only after it became obvious she would never appear that he finally allowed himself to doubt. Perhaps her absence was simply a rejection. Perhaps she had grown frightened — with reason! — and fled. But gradually, as he walked about the narrow, winding lanes of Ayiassos searching for her in the festival crowds, he talked himself out of that conclusion, too. He decided to go back to Ifestia the next morning and make her tell him to his face why she had failed to meet him.

For the first three days after his return, Alex waited every morning in the market square without success. She had told him she sold there three days a week, so he was certain he would find her; but for two days there was no market, and on the third Joyce was nowhere to be seen. So in the afternoons he took to wandering the town instead, hoping to bump into her. He visited the seafront, with its smell of fish and salt, the sparkle of sun on the waves, and the slowly rocking fishing boats. He walked through the white labyrinth on the hill, littered with dozens of emaciated cats. He investigated the back alleys with their widows crouched against the ancient walls, gazing at him with toothless implacability from beneath their black scarves. As soon as he reached whichever destination he had chosen for the afternoon, however, a panic would come over him in case he had missed Joyce in the town center and he would dash back, only to find the streets empty of everyone but old men and soldiers.

The soldiers mocked him, jealous that a boy like themselves was wandering uniform-less and free. "I'm English, we don't have a national service," he shouted at them in Greek, taking refuge in his dual nationality, as he often did the other way round in England.

"You better watch out, they'll get you!" the boys called back, laughing. Alex took to carrying only his English passport, just in case.

Gradually, the circumference of his wanderings shrank. He circled in more and more tightly, certain that Joyce would have to appear at the market eventually. By the fourth day, he had given up even trying to find her anywhere else. He sat in the market square all day long, waiting for her to come.

And, at last, she did.

It was late when she arrived, for she was there to buy, not sell. A few necessities they had run out of — Kastron was only a kilometer away from the house, a walk that had come to be nothing to her. She strode into the town, dressed in her usual drab skirt and blouse, her eyes cast to the ground, her face set in a fierce expression. It was her habitual protection against the soldiers.

He saw her enter the square just as the market was closing up and catapulted to his feet. He stopped himself from rushing at her, however, remembering her position, and watched her for a moment from a distance. She was smaller than he recalled — her presence had loomed large in his imagination — her body slight and her hair a shining dark blond. She was carrying a basket. Her skirt, a dull brown, hung to her shins. But she was real, and she was beautiful.

He approached from behind as she took a package wrapped in paper and put it in her basket.

"Joyce?"

She started. The blood drained from her face and she looked so frightened for a moment that he stepped back. "It's only me," he said, glancing over his shoulder.

Joyce said nothing. She walked rapidly away from the market, turning down a narrow alley. He followed at a discreet distance, trying to look as if he were merely out for a stroll.

When he caught up with her, she was leaning against a wall, her basket clutched to her waist. "Don't talk to me in front of people," she whispered urgently. "They're all going to ask about you now, about who you are and everything. They'll ask my mother-in-law. Jesus!"

"God, I'm sorry. I thought I was being careful."

"There's no such thing as careful here!" She was hissing. "It's no good, Alex, they'll find me out. I live in a fishbowl. We're not in Ayiassos anymore."

"I know. Look, please Joyce, let me just talk to you."

She stood up straight, glancing down the narrow alleyway. Her fear filled him with distress.

"I had to see you," he said quickly. "Why didn't you meet me at the festival?"

Joyce explained. "You found me just to ask that?" she added.

"No, I wanted to — I need to know what you want."

"What I want! Oh God, Alex, what I want." She spoke bitterly, and he understood. It made him happy, despite the danger and their predicament.

"I'll do whatever you think is best," he whispered, bold now in his joy. "I'm free, even if you aren't. I can stay as long as I want. What do you want me to do?"

Joyce looked up at him. His sunburned skin had darkened to a ruddy tan, and in the shade of the alley his blue eyes had turned nearly black. He looked wonderful.

"I mustn't see you," she said. "I can't." Her voice trembled.

"Why, because you don't want to?"

She stared down at her hands. "You know it isn't that."

"Then let me stay. I'll be careful. Please, I need to see you."

Joyce gazed at him in wonder. His face was strained, earnest, his expression nothing like the smooth smile Nikos wore when he declared love.

"It's too dangerous, Alex. I don't want to lose everything I've got here."

"But you want me, don't you?" He moved closer to her,

touched her forehead tenderly with his fingertips. "I certainly want you."

"Oh God." She shut her eyes. Even the scent of him made her long to succumb. "Stay if you want," she couldn't help saying. "But I can't promise anything."

"I'll stay if I can see you," he replied quickly, stepping even closer. "Just a few minutes a day, like this, so we can talk. Or if you have to go somewhere by yourself . . . don't you go to trade or buy anywhere? To pick in the fields? Don't they ever trust you to go anywhere but the market alone?"

Joyce looked down at her basket. He made her life with Dimitra and Petros sound like a punishment. Yet until she'd met him, it had not felt that way.

"Hardly ever," she said. "Even now is unusual. Only on Sundays after church and on festival days."

Alex ran his hand caressingly over her hair. "I'll wait for Sunday, then. If I can have a few hours with you on Sunday, I'll wait. I'll find a place where we can go alone."

"I can't, Alex!"

"You can. You must. Meet me while your mother-in-law is in church, the way we met the first time. Up on the hill above town."

Joyce put down her basket and let him hold her. His body hard and hot against hers. She wanted so much to resist him, but her desire, his words, were making her helpless. Closing her eyes, she wondered at his passion. In Florida, before Nikos, she had never roused such declarations in men. She had been just one of a bunch of girls there, her phone ringing occasionally for a date, but nothing special. She had not been a girl boys had crushes on. So many weekends had gone by with no phone calls, and so many months with no boyfriend, that at eighteen she had still been a virgin. What had happened to her since that men fell for her like this? Clinging to Alex, his desire palpable in the trembling of his arms, she felt suddenly powerful and womanly, yet in more danger than she'd ever felt in her life.

"All right, I'll meet you," she said at last. "Just to talk, okay? But this has to be the last time. It's too risky for me."

"I know." He pulled her tight. "God, I thought I'd lost you," he whispered in her hair. "I couldn't bear to lose you."

That night, Joyce lay in bed, thinking of Alex and his words. "I'm free," he had said, "even if you aren't." What did it mean to say you were free? Did it mean having noplace you had to go? Having nobody need you? But she'd had that kind of freedom already. She'd had it in Florida, bicycling to nowhere up and down the suburban streets, her mind occupied with soft-focus dreams of romance. If that was freedom, it was a sad thing to crow about. Freedom was supposed to bring happiness, wasn't it? Not a void.

Joyce turned on her bed to stare out the window. The moon was there, cut in half tonight, shimmering like an eye behind a veil. Perhaps that's why Alex is so eager to tie himself to me, she thought. Perhaps he doesn't like his kind of freedom any more than I liked mine.

VII

The house was thrown into turmoil the next evening by the unexpected return of Nikos. No warning letter this time, no greetings to wife or parents. He just appeared at the door, tired and unshaven, to claim his welcome.

Joyce started towards him, her joy at seeing him again making her momentarily forget her guilt. Seven months had passed since he had last been home, and he had grown more beautiful than ever. His hair still curled black and glistening over his brow. His eyelashes were still seductive as he lowered them slowly over his amber eyes. But he was almost twenty-eight now and looked more man than boy. His chest had broadened, his muscles grown thicker. Even his unshaven cheeks and tired gait made him seem more authoritative and worldly. He looked powerful in a way that Joyce had never seen in him. She wanted to fling her arms around his neck and squeeze. But then she remembered what she had done to him and stopped herself. What if he found out? What if he could tell? The sight of him standing there before her, solid and strong, suddenly filled her with terror.

Nikos looked at her expectantly, but she could not bring herself to move. His mouth tightening, he turned to hug his mother.

Dimitra was beside herself at seeing her son again. She sprang to life as if she had lost twenty years, stroking his cheeks, cooing in his ear. "You look so tired, my son," she lamented. "What have those skinflints on your ship been doing to my boy?"

He tossed his sailor's bag in the corner and dropped into a chair, running his rough brown hand through his curls. "I'm starving" was all he said. Dimitra scurried to serve him, pressing soup on him, then bread, covering his hands with kisses.

"*Mannamou*, please stop!" he snapped, and proceeded to eat and drink all they had in the house. Dimitra ordered Petros to go into town to buy more and Joyce offered to go in his stead, eager to make up to Nikos, but her father-in-law refused her. "You've not seen your husband for more than half a year. Stay with him, he wants you."

Joyce stood uneasily in the middle of the room. What would he do if he heard about Alex? Beat her up? Throw her out? Gather the villagers around to stone her and drive her out of town? She had heard of such things, she knew they were no myths. Her heart began to race.

Petros returned with a demijohn of local barrel wine and some bread from Alex's aunt. Nikos poured a glass and raised a toast to his parents, ignoring Joyce. He drank alone at the table, his parents and wife hovering around him like footmen.

"Sit down!" he cried at last, sweeping his arm at the chairs. "Don't stand there gawking at me! Are you not glad I'm home? Sit and drink with me!"

They did. Joyce had no glass and was not offered one. Petros picked his up and clinked it against his son's. "Thank God you are safe," he said, his old voice tremulous.

"Have you brought us any gifts?" said Dimitra at last. She looked suddenly small next to Nikos, round and old in her stained apron and baggy dress. Vulnerable.

"Of course I have, *Mannamou*. You think I would forget you? They are in my bag." He gestured to it but did not get up to fetch them. The family sat watching him eat in silence while he continued to ignore Joyce.

Finally, Dimitra sighed and put her hand on Joyce's arm. "Greet your husband like a proper sailor's wife," she said. "That is what he's waiting for. You must kneel at his feet and thank the Lord he is home safe. Then we can all relax. You have never given him the traditional greeting. It is time you learned."

Was that all it was? Joyce gazed at Nikos. He was looking at her eagerly, but to her it was not a look of welcome; it was the look of a man impatient to conquer. She could not make herself move.

"Kneel!" Dimitra shouted, and raised her arm as if to hit Joyce. Then she stopped herself, remembering their conversation in the church. She lowered her arm, looking sheepishly at her son.

"Mama." Nikos spoke warningly. "Have you not been teaching my Joyce the way I told you?"

Dimitra did not know what to do. She was trapped between two contradictory commands: that of her son to master his wife, and that of her heart to be kind.

"Perhaps if you say something more to her," Dimitra began, "make her know that you are happy to see her . . ."

"I've done enough!" Nikos roared. "I've written her love letters every week, I've sent money. She should kiss my feet, grateful that I have come back alive from the sea — that's how a sailor's wife is supposed to behave!"

"Be quiet, you spoiled brat!" The words rang out and everybody in the room fell silent, staring. It was Petros who had spoken. Little, withered Petros. He was glowering at his son, his eyes like dark, wet marbles.

"I never want to hear you shout at your mother like that again. You apologize or you leave my house forever!"

Nikos stared at his father, astonished.

Joyce was aching with the pain of what was happening. She knew that Dimitra's heart was torn between Nikos and herself, that it had been for some time. Petros's, too. If she had still been innocent, she might have fought for her own corner of those hearts, battled Nikos for them like two rats fighting over a rind of cheese. But she was not innocent, and all she could do now was try to smooth things over. She glanced at Dimitra and Petros. They were watching her from their chairs, the air in the room still with their hope.

"Thank you, father-in-law," she said at last, her voice wavering. "But Nikos is right. He has traveled the world while we stayed safely here, spending his money. He deserves at least to be greeted properly. Please, Mama, *Petheros* — she reached to take both their hands, as dry in hers as driftwood — "please do not distress yourselves."

Joyce rose and approached Nikos. She would not kneel — she was still too American for that. But she did, for Dimitra's sake, bend to kiss both his cheeks and to hug him. "Welcome again, husband," she said pointedly, then picked up the bottle and refilled his glass. Her hand trembled. She felt surer than ever that he was making all this fuss because he knew about Alex.

Nikos scowled. He was not certain what had happened, whether he was being obeyed or mocked. At last he raised his arm and waved Joyce away. "I wish to speak to my parents alone," he said coldly, and dismissed her from the room.

For a time, Nikos, Dimitra, and Petros remained silent. But at last, unable to contain herself any longer, Dimitra said, "What is the matter, my son? Your little Joyce is loving and obedient. What is troubling you so?"

Nikos drained his glass, then poured another. Leaning forward, his elbows on the table, he fixed his gaze on his mother, melting her as he had always done. "*Mannamou*," he said slowly, "tell me that I have not made a mistake marrying this American."

Dimitra narrowed her eyes. Petros cleaned his pipe.

"What mistake?" Dimitra said sharply, shifting her stout

body on the wooden chair. She folded her arms across her bosom and glared at Nikos, her square face suspicious. "What are you talking about?"

He looked down at the table, disconcerted. His mother was usually putty in his hands. But he forged on. "*Mannamou*, you saw how cold she is. She did not greet me as she always has. She looked at me as if I am a stranger."

"So?" Dimitra said scornfully. "Perhaps she is a little shy, so what? Are you so delicate you cannot overcome the shyness of a girl?"

Nikos frowned. "No, I think it is something else. She is growing hard and cold, like all women who have no children."

"What is this nonsense you are saying? What is the matter with you?"

"Mama, you want grandchildren, yes?"

"From your lips to the ear of God."

"But where are they? You see grandchildren coming out of Joyce's hole?"

"Nikos, watch your language. You are not on a ship here."

"Sorry, Mama. But we have been married two years and she still has no babies. I wait for good news by letter, but none comes. I wait and I wait, and still nothing. Then I come back and she looks and acts like a stone. Do you think there is something wrong with her?"

"Don't be foolish. Of course not. You have to be here to give her babies. What do you expect?"

"I expect a wife of two years to conceive a child, that's what I expect! *Mannamou*, I want a child so much it pierces me here!" Nikos thumped his chest, anguish distorting his young face. "You, of all people, must understand that! But look at her — she looks like a boy. . . . Mama, I want a son."

Dimitra grunted but did not move. Petros sucked on his pipe.

"Did you hear me? I want a son! Oh, God and the saints, why didn't I marry a nice, plump Greek girl?"

"Not so loud, Nikos. Control yourself," Petros hissed, taking his pipe out of his mouth and pointing it at the window. But, of course, it was too late. Joyce was standing outside, under the moonlight, and she could hear every word.

So that's what it's about, she thought, not Alex at all. She was relieved, yet at the same time strangely disappointed. Was this all that had become of their love — that Nikos wanted a brood mare? He had never shown any interest in children before, never dandled any coveted babe upon his knee. All he wanted was to prove his virility through her, his ultimate possession of her. Joyce knew this with a sudden and absolute certainty. And it filled her with disgust.

Dimitra unfolded his arms and leaned forward again, her heavy bosom pushing against the table, her gnarled hands splayed on the tabletop. "Nikos, don't make yourself angry at her. There is nothing wrong with Joyce. Give her your love and she will give you babies."

Nikos sighed. "I will try, *Mannamou*, but I don't know how much more my heart can take. I have been patient with her so far, but it is humiliating to be married for two years and still have no children."

Dimitra pushed herself to her feet, suddenly irritated. "I've had enough of this whining. You have your wife under God and the law, and she is obedient and loyal and here in my care as you wanted. She has done her duty to you, Nikos. Now you do yours to her!"

"But I have!" Nikos burst out. "I have been working like a galley slave for her. But she has lived under our roof all this time and given me nothing in return! What do I owe her?"

"Given you nothing? How can you say such a thing?" Dimitra cried. "She has given you faithfulness, the sweat of her brow, her love for us. You owe her your vows under the sight of God, Nikos. Your soul in the eyes of the Lord."

"But she is breaking my heart, Mama. People laugh at me, they say I am impotent and henpecked. A man cannot stay with a wife who breaks his heart!"

"Son," said the calm, cold voice of Petros again. "If you leave Joyce I will cut off your inheritance. Not one centimeter of this land will go to you, ever!"

Outside, in the pale moonlight, on the bare earth still warmed from the sun, Joyce sank slowly to the ground. She sat on her heels and leaned her head against the whitewashed wall of the house. It was hard and bumpy, but soothing, warm as Dimitra's hands.

Dimitra and Petros are willing to sacrifice their son for me, she thought. And I am nothing but a lie.

VIII

Alex had no idea of the events that were complicating his life. All he knew was that the wait to see Joyce was interminable. There was little to do on Ifestia if one had no work — one castle to visit, a couple of poky, run-down museums, a few ruins. He was tired of beaches. The tavernas were full of hostile, bored soldiers. The fishermen were too busy mending their nets to talk to a bothersome tourist. His aunt shooed him out of her bakery every morning, complaining that his gangly presence got in her way. Yet the ferry came only every third day. He was marooned.

He tried to think of what he could do for Joyce. For the first time he remembered birth control and that it was virtually unavailable in Greece. He had brought one or two condoms from England — after all, he had been seeking adventure — but they wouldn't last long. I should have used one the first time, he admonished himself. The last thing he wanted to do was make Joyce pregnant. He telegraphed a friend in England.

SEND FRENCH LETTERS STOP LOTS STOP WILL EXPLAIN LATER STOP

He would be ribbed about this for months, he knew, but he could think of no other way.

Meanwhile, he plowed through the rest of the week by reading, taking long walks, and continuing to explore, looking for a secret corner in which to hide with Joyce. One day he borrowed a cousin's moped and drove around the muddy Moudhros Bay, passing a huge military cemetery on the way, its immaculate lawns and regimented rows of white gravestones looking crisp and out of place on this wild, rocky island. Ifestia had been the principal base for the ill-fated Gallipoli campaign of 1915, and eight hundred soldiers lay buried here, many of whom had not lived long enough to push up a beard. Alex had learned that nowhere in this country could one forget the ravages of war. Reminders of death and starvation were everywhere. Mutilated men. Black-shrouded widows. Rotted teeth and stunted statures. A certain grimness. Deserted villages, their populations having fled to Athens for work and survival. Alex had come to think of modern Greece as a great tender snail. Whenever it poked its vulnerable, quivering tentacles out of its shell, it was bludgeoned by guns or dictatorships.

He forged east, along a narrow, winding road powdered by dust and gravel, until, his mouth dry, he stopped for coffee at a little northeastern village called Ifestia — the village that had given the island its name. Both names were derived from Hephaestus, god of blacksmiths, jewelers, and carpenters. Hephaestus had always seemed the least glamorous of the gods to Alex, as if a plumber had elbowed his way into the ranks of monarchs. Zeus had him given Aphrodite as a wife, a cruel joke: the sweaty, begrimed ugliness of the blacksmith united with the jewel of Mount Olympus. Hephaestus was ferociously jealous, so the legend went, and with reason. Aphrodite was revolted by her filthy husband and loved instead his boastful brother, the handsome and cruel Ares, god of war.

Alex wondered if that was what it was like for Joyce, being married to a Greek sailor. He imagined Nikos as ignorant, hairy, and ill-mannered. A lowly crewman with the raw machismo of a seafaring thug. Surely, he thought, she must yearn for escape.

The village of Ifestia still contained the ruins of a temple to Hephaestus, so Alex decided to take a look. But all he could find were a few broken pillars lying bleached and pockmarked in the blond grass. The temple was built to mark the spot where Hephaestus was supposed to have landed when Zeus hurled him in a fury from Mount Olympus, laming him forever. Zeus treated his son thus to punish him for interfering in a quarrel between his parents. Alex's mother had often joked that living on Ifestia has been a punishment ever since.

Alex walked around the toppled pillars, thinking again of the contrast between Joyce's flight to Ifestia and his mother's escape from it. The longer he stayed on this island, the harder it was for him to imagine his mother growing up here. She was so English now, an intellectual in dark brown suits, her black hair cut in a severe pageboy. She seemed to have lost all connection with her native Greece, except for a slight roll in her r's. For one thing, she had no interest in nature. Her passions were books, history, art. She was utterly devoted to her teaching — art history at a college in London — and to her galleries and museums. She only liked a tree if it was painted, a flower if it was marble. The real things left her cold. Furthermore, she was repulsed by anything that smacked of village life: gossip with friendly neighbors, obligations to local shopkeepers. She preferred the brisk anonymity of the city. He wondered what she would think of Joyce's decision to live here. Would she simply find Joyce ignorant, or would she see the courage and wisdom that Alex passionately believed Joyce possessed?

Having exhausted the scanty ruins of Ifestia, he remounted his moped and continued northwards. And there, on the tip of the island at Plaka, he found what he was looking for — the most beautiful beach in Ifestia, and a place to make love to Joyce.

It was late August by now, and the tourist season on this unpopular island was drawing to a close. The few Germans and Scandinavians who had ventured onto Ifestia had packed up and left, their bulky trailers filing back along the dusty roads like waddling elephants. The campsites were empty now but for an occasional car or tent standing alone as if left behind by a circus. Alex parked and walked over the white sand to the water, a gentle wind stirring his hair. The sea was suddenly full of jellyfish, which had considerately stayed away for the tourists. He could see them, some clear, some pink, bobbing in the water like little fat children's umbrellas. Over by a cliff some fishermen were beating their catch of octopi against the rocks, slapping them down again and again to tenderize them, then scrubbing the hard suckers off until the rocks were covered with bloody pink foam. Otherwise, the beach was long and empty and quiet.

This would be perfect for us, Alex thought. Miles away from Kastron and the people who know Joyce. Sand dunes to shield us from watchful eyes. We could make love for hours here. Wash ourselves off again in the sea. The only problem was how to get there — Alex's cousin would hardly let him have the moped day after day. He thought of his remaining traveler's checks in a drawer at his aunt's. Perhaps he could buy his own moped secondhand, then sell it again before he departed. It would leave him with little extra, but he might just manage it. I'm not really free, he said to himself, in spite of what I told Joyce. I'm too poor.

Alex was supposed to be traveling back to England by this time. Either that, or looking for a job. His parents had made it clear that now he was no longer a student he had to support himself. His most recent plan had been to return to Athens in late August and take a job teaching English until he could decide what to do with his life. Vaguely, he had thought of going back to university one day for a postgraduate degree and becoming a professor of political science. Or using some school connections to land a position as a foreign correspondent. Whatever he chose to do, he had decided, it would be in Greece.

For now, however, he was too bewitched to think of anything but the present, and the only full-time job he'd found was being a lover. He could think of nothing but undressing Joyce. Of making love to her in ways he had never made love to anyone. His every thought returned to her. Would she be pleased by this beach? Could he give her that trinket? What would she think if he showed her this village? All his inner conversation was directed at her. He tried to see everything through her eyes.

He walked up the beach, climbed onto the moped, and drove back to his aunt's, his body burning.

Alex's aunt, Eugenia Sarafi, was a small, sharp-edged woman who had been running the village bakery by herself ever since her husband had died five years earlier. Like all shopkeepers she was chained to her work, rarely free to leave the premises even for an afternoon, and the drudgery had made her efficient but sour. Her shop consisted of two rooms, divided by an open door draped with a rattling bead curtain. Built into the back was the *fourno*, a huge furnacelike oven in which she baked at least a hundred loaves a day. In the front were a counter and a series of slanting wooden shelves for displaying the bread.

Alex had tried to help his aunt in the bakery, feeling guilty for lounging about like a prince while she worked so hard, but she had resisted him. "You are clumsy as a goat," she had said when he'd tried to help her lift the loaves out of the oven or knead the great quantities of dough she kept in a stone trough on the floor. "You are your mother's son, you with your books and your skinny arms. Go fill your head with words and leave your old aunt in peace."

But Eugenia liked Alex. She'd had only daughters herself, and the boys she hired to help her bake tended to be sullen or disrespectful. She enjoyed having a conscientious young man about for company, even if he was as stringy as a grapevine. She liked his gentlemanly manners, courteous yet humble, and his fine way of speaking. She also liked that he had bothered to learn Greek, especially considering that his mother would never come home. Even his Englishness — a certain fastidiousness as he picked over the *kalamaria*, the gawky, self-effacing way he moved about her house — endeared him to her.

Sometimes at night, as they sat over a late meal, Eugenia stared at Alex from across the table and tried to see her older sister in him. He looked so tall and blond, however, that she found this difficult. Perhaps in the shadowy blue of his eyes, or in the turn of his head. On the whole, though, her sister's roundness and olive-dark features seemed to have drowned in Alex, to have been submerged under the more aggressive Anglo-Saxon looks of his father.

Eugenia had met Alex's father only once, when he'd come to Ifestia to marry Irini before taking her away, and she had not been impressed. The man had seemed so lifeless compared to a Greek, as pale as if all the fire in his blood had turned to dust. But even though he could speak no modern Greek, she could tell he was knowledgeable, an intellectual. Eugenia knew that her sister would like that.

Irini had always been bookish. Raised like all Greek women to be a wife, she had shown remarkably little curiosity about romance or the young men of the village. While Eugenia wove flowers in her hair for the May Day dances, Irini pored over books. When the mothers of boys came sniffing about, interested in the sisters' generous dowries — their parents had been well off for Ifestians — Irini refused to turn on her charm or even to gossip about them after they had left. Then, somehow, she convinced her parents to take her to Thessaloniki to have a last look at the museums before she was buried alive in a Greek marriage. And that was where she met her escape.

Given this history, Eugenia was not surprised that Irini never came home. Their parents were dead now, their brothers entangled in their own worlds of mishaps and adventures. Anyway, Irini had always been a misfit here. Her mother and father had been puzzled by her, although proud of her intelligence, but the young people of Kastron had not liked her at all. The boys thought her stuck up, the girls found her dull. She would have been miserable if she had married the old shopkeeper who had been chosen for her. Her flight had been a blessing to all.

Still, Eugenia mused as she watched her nephew, she did miss her sister. Although the work in the bakery gave her the chance to talk to everybody in the village sooner or later, she nevertheless found it lonely. She had no time to partake of the long, desultory conversations that build up an intimacy. Her only steady companions since Irini left had been her husband, now gone, and her daughters, who had all married and moved away. Her social intercourse these days was nothing but everyday pleasantries and snippets of gossip. So Alex, with his readiness to talk and his seemingly endless leisure, had been a welcome interruption to the lonely monotony of her baker's life.

Alex would have been surprised to hear this. To him, his aunt Eugenia was as brusque as his own mother was gentle. He had always thought of his mother as a sort of absentminded mole: sleek, plump, and distracted, but always available for a cuddle. His aunt was more like a water rat. Short and spare, her hair and eyes a gleaming black, she had a mustache that sprang from her upper lip in straight black points and an oval face that tended towards the dour. If she felt any affection for him at all, she only showed it in scolding and irritation. He couldn't shake the feeling that she did not want him there at all.

She did, however, like to gossip about the families of Kastron, he'd discovered. So when he got back from his explorations on the moped, he began to prod her. "I heard there was an American girl living here," he said, leaning against the door while his aunt swept out the bakery with a long twig broom. "I heard she married someone here. Is that true?"

Eugenia poked the broom between his feet. "Get out of the way, will you? Yes, it is true," she said, shaking her head disapprovingly. "She came two years ago I think it is now, brought home by that no good Nikos. God help that girl. She's given him no children. He'll throw her away like an old rag sooner or later."

Alex jumped back, saying nothing for a few minutes for fear of betraying himself. But eventually he added, "I wonder what it's like for an American to live here. Has she any friends? Do the women accept her?"

Eugenia grunted. "A married woman without children is neither girl nor woman, child nor matron, Alexi. She falls right between the cracks." She shook her head, clucking, and pushed him irritably out of the way. "She has some friends, yes. Marina Benaki, that young hussy from the mainland, a bad influence in my opinion. I see the two of them walking together. One or two others perhaps. But most of the young woman are suspicious of *Kyria* Nikos. They say she has bold eyes, that she looks at men like a prostitute. They think she will steal their husbands, the silly fools! The truth is they are afraid of foreign girls and their loose morals. And they're jealous."

Alex thought of Joyce as he'd last seen her, walking into the market with lowered lashes. Of the time he had saved her from the soldiers. She can't win, he thought. Enemies on every side.

"Why are they jealous?" he said. "Because she is —" He was about to say beautiful but stopped himself. "Because she is American and they think she's rich, I suppose?"

His aunt chuckled, but did not bother to answer.

Later that night Alex went to a seafront *kaphenio* to seek company for talk and a smoke, a few *ouzos,* a few debates. He went with his cousins, the children of his uncles, most of them fishermen, eager for some drink to warm their bellies after a long day at sea. They eyed the women passing by, making comments, and Alex looked them over, too. Many Greek women are lovely, he thought. Those dark eyes, black eyebrows. Those strong legs. Some were fair, their eyes flashing green. But he could only feign interest. Joyce filled his mind. She was like a creature from no world he had ever known. Half from the new, half from the old. Naive, yet worldly. Ignorant, yet wise.

How could he bear to wait until Sunday?

* * *

Nikos, meanwhile, stayed on. He did not approach Joyce in her bed, or indeed hardly at all. He was still too angry at her refusal, as he saw it, to give him either babies or subjugation. Instead, his eyes followed her mournfully, steeped in reproach and self-pity. And in defiance of his parents he talked incessantly about the son he wanted, his voice loud and deliberate so that Joyce could not fail to hear.

Joyce knew that he was waiting for her to beg. To ask his forgiveness for not bearing him children and to invite him back to her bed. To prostrate herself before him. And she wished she could. She longed again to feel the smooth muscles of his body, the worship he used to give her and the safety she used to feel. Above all, she longed to be sure that she still had a place in this life she loved with Dimitra and Petros, her Greek life, where she was necessary. But each time she tried to make herself stoop, to throw herself into Nikos's arms, she found herself turning away instead. Her pride would not let her demean herself this way. She was too modern, too defiant. So she withdrew from Nikos, even while she yearned for him — stiff, resentful, and still terrified that he knew or would find out about Alex.

Nikos would not tell them how long he planned to remain at home. One more day, a week, a month? He refused to say. Furious at Joyce's stubbornness, he took to going into Kastron to find his old friends, to drinking and lazing about and returning home late, morose and sorry for himself. He slept on his grandmother's pillows downstairs. His mother grew increasingly reticent, tired of scolding him. His father stayed out of the house.

Each night Joyce lay in her bed, listening for him. Why couldn't he drop this stupid pride and come to her? For months she had lain in that bed, missing him, yearning for his step, his caress. Now he was here, yet just as she needed him the most — to resurrect their marriage, to drive away her burning for Alex — he would not come. The waste of it filled her with rage.

* * *

When the next Sunday arrived at last, Dimitra hurried Joyce to church even earlier than usual. "You need to pray for my son," she said, and clung to Joyce's arm as they walked. "You must ask the Virgin to help him forgive you." She was smaller than Joyce by several inches, full in the bosom and belly but lean and strong in the legs, and usually she walked with the purposeful stride of a busy woman. Today, however, she seemed to hobble, leaning on Joyce as if she were truly old. Joyce had never seen her so enfeebled.

Joyce stared at the ground, feeling hollow and hypocritical. She had not even been thinking of Nikos just then, but of Alex and whether she should find him after church or avoid him for good. Her mind ricocheted between her husband and lover constantly now, uncontrollably. She frowned at herself. Her deceptions were multiplying, burgeoning, smothering her like layers of mud.

Before they reached the edge of town, she stopped and turned. "Mama," she said, "I want to thank you for defending me to Nikos. I know what he has been saying about me."

"Bah." Dimitra spat. "An empty barrel makes noise. What he has been saying is the foolish prattle of a young man. We will ask the saints to knock some sense into his head."

"But he is your son. He must come first. I understand that."

Dimitra shook her head, her long black scarf wrapped tightly about her hair and neck, her face square and creased within it.

"Yes, he must come first, little one. I know that in my heart. But my worry is that I cannot feel the truth of it." She paused, her hooded eyes troubled as she looked up at Joyce. "You have given me more love than I ever got from my son. To him I have always been like a mountain. There to climb and to suckle from, but never to give to. All his life he has taken from me without thanks. Yes, as you say, it is my duty to put him first in my heart. But is it right, *koroulamou*? This is what I must pray to the Holy Virgin about today. I must ask for her guidance."

They took a few more steps, both their heads bowed under

scarves, their black slippers scuffing the dust-covered stones. Joyce was moved by Dimitra's words, by the love and trust they expressed, yet she was mortified. Dimitra thought of her as a faithful wife, an obedient daughter-in-law, a devout Christian — everything she was not. The words of the English girls repeated in her mind, jabbing at her until the very idea of walking into that church filled her with revulsion. Sarah was right, she thought, I can't go on lying.

"Mama?" she said just as they reached the church door. "Mama, I cannot go in today."

"What?" Dimitra's neck snapped up in surprise. "Today of all days? You must pray to the Virgin for help with your husband!"

"No. I will explain later, I promise, but I have to . . ." She searched for a phrase Dimitra would accept. "I have to look in my heart first. I have to think for myself."

Dimitra clutched Joyce's arm, digging her strong fingers into her wrist. "You will offend the saints!" she exclaimed. "You will bring some terrible bad luck on yourself for such arrogance. Come back later to pray, at least. Promise me that."

"I cannot promise. I just don't know." Joyce looked steadily back at her until Dimitra let go.

"Let it be between you and God, then," she muttered, her tongue pressing against her teeth in disapproval. Then she turned her broad back on Joyce and shuffled inside.

Joyce stood for a minute, rubbing her wrist as Dimitra was swallowed by the darkness of the church. She was surprised that her mother-in-law had given in so readily — she had expected her to rail and shout.

The harder Nikos is on me, she realized, the kinder his mother becomes.

Because Joyce had not arranged to meet Alex until after the service, she had some time to herself, so she walked out of town and away from the marketplace and the seaside *kaphenia*, where the fishermen and soldiers would bother her or where she might even see Nikos. She chose instead a narrow path that meandered up the hill, past lumpy peasant huts and the most ancient of the stone houses left over from the Ottoman Empire, to the craggy gray rocks that rose above the town. She wanted to take this time to think, to decide what to do about her deceptions, but her mind was in such tumult that she could not hold on to one thought for very long. Guilt is a slippery thing, she was learning, sliding in and out of one's grasp like an eel.

Joyce was haunted by what she was doing to Nikos. She knew that she was hurting him terribly. He wanted her love, he was pining for it, even if he would only take it on his own terms. He was always sending her beseeching looks like a dog begging for meat. His parents were so fed up with him that he crept around the house like an outcast now, as if she had usurped him, become the blood child while he had sunk to mere in-law. Why couldn't she just give him what he wanted? Settle this business and go back to being a good Greek wife? Was it really only her pride that was stopping her, her revulsion at the idea of subjugation? Or was it her craving for Alex? Whichever the reason, she felt as if she were destroying Nikos with her stubbornness, perhaps destroying his whole family, and she was wrung with remorse.

Yet, even as these thoughts tormented her, here she was preparing to meet Alex in only a few minutes. Her conscience knew that she was doing wrong, but it was of absolutely no use to her. Her hunger for Alex seemed immune to any dictates of duty or decency. His body, his passion, his connection to modern life — these still intoxicated her even in the midst of her sorrow over Nikos. Her ardor for Alex seemed to have entwined with her love for her husband like the veins and arteries of a heart.

Joyce sat, tired from all these thoughts, pulled her church scarf off her head and leaned her back against a slab of rock, looking down over the town. Below her the umber roofs made a merry patched quilt, the white walls of the houses peeking out between them like tufts of snowy sheets. Fishing boats clustered at the marina, a crowd of bristling insects. And beyond, the sea shimmered in the bright morning sun, blue as Alex's eyes, stretching away down through the Cyclades, to Crete, Africa . . . to that huge world Joyce had never seen.

She shut her eyes, suddenly blinded. What was it that made her so willing to believe in Alex? She barely knew him. He might be another Nikos for all she could tell, domineering, changeable — she would be a fool to trust anything he said. On the other hand, she couldn't trust herself either. She had grown suspicious of her heart now. It seemed stupid, unschooled, like the foolish girl she had been two years ago. Nikos may have changed on her, but her own heart seemed the worst trickster of all.

She opened her eyes and glanced at the sun. It was the time she and Alex had arranged to meet. She would end it with him today, she told herself, that was her only possible excuse for seeing him again. She would end this misery, give herself back to Nikos, to Dimitra, and the family she loved. She would become again the honest wife she wanted to be.

Standing up, she tied her scarf back on her head for camouflage and brushed the dust off her skirt. She had chosen her nicest one, needing to entice her lover even while determining to renounce him. It was dark yellow, flaring past the knees but tight at the waist. Into it she had tucked a simple white shirt. Her long, smooth hair was fastened at the nape of her neck. It swung beneath her white scarf as she climbed down the path.

Alex was already there, pacing. He had been there all morning.

They caught each other's eyes, but some people nearby were heading home from church, so they both turned and walked on, as if unknown to one another. For some time they had to continue like this, Joyce in front, her yellow skirt swaying, Alex behind, trying not to reveal his longing as he watched her. At last, as they left the town for the parched fields above it, the

other people turned off to their houses and Alex could catch up
to her. "Follow me," he whispered, and led her up a rocky slope
and behind an empty sheep's pen, where they were hidden
from view.

There, looking large and conspicuous, sat a shiny red moped.
"Is that yours?" Joyce said.

Alex nodded. "It is now. I got it for us. It's our escape mobile.
Out of town, out of sight."

"But . . ."

"Don't but." He stepped up to her and laid a long finger gently across her lips. "Don't 'but,' please. It wasn't easy getting
this. I have it all planned out. A place to go where no one will
see us."

Joyce nodded. It was what she wanted.

The drive was like a cleansing of the spirit for Joyce. Sitting
behind Alex, her arms around his waist, the wind whipping her
scarf, she felt an exhilaration so powerful that she did not even
care if someone she knew saw her. She was about to lose Alex
anyway — what did it matter? "To hell with them all!" she cried
into the wind, startling him. She hugged herself to his wide,
bony back as if it were a mast, and tossed her head in defiance.

Plaka was really too far, so Alex had decided to make do with
Keros on the east coast, where the beach was also long and
sheltered by sand dunes. He parked, shouldered his rucksack
of food, and led Joyce by the hand. She followed him readily,
eager to surrender her will, as she had done on the moped. To
be swept up and away, making no decisions. Then she caught
herself. That was exactly the kind of thinking she had just
sworn to renounce.

Alex pulled her behind a dune, spread out a sheet he had
folded carefully in his rucksack, and invited her to sit. "I have a
picnic and everything," he said, suddenly shy. "We're all alone
here. We should be all right, don't you think?"

Joyce shrugged, yanked off her scarf, and lay down, her arms
behind her head, her yellow skirt spread around her like the

petals of a daffodil. "Don't ask me what I think," she said, closing her eyes against the sun. "I don't know what I think about anything anymore."

"Not even about me?" He leaned over her, shading her face.

"Especially not about you."

Alex gazed down at her. Her eyes were still shut, their lashes fanning along her cheekbones. Her lips were shapely but pale. Her brow was smooth, unmarked by any of her experiences. Her skin looked the light, golden brown of cooked butter.

"May I kiss you?" he said hoarsely.

She opened her eyes. "I have so much to tell you."

Alex had been imagining this scene for almost a week. At this point he was supposed to undress her, make love to her with all his pent-up desire, but she had rewritten the script. He swallowed and drew back to rest on his elbow beside her, still shading her face from the sun. He wanted her so much that his body was trembling.

"I'm listening," he said, his deep voice strained. "Talk away."

But Joyce said nothing. She opened her eyes slowly and looked at him. His long, reddish face, vivid blue eyes. Bright hair. Perhaps she would never find passion like his again. Perhaps this was the last time she would ever be with any man but Nikos. How could one more time make any difference?

"Take me first," she said, looking him right in the eye.

Why did I put it like that? she wondered as he began to undress her. Am I still so determined to give up my will?

Alex was more sure of his lovemaking this time. First encounters are often marked by the awkwardness of uncertainty, and passion grows, not dwindles, with the knowledge of a new lover's body. Plus Alex had imagined this so often that he knew exactly what he wanted to do. He pulled off her shirt, unhooked her bra, lifted it off like the shell of an egg, lying her gently back down on the sheet. He kissed her breasts softly, moaning. Then he pushed off her long skirt, eased down her underpants, until she was naked. "I have condoms this time," he mumbled, and she nodded.

"Good."

He stripped off his clothes and bent to her, slipping his hand under her hips. She closed her eyes and arched her back, feeling the sea breeze mingling with the brush of his hands, his lips, like a softer caress behind his, like the kisses of a ghost — as if she had two lovers at once.

Their lovemaking was fierce and wild. To Joyce it had the poignancy of a farewell, making her reckless and unrestrained as she cried out in pleasure. To Alex it was everything he'd wanted, feeding his obsession more than ever.

Afterwards, lying on his chest with the breeze tickling her skin, Joyce asked, "Alex, what is freedom to you?"

He was startled by the question. Then he laughed. "Is this your idea of a postcoital conversation?"

Joyce did not understand him. "No, I mean it. The English girls who stayed with me last week said you could never be free if you were deceiving the people you love."

"Oh, I see what you're getting at. Like with me, you mean?"

Joyce rolled off him, lying on the sheet with her legs splayed. Another kind of freedom, legs spread without fear or self-consciousness — so rare for a woman.

"Yes, kind of. But I mean it. I want to know, how would you define freedom?"

Alex tried to think, but thoughts were hard to muster just then. He felt weightless, drained and yet full, his mind giddy with satiated lust. And the sun was shining right into his inadequately pigmented eyes.

"Freedom . . . ," he began slowly. "I suppose for me it's being able to do what makes me happy."

"That's what I thought you'd say."

Alex sat up to look at her. Her long, narrow body was white

and gleaming in the sun, except for her brown face, neck, and arms. The tan on her feet looked like socks. Her nipples were pink flowers on a seat of white. Under his eyes she closed her legs. A freedom lost already in the gaze of a man.

"What do you mean?" he said.

"I mean your definition of freedom is typically male. Do what you want and to hell with everyone else."

"Oh! No, I don't mean that. I mean doing what I want without causing harm, of course. I agree with your English friends. If you have a guilty conscience, you can't feel free. Freedom should never be bought at the expense of anybody else. What's wrong with that?" He paused, answers to his own question already crowding into his mind. "Why?" he said, discomfited. "What's freedom for you?"

"Oh . . ." Joyce stretched and yawned, the blond tufts under her arms tangled by sweat and wind. "Right now I think freedom for me would be just to feel . . . safe." She smiled at him wanly. "I'm not feeling too safe at the moment."

"Why not?" Alex squinted at her.

"Oh, Alex. Things are a terrible mess." She sat up cross-legged, pulling her skirt modestly over her lap. "Can I have some food?" she asked plaintively.

"Of course." Alex unstrapped his rucksack and laid out a picnic, as he had before. Fresh whole-meal bread from his aunt. Olives. Stuffed vine leaves. Goat cheese. *Retsina.* Then he shyly handed her a bundle. "For you."

"For me?" Joyce was surprised. The bundle was wrapped up in a thin white towel. She undid it. Inside was a bikini, shampoo, and a comb.

"So we don't get caught out again," he said, blushing.

"Alex. You're sweet." Joyce put on the bikini top. It was too big, but they both tactfully avoided pointing that out.

Now that she was half-dressed, Alex felt he should be, too. He pulled his bathing suit on, smiling a little sheepishly. His long back curved gracefully as he sat down, cross-legged, his ribs visible on either side of his tight, muscular stomach, his buttocks lean and taut. Joyce gazed at him. She liked men's bodies. She hadn't know that back in Florida, when she had been a virgin and unawakened. Now she could assess a man's body like a seasoned lover.

He passed her the wine, which she swallowed greedily. It ignited the recklessness in her again, the urge to cut loose and follow her impulses, but she forced these thoughts away. She wanted, this time, to keep control.

"Well, are you going to tell me why things are such a mess?" Alex said at last. "Has something gone wrong?"

Joyce picked up the wine bottle and squinted into it. "Nikos came home."

Alex's face grew wary. He swallowed. "And?"

"I'm his wife, Alex."

Alex winced. "You want to stay with him?"

Joyce looked away. Out to sea, to the cerulean waves and the uncompromising line of the horizon. "I want to try."

"And where does that leave me?"

"I think this should be the last time." She put down the bottle and glanced at him. "I'm sorry." She reached for the bikini bottoms and pulled them on, as if to gird herself.

Alex looked at her, shocked. He felt as if she had reached into his chest and squeezed the breath out of him. In desperation, he took a gamble. "You don't mean it, do you?" he said quietly.

Joyce pulled up her knees and rested her forehead on them, closing her eyes. She tried to say yes. A simple affirmative. One word that would close the door as she had promised herself, as she knew she must do. But the strength seeped out of her. Ran onto the sand like leaking oil.

"I don't know," she whispered.

Alex folded his arms around her, holding her against him. His voice was low and serious. "Come away with me, Joyce. I'm mad about you, you must be able to tell that. I can't think of anything but you. We can go to Athens. I'll get a job teaching

English — we both could. There's lots of demand. We'll rent a flat, make some money, travel the world. You don't really want to stay here. Come with me."

"Don't be silly," Joyce said crisply, pushing him away and standing up. "I hardly know you." Turning her back on him, she ran to the sea, her thighs flashing white in the sun.

"Watch out for the jellyfish!" Alex cried, but she could not hear him. His voice dissipated into the air, the thin cry of an Englishman, and he felt suddenly timid and foreign. If she is not afraid of their stings then nor shall I be, he told himself. And plunged after her.

Later, as they sat drying on the sheet, examining the jellyfish welt on Alex's thigh, he decided not to ask her any more about Nikos. He preferred to dwell in the moment, grab what he could. Then Joyce startled him by throwing another peculiar question his way. "What would you think," she said, "if I was Jewish?"

He laughed. "What is this, a test? You'll be asking me to string a bow next."

Joyce frowned, once again not understanding him. "Go on, answer me." She looked at him until he stopped laughing.

"But you're not. You go to church every Sunday. Why are you asking me this?"

"Deceptions, remember? I am Jewish. I always have been Jewish and I always will be Jewish. It's just that I never told them." She glared at him challengingly.

Alex stared at her for a moment. "God, you have got yourself in a tangle, haven't you?" he said at last, his voice gentle. "Come here, my sweet."

He put his arms around her back and lay down, pulling her head onto his shoulder. "Can't you just say to hell with them all?" he said then. "What does it matter what those old people think? They're from another time. Their ideas are frozen in ice. You can't let yourself think like them, they belong to the Stone Age. This is the nineteen seventies. You can be as Jewish as you want."

Joyce moved her head to his chest and for a time said nothing. Just listened to his heart beating, echoing the sound of the waves beyond. His words were kind, but they merely brushed the surface.

"I love them, that's why their ideas matter. Dimitra and Petros are my parents now. Nikos is their son. They've sacrificed so much for me. I can't keep deceiving them and I can't run out on them either. I can't break all my promises."

Alex frowned. "But you didn't marry your in-laws, Joyce. We all have to leave our parents eventually. Real or adopted ones."

"I know. I've done that already."

He shifted to his elbow so that he could look down at her. Her bikini top hovered above her breasts like an irrelevant remark. Her hair, wet from the sea, clung to her cheeks. "Haven't you ever wanted to go home? Even for a visit?"

"Nope," Joyce said, her voice turning bitter. She sat up. "I didn't run away just to run back again."

"What do you mean, run away?"

"I eloped," she said mockingly. "They didn't want me to marry Nikos, so we ran away together. Didn't I tell you?"

"No," he said slowly. "You didn't tell me. Are they angry?"

She turned her head away from him, hiding her expression. "I guess so. I've been writing to them the whole time I've been here, but they've never answered."

"That's terrible. Can't you phone them?"

Joyce shut her eyes, tilting her sharp face to the sun. "I did phone them. They were a pain in the ass. I don't care, anyway. To hell with them."

"But . . ." Alex paused. "Why do you hate them so much? What did they do to you?"

Joyce threw herself back on the sheet, lying rigid and glaring up at the sky. "They dumped me," she said harshly. "But I don't hate them. I just don't like them."

"You like your family here better?"

"Yes." She squinted up at his face, her eyes like green onyx. "Much better."

"And you still like me?"

She softened. "Yes, Alex."

He reached out to caress her face. "I like you, too," he said. "Turn over." And he entered her from behind, as Nikos sometimes had, thrusting deep into her, as if to touch her soul.

At home that night, peeling onions in the dark courtyard, Dimitra told Joyce that she had found a solution to her troubles with Nikos. Joyce was slicing potatoes beside her, both of them crouched on their haunches over their buckets, their only light the kerosene lamp shining from the back window. Shadows stretched across the courtyard like ghouls.

"I prayed to Saint Dimitrios and the Virgin and now I know what is wrong with my boy," Dimitra said, her rough voice firm. She leaned forward and gripped Joyce's arm with her oniony fingers. "Bear him children, little one, and his complaints will end."

Joyce wiped her sleeve over her face, the onion scent stinging her eyes. "Yes, I know he wants children, Mama," she said impatiently. "He keeps saying so. A son."

"The Virgin showed me," Dimitra went on, ignoring her. "Nikos feels that he is not a man without children. He feels shamed in front of his friends. That is why he is sulking like a child. Take him back into your bed and he will leave those *puttanas* in the brothel and return to you."

Joyce looked up. "Brothel? What do you mean?"

Dimitra tossed the onions into a pan beside her, her own eyes unaffected. "It is nothing to make a fuss over. Women put up with this all the time. I have been lucky . . . if you call it lucky. Petros has no eye for other women, but then" — she lowered her voice — "he is only half a man."

"Are you telling me that Nikos has been going to a brothel all these nights?"

Dimitra shrugged. "Of course. What did you expect? If you ban a husband from your bed, what is he to do?"

"But I didn't ban him from my bed. He just stopped coming!"

Dimitra shook her knife at Joyce. "Do not be such a fool, little one. It is your own fault."

Joyce went back to peeling her potato, the shock sinking into her like a weight. So her conjectures were right. But she was stupid to be so surprised — Nikos was a sailor, after all. He must have been visiting brothels all over the world.

"Why should I put up with that?" she blurted, spitting in her indignation.

Dimitra shoved her knee. "*Koroulamou*, don't be so proud. I have told you before you must suffer to be a wife, yes? He will tire of his whores. When he has a baby in you, everything will change, you will see. Make him forgive you and he will lose interest in his *puttanas*. And think what beautiful babies the two of you will make!"

Joyce squinted down at her potato. The lamp was dimming and it was hard to see. Nikos had become a stranger to her. Sulking, sending her reprimanding looks, waiting for her to crawl — and now going to brothels like the lowest of booze-sodden sea scum! She tried to remember him as she once thought he was, generous and heroic, but it didn't work. That Nikos was gone, he had faded away to a memory, or perhaps only a dream. The thought of making love to the Nikos she knew now, this sullen, dissipated man who called himself her husband, filled her with revulsion.

"I don't know if I can," she muttered. "I don't know him anymore."

Dimitra dropped her knife and stared at Joyce in amazement. "You silly girl! He is your husband, of course you know him! What you feel doesn't matter! Go do your duty as a wife and let me hear no more of this nonsense!" And she pushed Joyce away in contempt.

But Joyce knew she could not expect Dimitra to understand.

What, after all, did her mother-in-law know of the capriciousness of desire? She had lived a life entirely without it. Her passions had been diverted to other things — to war, to her son and her land, to Joyce herself. Why should she have patience with the reluctance of a girl? She did not believe that any decent woman actually enjoys sex.

At dinner that night Nikos was more cheerful than usual, almost as if he knew of his mother's plotting. He had been drinking all day, but slowly, enough to make him sentimental rather than sulky, and he decided to try a gentler approach to Joyce. Perhaps, he acknowledged in his sloppy mood, he had been too proud. Perhaps he had only to be forgiving and she would again melt willingly into his arms.

Ever since his return, Nikos had only wanted to win her back. He missed terribly their former passion, her cries of pleasure, the certainty he had carried over the seas that at home he had a beautiful wife who worshipped him. When his companions had mocked him for being married, teased him about the notorious unfaithfulness of sailors' wives, he had been able to say, "My wife is different. She will wait for me, I know." After all, he had brought her home an empty, directionless girl, a girl with no faith, and he had given her a life, a purpose, even a religion. How could she not be grateful? How could she not love him for this? He should give her another chance, that's all. Remind her of their love.

So during the meal that night, Nikos decided to seduce her all over again. He put on his old charm, a charm he had lately been allowing to slip beneath resentment and self-pity, and made his family laugh the way he used to. He told raucous stories of his shipmates at sea. Drank until he was singing. Looked his wife over with a wink and gave her a friendly pat. "Tonight you remind me of how you were in America," he said at one point. "Look at her, Mama, is she not pretty? A light comes out of her skin like a lamp."

Joyce picked up the dishes and left the room.

Nikos smiled to himself. She was moved — this was a good beginning. He stretched himself out on the Turkish pillows and squinted up at the ceiling. "I have not had this much rest in five years," he said to Petros once the women were gone, his words slurring. "At sea it is work, work, all day long. Sometimes all night, too. You never sleep in peace. The snores of the other men, the waves slapping in your ear. It is so quiet here. Silent." He folded his muscular arms behind his head and stared up at the strings of onions dangling above him. "I am almost ready to become a farmer like you, Father. I am growing tired of the sea."

Petros grunted. He was sitting at the table, his chair angled to one side, his head turned away from his son. He was fingering his worry beads compulsively, a habit he had renounced until Nikos came home. "You will lose your pension if you leave now," he commented.

Nikos raised his head. "But I could help you on the land, *Papas*. Would you not like that? The work must be getting hard for you at your age."

Petros eyed him in silence. He did not believe a word of this claptrap. He knew Nikos had the sea in his blood, that he would never be able to tie himself to a farm. It was Joyce whom Petros was grooming to look after his land. He would no more trust it to Nikos than he would trust a scorpion not to sting him if he sat on it.

Nikos dropped his head back down to the pillow. "Joyce?" he called suddenly. "Where is my woman?"

Hearing him in the courtyard, where they were now washing saucepans under the pump, Dimitra gave her a shove. "Go to him," she said. "Pet him. Excite him. Get a baby from him tonight."

Joyce was shocked. She had never heard Dimitra be so coarse.

Wiping her hands on her apron, she stood up and reluctantly went back into the house. She was still tender between the legs from her lovemaking with Alex. He had become a trifle rough with her in his excitement, entering her from above and behind, over and over. Complaining about the condoms.

"Yes?" she said.

"Come here, little wife." Nikos's voice was jovial. He reached out an arm and beckoned. "Come rest on this pillow with me."

She trailed over, taking off her water-soaked apron. She was still wearing her church clothes, her Alex clothes. The yellow skirt and white shirt, cinched tight at the waist. She crouched down to the pillow and let Nikos take her in his arms.

He pulled her to his shoulder and kept her there, his arm locked around her. She could feel his will in the strength of his embrace, and it frightened her. Alex had a casual, relaxed strength, not taken with itself. Nikos's strength was tense and threatening, like that of a leopard about to pounce.

"It is wrong for us to fight," Nikos said, still clamping her to his side. "It is trying on a marriage to be apart so often. We become strangers. We must get to know each other again, yes?"

Joyce closed her eyes, her throat tightening. In spite of her anger at him, his words softened her. The chance to start over, to find again the love that had once enclosed them, to retrieve this life she felt slipping away — all this she still wanted desperately. "Yes," she said, her voice cracking. She cleared her throat as if to say more, but nothing would come to her.

Nikos watched her, moved. "You know I think of you all the time at sea," he said then, his voice tender. "When I am wet and cold, when I am tired, when I am lonely, it is you, my Joyce, I see in my mind. Always. I come back to feel alive with you again. Do not destroy this for me."

Tears slipped out from beneath her eyelids. "I won't, Nikos," she whispered. "Of course I won't."

"I will stay for a while, then," he said gently. "We will make our love grow back like watering a seed, right?"

She nodded, wiping her eyes.

"And I will make you eat!" he added with a laugh. He

pinched her rib, hard, and she jerked away from him. "I've married a stick!" He laughed again and rolled over to kiss her, his mouth pressing down on her lips. He tasted of cigarettes and *ouzo*, licorice soaked in booze and ash.

"Tonight I come to your room and we will make love like newlyweds," he whispered in her ear, then pushed her to her feet. "Go help Mama clean the pots."

Upstairs later that night, Joyce tried to gauge her feelings. Was she afraid of Nikos's desire, or did she welcome it? She had never faced lovemaking with such uncertainty before. Oh, back in Florida she had made out with plenty of boys she didn't like, let them put their fingers in her, suck her nipples like babies, but she had done that as a kind of requisite initiation rite. To be able to tell her friends that she had. But real lovemaking had become sacrosanct to her. It had always been an expression of genuine passion. She wanted to keep it that way, guard its preciousness, guard herself. And although Nikos had been the one who had ignited all this, although she wanted so much to love him again, the idea of sex with him now, with this man who played her emotions like a fiddle, who changed from moment to moment, who betrayed her with prostitutes while determining to conquer her with his will and his traditions, terrified her.

So she sat on the bed, waiting, her heart tight with anxiety. She was afraid not only of the sex but of what he might find out. Would he be able to tell that she had made love that day, three, four times? She had bathed in the sea, even used the shampoo between her legs, but what did she know of what men could feel? And if he found out, what would he do to her?

Joyce looked hurriedly about the room. Up on a crude shelf Dimitra had propped a wooden crucifix. It was the only weapon Joyce could see. Quickly she stood, grabbed the cross, and hid it under her pillow. How she would use it she did not know. But she would if she had to.

She heard Nikos climb the ladder. He was singing to himself, softly, sexily. She sat on the edge of the bed, still dressed, her knees pressed tightly together. One hand she kept under the pillow, gripping the crucifix.

Nikos came in without knocking and kicked the door closed behind him. He peered at her in the darkness, saw she was fully dressed, shrugged, and took off his clothes. In spite of Joyce's uncertainty, she could not help but admire his body as she used to. He was like a sculpture, like the gods of his history — his waist tapered, his torso muscular and lithe. He came over and sat beside her.

"Come," he said. "Let me see again how beautiful you are."

He kissed her, softly this time, and slid his hands up her shirt to her breasts. His touch was gentle, teasing, just as it had been when they first courted. He rubbed her nipples until they stood out.

"You smell beautiful, my little wife, like the sea," he whispered, licking her ear. Joyce stiffened at his words, worried that he was implying something, but then he reassured her by running his tongue down her neck. Slowly, he undid the buttons of her shirt and slipped it off. She let go of the crucifix and put her hands on his back. It was smoother and more muscular than Alex's, swelling under her touch in waves. He lowered her onto her back, sliding his tongue down her chest to her nipples, her belly. She moaned as he pulled off her skirt and underwear and opened her legs, her labia, his tongue flickering over her, into her.

She whimpered, arching helplessly to his touch. Memories of Alex's lovemaking merged with Nikos's, enhancing her lust. She felt wild, insatiable. She cried out with longing, and begged Nikos to enter her.

"Yes, my wife," he said, "beg. That is what I want to hear."

The next morning, Joyce got up and out before Nikos stirred. She had spent the night on the floor, having cautiously pulled a blanket off the bed to sleep on. His words of triumph had turned her cold, furious, had killed off her arousal at the very minute she should have been fulfilled. How dare he manipulate her like that! She had not wanted to sleep in the same bed with him. But she was sore — the floor was hard — and illrested. Dimitra kept looking at her, her thick eyebrows arched suggestively, but Joyce gave nothing away. Let her have her dirty thoughts, she told herself angrily. Her son is not the man she thinks.

Nikos came up to her later that morning when she was bending over in the vegetable patch to weed around the beans, and grabbed her hips from behind. He rubbed his groin against her buttocks. "That was good last night, my little sweet," he whispered in her ear. "More tonight, yes?"

She stood up quickly, knocking him off her, and looked at him with contempt. He smiled, trying to leer, but his face betrayed uncertainty when he saw her expression. He doesn't even know how offensive he's been, she realized. He doesn't know me at all.

She wrapped her arms around her basket, turned her face away from him, her mouth clamped tight, and walked off, leaving him hurt and puzzled behind her.

For the rest of the day, as she was tending the animals, weeding and picking, she tried to figure out what kinds of power a woman can wield over a man. If she were to stay she had to know this, for she could never be a willing slave. She had to find a way of conquering Nikos so that he would never dare treat her like that again. So that she could have him on her terms, not his.

That was the only way she could think of to keep everything she wanted.

I X

P etros sat outside a *kaphenio* at six in the evening, having his customary *ouzo* with friends before he returned home for dinner. His cap was slanted over his brow, as always, shadowing his gaunt face, and his tiny shot glass was clasped like a thimble between his thumb and forefinger. It was an old *kaphenio*, shabby and well-used like Petros himself, the doors thrown open to allow the scraped, painted-tin tables to spill out onto the street. Surrounding the fraying vine-woven chairs was a row of tubs filled with red geraniums, which formed a kind of territorial marker to keep out tourists and women. Any such person who dared step within the invisible border line was scrutinized in silence until he or she turned tail and fled.

Usually, as Petros sat with his friends, he talked over the news, for, like them, he was disappointed with the election of Karamanlis and his *Nea Dhimokratia* party. Petros and most of the men had voted for Papandreou and his socialists in the '74 elections, suspicious of anyone with power yet eager for a leftist government; but their party had lost, the country preferring to play safe. Nevertheless, Petros's friends were still in a celebratory mood, high on the fall of the Colonels and certain that soon their day would come.

That night, however, Petros sat apart from the conversation, sipping his cloudy white drink and fingering his worry beads as he stared into the distance. Ever since Nikos's return, Petros's friends had noticed, the old man had been unusually withdrawn, sitting alone, turned into himself. He was having son troubles, they muttered to one another. It was never easy when the sailors came home. They came back with big heads, swaggering. Boasting of all the corners of the world they had seen, the women they'd had in all shapes and colors. Many of their boys were the same. They looked on their old parents as provincial and ignorant, as if everything these same old people had been through in the wars, all the suffering they had undergone, meant nothing at all.

But for Petros it was more than this. He was feeling not so much humiliated by his son as ashamed of him. Nikos had always been self-indulgent — his mother's fault of course — but at least he had been dutiful. He had held a good job, sent his money home every month, and Petros had been proud of that. Now, however, Nikos was so steeped in his own troubles that he had become an embarrassment. Petros could not bear the sight of his glowering looks, his mournful sighs. Just because of a little trouble with his wife, which any grown man should have been able to handle, the boy was sulking like a baby. Frequenting bars and brothels, trailing self-pity over the house like an odor, acting rude and indifferent to his parents. Petros did not care about this for himself — he was a humble man and needed to be worshipped by no one. But he could not bear to see Nikos trample Dimitra's heart.

Petros had never been close to Nikos. He had been at war when the boy was born, so he missed his infancy, and afterwards Nikos had always seemed to avoid him, preferring the doting love of his mother. Yet as critical as Petros was of his son, he still knew the sweet ache of parental love. It had once saved his life. And it was why he suffered now.

When Nikos was born, in 1947, Petros had been on Lesbos, his native island, fighting on the side of the Communists in the civil war. For five years after the end of the Second World War, two groups of rebels, the Communist-backed Democratic Army on the left, the fascist government's National Army on the right, who had formed initially to fight the Germans, fought instead over possession of their own people. Families split down the middle, brother slaughtering and betraying brothers. Guerrilla armies swept into villages and massacred mothers and old women to demonstrate what would happen if people resisted their cause. Armies on both sides tortured and murdered their own people in the name of revolution.

Petros had chosen to return to Lesbos because there the Communists were winning, yet his heart was not in it. He couldn't get over the notion that he and his comrades were like toy soldiers in the hands of their commanders, forced to fight less for ideology and the future than for opportunism and revenge. When they had been united against German Fascism, war had made sense, but in the *andartiko* both sides began to seem like nothing but fanatics to him, looters and thugs using ideology to excuse their greed and rapaciousness. As the war escalated, which side any given peasant took depended more on who bullied him the most rather than on his own beliefs — few dared to stand up for what they really thought. Most of Petros's comrades in the Democratic Army were too young to understand politics anyway, girls and boys between fourteen and twenty-five who had known nothing but propaganda their entire short lives. Almost all of them had ended up dead on the mountains of Macedonia.

He saw youths of fifteen dragged from their houses and beaten with ropes until they agreed to join the Communist guerrillas, the *andartes*. He saw fascist louts from tavernas raping women they had known their whole lives in the name of purging the left. Many of the peasants he came across couldn't even tell the sides apart. "Are you the White Terror or the *andartes*?" they would ask, trembling. "Why don't you leave us in peace?"

He envisioned Zeus, or God, both of them equally shameless and unforgivable shits, reaching down from the heavens with a huge wooden spoon and stirring up Greece until every inhabitant was mad with disorientation and terror.

Petros came back from the war emaciated, infested with lice, and with his eyes fixed wide with horror. His skin was covered with red welts, his hair moved by itself — Dimitra had to put him in the hottest water he could stand, shave every hair off his body, and baste his skin with paraffin. For three months he did not speak, except to scream in his sleep. He had lost his faith not only in God but in man. For a time even Dimitra was nothing to him, a figure in a dress who ministered to him but whom he wanted neither to hear nor to touch. His illusions shattered, he wanted only to die.

Then he began to notice Nikos. It was 1949 by now, and in spite of the scarcity of food, his son had grown into a healthy and beautiful two-year-old. He was thin but strong, his cheeks pink, his eyes watchful. Thanks to Dimitra's sacrifices and industry he had thrived, untouched by death, evacuation, or mutilation, as if the gods, having slaughtered one generation of youths, had decided to save the next.

Petros watched Nikos totter across the room, and his heart succumbed. His son's curious eyes, buttery skin, and sweet-milk smell reminded him that there was still a reason for even a battered man like himself to exist in the world. His son, who had done no harm to anyone, needed him. And so he regained the will to live — if not for himself, then for his child.

By the time Petros was better, however, Dimitra had grown obsessively protective of the boy, sure that everyone in sight was poisoned with envy over her darling baby. She rarely let Petros touch the child, and when Nikos reached adolescence, Dimitra refused to allow Petros to take him off for manly rituals such as introducing him to the local brothel or getting him drunk with friends. So Petros had learned to watch Nikos from afar, holding his tongue when he saw something wrong, preferring the silence of private worry to the storms of public quarrels. And over the years, as Nikos had grown more beautiful and arrogant by the day, Petros had withdrawn further into the secret life of his mind, leaving his wife and son to their own mistakes. Petros's mind was surprisingly rich. He was not wholly occupied with thoughts of crops or money, of what to mend and what to sell, as one might expect of a poor peasant. His greater interest was human nature. He had always, even as a child, loved to study the people around him — perhaps the result of being the youngest son in his family, shunted off by himself and ignored by his elders. He was fascinated by the customs of his countrymen and of his adopted village. For long hours as he worked he would turn over all he had seen and heard, analyzing how people talked, what they revealed unwittingly about themselves, the vast gaps between what they said and how they behaved. If he had been a learned man, he might have written a book about the weaknesses of humanity, or traveled to study cultures different from his own. But he was confined to his little island and to those close by. He did not complain. He knew that one did not need to travel to learn about the complexities of human behavior.

So Petros camouflaged himself as an unremarkable peasant, seemingly unaware of the world, while in reality he watched and remembered everything. For instance, he knew about Alex. He had known since the festival.

Petros had seen Alex talking to Joyce in the market square of Ayiassos. He had gone out for a walk, needing to escape the boasts of his brothers, and had spotted him leaning over her in front of the clothes shop, his body bent like a worshipper's. Later, like Dimitra, he'd seen the salt on Joyce's arms, but unlike his wife had allowed himself to guess that Joyce had been frolicking in the sea like a tourist. And until Nikos had come home, Petros had noticed a change in his daughter-in-law. She had bloomed like a spring flower, her tight bud of a heart growing open and tender. She had even begun to stand differently, upright and proud, the stance of a woman who, having been neglected, has discovered again that she is appreciated.

So Petros decided not to interfere. He trusted Joyce — it never occurred to him that she might be unfaithful — but he was pleased that she had an admirer. All along he had felt uneasy for her. A girl brought home like a pet by his son. A girl from another world who, hard as she might try, would never belong to this one. Who did Nikos think he was to capture a human being like that and cage her with his parents? Petros knew nothing of the social revolution that was to sweep the country over the next decade, that would do away with dowry, guarantee pensions to peasant women and equal rights to all women under the law. He knew nothing of all this, but he did know that war had made him lose respect for tradition. He had seen the very same men who had spouted self-righteously about protecting their wives and mothers raping the wives and mothers of others. He had watched the village elders he had heard pontificating about loyalty and courage betray their own neighbors for a slice of bread. These sights had killed his faith in the Greek traditions of male superiority and chivalry. Even of family honor.

Petros therefore decided to say nothing about Alex. Joyce deserved some pleasure, he thought. She was a good girl, it would be nothing more than a trifling flirtation — what harm would it do? Nikos did not realize what a prize he had in Joyce. Perhaps if he saw that she was admired by other men, it would make him recognize her value. Perhaps it would make him see that if he wanted her back he had to win her with love and respect, the way Petros himself had won Dimitra.

"Petros, why such a long face?" his friend Yiorgos shouted. "Come over here and drink with us." Yiorgos was an old man who, like all those in the *kaphenio*, had worked himself over the years to nothing but a shriveled husk. He and Petros had been friends since they were young and first married, without a line on their brows.

"All right, all right," Petros muttered in a show of irritation. He finished his drink and stood, running his eyes affectionately over his friends. Look at us, he mused. Look how ancient we have grown, stooped and dusty and thin like scraggly old chickens, sitting in the old men's *kaphenio* of the village. We used to make fun of places like this, where the old wrinklers go, but now it is we who sit here. Life has flashed by like a comet and here I am already, tucked away with a bunch of old grumblers who have nothing better to do than cheat each other out of our hard-earned money.

He scraped back his chair and joined the others around a table. They were playing dominoes, betting on the winners, drinking and smoking and fiddling compulsively with their chains of *komboloyia*, their worry beads, but he was content to pull up a chair and watch. He felt a great love for these old rascals. They had all had their hard times. Fotos over there, the thick, bent man, still handsome in the firmness of his jaw, lost his wife to cancer when he was only thirty and refused ever to marry again. Alki, the one with a gray beard, had two little sons die of hunger in the civil war. Yiannis, the pale one with a pot-belly, had never married, despite every girl and widow on the island setting her cap at him — Petros thought he really liked other men. And Vassilis, kind old Vassilis, who was blind now in one eye, his was the saddest case of all. His beloved wife and two baby girls had all been killed at once in a massacre by Petros's own comrades, the so-called Democratic Army of Greece.

We have all had our bad times, Petros mused. And we have all committed our sins. Whoring, cheating, stealing, deserting the army, beating our wives, neglecting our children, betraying our friends — each one of us has done some of these things, or more. Yet look at us, sitting around here like a crowd of old tarts, waiting our turn for heaven, as unconcerned as if we have always been angels.

He glanced at the sun. "It is time for me to go," he said quietly, tucking his *komboloyia* into the pocket of his rumpled jacket. The others waved, took little notice. They were too absorbed in winning money. Petros patted the nearest man on the back and stepped out into the street.

Before he went home, however, he decided to stroll along the waterfront to look for Nikos. The boy was coming home later and later these days, sometimes not at all, and because Dimitra insisted on waiting for him before she and Joyce could eat dinner, Petros often had to eat alone at the family table. He did not like sitting by himself while the women hovered over him, trying not to show their hunger. If he could round up Nikos early tonight, perhaps for once they could all eat together.

Leaving the side street by the market square, where his old men's *kaphenio* was tucked away from the bustle of town, he walked down to the seafront, his thin back upright but his steps slightly faltering. Petros was seventy-two, and his food no longer gave him the strength it used to. His body was habituated to hard work and still performed like a well-oiled if somewhat creaky machine, but now it ached constantly. His feet, his knees, the joints around his knuckles and wrists; there was never a moment when he did not feel pain. Petros said nothing of this, however, not even to Dimitra. He knew it was only old age. What was the use of complaining?

The seafront was bustling now, as it always was at this time of day, the wealthier families out on their *peripato,* their promenade, the unmarried girls parading, their mothers and sisters on guard, and all those soldiers on the hunt. The men walked a few paces ahead while the women strolled slowly behind, arm in arm, their skin glowing in the golden light of early evening. Petros loved this. He loved the sway of the women's bodies, the supple swing of their legs as they drifted by. He loved the gleam of the late sun on their hair and the barely suppressed excitement on the faces of the boys who watched. He even loved the arrogant husbands, walking in front like kings. Humanity displaying itself, as foolish as peacocks shaking their tails.

Beyond the promenade the street ended abruptly at a stone curb, which dropped straight down to the water. Having failed to find Nikos, Petros stood for a moment and looked out to the horizon. Three fishing boats rocked lazily nearby, their bells clanking in the soft breeze, black silhouettes of simple grace, but otherwise nothing interrupted his view westward towards the mainland. The Aegean was calm this evening, its gleaming, indigo surface darkening to magenta as the sun slid into the sea. A few distant streaks of clouds were turning scarlet, the sky around them an audacious gold. The light suffused every-thing Petros saw with a soft, reddish glow. Good weather to-morrow, God be praised, he thought. I will be able to ready the earth for the autumn plantings.

Thinking of work made him hungry, so he gave up on find-ing Nikos and turned homewards at last. And that was when he spotted Alex.

Alex was sitting outside a seafront *kaphenio* across the road, reading a newspaper with a coffee in front of him. Even though Petros had seen him only once, he was not hard to recognize, tall, blond, and burnt as he was. He was alone at a round mar-ble table, dressed in white trousers and a short-sleeved shirt, a lanky Anglo-Saxon who looked both at ease as he read in his rickety chair and yet unmistakably foreign.

The boy is so young, Petros thought in surprise. Younger even than Nikos. But look how absorbed he is, how he reads with such concentration! Petros had never seen his own son read like that. The foreign boy looked intelligent just from the way he was sitting. Petros wished he knew more about him. Was he a German? What line of work was he in? What educa-tion had he had? Would he offer Joyce respect or was he just chasing a skirt?

Deciding it was his duty to find out, Petros strolled over, took a table next to Alex, and ordered a strong cup of the local Turk-ish coffee. Then he waited until he saw an opportunity to strike up a conversation. It came when Alex separated the newspaper and put down a section beside him.

Petros leaned over. The first surprise was that the newspaper was Greek. He was even more impressed: a tourist boy who not only read like a man of the world but read Greek! Perhaps he was Greek, although not from these parts — there was clearly no blood of the Turk in him.

Petros cleared his throat. "Excuse me, young man," he said slowly. "You have finished with that section? May I . . ."

"Certainly, *Kyrie,* of course," Alex replied with perfect politeness. He handed over the section. "It is the national news. If you prefer the international I have it here," he added, offering the paper in his hands.

"No, this is fine. You speak excellent Greek for a tourist. How is this?"

Alex colored at the compliment. A sensitive boy, thought Petros. The local lads would skin him alive.

"Thank you. My mother is from this village. Irini Konsaki, you know her? My aunt Eugenia owns the bakery."

"Oh, the English nephew! So that is why you speak our language. Yes, I have heard much about you." Petros gazed at him, relieved. Thank God the lad was not German. Petros had never been able to abide Germans, not since the occupation. He was also grateful that the boy was not an unknown, not some English tourist here only to fuck the girls and leave. No, he was a gentleman. He might flirt with Joyce, but he would know to respect a married woman.

"I remember your mother," Petros said at last. "She is famous here for having escaped."

"You knew her?" Alex was pleased.

"Oh, yes. She was very smart. She read a lot of books, I remember. People were afraid of her!" Petros chuckled.

"Come, sir, please join me," Alex said then, eager to hear more. He liked this old peasant. He looked as ancient as the mountains, but he seemed sharp and more curious than many in this place. "I'll buy you a drink, another coffee."

"No, no. You are the guest." Petros moved to Alex's table, waved down the waiter, and ordered two *ouzos*. "To welcome you home," he said with some irony.

"I would like it to be home," Alex said sincerely. "I love Greece."

"Good, good," Petros answered. "But it is difficult, I think, to love Ifestia."

Alex was surprised at this. The old man had to be from elsewhere — a native would never say such a thing, unless he had escaped like Alex's mother. He reappraised Petros. A tiny face, wrinkled as bark and bare of the usual mustache. Beady brown eyes, dark and watchful. Peasant clothes — battered work cap, a blue shirt, a worn brown jacket. Baggy black trousers. He must have been a delicate-looking youth, Alex thought. He was as skinny as a goat, and he looked as if he stood no more than five foot two. Yet he had a certain irreverent twinkle about him that Alex liked.

"My mother was glad to leave, it's true," Alex said cautiously. He reddened again, in case he had offended. "I hope you don't mind . . ."

Petros dismissed his concern with a wave of his hand. "Do not worry, you cannot offend me. Even the ancients knew this island was no good. Three hundred years ago the Turks banished their criminals to live here in exile, so you see how we feel! Our earth — the earth I try to make a living out of — was considered so astringent in ancient times that it was used to treat snakebites and wounds. Even Ayios Dimitrios, our patron saint, we had to borrow from Thessaloniki because no saint ever bothered to work his miracles for us. You have a guidebook?"

"Uh, yes," Alex said, rather stunned by this diatribe. "I have the Blue Guide."

"Is there anything in it about this island?"

"Well, to tell you the truth, no. Although I did find it in another book." Alex grinned. "It said not to bother to come here because it's so boring."

"There, you see!" Petros said triumphantly. "Even the Tourist Board considers the place cursed."

The drinks arrived with the customary tumblers of water and plate of *mezedhes*: cucumber slices, cubes of cheese, tomatoes, and an ungenerous serving of marinated octopus. Petros poured a touch of water into his *ouzo*, clouding it to white, and picked up his stumpy glass. "To Irini, the prodigal daughter, may she never have to return," he said, pleased with his own joke. *"Yiassas!"* and they clinked glasses.

"Your mother, what is she doing now?" Petros asked after allowing the full taste of anise to saturate his tongue. He ran his discerning eyes over Alex. He is a well-mannered youth, he thought. Privileged. Clearly with an expensive education. He must be good company for Joyce, a welcome break from all us rough peasants.

"She teaches art history in a local college. My parents are both professors, actually." Alex popped a piece of cheese in his mouth.

"Your mother is a professor?" Petros was glad. He had always hoped Irini would astound the village with fame and glory — he remembered well how she had been mocked for her brains. "Yes, teachers are good," he said. "It is the most important work we can do to teach the young. You want to be a teacher yourself?"

Alex thought of his parents' complaints. The bored students. The uninspired papers they had to mark year in and year out. The drudgery.

"I think the work of growing food and fishing the waters is the most important work a man can do," he said. "Children will teach themselves."

"Teach themselves to become savages!" Petros declared. "I never finished school and I have regretted it my whole life. You are not even half a Greek if you do not believe in education!"

Alex laughed. "Of course I believe in education. That's not what I meant. I just think we do it wrong. All that force-fed rote learning, it's guaranteed to stultify the mind. Children should learn by practice. Don't read about Africa, go there! Don't listen to lectures about the fishing industry, work on a boat for a summer!"

"Ah, newfangled fiffle-faffle," said Petros, but his remark was good-natured. He cocked his head to one side, like a sparrow. "But you have not answered my question. You want to be a teacher?"

Alex turned away, pondering his answer. He had forgotten to think about what he wanted to be. Ever since meeting Joyce, he had forgotten to think much at all, except about what to do to her, how to save her. "I might go into journalism and cover politics," he said. "Or maybe take a higher degree in political science."

Petros's eyes brightened, and soon they were deep in discussion about Greek socialism and the new democratic party.

An hour later, when the sun had sunk low enough to turn the sea and their faces a fiery red, Petros remembered that he had to go home. He stood, wobbling, to shake hands with Alex. He was full of joy, the joy one gleans from a good discussion with a new companion who is both deferential and knowledgeable. He would do Joyce a favor, he decided. Bring her friend home as a nice surprise, and show her how liberal and advanced her old father-in-law was while he was at it. Then she would not have to hide her little flirtation from him and Dimitra any longer. Anyway, why shouldn't they allow her a friend who spoke her own language, even if he was a man? Perhaps she would not be so lonely with such a friend, so cut off from her past and her home. Perhaps she would be more content to stay.

Pleased with himself, Petros grasped Alex's shoulder. "Come to my house!" he cried. "Come have some food, visit my family! It will be an honor to have you dine with us." He chuckled inwardly. This will be entertaining to watch, he thought. This should give a jolt to my slouch of a son. Alex will show him how a gentleman should treat a lady.

Alex accepted. He needed distraction. They quarreled over who would pay for the bill, Alex won, and they began to stagger home — or at least Petros staggered; he was not a habitual drinker and had consumed many more *ouzos* than usual. Alex walked discreetly close to him, ready to catch him if he fell.

When Alex stepped into the little house, ducking through the front door, he seemed to Petros to fill the room. The place was empty just then, although they could hear the clanking of pots out in the back courtyard, and it smelled of roasting chicken and garlic. The family had been eating well since Nikos's return.

"Sit," Petros said, taking off his cap and jacket to hang on a peg by the door. "My wife and daughter-in-law are preparing the food. I will tell them we have a guest."

He scuttled out, leaving Alex to look around. It was a classic peasant cottage, lit only by a smoking kerosene lamp on the rough table — clean but timeless, no different than such a house might have been five hundred years earlier. Alex stood, feeling huge and strangely futuristic under the rafters hung with herbs; an alien beamed back to the past.

Petros scurried outside, where the women were crouched to remove various platters from the oven. He was eager to tell his news.

"Ah, there you are! Two hours late!" Dimitra exclaimed, straightening up with a platter of chicken in her hands. It was so rare for Petros to miss dinner, however, that she refrained from scolding him. "We have waited for you. Nikos, too, is not home yet. Is something happening in town?"

"Nothing special, but I have brought a guest!" Petros said triumphantly. "It is the English nephew of Widow Sarafi. Remember the story? He speaks perfect Greek, Dimitra. Better even than Joyce here."

"Irini's boy?" Dimitra was delighted. This would feed the gossips for weeks. "He is here in Kastron?"

"Yes, to visit family."

"Hah. That is more than his snob of a mother would ever do. But good. I will go in to welcome him. Joyce, you bring in the *yemista*."

Petros sneaked a look at Joyce. She was squatting on the ground, utterly still. He couldn't see the color of her face in the dark or read her reaction. But, for the first time, it occurred to him that she might not welcome this surprise. Perhaps she would be embarrassed to see her educated friend here. Perhaps he should have given her some warning.

Inside the house Dimitra was already fussing over Alex. She poured him water, wine. She gave him the place of honor at the table. "You look just like Irini," she lied. "We used to play as girls. Why have we not seen you here before?"

Alex answered graciously, telling her that the last time he had visited Kastron he had been a pimply teenager, unmemorable to anyone. He was courtly yet unassuming, endearing himself to Dimitra immediately. Then Joyce walked in and he turned white as ice.

Luckily Dimitra did not see. She was taking the dish of stuffed peppers from Joyce's hands. Joyce's cheeks were burning. She had never wanted Alex to see her like this, a housewife in a peasant home, serving the men like a maid. She had felt his worship of her, that he saw her as wise and mysterious, not as the servant she was here. Humiliation bit into her too deeply to allow her to speak.

Dimitra looked at her in surprise. "What is the matter with you?" she scolded. "Greet our guest!"

Alex recovered enough to get to his feet. But when he opened his mouth nothing came out.

"She is American!" Petros said quickly. "You can speak to each other in English and we won't understand a word!" He laughed as if it were a great joke, but he knew what he was doing.

"Hello, pleased to meet you," Alex at last managed to say, although in Greek. Then he added quickly in English, "I'm sorry. I didn't know."

Joyce nodded. She wanted him not to talk, not to risk anything. She rushed out of the room.

At last all the food was on the table and they sat down to eat. They would have waited for Nikos if it had not been for their guest, but guests took precedence even over husbands and sons in this land that revered hospitality. Dimitra and Joyce served the men, then each helped herself to a smaller portion of chicken than usual to leave enough for Nikos.

Alex could barely swallow. The situation was agonizing, not so much for him — he was in fact thrilled at the chance to see Joyce's home and to know more of her life — but because he could tell how much his presence pained her. He did his best to put her at ease, complimenting the food, which was rich and fragrant, taking as little as possible without seeming rude so as not to deprive them, and answering Dimitra's questions about his mother. Joyce, meanwhile, got up from the table to serve every few minutes. They sent her for more wine, more water, for olive oil and bread. They treat her like a slave, he thought, and his cheeks turned dark with anger.

Petros was uncharacteristically garrulous. He realized now that he had made a mistake, but all he could do was try to save the situation he had created, and do it without rousing Dimitra's suspicions. She was already looking at him in wonder, for he rarely talked at all in the house, let alone like this, but he forged on anyway, telling the story of how he had met Alex, of what Alex had said about his family, of their discussion about education and politics. Alex tried bravely to keep up with him. Joyce sat silent and still.

"So, Mr. Englishman," Dimitra said jovially at one point.

"What does little Irini say about the old home she never visits, eh? What has she told you about the Greek blood in your veins?"

Petros chuckled. He loved watching Dimitra grow heated in defense of her nationality.

Alex eyed him, feeling caught. "She has told me how beautiful it is here, and of course that Greece is the basis of our civilization, *Kyria* Koliopoulou. That is why she has made sure I go to Athens every summer to study."

"Hah," Petros said. "She says it is a prison here! A hellhole!"

Dimitra turned to Alex, indignant. "Pay no attention to my rascally husband. He is from Mytilene — Lesbos, you English call it. He knows nothing about this place. But is this true? She says such things about our beautiful island?"

Alex reddened. As a guest, he could not possibly denigrate his host's homeland. "Not exactly," he replied evasively. "She is very proud of being Greek. She teaches the history of Greek art at a college."

"She is a teacher?" Dimitra gazed at him speculatively, her shrunken mouth slightly open. Irini always was bigheaded, she mused, she always thought herself too good for the rest of us. But all Dimitra said aloud was "Well, I hope she remembers to thank God for her luck."

At last, after an hour more of this delicate conversation, during which Joyce remained sunk in silence, Nikos stomped in with a great banging of doors and clearing of throat. He was in a terrible mood, hungry and irritated. He had gone fishing earlier and caught nothing. His friends had been mocking him all day — God he was sick of being on this poky shell of an island. He felt stuck. With his parents, reeking of disapproval, with his friends, who refused to admire him. And worst of all with his silent, unhappy wife, who would not let him into her heart.

When Nikos walked in, Alex was stunned. He had expected a monster, or at least a grizzled, brutish man with a belly and the stink of a sailor — the Hephaestus he had imagined to

Joyce's Aphrodite. Instead, here was a youth of dazzling beauty. His face was sculpted in perfect proportions, his body moved with the subtlety of a cat. His coloring was vivid with health — now Alex understood his aunt's remark that the women of the island were envious of Joyce. He felt wretched. He had known that he had to woo Joyce away from the love of her in-laws, even from the safety of her captivity. But he'd had no idea he had to win her away from an Ares.

Nikos noticed nothing. Upon seeing his guest he controlled his temper enough to shake hands and welcome him, then joined his family at the table. Seizing a tumbler, he poured himself some wine, clinked the other glasses without waiting for a toast, and drank. With a shove from Dimitra, Joyce stood up once more to serve him. The tale was told again of who Alex was, why he spoke Greek, how Petros had found him. Nikos nodded, asked a few questions, and quickly lost interest in this overeducated tourist. Nikos liked men of the earth and sea, not erudite Brits with Athenian accents.

Alex was mortified. He felt horribly ungainly compared to Nikos, awkward and clumsy, like a giraffe in a cage — all knobs and points and gracelessness. Nikos oozed sexuality. His heavy-lidded eyes, wide and sultry. His sinuous movements. The flex of muscles in his jaw, his back. The longer Alex sat at that table, the more bony and colorless he felt, like an overgrown schoolboy trying not to knock over a tea set. He could no longer understand how Joyce could have desired him.

He stole a look at her. She was staring down at her plate, unable to eat. Her whole body was tense, he could see it, her fingers tight, her neck taut. Every now and then she glanced at Nikos and Alex saw fear in her eyes. She would not look at him.

Is she sleeping with him? Alex wondered. He hadn't dared ask her before, but he'd had the idea she wasn't from all she'd told him, and from her passion on the beach. He could feel the body heat pulsing off Nikos, who was sitting beside him. He could smell the sea and tobacco on his skin: smells of manhood and authority. It made Alex want to sink through the floor.

He left as soon as politeness allowed, thanking Dimitra and Petros effusively, promising to visit again. Nikos nodded absently at him. Joyce avoided his eyes.

Stumbling back down the path to town, Alex was consumed by despair. He had misunderstood everything! He had thought that Joyce needed rescuing, that she wanted escape. He had thought she was starved of love. Now he feared that she was only using him to win back her husband. That she cared not one jot for Alex's gawky body, nor for his naive, credulous self.

"He is a fine young man, is he not?" Petros said after Alex had left. He eyed his son. "He has the manners of a gentleman, Nikos. You could learn a thing or two from him."

"Know a thousand things and ask ten thousand questions," Nikos muttered contemptuously. "He is a stuck-up Brit." He looked over at Joyce. "I am glad you did not talk to him, wife. You were right to ignore a *malaki* like him."

"Nikos, your language!" Dimitra said. Then she turned to beam at Joyce. "Yes, you behaved like a good wife. Did she not, Nikos? Did you see how she kept her eyes lowered? No bold glances? She did not even speak to him in English!"

"Yes," Nikos looked at her, considering. "Maybe she is learning, eh? Anyway, why would she want to flirt with a stork like that when she has me?" He winked and pulled her to him, kissing her neck.

Petros sighed. So much for his lesson.

Joyce stood passively in her husband's arms. I might as well be a tree the way they talk about me, she thought. Alex won't want me anymore. He has seen what a nothing I am.

For the past few nights, Joyce had accepted Nikos again into her bed. She had not been able to find the key to wielding power over him as she'd hoped, but she had tried to make it clear that she would turn him away unless he treated her with more consideration.

"I will not want you unless you are kind to me," she'd said the next time he'd come into the room for lovemaking. "When you bully me like you did the last time, it makes me turn cold. You don't want a cold wife, do you?"

He'd stared at her in bewilderment. "What do you mean?" he exclaimed. "You have always liked the way I make love to you before. You have loved it!"

"Yes, but you've changed, Nikos. Sometimes I feel like I don't know you anymore. You're not gentle and considerate the way you used to be. You used to make me feel worshipped. Now you make me feel like a whore."

"Worshipped! What are you, a princess? Why should a man worship his wife?"

"I don't mean that. I mean I just want to feel respect."

Nikos sat next to her on the bed. "But I do respect you!" he said. "Have I not said I love you? Have I not told you how much I long for you when I am away? That I miss my wonderful wife? What about my letters? It is not me who has changed, it is you!"

"I'm sorry, Nikos. I'm doing my best, but I can't stand it when you bully me."

"Bully you? But I am the man, the husband. It is natural that I hold the reins."

"No. Not for me. Not for sex."

"I do not understand. What do you want, for God's sake?"

Joyce covered her eyes with her hands, as much to shut out his voice as his face. I want to feel love, is what she needed to say. I want to feel the kind of love that Alex gives me, not your kind. But she couldn't say that. "Just be gentle," she said. "Just be the way you were before."

Nikos shrugged. "I am no different. I don't understand you. Come, enough talk. Take off your dress."

So now, every night, she lay on the bed, let him climb on top of her, let him saw away inside her until he was done. Sometimes, if he was kind, attentive, his kisses could still arouse her. But other times, on the days he was impatient or imperious, her body felt dead. Then she would shut her eyes and clamp her teeth, praying that he would be quick. He seemed to feel heavier on those nights, his weight on her chest squeezing the breath out of her. She tried to pretend he was Alex so that she could feel some pleasure, but it didn't work. It was too much like unfaithfulness itself. So instead she told herself that her lack of desire for Nikos was temporary, something every wife went through once in a while. I'll get over this, she said to herself. I'll want him one day. After all, he is beautiful, he still adores me. It must be that I only feel this because of Alex. If I get rid of Alex, then I will be free to enjoy my husband again.

PART TWO

X

Nikos dangled his legs over the harbor wall, gazing disconsolately out to sea. It was early evening and the low sun had turned everything a dusky gold, the sky deepening to amber towards the horizon, the sea a thousand golden shoulders flirting with the sun. But Nikos was immune to all this beauty. He could only think of how much he longed to be on a ship again, sailing down the Aegean and around the southern tips of Greece and Italy, away from his disappointed mother, the cold silence of his father, and the furtive rebellion of his irritating wife.

All Nikos's dreams of marital contentment had come to grief. Joyce ignored him when he told her what to do. She put his mother first, catering to Dimitra's needs before she paid any attention to his. Took her side in arguments, Petros's, too. His parents praised her constantly, while for him they had nothing but criticism. Why, Joyce even turned her face from him in bed sometimes, pushed his hands off her body — she lay beneath him like a sacrifice, not a lover! The humiliation was driving into him like nails. His wife was making him feel like an outcast, an intruder, when all he wanted was to be adored, the way a man is supposed to be adored.

Scowling, he clambered to his feet and walked along the seafront. He should have been heading home for the evening meal but decided to go to his customary taverna for a drink instead. To hell with them all, he thought. I'm going to get drunk.

People were coming out for their evening *peripato*, and they nodded and greeted him as he walked by, the women eyeing him appreciatively. In spite of his bad mood, Nikos was obliged to stop and chat. He had always caused a stir in town. Women could not stop themselves from staring at him, from flirting and vying for his smiles, and, in jealous compensation, the men were also eager to engage him, if only to show off their superior wit and knowledge. All his life, Nikos had attracted the admiration of women and the dislike of men.

Before he reached the taverna, however, he ran into his father. Petros had been out looking for him again. "Son," he said briefly, his little face grim, "come with me."

"But *Papas*, I promised to meet Vangelis and the others."

"They can make themselves drunk without your help. I wish to talk to you."

Reluctantly, Nikos obeyed. He dreaded confrontations with his father, rare as they were. They always consisted of reprimands, criticism, or worst of all, silence.

To Nikos's surprise, however, Petros led him not home but to another taverna, a small, smoky place that neither of them usually patronized. They sat at a rickety metal table and Petros ordered two glasses of the local plum brandy that shot right to the brain and burned the stomach.

"*Yiassas*," the old man said automatically, clinking his glass against Nikos's. "It is time for us to talk like father and son, yes?"

Nikos glanced at him, puzzled. "Yes, *Papas*," he said sullenly, and braced himself for a lecture. "I am hungry though. May we go home soon to eat?"

Petros ignored him. He took his *komboloyia* out of his pocket and began to rub them between his thumb and forefinger, gazing at Nikos with a frown. "Drink," he said, waving at his son's glass. His own remained on the table, untouched.

Nikos swallowed his brandy, and Petros ordered him another. Usually he tried to cut down on his son's drinking — Nikos could not understand it.

"What is it you wish to say, Father?" he asked, shifting uneasily in his chair. "Is it some bad news that you are making me drink like this?"

"No, no." The old man took off his cap and put it over his knee. He continued to rub his worry beads, which shone a dull brown in his fingers.

"If you are going to scold me for my visits to the brothel, as Mama does every day, you are wasting your breath. You know what they say: 'I want to be a saint, but the demons won't let me.' Anyway, that's over now." Nikos scowled.

Petros rubbed his face wearily. "No, that is not why I brought you here. I only want you to tell me what's on your mind. I can see that you are unhappy. Is it the sea? Do you miss it? Or is it your wife?"

Nikos shrugged his broad shoulders, his mouth bitter. "Of course it is my wife. You know that, *Papas*, why even ask? She has turned against me. She will not treat me with respect."

Petros looked down at the table, his walnut brown face suddenly sad. "She has not turned against you, Nikos. You do not understand her. Joyce is a good girl."

Nikos shifted angrily in the chair. "This is what I hear from Mama all day long. You might not see it, *Papas*, but Joyce has changed. She has grown cold and defiant. She won't do anything I say. She is not the woman I married."

Petros did not reply at first. His son's words irritated him, although he had to admit they were heartfelt. "What are you trying to tell me?" he asked at last, his lips tightening. "Is it that you want your freedom?"

"No!" Nikos cried out, making Petros start in his seat. "No, I have had years of wandering loose about the world, seducing women — I need that no longer. I want a wife, that's all! I want to come home to a woman who loves and respects me, not who treats me like a worm! It's only what every man is entitled to. Why am I the only one denied this?"

"Shh, my boy, calm down," Petros muttered. "You want the whole town to hear?" He gazed at Nikos a moment, his dark eyes sad. "If you want a woman's respect, you must earn it. Just being a man is not enough."

"Earn it?" Nikos threw himself back in his chair. "What am I to do, stand on my head? I go to sea, don't I? I live away from home for months on cramped, stinking ships, weathering storms to bring home money for her and for you. Why is that not enough to win her respect?"

Petros sighed. "Perhaps if you are more patient, more tolerant of her American ways, you can make your love grow again. For love to work a man must bend to his woman. He cannot stand still as a tree and expect her to wind herself around him like a vine. You must try harder."

"I do try! You don't know how hard I try!"

Nikos rested his elbows on the table and stared down into his brandy glass. His head hung low between his shoulders, his curls dangling over his smooth, dark brow. *"Papas,"* he said at last, "I felt so lucky when I found Joyce. My golden American. I felt on top of the world, the luckiest of husbands." He looked up at Petros, his amber eyes glistening. "You don't know this, but of all the women I've had in my life, Joyce was the only one whose love made me feel fulfilled. She loved me so deeply! She had no purpose when I met her, you know. She was brought up with no destiny, no religion." He shook his head and sighed. "The women in that country are empty, *Papas,* and Joyce's family . . . I have never met people so lazy. Her brothers are cowards, her father a man dead on his feet. They never go to church. Her mother is fat and purple like a stuffed eggplant — she has taught her daughter nothing of respect for God or for men. My poor Joyce, she had no path set out for her."

"Not like a Greek girl, who knows she is born for marriage,

motherhood, and nothing else?" Petros said. But Nikos missed his irony.

"Exactly. Greek women know their role in the village. To marry, to have children, to uphold the family honor. I wanted to give this to Joyce. My gift of love. To give her a destiny."

"So you left her alone with us to work like a servant."

Nikos darted a surprised look at his father. "No! Well only to train her, to get her used to Greek ways. But it has done no good *Papas*. I am afraid that she is too corrupt for me. The rotten soul of her family has polluted her."

"There is nothing corrupt about Joyce," Petros replied sharply. "We know her better than you, Nikos, do not forget. We have lived with her for two years, you for a few weeks. Do not speak about her like that."

"Then what is it, *Papas*? How can a woman change so much towards her husband?"

Petros shut his eyes. "She is an American in a strange country, Nikos. You have left her alone for months. The last time you returned, it was only to quarrel. Now this time you come back proud and arrogant, expecting her to grovel because she has not borne you children. Then instead of giving her some love and attention, you go off with those *puttanas* at the brothel. She is not a Greek woman, brought up to be treated like a mule. Does this not tell you something?"

"Bah! I would not need the brothel if she gave me her love. And that fight only happened because Joyce was so rude to me, and even so I have apologized out my asshole for that. Excuse me."

"Son, why have you not tried to make some adjustments for Joyce? She is from another world, remember. Have you not listened to your uncle Sophocles? American women have machines to do the work for them. They have money to spend in shops, pills to take when they feel sick, cars to drive wherever they want. She was not born a peasant, yet she has worked like one for us. You must show her that you appreciate this."

Nikos thrust his shoulders back in disgust. "But she was not born a queen, either! No, it's useless. She has set herself against me. She acts like the officers on my ships, as if I am nothing to her, a nobody! And she has done something I cannot forgive."

Petros picked up his plum brandy at last, annoyed. "And what could that possibly be?"

"She has turned Mama against me."

"What are you saying, boy? What goat shit is this?"

"No, *Papas*, I mean it. Have you not noticed? If I ask Joyce to fetch me a drink, Mama tells her to get a loaf of bread instead. If I invite Joyce up to bed, Mama insists she needs her downstairs for longer first. It is as if they are forming a battalion against me, a fortress to keep me out!"

So that's it, Petros thought. My son is still a child, as jealous of his own wife as he would be of a rival sibling. He gazed at Nikos for a moment in wonder. How had two people like himself and Dimitra, people who had lived through war and famine, who had even had their moments of heroism, turned out such a ninny of a son? Yet Petros had to admit that Nikos was not entirely wrong. Dimitra did seem to have set herself and Joyce against him lately, it was true. She was treating Joyce like a beloved daughter and Nikos like an intruder, as if she had transferred all the power of her mother love to her daughter-in-law. Petros sighed and lit his pipe, gazing pensively into its bowl. It is time for me to admit that the love between Joyce and Nikos is dying, he told himself. A modern American and a peasant Greek — a marriage like this was bound to have troubles. And my wife is making it worse.

For the next two days, Petros searched for a way to bring harmony back to his family. He realized that he could not be too obvious, for Nikos would only be insulted again if Petros suggested that he treat Joyce with less arrogance. So he watched Dimitra glowering at their son and petting their daughter-in-law until he could bear it no longer. I must talk to Joyce about this, he decided. *I know I cannot change Dimitra's behavior, but if I can persuade Joyce not to ignore her husband so much in favor of her mother-in-law, perhaps I can help her marriage grow strong again.*

Petros picked an afternoon later that week, just before he was about to settle down with a newspaper for siesta. "Joyce?" he called. "Where are you?"

"Here, *Petheros*," she called from behind the house. She had never stopped addressing him formally as father-in-law. She felt it suited his modest dignity. The familiar address she reserved only for Dimitra.

Petros found her in the vegetable patch, pulling dandelion roots from the ground. She was wearing his old work gloves, he noticed. The muscles in her upper arms strained and snapped like those of a young boy.

"Put that down, *koroulamou*, it is work too hard for a pretty young girl," he said guiltily, thinking of Nikos's complaints about her stringiness. "I want to talk to you."

Joyce straightened up, wiping her brow. Struggling with dandelion roots was like pulling chains from seaweed. She was panting with the effort.

"Little one, come sit with me inside where it is cool. You need some rest and what I have to say will take time."

"I have so much to do, *Petheros*."

"You can rest," he said impatiently. "Your mother-in-law works you too hard. Come." He turned, his frail body determined, and led her inside.

Dimitra was in town visiting a sick friend, and Nikos was at a seafront *kaphenio*, as usual, so they had the house to themselves. Joyce poured them each a cold glass of water from a jug in the pantry, then threw herself down on the kilim pillows while Petros took a chair. "Yes, *Petheros*?" she said. "What is it?" She felt distracted, eager to get back to work.

Petros told her of his worries at some length. He explained what Nikos had said in the taverna, and how Dimitra was making him feel unappreciated. "Nikos is afraid that he is losing the love of his mother to you," he said. "You must be careful to avoid this. After all, you are married to him, not her."

"I know," Joyce said quickly, frowning down at her callused hands. "She only does this because Nikos will not be kind to me. He never talks to me with the respect you talk to *Pethera*. He tries to boss me like a servant. It makes Dimitra angry. It make me angry, too."

"I see this, little one. But perhaps if he feels more respect from you, he will be able to give you more in return."

Joyce nodded, still gazing at her hands. "I will try, *Petheros*," she said. "You give good advice."

Petros yawned. "Good. Now I have a favor to ask. Dimitra asked me to get some bread from Widow Sarafi today, but I am too tired. Will you go for me, little one? Tell her some good words about her English nephew. And if you see the boy, give him this. It is about something we discussed, and I think he will be interested." He took a folded newspaper out of his trouser pocket and handed it to her, his old fingers trembling.

Joyce sat up on the pillows, startled. She didn't want to go chasing after Alex in town, not now that she had decided to end it with him. She had been avoiding him, putting it off, frightened that she wouldn't have the strength. She didn't feel ready to go yet. "But Mama told me to rake the yard after I finish pulling the weeds," she said quickly.

"I will explain to Dimitra that I needed you for an errand. Off you go!"

"Can't I go tomorrow instead? I also have laundry to do today."

Petros frowned, pushing his cap off his eyes to squint at her. "Daughter-in-law, do not argue with an old man. It will look impolite if we do not let the widow know we met her nephew. Now go."

Joyce sighed. "Yes, *Petheros*. Perhaps I should take some eggs to sell. The chickens laid well this morning."

"If you wish. But hurry before she closes the bakery for siesta."

Joyce walked to Kastron full of dread. It was nearly September by now, and the air was cooler, smelling of rain and the gusting winds from Macedonia to the north. She wore a loose, short-sleeved shirt, woven by Dimitra, which she believed made her look bulky and old. On her feet she had cheap rubber flip-flops. She stared down at them as she walked along the stony path, noticing vaguely that her toenails were chipped and dirty. Joyce had lost all confidence in her strength. Her troubles with Nikos had sapped her of willpower. She was feeling defeated and confused, needy. In this state how could she even greet Alex, let alone find the courage to tell him good-bye?

She took her eggs, packed carefully in a basket, to the grocery shop, but she had come too late to sell them for a good price; better to have waited until the next morning's market. She sold them for what she could, but she knew Dimitra would be angry. Then, reluctantly, she approached the bakery.

Eugenia was in the bread shop, as always, busy behind the counter. She was surprised to see Joyce, for she and Dimitra usually made their own bread. "*Yassou,* my child," she said, raising her eyebrows. "What can I do for you?"

Joyce found herself blushing. "*Kalispera, Kyria* Sarafi. My father-in-law sends his greetings." She stumbled over the words. "He asked me to tell you that he met your nephew the other night and that he is a fine lad. He sent me with a package for him."

Eugenia's black eyes flashed with pride. "Yes, he is a good boy. My sister Irini has raised him well. He told me of his night in your house. You will all come to me soon, yes? Your husband, too. Alexandros is upstairs. He reads up there a lot — the boy will make himself blind. Wait a minute and I will fetch him."

Eugenia finished serving a customer, brushed the flour off

her hands on her apron, and walked through the beaded curtain in the back of the shop to call up the stairs. "Alexi, somebody has brought you a package!" She returned to Joyce. "Come out here, please. Sit at the table and make yourself comfortable."

She ushered Joyce through the curtain and past the hot and fragrant *fourno*. In the courtyard outside sat a round metal table, two flimsy plastic chairs, and several rows of flowerpots growing herbs and spices. Morning glories climbed the whitewashed walls, delicate trumpets of red and violet. A small mulberry tree grew out of one vast pot in the far corner, its black berries dripping inky juice onto the flagstones below.

Joyce sat, her basket clasped on her lap. Nervously, she fiddled with her ponytail.

A second later, Eugenia reappeared with a glass of cold water and a spoonful of jam on a plate. "Please excuse me, I will join you as soon as I finish with my customers," she said, putting these down in front of Joyce. "Alexi is coming. You can give him the package then."

Joyce felt him before she saw him. His shadow hesitated behind her, standing in the doorway. She did not turn to greet him.

Alex didn't know what to think. He was thrilled that she had come, but he could see that her back was stiff and her head bowed. He had waited all week to talk to Joyce again in the hope he had somehow been wrong about her husband. Now he was terrified that she was here only to bid him farewell.

He walked around the table to face her. "This is a nice surprise," he said cautiously.

Joyce cringed. He sounded so cold. "I," she began, but she could not bear him standing over her like this, towering like a schoolmaster. "Would you sit?" She glanced up at him, squinting against the late morning sun.

Feeling reprimanded, Alex sat quickly in the chair opposite her, his long body folding awkwardly.

"My father-in-law sent me," she began formally. "He wanted

to give you this, and since I was coming to town to sell eggs . . ." She handed him the paper.

So that's why she's here, forced by Petros, Alex thought. Not because she wants to see me.

"Thank you," he said stiffly, and took the folded paper from her hand.

They fell silent. Joyce stared at her sweet on the table. She knew she must eat it so as not to insult *Kyria* Sarafi, but the thought sickened her. On the other hand, the longer she delayed eating it, the longer she would have to stay here under Alex's cold eye.

I gave myself to him too quickly, she thought, and suddenly the passion with which she had cried out on the beach came back to her, her animal lust echoing against the dunes for all to hear. The memory filled her with shame. I made myself cheap, she chided herself. I behaved like a slut.

Slowly, her stomach lurching, she began to nibble at the sticky jam on her spoon.

Alex watched her warily. He couldn't tell if she was unhappy or merely embarrassed. "Look." He cleared his throat. He had to speak quickly, before his aunt returned to chaperone them. "I'm really sorry about coming to your house the other night. I had no idea who Petros was. I would never have sprung myself on you voluntarily, I hope you know that. I'm sorry if it was awkward for you."

Joyce took a sip of water. She could not even begin to express how painful that night had been for her. How everything Alex had done, his every word and gesture, had made her long for him. The way he had eaten so little — she noticed, and knew it was because he had been considering their poverty. The way he had been so courteous to Petros and Dimitra, so considerate of her. And there was Nikos sneering beside him, gobbling his food, mocking him with the tone of his voice, the use of his words. It had been intolerable to Joyce, rubbing her face in all her bad choices.

"I know you couldn't help it," she said at last. "I'm just sorry it had to happen."

"Does . . . does anyone suspect?" Alex said at last.

"No." Joyce looked away. If she ate another bite she would gag. "Of course not. They thought I was being a good Greek wife not talking to you."

"Joyce, how —" It was a cry of pain and Alex stopped himself. He sensed that she did not want to hear his questions, his sympathy. That she did not want to hear from him at all anymore. He was stupid to have even hoped. She had her handsome husband back now.

Joyce waited for him to finish speaking, but he was silent. At last she looked at him. His face was guarded and cold. Was he angry at her? She couldn't tell. She only knew she hadn't the strength to say anything significant.

"I better go," she mumbled. "It'll look strange if we stay here talking any longer."

She stood up, still clutching her basket. "I should go thank your aunt and buy my bread."

Alex stood, too. His sunburned face was tense, whitening around his clenched lips. "Tell your father-in-law I'll read this article and that I'm grateful," he said stiffly. "And I hope . . . I hope you'll be all right."

He is saying good-bye, Joyce realized. I don't even have to do it myself. He cannot bear me anymore. She spun quickly on her heels and hurried into the shop.

The pain began later that week. It stabbed at Joyce as she was huddled under the old cow's belly, trying to coax half a bucket of milk out of her shriveled udder. One minute she was teasing a few drops from Hera's teat, the next she was on her knees, clutching her stomach, moaning.

A fire seemed to be burning inside her, flames searing deep in her womb. Joyce realized that she has been feeling twinges like this for several days. A bruised sensation when she sat down, a tenderness when she lifted her legs to climb the ladder to her bed. And two nights earlier, the last time Nikos had made love to her, his plunging had hurt deep within her, making her cry out and push him away.

Shoving the bucket into the corner so that Hera would not kick it over, Joyce stumbled to the outhouse, still bent and clutching her stomach. It was dark in there, but she could see that there was no blood. What is the matter with me? she thought. Is it pregnancy? But why does it hurt so much?

Joyce knew almost nothing about pregnancy. She knew how it was caused, but nothing about how it felt. She left the outhouse and limped back to Hera, then sank onto the milking stool. She had used no birth control with Nikos; none with Alex the first time, either. "Oh God," she cried out, thinking of her foolish wish in the marketplace with Marina. "What will I do if I'm pregnant?"

For half an hour, Joyce sat paralyzed on the stool. The burning inside her grew more and more intense until she could envision some creature within gnawing at her flesh. She doubled over again, but that hurt more, so she stretched out on the straw. Nothing relieved the pain. Unknowingly, she moaned. Suppose the child came out looking like Alex? Suppose it was a girl? Greeks don't want girl children. "May you have male children and female sheep" was a common blessing.

Dimitra found Joyce forty minutes later, still lying on the straw, groaning. "What's the matter, *pedhi mou*?" she cried in alarm and bent down to her. She took Joyce's head in her lap, smoothing the sweat from her brow. "You are sick, little one, you head is hot and damp."

"It hurts here," Joyce answered. She touched her belly, low below the navel. "Deep in here. Is this what it's like to be pregnant?"

Dimitra frowned. It did not seem right to her, unless the girl was having a miscarriage. "Is there blood?" she said.

"No blood."

Dimitra clenched her lips. "Come," she said angrily, "we will go to the doctor."

My son has given her sailor's clap, she thought. My son the whore chaser!

Joyce had to ride on Phoebus to the doctor in Kastron, for she couldn't walk, and each bump was like a knife in her guts. The doctor examined her, making her lie curled up like a fetus while he poked inside her from behind, both of them horribly embarrassed. "Gonorrhea," he pronounced, and wrote out a prescription for penicillin pills. "Send your husband in for a shot. Your case is advanced. It may prevent you from having children."

Joyce lay on the examining table, hugging her ribs. As soon as she heard the doctor's words, she swung from not wanting children to wanting them desperately. Perhaps this is my punishment, she thought. Perhaps this is how God treats a Jew who worships idols. Or a wife who is unfaithful.

"Come, *koroulamou*," Dimitra said gently. "I will take you home and put you to bed." Joyce rode back on the donkey sidesaddle, like some polluted Madonna, clutching her womb.

That night, while Joyce lay writhing upstairs in bed, Dimitra had a terrible scene with Nikos.

"You have brought home your filthy diseases like a common whoremonger, the lowest sailor scum!" she shouted. "You, who boasted of making sons! You have poisoned your future children. You have made your wife barren!"

At first Nikos acted indignant. "I am clean!" he protested. "It must be her. She has betrayed me — she has been sleeping with any soldier she can find!"

That was when Dimitra hit him. Hard, harder than she had ever hit Joyce. Whack across the cheek. Joyce could hear the slam of flesh on flesh from her room.

"Never talk about your wife like that again!" Dimitra screamed. "I know where you have been all these nights you did not come home! Go to the doctor like a man, get your shot and pray for forgiveness. You have disgraced our family. You have disgraced your own mother!"

Then Nikos cried. He got on his knees, clutched his mother's legs like a baby and cried. "Forgive me, *mannamou*, I don't know what I am saying," he wailed, gazing up at his mother, his eyes wide and tearful. "Don't turn against me! It is because I was so lonely. I meant Joyce no harm. I want a son, oh, God I want a son."

"Don't cry, silly boy," Dimitra said, surprised, and stroked his glossy curls. They tickled her palm just as they had when he was little, and she felt her anger drift away. "Don't cry anymore, my son," she said again, gently. "The doctor told us only maybe the disease will hurt her; she might be all right. Light a candle to the Virgin tonight and pray hard and perhaps she will still give you sons after all. But you go get your shot. And you stay away from Joyce and those *puttanas* until the doctor says you are both cured."

"Yes Mama," Nikos sobbed. "I will do all you say."

Upstairs Joyce lay in her bed, listening in misery and confusion. Supposing Nikos was right and she had given him the disease? After all, what did she know of Alex and his affairs? If so, would Nikos finally realize she had a lover and turn her out? On the other hand, perhaps she had carried it from Nikos to Alex. She was in too much pain to remember the chain of events. She was too afraid to think straight.

Nikos wiped his tears on Dimitra's skirt, and the next morning went jauntily off to the doctor, basking in his mother's forgiveness.

Sunday came and went, the previous meeting time between Joyce and Alex passing unmarked while the lovers hid in their separate uncertainties. Joyce swallowed her penicillin pills and waited, fretting, for the pain to recede. Alex gazed forlornly at the red moped he had parked in the side alley and tried to make himself leave.

When he thought of Nikos and his sultry beauty, Alex's impulse was to give up on this whole messy adultery business and run. In this mood, he would start to pack in a fury, hurling his books and clothes into his duffel bag in a haphazard mess. But then he would suddenly remember Joyce's uncertain face in his aunt's courtyard, sit on his bed and stop. Was she dumping him or not? Had he understood her too well or not at all? How could he even think of leaving until he knew? And so he would unpack all over again. He repeated this ritual over and over until he was in a paralysis of bewilderment. But eventually, his natural optimism won out. He had always got what he wanted out of life so far — why not this time? He still had some money left, he had nowhere else he had to be — he could do as he pleased. I'll damn well stay if I want, he muttered to himself. I'll stay until this is all sorted out.

To pass the time until he could talk to Joyce again, Alex persuaded his aunt to let him work in the bakery after all. He was tired of being a tourist, hanging about in tavernas with his fishermen cousins, lazing through the island's dreary museums and ruins. He wanted some purpose, something to distract him from Joyce. Nevertheless, it took him two entire days to persuade Eugenia to let him help her. "You will get in my way," she said grumpily. "You will dream over the ovens and burn everything. Head in the clouds, feet in the cow shit, that's you."

"No, Aunty. Give me a chance. I'm a good worker."

"Work! What do you know about work? You have the muscles of a grasshopper."

Once he had broken her down, however, she slyly gave him the most arduous job in the place — lifting the bread out of the oven.

"All right, English boy," she said. "Watch me carefully. When I flip the bread, you catch it." She grasped the huge, eight-foot oar she used for the task in both hands. "You slip it deep into the *fourno* like this, see? Ease it under the loaf, one, two, three, straight under. You are paying attention?"

"Yes, Aunt. I've got it."

"Huh. So says the fisherman just before he loses the fish. Very well, you slide it under like this until the loaf is square in the middle, like a hen in her roost, yes? Then you pull it out in one smooth movement, flip the loaf. . . . Watch it!"

Alex flailed his arms wildly as a steaming hot loaf came flying through the air at him. Despite a series of mad dashes and a pirouette, he managed to miss it entirely. It landed with a thump at his feet.

Eugenia dropped the oar and put her hands on her hips. "What, you have flippers for hands?"

"Sorry. I wasn't expecting it to come so fast."

Eugenia clucked her tongue. "Pick up my bread, go on, it is not a floor sponge. Come, now you take the oar. It is man's work, anyway. I'll catch the loaves."

Alex picked up the oar, which was so heavy that he was amazed his aunt had been wielding it alone all these years, and shoved it into the oven.

"Not like that, you sheep's brain! You will knock all the loaves into the fire. The saints help me. Slide it in flat."

Alex managed to get a loaf onto the oar, but as he was pulling it out, he tripped over his own feet and knocked a whole rackful of bread into the coals.

"Oaf!" Eugenia shrieked, while he stood there sheepishly watching the precious manna go up in flames. "God help the weak and learned! Come, from now on you will practice with bricks."

Eventually, after another hour of curses and instruction, he learned to flip the oar so that his aunt could catch the bread, which she then swiped with a damp sponge to make the crusts shine. The work was hot, the room filled with flour dust. He understood her cough now and her solid, muscular arms. Yet he found it satisfying. He liked the way the line of loaves grew steadily longer as he tossed them off the paddle. He liked the cozy, sweet odor of rising dough. And he took pride in his new skill.

The next few days were so busy they passed quickly for Alex, just as he had hoped they would. Up at five in the morning, an hour he had never known existed in England. A quick cup of strong black coffee, half of which was left as powdery grounds in the bottom of the cup. A few minutes to allow his aunt to read the grounds for his fortune, taking delight, it seemed to him, in predicting gloom and doom. Then to work. Building a fire in the huge *fourno*, kneading the dough, flipping out the loaves. Over and over. They would work all morning, stopping only for coffee and some of their own bread later on. Then lunch and, at last, siesta, after which the village wives came with the casseroles and roasts they wanted baked for a small fee, as their own ovens were not big enough. The evening stretched into a night of work and more work until, at one in the morning, Alex and his aunt would drop from exhaustion.

Alex liked the hard work, but it didn't help him sleep. Siesta was a particular torture to him. His northern European body could not get used to sleeping in the afternoon, especially now that September had arrived and the weather was no longer enervatingly hot. His muscles might be aching from the hours of standing, kneading, lifting the oar, but his mind was wide awake and restless, roaming about like a frantic animal. He lay on his bed, his eyes fixed on the beams of the ceiling, admonishing himself. Confront Joyce. Find out if she wants you or not. Move your paralyzed arse!

At last, unable to bear his own scolding any longer, he took to slipping out for a swim during siesta if it was warm enough, or to strolling up the mountain to clear his lungs of flour, then returning for a few minutes' nap. And in the evenings, if his aunt could spare him, he wandered the streets looking for Joyce and Petros.

*   *   *

When Joyce came into the bakery late one morning a few days later, Alex could not hide his delight. He put down the oar and greeted her happily. In his surprise he forgot to be wary, and she was encouraged by his unexpected warmth.

"My father-in-law has sent me with another message," she said to him formally, after greeting his aunt.

"Have you got time for a coffee?" Alex said quickly in English. In Greek he added cunningly, "You and your father-in-law must be tired after your long morning at the market. Aunt Eugenia, may I join *Kyrie* Koliopoulos and his daughter-in-law for a coffee?"

"Yes, yes," his aunt said, preoccupied with a sale, and waved them out. "Hurry, you are blocking the door!"

They went outside and slipped into an alley. As always on market day, the streets were busy and Joyce was worried that they would be seen.

"Where do you want to go?" Alex said. "I don't suppose you have time to take a drive with me?"

"No, I only have a few minutes. And I have Phoebus here." She gestured to the old donkey, who stood at the end of the alleyway, lazily sweeping away flies with his tail, his head hanging low in the morning sun.

Alex blinked in surprise. He hadn't known Joyce drove a donkey. He thought it charming, but the anxiety on her face stopped him from making a comment. "Are you all right?" he said, concerned. "You look upset. Has something happened?" A sudden dread gripped him. Had her family found about him?

"I can't talk here," she said, and looked about her despairingly.

"Perhaps we'd be better off in the back at my aunt's table. I can always say Petros went home."

"No. I can't risk anyone hearing."

Alex regarded her uneasily. "Come," he said in a firm voice. "I know it's risky, but we have to get out of town. It's the only choice."

He led her to his moped, parked down a back alley, waited

while she wrapped her scarf around her face and hair, and drove them quickly down the emptiest streets and out of Kastron. Determined to get her away from everyone she knew, he took the road up to Kondias, a small, semicircular village of ancient Turkish houses topped with moss-covered roofs. Once there, they dismounted and he turned to her. "There's a *psistaria* here. You want something to eat?"

"No. I'd rather go somewhere away from people."

She did not look well, Alex noticed. Her face seemed tight, her usual glow faded to a yellowish tinge. He wanted so much to reach out and take her hand, hold her and comfort her, but he did not dare.

Leaving the moped beside the road, they climbed up the stony hill until they reached a rock flat enough to sit on. No one would notice them here, but Alex still wished the damned island had some trees.

"Are you comfortable?" he said, still formal.

Joyce pushed her scarf off her face. Pulling her knees up under her long brown skirt, she rested her forehead on them. She was so ashamed that she could barely speak.

"I've got something awful to tell you. To ask you," she forced herself to say. She raised her head and looked at him pleadingly.

"What is it?" Alex said, bewildered.

She hesitated. How hard it was to spit out the words.

"I'm sick," she finally said, her voice dropping to a whisper. "I've got a disease."

"What kind of disease?" Alarmed, he sat beside her in order to hear her better. "Something serious?"

She swallowed. "Dimitra calls it the clap."

"The clap? Nikos gave you the clap? That fucking bastard!"

The words shot out in angry jealousy before Alex could stop himself. So she has been sleeping with her Ares, he thought bitterly. She's been bouncing between us like a ping-pong ball!

Joyce shook her head. "You think I did get it from Nikos? I

mean, I'm sorry to ask you this, but it's not from . . . I mean, you don't think you might have it, do you?" She looked at him, squinting anxiously. Why did lovemaking have to come down to this? To diseases and doctors and sordid conversations on pieces of rock?

Alex stood up. "If I have it," he said firmly, "it would only be from you. I haven't been with anyone else, if that's what you mean."

"Don't get angry." Joyce's voice trembled. "I only told you so you could go to the doctor."

"I'm not angry," Alex lied, trying to sound reassuring. Looking at her, he realized that he had never seen her face so vulnerable, not even while they were making love. Her lips were tight and pale with anxiety.

"Don't worry," he said more gently. "It's nothing. I'll go to the doctor and get a shot today, if you think it's necessary."

For a time they were silent. Alex stood beside her, his hands in his pockets, gazing out over the mountain to hide his humiliation. Joyce remained seated, words tumbling about in her head. She didn't know how to defend herself, whether she even should. She was still too confused to realize that she could not have given Alex the disease, for she hadn't made love with him since Nikos had reclaimed her.

"How do you feel?" Alex asked at last, making an effort to sound kind. He turned to face her again. "Did you feel any pain?"

Joyce shrugged. His sympathy was making her throat swell, another impediment to her speech. She longed to weep. To weep in his arms and tell him that she wanted her marriage to work, that she wanted him, that she didn't know what she wanted. But she knew that she couldn't say any of these things. She must be disgusting to him now, bringing him diseases like some sailor's prostitute.

She had no choice but to sit there alone, the few feet between them as wide as the sea.

"I better get back," she said at last, struggling to control her voice. "You know where the doctor lives?"

"I know." Alex paused. His sympathy for her was still wrenching his heart. But his jealousy of Nikos was stronger. "I just want to ask one thing before we go," he added, his voice hardening.

Joyce flinched. She had never heard him sound so bitter.

"I just want to know if I meant anything to you at all."

She looked directly at him when he said that, too shocked to stop herself.

"You don't seem to realize this, Joyce, but it's cruel to use people."

"Use people? What do you mean?"

Alex heard the pain in her voice. She was trying to deny it. He must have hit the truth.

"Never mind," he said, turning away to hide the hurt on his face. "There's no point in belaboring it." He took a step down towards the road. "We better go."

But Joyce remained sitting. He sounded as if he hated her, and this she could not bear. Hot, unwilling tears slid from the corners of her eyes, spreading over her cheeks like a web.

"Are you coming?" he asked. His back was to her and he did not realize she was crying.

Joyce fumbled to get up. She could not see. Everything was a blur of gray and brown and pain. She turned her back to him as she rose to her feet, surreptitiously wiping her eyes on her skirt. He was already walking down the hill to the moped.

As they drove home, the wind dried the tears on her face to an invisible mask of salt.

The next day Alex sold his moped. Then he went to the doctor and suffered a humiliating jab in the buttock with a needle. Some romantic adventure this, he admonished himself, some experience of ancient Greece. A sordid affair with a married Yank and a case of the clap. Wonderful.

Upstairs in his room, he found a packet from England on his bed, where his aunt must have put it when the postman came. It was full of condoms, wrapped in a teasing letter from his friend.

Alex. I can't imagine what you could need these for. Preserving pickles? Fish bait? Or are you planning to blow them all up and float home? Your envious friend, Peter

Suddenly he remembered that he had used condoms the last time he had been with Joyce, on the beach — he could not have contracted the clap from her then. If he had it at all, it would have been from the first time they made love, on the mountaintop at Ayiassos.

If that was the case, Alex realized, she must have thought she'd given it to him long before Nikos came home. So she had been lying when she'd said that she had never gone off with anyone before — she could be screwing half the town for all he knew! No wonder she wouldn't listen to his offers of rescue.

Some Penelope she, he thought. I'm obviously nothing but a bead on her string.

XI

September was a busy time of year for the family, a time to preserve fruit and pickle vegetables, to nurse the tomatoes and squash off their vines, to collect the last of the summer sesame; and Dimitra kept Joyce working hard. Everything delicate that managed to grow on their parsimonious slice of land had to be plucked and coddled before the first northern frost crept up in the night to kill. Even Nikos was persuaded to leave the seafront a few hours a day to help. Joyce tried as usual to bury herself in all this work, but she had never felt so crushed. All her optimism, all the determination she had felt to make this life with her in-laws a success, seemed to be disintegrating at her touch.

Nikos, at least, kept away from her, even after her course of penicillin was done. He avoided her now, ashamed, and either worked beside his father or disappeared into town. Petros and Dimitra were their usual silent selves, going about their chores with the fixed determination of farmers who must race against time. Joyce was left to the cacophony of her own thoughts, which clattered about in her head while she worked through the day in outward silence, like the echoing of drums in a sad, empty building.

The thoughts in her head were nothing like the thoughts she

used to have back in Florida. There she had worried about such matters as fights with her mother, whether she was gaining weight, and who would call her for a date on Saturday night. Those worries had loomed large at the time, but now she knew they were the concerns of a child. Now she felt as if her every thought, her every decision had the power to ricochet throughout her future, altering it forever. She remembered saying to Alex once that her life here was pure and necessary compared to her life at home. Suddenly, all that had changed. Nothing was pure any longer. Her love for Nikos was soiled, her passion for Alex perverted by disease and suspicion, Dimitra's trust violated by Joyce's own lies and betrayals. How, she wondered, as she knelt pulling weeds out of the rocky earth, how had everything turned so sour so fast?

She looked over at Dimitra, who was squatting on a milking stool by the back door, her knees spread, a pile of haricot beans poured into the lap of her old blue dress. Her head, its gray braids coiled about her crown, was bent over, concentrated. Her sun-blotched hands trembled slightly as she picked out the beans that had rotted. She appeared suddenly frail to Joyce, who frowned in consternation. Joyce was used to seeing her mother-in-law as all-powerful, as tough and unyielding as the trunk of an ancient olive tree. Yet there she was, nothing but an aging peasant, her eyes dimming, her limbs increasingly stiff and unreliable. Nevertheless, Joyce was filled with an aching, grateful love for this woman. Dimitra had stood up for her in ways Joyce had never expected. She had defied her son for her, criticized him. Even hit him. And she had done all this for a Joyce that did not exist.

Swaying on her knees, Joyce spread one hand on the rough earth to steady herself. For the first time since she had become used to this rocky, primitive island, she felt not protected but in danger, not moored but frighteningly loose. As if at any moment she might break free and sink.

* * *

On Sunday morning, after the only few hours that week when Dimitra allowed anybody to rest, she ordered Joyce to church for the first time since her illness. "Here, put on your scarf quickly," she said, thrusting Joyce's usual white head wrap into her hands. "We have not much time. Today you must pray to the Virgin for children." She pulled a woven shawl around her shoulders and lifted something off the mantelpiece. "You must pray that this cruel disease has done you no harm. Look what I have bought you."

She held out a small *tama*, an oval votive of silvery tin. On it, painted in the childish style Joyce recognized from a local artist, was the curled fetus of a baby boy.

Dimitra must have spent a fortune on this, Joyce thought, money they could hardly spare, yet it repulsed her beyond words. I am not a primitive, she found herself thinking. I can't do this! The idea of kneeling in that church, kissing those painted hands, propping that crude silver womb at the Virgin's feet, made Joyce feel sick. She thought of the English girls' words again, of their warning about how deception can lead to slavery. I owe it to Dimitra to tell her the truth about this, at least, she admonished herself. I owe it to myself.

"I cannot, Mama," she said at last, looking at her mother-in-law steadily. "I cannot go to church. I cannot put that thing at the Virgin's feet."

"What do you mean, child?" Dimitra cried, crossing herself rapidly. She thrust the *tama* at her. "I have never heard such nonsense. Come, take it and put on your scarf."

Joyce backed away. "Dimitra, please listen."

Dimitra looked at her, surprised by her tone. Joyce rarely sounded so grave. "Well, what is it, *koroulamou*? What is the matter?"

"I have something I have never told you. Please forgive me, but . . . it is to do with my home back in America."

Dimitra's eyes darted away from Joyce in a strangely guilty glance, but Joyce was too afraid of her own confession to notice.

"Go on, quick," Dimitra said then. "Out with it."

"I cannot go to church with you anymore because — "

"Holy Virgin, what is she saying?" Dimitra crossed herself again. "What evil spirit has possessed you, child?"

"Mama, stop!" Joyce shouted. "I'm trying to tell you something!"

Dimitra quieted down and stared at her. She was suddenly afraid, and her arms trembled.

"I must sit, I need to sit," she mumbled and put the *tama* down on the table. She pulled out a chair and sank onto it. Clutching the apron she wore around her waist, she said, "All right, I am ready."

Joyce took out another chair and sat down, too. "Mama," she said, leaning forward. "You have never asked me about my church in America."

"I do not want to know!" Dimitra exclaimed. "I do not like those modern, heathen ways. The Greek Orthodox is the old way, the pure way. We do not meddle with the word of God. Anyway, Nikos told me you had no church in America."

"That is not true. Please listen."

Dimitra calmed herself. Her dark blue dress, covered with tiny white dots, was open at the collar, revealing splotchy skin and a wrinkled neck. Her hair was hidden under her usual black scarf, which she had wrapped around her head like a cowl. Her heavy face was sun-stained and creased, her mouth folding over missing teeth. She stared at Joyce anxiously, her dark eyes hooded and wary. She looks timeless, Joyce thought. She looks like the mother of the earth.

"I was afraid to tell you before," Joyce finally said, fiddling nervously with the corner of the woven tablecloth. "I should have told you right away, but I was too afraid." She swallowed and took a deep breath. "I am not a Christian, Mama." Joyce looked up from the cloth, her hands still kneading it. "I am a Jew."

Dimitra's mouth dropped open. She sat in frozen silence, staring as if her daughter-in-law had burst into flames. Then she shot to her feet, widened her puckered lips, and let out such a bellow that the chickens outside squawked and scrambled for their lives.

Joyce, too, leapt up, terrified. She ran to the pump to wet a rag with cold water — she was afraid that Dimitra was having a fit. But then she heard Dimitra shouting. "Come back in here!"

Joyce ran back in. Dimitra rushed at her, her hands raised. "You traitor! You devil! Infidel! How dare you, how dare you!"

Dimitra hammered blows on Joyce's head and ears, smashing her fists down as hard as she could, over and over again, slamming Joyce's face, her shoulders, her jaw, and finally landing a mighty punch in one eye. She hit and hammered until she drove Joyce out the front door, sobbing, her head clutched in her hands. Not content with that, Dimitra chased after her, stumbling and shrieking curses, her fists striking out at Joyce's fleeing back in uncontrollable rage.

"What is this?" It was Petros, returning from his field with Phoebus, who also started in surprise at the violent scene. "Stop that, Dimitra!" he cried, and stepped between them to shield Joyce. "What are you doing to the child?"

"She is a Jew! A filthy, lying Jew!" Dimitra screamed, and tried to push past Petros to attack Joyce again. But he barred her way.

"What is the matter with you?" he said sternly, surprising Dimitra into silence. "This is Joyce, our daughter. Why are you treating her like this?"

Dimitra was panting, her wrinkled lips drained white. "She has kissed the Holy Virgin!" she spluttered. "She has prayed beside me in church! She has blasphemed!"

"Dimitra!" Petros barked at her, his feeble voice cracking with anger. "Go back in the house. You are making a fool of yourself." He turned to Joyce, whose eye was already swelling. She was sobbing too hard to speak.

"Come, little one," he said. "Come with me." And he tied up Phoebus, put his bony arm around Joyce's waist, and escorted her gently down the path to town.

Once they had rounded the bend, out of sight of Dimitra, he handed Joyce his handkerchief in silence. Taking a deep breath to control her sobbing, she wiped her face and gave it back. "Keep it," he said quietly. "We will find you something cold to put on that eye."

"I am so sorry, *Petheros*," Joyce said, her voice still shaking. "I have brought nothing but trouble on your house."

"It is not you, it is Nikos," he said firmly. "Nikos brought you here."

"But he didn't force me. I came because I wanted to."

Petros waved his hand dismissively. "You were a child. He should have known better. Come, don't cry anymore." He gazed into her face a moment. "Is this true, what your mother-in-law says?" he said gently. "Or is she making this up because she is angry about some other thing?"

"It is true," Joyce paused, still trembling. "I should have told you before. I was too afraid. I was a coward."

Petros sighed and walked on a few paces in silence. "Do not blame yourself, *koroulamou*," he said at last, his voice low. "You were in a strange country, with a strange family. A country where we have killed so many Jews that their blood will never wash from our hands."

"You didn't kill them, *Petheros*. The Nazis did."

"But some of us helped. If nine of our men fought against the Germans and one man helped them, the blood is on all of our hands forever. The sin of one collaborator outweighs all the good of the rest."

Joyce looked at him, thinking of her discussion with the English girls. "Couldn't you see it the other way round?" she said tentatively. "Can't you take pride in those nine men and only feel ashamed for the one?"

Petros shrugged. "That is the difference between the young and the old, *pedhi mou*. The young see what is gained, the old only what is lost."

"I'm lost, aren't I?" Joyce said then. "I can't stay after this. Dimitra will never have me back."

"Shh, do not say such things. Come, we are here."

He had brought her to the northeastern edge of town, where he stopped in front of a small house. Leading her around to the courtyard at the back, he whistled at the door. A tall, plump woman appeared, perhaps in her fifties, her hair pulled back in a gleaming black bun and her figure erect. Her cheeks were round and firm, and thick eyebrows arched over her oval gray eyes, giving her a look of kindly but amused self-assurance. She was dressed in a loose, belted gown of widow's black.

"Petros," she said calmly, opening her arms. They embraced while Joyce watched in astonishment.

"This is my daughter-in-law, Joyce, the American," Petros said then, pushing Joyce forward. "Joyce, this is Maria Kofa, an old friend of mine. Maria, do you have something cold for her eye?"

"Yes, of course. Come in, come in." The woman led them into her house, not unlike their own, and bade Joyce sit at the table, bringing over a bowl of cool water and a clean rag, along with the usual tray of glasses and sweets. "Put the cloth over it, like this," she said. Quickly dipping the rag in the bowl, she squeezed it out and laid it gently against Joyce's face. "Who did this to you, child?"

"I will explain," Petros said. "Excuse us a minute," he added, addressing Joyce. He signaled to Maria and they both stepped outside, leaving Joyce alone.

Holding the cold rag to her eye, Joyce looked about the room in confusion. It was a simple room, with a frame containing an icon of the Virgin nailed to one wall, under which burned a fat yellow candle. An iron pot hung over the hearth, and the table at which she sat was covered with a crisp white cloth, embroidered around its edges. Above the table, a gilt-edged mirror dangled by a single nail. The only other decoration was a thin wooden shelf lined with bottles, glasses, and, a surprising sight, books. As bare as the house was, however, it looked better off than their own, newer, with smoother walls and a red-tiled floor instead of their unpolished wood. It smelled of fresh whitewash and lilacs. Could the owner of all this be Petros's mistress? Joyce wondered. Little Petros, whom Dimitra called half a man? Was he like all the other Greek men after all?

Petros and Maria returned, this time bearing a small bowl of ice they had borrowed from a nearby *kaphenio.* "Joyce, I want you to stay here with *Kyria* Kofa for a few days until Dimitra returns to herself," Petros said. "You will be safe here. Dimitra does not know of it, and I will come to see you."

"But . . ." Joyce's confusion choked off her words.

"I will bring you clothes when Dimitra is out at the market." Petros bent over her, frowning with concern. "Do not be upset, my child. Your *pathera* loves you too much for this to last. I will talk reason into her."

"What about Nikos?" Joyce said, her voice still shaking. "What will he do when he finds out?"

"Nikos is leaving, *koroulamou.* I made him sign up on a ship that sails tomorrow. He is saying good-bye to his mother now. He will go to Skiathos today. He has caused too much trouble, too much grief. I have told him not to come back until he can behave himself."

"Nikos is gone?" Joyce looked at Petros in dismay. Now it would be months until they were reconciled. Months of uncertainty and worry. It would be torture!

"Maria will look after you, don't worry," Petros said quietly. "She is a good woman. Now put some ice on that eye." He touched Joyce quickly on the arm, kissed Maria, and left.

*   *   *

As Petros toiled back up the hill towards Dimitra, his cap pulled down over his eyes to shut out the sun, he felt unusually fierce. He knew his wife had grown up in a family torn by religious and political differences, the Turks and Greeks warring sometimes even in her own blood, but he'd be damned if he was going to allow her to bring all this strife into his own family. He did not care if Joyce was a Gypsy or an idol-worshipping heathen, let alone a Jew; she was still their daughter-in-law, and she was still a loving, kind girl. She had never spoken a cross word to him or Dimitra in all the months she had lived with them, except that one time after Dimitra had hit her. She had never refused tasks. She had never taken more than her share of food. She had never even complained. She has been enslaved by us, he thought as he shuffled slowly up the path, captured by my son Nikos and now perhaps made barren by him, too. I owe it to her — we all owe it to her — to treat her with mercy.

He found Dimitra shrieking on their bed. Prostrate, her apron thrown off, her dress unbuttoned to reveal the thick bands of cloth she wore as underwear, she was wailing and beating her breast. "She is a devil!" she screamed as soon as Petros walked in. "She is possessed! She has stolen my heart from my son and now she tells me she is a filthy Jew! I have lost everything because of her — my beloved Nikos, my grandchildren. Now he is gone to sea to be swallowed by the cruel waves before I ever had a chance to welcome him back to my bosom. Oh evil girl, demon! My son, my heart, how could this happen to me?"

"Dimitra, calm down," Petros called out to her. "Get control of yourself." He sat on the edge of the bed, took off his cap and grasped her hand. "Hush."

For a long time Dimitra ignored him. Furious tears streamed down her cheeks, her voice bellowed loud and strong. But finally, her rage spent at last, she quieted enough to listen to him.

"Dimitra, you are making too much of this. A Jew is not a heathen. She prays, does she not? Did you ever give her a chance to tell you her beliefs, did any of us give her a chance? No, we did not. We took possession of her as if she were an empty vessel. We forced her to follow our ways without ever considering her past."

"She blasphemed!" Dimitra sobbed, her voice a hoarse whisper now. "She kissed the Holy Virgin — a Jew!"

"The Virgin was a Jew, and so was her Son."

Dimitra clutched her head. "Don't preach to me, old man! She is a Judas! Her people killed that Son."

"Dimitra, the Romans killed Christ. But let us not talk of this. It is Joyce who matters. We have bullied her, given her no respect. It is not surprising that she was afraid to tell us the truth."

"Respect! And who respected me when I was childless? I was nothing, treated as dirt by your brothers, your sisters-in-law . . ."

"And by me?" Petros smiled at her tenderly. He sensed that Dimitra was weakening. Inside her tough hide she adored Joyce, he knew this.

"Hmmm." She grunted, not yet ready to give in. Then her face crumpled again. "But my Nikos. He has gone again, and who knows if I will live until he returns!"

"Dimitra, you will live to be two hundred and twenty, I know it. You are as strong as the mountain. Nikos will be old and gray before you even look at a grave."

"Petros, you will tempt the evil eye with such nonsense," Dimitra said, spitting on the floor. She held out her arms. "Oh, my husband, my heart is breaking."

"*Manoula mou*," Petros said tenderly, and leaned down to hold her in his arms until, exhausted, Dimitra fell snoringly to sleep.

Once Petros was sure his wife was deeply unconscious, he

slipped his arms out from under her bulky frame and tiptoed to Joyce's room. There he gathered some of her clothes, bundled them into a roll and made his way back to Maria's house. Dimitra would not be ready to speak to Joyce for another week at least, he reckoned, but even if she were, he wanted to keep them apart for a while. He wanted Dimitra to miss her little *pouli*, to recognize the tenderness in her own heart. And he had other plans for Joyce as well.

He dropped off the bundle and whispered a conference with Maria. It was siesta time by now, and Joyce, like her mother-in-law, had fallen into the deep sleep of emotional exhaustion. Petros had no time for rest, however. He kissed Maria good-bye and slipped away into town. He wanted to find Alex. Joyce would be feeling abandoned, he knew. She needed a friend of her own kind. Someone to help her feel anchored. Someone who might even tempt her to stay.

The bakery was closed as it was Sunday, so Petros had to walk around the narrow side alley, dodging cats and loose, treacherous stones to reach the back door. The beaded curtain hanging over it rattled gently in the breeze that had sprung up since noon, and he could feel the leftover heat from the *fourno* radiating through the door like dragon's breath. Taking a last gulp of fresh air before he stepped inside, Petros called quietly, "*Kyria* Sarafi? Alexandros?"

A pause. "Who is it?" an irritated voice replied at last from upstairs.

"Excuse me, it is Petros Koliopoulos. May I speak to you?"

Eugenia appeared, looking crumpled with sleep. Her mustachioed, oval face was furrowed and cross.

"*Kalispera*," Petros said hurriedly. "I am sorry to interrupt your siesta but it is a matter of some urgency. Is your nephew at home?"

"I hope nothing terrible has happened, God protect us!" Eugenia crossed herself quickly. "No, I am sorry, my nephew has left. He caught the ferry today."

"Is he going to come back?" Petros asked, surprised.

Eugenia shrugged. "Who knows? These foreign students, they have no obligations, no place they have to be. He does not even send money to his parents. I do not understand these English, they have no sense of family at all. They must be a cold people, do you not agree?"

But Petros was too disappointed to answer. "Yes, yes," he said, not really listening. "I must go, excuse me . . . ," and still mumbling, he rushed out the door.

Because it was Sunday, and on Sundays the ferry timetables were even more erratic than usual, Petros had hope. He hurried down to the seafront, praying that he would find Alex lounging about like the other passengers, waiting for the ferry to depart. He spotted the boat in a minute, still lying, as he had expected, like a great lazy fish in the harbor. But when he approached the quay where the passengers sat, numb and listless in that way of waiting passengers all over the world, he could not see Alex. On this island it was easy to spot this English boy. The Greeks here were so mixed with the blood of the Ottomans that most of the blond and tall had long since been bred out of them. Alex stood out like a palm tree.

Petros walked up and down the quayside, looking for Alex anxiously. But he was nowhere to be seen. The waterfront was small, there was no chance that Petros could miss him. The boy must have caught a motorboat or a fisherman's caïque to Mytilene instead of waiting for the ferry. He must have grown tired of this claustrophobic island after all and fled.

Two *kaphenia* away, on the other side of the harbor, Alex sat in a corner with his sleeping bag and his rucksack between his legs, utterly miserable. On the table in front of him were a beer and a plate of *kalamaria,* but he could not eat. If the ferry had left on time, his decision would have been made. But it hadn't, and now he was caught in limbo. He looked out at the bright sea, the famous Greek light dancing and sparkling off its waves, as carefree as a nymph, and a weight closed over his heart like a hand. He felt as if he had done a great wrong. But he was not sure why.

He finished his beer and paid without eating the squid, much to the disapproval of the proprietor. Hoisting his bags on to his shoulder, he headed back along the seafront. If I stay, he thought, what would be the purpose? To see Joyce one more time and rub my face in her indifference? Let her use me again to make her husband jealous? I'm so bloody naive!

But when Alex thought like this, he did not feel quite honest. It was as if those thoughts belonged to someone else, to some other man who was acting Alex but who was not really him. Those were the thoughts of a rejected lover, of hurt pride, he told himself. They were not necessarily the thoughts of reason.

Alex puffed on, his bags heavy in the afternoon glare. If I'm to believe she just used me, he said to himself, trying to think straight, then I'm deciding that almost everything she told me is a lie: that she had never gone off with any other man before, that she'd been alone with those old people for the better part of two years, that she'd tried to love Nikos. Alex found it hard to believe that Joyce, who had seemed so ingenuous to him, even in her mystery, could lie about all that.

Nevertheless, he thought fretfully, maybe I could still be spinning these excuses out of hope. How pathetic. It's time to save my dignity and get out of this mess.

"Alexandros!"

He heard Petros's cry immediately, for the afternoon was still sleepy and quiet, most shutters closed against the wind, most people not yet up from their beds. He turned to see the little man on his feet at a *kaphenio*, waving wildly. Alex walked over to him.

"Are you leaving?" Petros exclaimed. He pointed to the bags in horror. "You are leaving without saying good-bye to your friends?"

Alex blushed, suddenly realizing how rude he must seem. "I have stayed too long. I must go back to Athens and get a job."

"Bah! What silliness! Sit and have a coffee with me."

Of course Alex obeyed. He wanted to.

"So you are tired of us, is that it?" Petros said teasingly after Alex settled himself. "Boring provincial islanders, that is how we must seem."

Boring was the last word Alex would have used for these past few weeks. "No," he said earnestly, "no, that's not it. I could live here forever, but I have to make a living."

"Does your aunt not pay you for your work in the bakery?" Petros asked innocently. Alex didn't know this, but the sight of him covered with flour in all his English gawkiness, at the beck and call of the fierce Widow Sarafi, had made him the laughingstock of the village.

Alex shrugged. "Only in food and board. She believes the English are all rich, so she won't take my need for money seriously. Sometimes she tips me a drachma or two if she's in a good mood." He grinned sheepishly.

Petros chuckled. "A bean at a time will fill your sack. If you had seen how we starved during the war, you would understand. But I have an idea. Don't leave today. The Sunday ferry is a lazy thing anyway, and the wind is making the waves leap about like spring frogs. You will lose your guts on that boat if you go now."

Alex looked over Petros's shoulder at the sea. It was true, the waves were choppy, and the ferry was already rocking like a toy boat. The Aegean was famous for making people seasick.

"But the next one doesn't leave for three days and I'm running out of money," Alex said, laughing. "You Greeks hate to see a guest go, don't you?"

"Yes, it is true. It always feels like a rejection, it hurts us here." Petros thumped his bony chest. "Do you want to hear my idea?"

"I do." Alex smiled. He couldn't help liking this old man. There was something so gentle and intelligent about him, yet he seemed full of unaccountable mischief.

"You go back to your aunt for a day or two — she will be happy to see you again. It is hard work in her bakery all day, and the boys she hires to help her are a great deal more expensive than you." Petros chortled. "You go back to her. Then in a few days, come have a farewell celebration with me so that you can take your leave like a real traveler, not like some tourist sneaking out with his tail between his legs."

"No, no, I can't. Thank you but . . ." The thought of appearing again in Joyce's house to face the jeering Nikos filled Alex with horror.

"Wait." Petros held up his claw of a hand. He sensed that he had to be subtle about Joyce. "You have not heard me out. My son has gone back to sea, my wife is grieving as if he has died, and my daughter-in-law is not feeling well. So this is not the time for celebration in my house. But I have a friend in town, a good friend" — he winked — "and she is a cook like no other. You go there, I will invite some friends, and we will drink and dance until your heart is brave again. 'If the pot boils, friendship lives.' Yes?"

"But I must leave on the next ferry."

"Yes, yes. Well, maybe I will let you go if you agree." Petros's eyes seemed to dance. "You like my plan?"

Alex succumbed. Perhaps this is what I need, he thought, a good booze-up with a bunch of men. A cozy ring of male camaraderie to protect me from the barbs of love.

"But first," Petros said cunningly, "you must come with me now so I can show you the house. You will meet my friend, and if she likes you she will be willing to cook us a feast. You must charm her first, however — she would not do this for everybody."

"All right," said Alex, laughing. What a rogue this little peasant was turning out to be!

They finished their coffees, Alex heaved his bags back over his shoulder, and Petros led him up the hill through the winding cobbled lanes of the village. The houses here had all been recently whitewashed, the marble dust and water slapped on with brooms, mops, or special brushes called *vourtza*, and they gleamed in the afternoon light, burnt orange roofs topping each one of them like sugar icing. Ifestian houses had always made Alex think of little cakes, tiny and tasty-looking, like the petits fours his English grandmother used to serve for tea.

At Maria's house, Petros stopped, winked at Alex and knocked on the front door. The green wooden shutters were still closed for siesta, making even the house look asleep. Red and yellow hibiscus trailed down from pots along the top of the outside staircase, their bright tongues pointed saucily at Alex. A stream of soapy water trickled by their feet. The smell of ammonia mingled with the scents of jasmine and feces.

The door opened and Alex saw a black-haired, matronly woman staring at him in surprise.

"This is Alexandros Gidding, the nephew of Widow Sarafi, the English boy I told you about," Petros said quickly. "He is a good lad, but I found him trying to slip away without saying good-bye. Alexandros, this is my friend *Kyria* Kofa."

"Come in, come in," Maria said, looking at Petros quizzically. In the twenty years she had known him, he had never brought people over. Now, within a day, he had brought two. "Your daughter-in-law is still asleep. She does not seem well, poor girl."

At these words, Alex froze. He turned to stare at Petros.

"My daughter-in-law is here?" Petros said in astonishment. "Tut, tut, she must have had another fight with my wife." He shrugged while Maria gaped at him. "You do not mind, do you?" he said to Alex. "Sometimes she takes refuge here when my wife's sharp tongue drives her away."

Maria swallowed. "Sit," she said faintly. "I will tell her you are here."

Alex didn't move. A suspicion that he was being set up filtered into his mind, but he quickly dismissed it. If Petros had any idea of what was between him and Joyce, he would never throw them together. If I were wholly Greek I'd believe this is fate, or that my saint is trying to tell me something, he thought. As it is, I'm flummoxed.

"Sit down, my boy," Petros said casually, and waved him to the table. "It is nice and cool in here, is it not?"

"Uh, yes," Alex managed to say. Sweat was soaking through his clothes.

Upstairs a few minutes later, Joyce was blinking at Maria in disorientation. She had slept deeply, dreaming of Florida, of her brothers bobbing in the sea while they mocked her, their faces leering like Nikos's. Now it took her a long moment to remember where she was. The room was unfamiliar, as was the face of Maria bending over her, talking about something. Joyce yawned and felt the pain of her swollen eye.

"Petros is back," Maria was saying. "He has brought a guest. We must go down and pay our respects."

Joyce sighed. She was in no mood to entertain, but she knew her duty. "Yes, I'm coming," she said and swung her legs off the bed. She slipped her dress back on, the faded pink one she wore for chores. Her head felt heavy and sluggish from sleep. Usually she woke herself up from siesta with coffee and a splash of water from the pump, but today she had no such luxury.

She combed her hair quickly, tying it at the nape of her neck, then touched her eye. There was no mirror in the room, but she suspected that she must look a sight, for her eye felt puffy and sore. She had no way to hide it, however, so she smoothed out her dress and climbed reluctantly down the ladder, preparing to greet the stranger.

And there was Alex, alone in the room and staring at her. Joyce gasped and reached out for the ladder to steady herself.

"God, what happened to you?" he exclaimed. He stepped

towards her. The sight of her eye horrified him. It changed everything. It turned his view of Joyce full circle again, from callous user of men back to captive. "Did Nikos do that to you?"

Joyce ignored the question. "What are you doing here?" she stammered. She looked around in a panic, but Petros and Maria had disappeared. "How did you find me?"

"I didn't know . . . it's like the last time. Petros keeps leading me to you."

"Are you leaving?" Joyce pointed to his bags lying by the door.

Alex swallowed. "Yes. Well, I was, but Petros persuaded me to stay until the next ferry."

Joyce made her way to one of the chairs at the table. She sat, put her head in her hands, and stared down at the tablecloth. Her face was distorted, swollen and purpling beneath her eye. One side of her mouth was puffy, making her look as if she were sneering. It was obvious to her now that her father-in-law was throwing Alex her way. She wondered if Petros was trying to get rid of her — handing her over to some other man like a pair of secondhand boots. Or was it only that he wanted her to be happy?

"You were going to leave without telling me?" she said tonelessly.

Alex did not reply. He was trying to read her. She sounded more defeated than he had ever heard her. The bravado and quiet wisdom he had always seen under her naiveté seemed to have been battered into a despairing calm.

He sat down at the table across from her. Then reached for her hand. She let it lie quietly in his grasp.

"Joyce, tell me what's been happening to you."

But Joyce was frowning down at the table. "Are you still angry?" she asked. "At me, I mean." She was speaking dully, her voice weary and flat, as if nothing she said mattered anymore.

"Angry?" he repeated, stalling. "Of course not."

She pulled her hand out of his. "Is it because of that disease?

I shouldn't have accused you, I realize now. I didn't mean to insult you. I did get it from Nikos. The doctor said he had it. So you and I couldn't have given it to each other."

Alex stared at her, his long face confused. "You mean you didn't have it when we first . . . you know, in Ayiassos?"

"I told you, I got it from Nikos. Why are you saying this?" Joyce gazed at him, puzzled, then understood. She sat up straight, her cheeks flushing. "You mean you thought I got it from somebody else? Oh, Alex, you're just like all the Greek men. You think I sleep around with everybody, don't you?"

"No," he said quickly. "I'm not like that. I just didn't understand. I didn't mean to imply anything."

"Like hell you didn't." She stared at him a moment. "What do you care, anyway? You've packed your bags. You're free, you've boasted about that enough. So why don't you just get on your damn boat and go?" Her voice choked up at this point, more with anger than with sorrow, but she controlled it. I will not break down, I will not appeal to his pity, she swore to herself.

"If you would only explain," Alex said desperately. He stood up and began to pace in his frustration, looking elongated and gaunt in the darkening room. This is like starting an avalanche, he thought. Every move I make, every word I say brings us closer to catastrophe. At last he turned to her and spoke, his voice low and urgent. "Joyce, I will stay if you want. I do care, I've never stopped caring. I thought you were the one who didn't. I thought you never cared for me at all."

But Joyce had had enough of lying men. Even Petros, whom she had thought of as the most honest and pure-hearted man she had ever met, turned out to have a mistress. She sat in silence, her arms still folded, her bruised face turned to the wall. Their precious moments alone ticked away.

Alex leaned over her. "Who hit you?" he said. "Tell me that at least."

Joyce looked away. "My mother-in-law," she said reluctantly.

"She hit me because I'm Jewish." Her mouth twisted into an inadvertent smile. "I guess it sounds kind of funny now."

Alex straightened up. "Because you're Jewish?" he repeated.

"Yes. I finally told her." Joyce looked over at him with a shrug. "Petros is hiding me out here until it all blows over."

"Jesus. Are you all right?"

She stood up. "Of course I'm not all right," she replied calmly. "How could I be all right?"

Alex took both her hands in his. "Is it Nikos? Are you sad he's gone?"

"Sad?" Joyce broke from his grasp and turned away. "God, I don't know. All I know is that now everything'll be up in the air for months. It's all falling apart." And at those words, she collapsed back into her chair. "Anyway, what's it to you?" she added bitterly. "You're leaving."

But Alex was so thrilled that Nikos was gone, he risked being honest. "I was jealous," he said simply. "I thought you loved him."

Joyce looked down at the table. "I did. Maybe I do. I still want it to work."

"But why?"

"Oh . . ." She put her hands over her face. "Because I like it here. Because I love Dimitra and Petros. Because I don't have anywhere else to go."

"You do have somewhere else to go," he said gently. "Come here, my love," and he opened his arms wide, until Joyce stepped into them.

XII

Later that evening, when Dimitra awakened, calmer now from her nap, she was surprised to find the house and the yard empty. Phoebus was there, chewing on a lonely tuft of grass and flicking his tail at the flies, but there was no sign of her husband or Joyce. Where on earth have those two devils gone? she muttered to herself. But she could not worry about that now. More pressing matters weighed on her mind. She would make a cup of coffee, then go straight to the church and consult Father Poulianos. She had been harboring an infidel in her house, her heart was in tatters — she needed help.

Dimitra was still terribly shaken by Joyce's confession, but it took only the walk from her house to the priest's cottage to send her resentment of her daughter-in-law spinning even deeper. How dare that girl corrupt my house with her lies! she thought as she strode down the path, a solid, stalwart figure shrouded in a dark blue dress and head wrap. "How dare she corrupt my son!" She felt as if he had been polluted. Worse, as if her mother love had been polluted. She was haunted by the remarks she had made to Joyce — that Joyce showed her love more than her son did, that she had been grateful and generous in a way that Nikos would never have dreamed. How could she have uttered such words about her own beloved boy, let alone shouted at him, hit him as she had just this past week? How could she have let Joyce shove Nikos aside in her heart? Worst of all, how could she have blamed her innocent son for the rift in his marriage when all along it was Joyce who had been deceiving and lying?

Joyce had committed the worst of all sins, Dimitra decided. She had made Dimitra turn against her own flesh and blood.

Dimitra found Father Poulianos standing outside his dilapidated house behind the church, varnishing somebody's dinner table in the evening's waning light. He had cast aside his black robes in favor of old trousers and a workman's apron, over which his long, bushy beard dangled incongruously. When Dimitra appeared, panting and wringing her gnarled hands, he was bent over the tabletop, stroking it with a paintbrush.

Father Poulianos had spent the thirty years of his adult life locked in a struggle against poverty. Neither highly educated nor even respected, except by a few old women of Kastron, he played confessor, doctor, and psychiatrist for the entire town while also performing his duties as priest — all for pay too low to support his wife and four children. So he took on what extra work he could. He mended people's cabinets and tables. He painted and he varnished. And, for a small fee, he exorcised the odd demon from a villager's home, spouse, child, or cow.

He greeted Dimitra wearily, invited her to sit, and asked if she minded if he continued his varnishing while they talked. Dimitra murmured assent and sank onto a rickety stool beside his back door, sighing deeply. She looked about the shadowy courtyard with a critical eye. The priest's house was in much worse shape than her own, more like a series of overlapping stone huts than a respectable home. Its walls were mossy and cracked. One side was sinking into the ground. Many of the roof tiles were chipped or missing, and the patch of dried earth where she sat was littered with pieces of broken furniture. An occasional child peeped around the corner at her, black eyes winking in insolence. The whole place looked shockingly unkempt.

She turned her gaze severely on the priest. He breathed heavily as he worked, the fumes of the varnish causing him to distort his hairy face into a snarl. Dimitra watched in alarm as the varnish splattered over his magnificent gray-streaked beard.

"*Patris*, may I speak?" she asked at last. Dimitra was not a woman to fear priests.

"Yes, yes, my daughter. Speak. I am listening." Poulianos crouched with a groan to paint the legs of the table.

"O *Patris*, have pity on me! I have such problems in my house I do not know what to do." She paused, but he did not react. "It is about my daughter-in-law," she added pointedly.

The priest nodded, concentrating on the oily paintbrush in his hand. This was only too familiar. "She is rude and insubordinate?" he asked, his patriarchal voice deep and rumbling.

"No, no. It is not that."

"She is lazy?"

Dimitra drew her shawl about her and shivered slightly in the cooling night air. "No, she works hard."

Shrugging, he hobbled, crablike, around to the other side of the table. He was a big man, broad across the shoulders and stout in the belly, and his movements were clumsy, a bulldog trying to walk sideways. "She will not give you grandchildren, is that it?" he said.

"This is true, but she is trying. My son gave her a disease, and now, God forgive him, we do not know."

"What is it then?" he said irritably. The varnish was drying too quickly, and it was making the table look splotched.

Dimitra cleared her throat. "She is a Jew."

The priest stood up and stared at her. "What? Little Joyce?" He thought of her weekly visits, her kneeling and kissing the hands of the Holy Virgin. He spluttered indignantly, then fell silent.

"Yes, *Patris*. She told me only this morning."

He crossed himself. "This is beyond anything I have ever heard!" he cried. He was deeply affronted that a Jew had masqueraded as a Christian in his own church, even hoodwinked him into thinking her a devout young woman. "She has lived with you for how long and never said this before?"

"It has been more than two years, *Patris*." Kneading her hands again, Dimitra began to rock on the stool in distress. "She has been lying all this time. Lying! Can you believe this?"

Father Poulianos stared at her, his gray eyes bulging from beneath their bushy eyebrows. "She is never to come into my church again!" he bellowed.

"I know, I know," Dimitra moaned, still rocking. "My son knows nothing of this," she told the astonished priest. "My daughter-in-law has deceived him, too. *Patris*, do you think this is grounds for annulling their marriage?"

The priest frowned. He stared down at his table, which he dimly realized was looking leprous and blotchy. "I will have to think it over," he said. He ran his big hand over his mustache and down his woolly beard, smoothing it over his chest as if it were a cat. "Were they married in the Greek Orthodox Church?"

"My son said they were, but I have no way of knowing. They were married in America."

Poulianos looked at her sharply. "Are you sure they are legally married, *Kyria* Koliopoulou? I don't mean to offend, but some young people these days have ways of . . ."

"No, no!" Dimitra said, shocked. "I have seen the papers. Of course they are legally married. My son would not lie to his own mother, even if his wife is a snake!"

The priest mumbled dubiously into his beard and turned back to his work, shaking his head in disgust. "I have never heard of such a thing. A Jew sneaking into our church! I am speechless."

"But *Patris*," Dimitra moaned again, "there is something worse."

"Nothing could be worse!"

"It is worse! She has poisoned my love for my son!" And Dimitra began to wail. "She has driven the sweetness out of him. She has even made me fight with him, my own boy! And now he has turned against me and gone away to sea, without even my blessings to keep him safe. O *Patris*, this demon has come to destroy my life!"

"Never let her in your house again!" the priest thundered, waving his paintbrush for emphasis. "She is a devil, it is clear. You must pray tonight, pray to the Holy Virgin to protect your family from this American demon. Throw her out, *Kyria* Koliopoulou, throw her out!"

"I will, I will," Dimitra cried, rocking on her stool in an ecstasy of revenge. "She will never set foot in my home again!"

For the first two days after Joyce's departure, Petros steered clear of Dimitra. She slammed about the house and yard with all the violence of the Three Furies, so he did his best to stay out of her way. She bought candles and lit them under their household icons, praying loudly to the Virgin and Saint Dimitrios to purge the house of Jewish spirits, making sure that Petros could hear every word. She boiled and pounded Joyce's sheets, which were perfectly clean, grumbling about the stains of sin. She even invited Father Poulianos to the house, much to Petros's disgust, and asked him to sprinkle holy water over her and all the rooms with a sprig of basil in order to exorcise them of Joyce's demons. Then she bundled up the rest of the girl's clothes and her few belongings, and thrust them into Petros's arms.

"Get rid of these. Burn them for all I care. I do not want to know where you have hidden the girl. And never mention her name in front of me again!"

Petros waited for all this venom to subside. Meanwhile, the house grew sad and empty, just as it had during the days after Nikos first went to sea when he was seventeen. Sometimes, after he had left, it had felt as if they'd never had a son, as if the sounds of his childish laughter, his prattle, his footsteps had all been a dream — as if they had never escaped those lonely, aching years before he was born. Now, with Joyce gone, the house again was silent and cold, the garden dull, the fields bleak. Petros continued to dig and weed, to cut and harvest — harder than ever without Joyce to help him — but it seemed pointless now. Just a lot of work to keep a couple of lonely old bags of bones alive.

Finally, after forty-eight hours of furious purging, Dimitra growled to Petros as they sat at their evening meal, "Well, what have you done with her? Sent her back to America?"

"Of course not," Petros answered carefully. "She has no home there anymore."

"She has no home here, either. She is a snake and a demon. I never want to see her Jewish face again."

"Stop it, Dimitra," Petros said, his patience exhausted at last. "You are too good to hold hatred like this in your heart. We did not fight the Fascists for this." He looked at her, his old eyes damp and soft. "Dimitra, *manoula mou,* tell me what it is that makes you so unhappy. It is not this business of religion alone, I know it. What has Joyce done to make you rage at her so?"

At first Dimitra would not answer. She was ashamed of her fuss about the Judaism. She knew it was an excuse.

"Dimitra, little wife, don't be a stubborn old mule. Tell me what is wrong." Petros leaned towards her. They were at their rough table, eating bean soup by the light of one candle.

"It is her lies," Dimitra muttered at last. "How could she lie like that to people who love her?"

"She was afraid. Can you not understand that?"

Dimitra scowled. "She who has never faced a gun — afraid? Bah. She is a coward."

"What else is it, Dimitra? Tell me."

Dimitra took a spoonful of beans and gummed them slowly, the few teeth in her mouth too weak to chew. "It is Nikos," she said at last. "She has poisoned my heart against him. She has made me turn away from him. My own son, for whom I would give my life!"

Petros frowned. This he had expected. He had wondered when Dimitra would wake up and realize that she had allowed her daughter-in-law to supplant her son in her affections. He had wondered, too, when Dimitra would finally recognize Nikos's faults.

Petros himself had felt the pain of his disappointment in Nikos for years. He had struggled again and again to keep alive the hope that the boy would learn some magnanimity — he still struggled with it. But Dimitra had always been blind. It was normal for a Greek mother to be devoted to her son — it was through a son, after all, that a woman won her glory. Her son's achievements were more important even than her husband's, for she had made the boy with her own body, while the husband had come from the loins of another. Dimitra, however, had carried this to an extreme. She had always thought her son perfect, a saint. All his life she had blamed his faults on the envy of others. Only now had she begun to see how weak he was: that he was a boy who expected worship without earning it, who thought his beauty alone would win him the respect of a woman as good as Joyce. Who whined like a child if denied what he wanted. But instead of turning her anger on Nikos, Dimitra had turned all her blame on Joyce.

"Joyce did not make our Nikos so spoiled," Petros said. "It is the sailor's life that has done it, the company he keeps. It has taught him to think only of himself." Petros would never say what he really thought: that it was Dimitra's fault for over-indulging their son, and his own for not stopping her.

"No," Dimitra said, crossing her plump arms. "If he had found a nice Greek wife who did not question him, who obeyed him, who did not lie like a demon, he would never have run away like this. He would have faced his responsibilities. It is because she is an American and corrupt."

"You are not being just, *manoula mou.* Joyce loved him devot-
edly when she first came here."

Dimitra spat on the ground in disgust, her arms still clamped
defiantly across her chest. "Huh. Who knows what she felt? We
can trust nothing about her, this snake, this liar. My Nikos
trusted her, old man! He loved her, he loves her still. I thought
it was he who was unfair to her, but now I see my mistake. It
was *she* deceiving him! She has caused him such pain, my ten-
derhearted boy. I could kill her for this alone!"

"But, Dimitra, she was trying so hard. Could you not see
this? Nikos came home, after being away for months, behaving
like an emperor, expecting her to fall at his feet and obey him
like a Greek wife. She has not been brought up to this. What he
expected of her was not reasonable."

Dimitra stared at Petros, openmouthed. "What nonsense you
are talking! What is wrong with wanting a wife who obeys
him? It is his right!"

And have you granted me such a right? Petros wanted to say,
ready to laugh. But he refrained. "The mother can be indul-
gent," he said. "The wife can add spice."

"But she has made me turn my back on my own son!"

Petros looked at her, his tired face affectionate and sad. "He
will forgive you, do not worry. You can do no wrong in his eyes.
He loves you. Nobody can take a son's love from his mother."

"Not even a wife? Perhaps she has hurt him so much he will
never come back!" Dimitra looked at him, her eyes narrowed
and fearful, and he saw that she was genuinely terrified that
Joyce had driven her son away forever.

Petros sighed. If his wife kept thinking like this, she and
Joyce would never reconcile. Joyce had come between a mother
and son. There was no mercy for that.

So Dimitra dragged around the house and the yard, bereft
and lonely, tending the animals and the plants, cooking her
food, and preparing for the coming winter. And Petros looked
after Joyce.

Petros had never been so duplicitous in his life. True, he had kept his affair with Maria a secret for twenty years now, but he had persuaded himself that there was nothing sinful about it. He only saw her once in a while, sometimes not even for a month, so he was able to tell himself that he was not depriving Dimitra of his company. He gave Maria few gifts and no money, for she was richer than he, so he took nothing from Dimitra to be with her. Maria talked over village matters with him but asked him nothing of his family life, so he betrayed no confidences — he had been much more considerate than most men were about their mistresses. He loved Dimitra. It was just that he went to Maria for a rest, he told himself, for the chance to be with a woman of more learning than his wife, who was not frantic with work and mother love. He did not think that Dimitra might have welcomed the conversation and seed he had squandered on Maria.

But now, for the first time in his life, Petros had to plot, not merely hide. He had to devise ways to slip Maria a few drachmas to help cover Joyce's food and board. And he had to conceal Joyce's whereabouts from Dimitra so that she would not find out about Maria.

Joyce, meanwhile, was trying to earn some money. Maria was a seamstress, working all day in either her home or her courtyard, so the morning after Joyce arrived in her house she asked Maria to teach her the skill. Without her own money, Joyce knew now, she would always be at the beck and call of others.

Maria agreed and, wheeling her old sewing machine out to a sunny spot in the courtyard, placed Joyce beside her so they could talk together while they worked. Joyce enjoyed this. She liked the warm cobbles of the courtyard that made her chair rock beneath her, the scent of the flowers and herbs in the pots around them. She liked, too, the whirring of the machine, which Maria pedaled with both feet like a cyclist, hemming sheets, tablecloths, or bridal nightgowns. Joyce only didn't like the sewing. Maria had given her handkerchiefs to embroider, and she found the work so irritating that she could hardly refrain from ripping up the delicate squares of cotton and throwing them over her head.

One day, to relieve the tedium, Joyce asked Maria how long she had been a widow.

"Almost thirty years," Maria replied, her round face looking over at Joyce, her gray eyes lively. "That's longer than a lifetime to you, eh, little American? I was engaged at thirteen and married at sixteen, during the brief euphoria we had between the world war and the civil war, God forgive us Greeks."

"You were only sixteen?"

"Yes. It may seem young to you, but we felt old. My husband, Grigoris he was called, he was a local fisherman's son I'd known all my life. We used to play as children." She smiled wistfully. "He had only the softest fuzz on his upper lip. It tickled me when we kissed. He proposed to me on the beach. 'After I come back a man from the war,' he said, 'we will marry and have forty children.' He gave me a piece of pink coral — who could afford a ring those days? — in which he had bored a small hole. I threaded a thong through it and wore it all the way through the war until the Nazis tore it from my neck."

Joyce looked over at her. "The Nazis captured you?"

"Let me tell you," Maria answered. "It is good for you Americans to hear these things. You see, when my Grigoris left to fight the Fascists he was still a boy. Skinny as the stalk of a poppy, his shoulders thin, his legs scrawny — like a newborn lamb he was. I remember the down on his cheeks glistening in the sun. But he was very beautiful to me, little Joyce. His eyes were so blue, wide like a baby's. When I first saw him in his uniform and that enormous rifle slung over his shoulder, I cried because his face looked so lost."

Maria paused and gazed at Joyce contemplatively. "You modern kids, you don't know how young so many of the soldiers were. My Grigoris, he was so green that when he kissed me good-bye he missed my lips. We were just children. I tucked one ankle behind the other and blushed. My breasts ached, I remember — they were still growing, still tender like buds on my chest. But my feelings were strong as an adult's. 'You don't have to go,' I told him. 'You're too young.' He was only fourteen, but Italy had invaded and no Greek man or boy worthy of his name could refuse to fight."

"How long was he gone?" Joyce asked.

"Three years. It felt like three lifetimes — but then, you know what it is to wait. Finally he returned, miraculously alive, although crisscrossed with scars. He found me bone-thin and weak. My skin was dull and rough from starvation — I had suffered too in this war. He himself looked twenty years older. His face was lined, his hair thin, and he shook like an old man. He screamed in his sleep every night, but when the bells rang out, proclaiming victory against the Germans, he said to me, 'I am not much to marry anymore, but perhaps we can still make a life together.'

" 'I have waited for nothing else,' I told him.

"So we married. It was early in 1946, and we looked like two scarecrows hobbling to the altar. I remember looking in the mirror at my wedding gown and seeing that it hung off me like a shroud. I had made it when he first went away, never suspecting what war would do to me. But still, we had survived, we were together again, and that was a miracle for those days.

"For two months he stayed with me. Then the *andartiko* reached Ifestia, may they all rot in hell. Grigoris would not fight. 'I will not give my life to fight my own people,' he said to me. I thought he was right. What we did not understand was that he had no choice. One night as we lay in bed, the door flew open and three men with guns came in. They dragged Grigoris out of bed at the point of a rifle. 'You join us or die,' they said.

"I screamed curses at them and lunged for the rifle. I had

grown brave and angry during the war. But one of the men knocked me flat out with the butt of his gun."

Maria looked down at her lap. Her sewing lay forgotten on her knees. Joyce watched her, waiting.

"When I woke up," Maria at last continued, her voice quiet, "I found my head oozing from a wound. My mouth was split and swollen, and a stranger's semen was spilled on my thighs. Next to me, on the floor, lay my Grigoris. His chest was exploded by bullets, and a wide, gory smile had been sliced into his face."

Maria glanced at Joyce, her round cheeks bright. "Never let anybody tell you the civil war was worth it," she said. "Never listen to those bastards who say they fought for a cause." And she spat on the ground, three times.

Joyce stared at Maria in a horrified silence.

Maria picked up her sewing. Not once during her story had her voice wavered or the brightness faded from her eyes. "Seven months later," she continued, "the gods took pity on me and I bore twin sons. A Greek widow's salvation, twice over, yes?" She looked at Joyce, smiling. "They are survivors, like their mother. Sometimes I think they learned to battle in the womb, fighting off the invasion of those filthy soldiers and their rape. They survived, the little darlings, and they both look exactly like Grigoris."

Joyce still found it hard to speak. "They are in America now?" she managed to say.

"Yes. As soon as they were grown, they went. They entered the hotel business together, and they have been very smart. They visit me every few summers, and for years now they have been sending me money. Two strong lads, they are, built like tugboats. I see in them what Grigoris would have been."

Joyce nodded. She realized that Maria's sons' money must account for her newly plastered house and her casual independence.

Maria's independence fascinated Joyce. Despite the horrors Maria had undergone, she had an autonomy that Joyce had never seen in married women, not even in her mother back home, and Joyce suspected that Maria had remained unmarried less out of custom than because it suited her. She arranged the sequence of her days without having to accommodate anybody. She decided how much work to take on according to nobody's needs but her own. She received Petros with calm acceptance but little inconvenience. She did not even seem jealous or curious about Dimitra. Not once did she ask Joyce about life in that house. Instead, she was self-contained, she ate and slept well, and observed all around her with an ironic remove.

Maria also had a lively mind, Joyce discovered. She liked to discuss politics as well as her past while the two of them sewed, and to deride the newspapers she brought home from her customers. Like most people in Kastron, Maria wished heartily that the Socialist Party had won the elections. "PASOK will be good for women," she told Joyce one day. "They will clean up the corruption and bribery, sweep all the vermin away. You wait and see. Papandreou will have his turn soon."

She leaned forward, gripping Joyce's arm enthusiastically. "You know what he has promised? Peasant women will get pensions just like the men! Yes! Three thousand drachmas a month!" Maria rubbed her hands up and down her round arms in a delighted hug. "It will serve the old goats right. It will be a time for women again, just as it was for us during the Resistance."

"Weren't you too young to be in the Resistance?" Joyce asked in surprise.

"Too young? No! If Grigoris was not too young at fourteen to fight, I was not too young at thirteen to resist the Fascist vermin. Many girls and boys younger than I joined in."

"What did you do?" Joyce had never grown tired of hearing these stories, even though Dimitra told them so often. The women of Kastron, she had noticed, talked of their roles in the

Resistance with the same pride and defiance with which men recounted their triumphs on the battlefield.

"Oh, what I did!" Maria rocked back in her chair, letting her embroidery drift again to her lap. Her cheeks were flushed, and her straight hair, which she wore up in a tight bun, gleamed in the bright courtyard like a wet black olive.

"I helped to smuggle prisoners away from the Nazis," she said proudly. "We made a chain in the village, a chain of secret houses to pass the soldiers to in the night. Greek boys, English boys . . . boys like my Grigoris who had been caught, imprisoned, some of them tortured. We kept them in basements and henhouses, even in our dowry trunks. Then we sneaked them onto fishing boats in the dead of night so they could sail away free."

"That must have been incredibly dangerous."

"Of course, but what difference did that make? The Nazis had taken over the monastery — you know, up on the mountain — and made it their torture chamber. The screams of those boys — we could hear them all the way down here!" Maria looked at Joyce intently. "No human being could listen to those screams and not be moved to do something." She leaned forward again. "It was not just soldiers they tortured. It was anybody they thought was collaborating with the Allies or struggling for freedom. Mothers, grandmothers, even little girls like me."

"I know," Joyce said quietly, thinking of Dimitra's tales about Natalia. "Did you ever get caught?"

Maria unbuttoned the front of her dress and pulled it down almost to her nipples. There, across the tops of her full white breasts, was a row of deep scars, each one round and ragged. "They burned me with their cigarettes," she said. "Over and over, to make me talk."

She closed her dress again, buttoning it to her collarbone. "But I did not talk, little Joyce, I did not. The other women in the prison, they had been through this and they knew how to give me courage. They sang to me, they told me stories through the bars of their cells. Together we refused to sign statements of repentance, no matter what they did to us. Those of us they decided to kill never showed fear, so as to give strength to the others. We danced and we sang with the condemned women on the eve of their executions. We gave each other lessons, we taught one another whatever it was we knew, just as I am now teaching you to sew. We shared our food, we sang our songs. We made a circle that no Nazi could break." Maria glanced at her with pride. "We discovered how to prevent each other from losing heart."

"How long did they keep you locked up?"

"One year, until I was fourteen. But I was lucky; they spared me. One of my friends, also only thirteen years old, was shot against the wall like a dog."

Maria once more grasped Joyce by the wrist. "We did this for freedom, little Joyce. You Americans, you take your freedom for granted. You spilled your blood for it long, long ago. We have been fighting for it my whole life. Even now. But I will tell you a secret — the big fight is still to come."

"What do you mean?" Joyce said, her wrist aching in Maria's fierce clasp. "You have freedom now for the first time in years and years. You have democracy. Isn't that what you were fighting for?"

Maria let go of her and leaned back again, smiling mysteriously. "You Americans are so naive! You know what I came to see in all my years of prison and war?"

She raised her eyebrows expectantly until Joyce said, "What?"

"I came to see that freedom is in the eye of the beholder. To dictators like Hitler, Mussolini, General Metaxas and the Colonels, even to the monarchists, freedom is nothing but power in their own dirty hands. To the Communists in our civil war, it was an idea, just an idea, but they thought it was worth killing and torturing their own brothers for it. Greek men and women, my little Joyce, they have been dying and killing in the name of freedom since the beginning of history."

Maria's gray eyes were intense, fixed on Joyce but hardly seeing her. "But what have women got out of it, eh? The government may call itself a democracy, but in the home every woman in Greece is still living under a man. Our husbands, our fathers and brothers, even our sons. Can you walk about by yourself whenever you want? Can we marry if we have no dowry? Do we own our own property once we are married? Are we paid equally for our work, or considered the same as men under the law? No, no, no, and no. You must have learned this for yourself living here. Women have been sacrificing themselves all this time for the freedom of men, little Joyce, not for their own."

Joyce listened, fascinated, and a surge of outrage rose in her at Maria's words. It was true, she realized, Maria was right. Why had she not minded this before? Why had she not objected? Now she, too, wanted to fight for justice, be a hero. She, too, wanted to be able to interpret the world around her with a critical eye. When she marketed for Maria the next day, she looked at the old women of Kastron with new curiosity. Had this one been raped like Maria? Had that one been tortured for the freedom of men? Did this or that housewife mind her inferior status — did she even recognize it? These thoughts made Joyce feel more restless than she had in years — longing not merely to run or walk wherever she wanted, to wear her jeans or climb a mountain with Alex, but to make her mark on the world.

In reality, however, since her arrival in Greece, Joyce had never been so paralyzed. She realized that her chances of hanging on to her precious Greek life were wearing thin. Yet if she decided to leave, too many things held her back. She wanted to make peace with Dimitra before she left, but Dimitra would not speak to her. She knew that she could go with Alex, but she never wanted to depend on a man again. She needed money, but had none. And every time she considered writing to her American family to ask for some, humiliation crushed her words. It would be such an admission of failure — as a wife, as a lover, as a person who had thought she'd known her own mind. And after their silence in the face of all her postcards, writing again would feel like crawling. Sitting in Maria's stark house, she closed her eyes and pictured what it would be like to return home. The jeers of her brothers, the pitying looks of her friends. The sneering triumph of her mother. "I told you not to marry him and sure enough you made a mess of it," she could hear mother saying. "You're just as stupid as I thought."

XIII

On the fifteenth day of September, the morning after the last festival of the summer — the Exaltation of the Cross — the women of Kastron marked the end of the season by shaking out their handwoven blankets for the coming winter. They stood in rows in their dark clothes and headscarves, or leaned out of their windows like a collection of plump dolls, and beat the blankets with wooden cooking spoons, all the while calling friendly insults back and forth across the rough stone lanes. The lengths of colored wool flapped against the whitewashed houses like a row of bright flags. Women's voices echoed along the streets. Dust and the smell of autumn dissipated in the cooling air.

Alex propped himself against the frame of the bakery door, watching while he smoked a powerful local cigarette. He had been at work for six hours already, yet it was not even lunchtime. His sleeves were rolled up, revealing tanned forearms, sprinkled now with the burns and scars of a baker, and his shirt was dusted with flour. Lounging against the door like this, his hair swept back and his face browned and tired, he looked more the Greek within him than he ever had in his life.

He took a drag of the cigarette, holding it between thumb and forefinger like a working man. It had been instructive living his days as a village baker — it was just the kind of out-of-classroom education he had touted to Petros. But he had been on Ifestia for over four weeks now, and he felt the island closing in around him. The streets of Kastron were no more private than a vast sitting room, the villagers as close as one family. Everyone knew who thought what, who owned what. Little went on behind a wooden shutter that could not be heard. He was unable to see Joyce without putting her at risk; he could not even talk to her in public — after the wildness of his time at university, a time of breaking rules and flouting convention, these medieval restrictions were chafing at him sorely. He missed urban anonymity, sophistication, and luxury, his educated friends and hot baths. He wanted to walk down a street holding Joyce's hand. To kiss her in a shop. To eat ice cream in a cinema. Above all, he wanted to take her to his bed without danger or interference.

Instead, however, Alex was working harder than he had known possible. After Petros had brought him to Joyce three days ago, he had returned to explain to his bemused aunt that he had decided to stay after all, and ever since he had been throwing himself into work like a man before a whip. Mornings he mixed dough, up to his elbows in the stone trough at the back of the bakery. Afternoons he wielded the long oar, flipping loaves to Eugenia with ever increasing skill. Evenings he emptied and cleaned the vast baking trays that each held a dozen rows of giant, round whole-wheat loaves. Look at me laboring like a peasant, he mocked himself. What wouldn't I do for love? But he kept at it anyhow, working away the time until he could be alone with Joyce.

Grinding out the cigarette with his foot, he asked his aunt if he could take a walk. "Yes, yes," she snapped, waving her hand at him. "Now the festival is over I can spare you for a few hours. Go cough the flour out of your lungs. And bring me some coffee. You are drinking up my whole supply."

Alex said he would and headed down the street. The sky was clouding over, the air felt damp and cold, and he shivered. It was market day, and he was going to see if Joyce was there. He wanted to arrange to visit her during siesta. They had not been alone since he had seen her at Maria's house. They'd had no chance even to talk. Every time he had dropped by during the past three days, Maria or Petros had been there, forcing him into jovial conversation. It was driving Alex mad.

He spied Joyce as soon as he entered the market square. She was standing at a vegetable stall, bargaining for a basket of tomatoes. Like his, her blond hair shone out in the crowd, making her easy to find. He approached her cautiously. "Joyce?"

She started when she saw him. Her black eye had faded to a jaundiced yellow, but she still looked beautiful. Just standing beside her made him weak with desire.

"Hello," he said gently. "Are you going to be alone any time today? My aunt's given me a little time off."

Joyce suddenly became aware of two housewives beside them, watching, so she walked away quickly. Alex understood. He pretended to browse among the onions until he could leave unobserved and follow her into their usual alley.

"Well?" he asked.

Joyce's cheeks were flushed. "If those old crones gossip about me to Dimitra, then I'm really finished. I wish you'd be more careful, Alex. If anyone tells her they saw us, she'll never talk to me again."

"I'm sorry. But why do you care what she thinks after what she did to you?"

"She's a mother to me, Alex. I've told you."

"She's cruel."

"No." Joyce looked up and down the alley nervously, clutching her basket with both arms. Her hair was pulled back in a severe bun, her clothes their usual sacklike shape. Her narrow face looked tired and worried. "She's just . . . stubborn."

"And anti-Semitic."

"And loving."

Alex sighed. "Just tell me," he said at last. "Do you want me to come today or not?"

"Of course I do." Joyce thought a moment. "Come right after lunch. I think Maria might be out. Now go away before you get me in trouble!"

Giving her hand a squeeze, Alex obeyed.

After he left, Joyce headed up the hill to Marina's house, her shoulders hunched against the soldiers' leers and the few raindrops that had begun to fall. She hadn't seen Marina since Dimitra had thrown her out, and Joyce knew that the gossip must have reached her friend by now. She wanted to sort out the truth from the lies.

On the way, she wondered nervously what would happen. If Marina had heard only about the fight with Dimitra, the conversation would flow easily, for feuds between wives and their mothers-in-law were nothing unusual, as Marina herself knew only too well. But suppose she had heard something about Joyce's Judaism? Or, worse, about Alex? If that were the case, it was possible that Marina would not talk to her at all.

Marina lived high up on the hill, in a house that she shared with her husband's numerous family. Unlike Joyce's home with Dimitra, this one was bursting with children, voices shouting from room to room, buckets and wooden cars and the sticks and broken tools that served as toys littering the tile floors. Joyce liked it, though. She missed the presence of children. She had grown up surrounded by them, her Miami block full of young families. Dimitra's house, with just the two old people and Joyce, had often felt lonely.

"Marina?" she called tentatively, approaching with the tomatoes in her basket as a gift.

Marina poked her head out of an upstairs window. Her house was one of those in the white labyrinth, and even though Joyce had visited it many times, she was still not sure where Marina's house ended and the neighbor's began. *"Yassou!"* her friend called, her flaxen braid falling over her shoulder in a thick rope. "I am ironing the laundry. Step over the children and come on up."

Joyce rubbed the heads of Marina's nieces, two grubby little girls who were playing with stones on the outside staircase in spite of the rain. She climbed over them and up to the house, pushing through a curtained doorway at the top. *"Kalimera,"* she said. "I've brought you some tomatoes for lunch." She put the basket down in a corner.

The room smelled of fresh soap and steam and was stiflingly hot. Marina was standing beside a huge pile of shirts and linens, ironing on the tabletop. Next to her the stone fireplace was stoked with coals, three irons heating on the range. Her light blue dress was stained with sweat, and perspiration kept running into her eyes. The baby was crawling about on the floor.

"Thank you," Marina said, wiping her brow. "I will make a salad with them. Yiannis there loves tomatoes."

Joyce crouched down to coo at him. He crawled over and began to poke at her sandals with a soft, fat finger. "How are you, Marina?" she said, still unsure of her welcome. "Has the harvest treated your family well?"

"Oh yes." Marina shrugged her wide shoulders. "My father-in-law is very pleased with himself, the old bastard. His field produced more potatoes this year than ever before — we are drowning in them." She reached into a bowl in front of her and sprinkled a shirt with water. As she pressed the iron over it, the water hissed pleasantly. "All day long now I peel potatoes, I cook potatoes, I eat potatoes. I even dream potatoes. And the more money the old bastard makes, the more shirts he buys. I will be up all night ironing these. Such a vain old cock, he is."

Marina replaced the iron over the fire, flung her long braid back over her shoulder, and picked up a stack of undershirts. "So, what happened to you? You had a fight with an olive tree?"

Joyce's hand went to her eye. "Yes, something like that."

Marina clucked her tongue. "An olive tree who has thrown you out of her house, I hear."

Joyce stood up to face her, leaving the baby to examine her sandaled feet on his own. "What did you hear?" she said, her voice shaking.

Marina spread out an undershirt and looked at Joyce seriously for a moment. "I hear things I would be ashamed to repeat, my friend. This town is full of small-minded, vicious bigots, specially the old crows. Be careful, or they will be stoning you in the streets."

"What are they saying?" Joyce was unable to keep the fear out of her voice. "Tell me, please, Marina."

Marina rolled her eyes. "It is embarrassing."

"Please. I understand it's not your opinion."

"Well." Marina picked up a newly heated iron. "They say you are a blasphemer and a heathen. That you have put a curse on Dimitra that will make her die before her time. This I know is nonsense. Stupid old gossips."

"I am Jewish, Marina. That is what they mean. That's why my mother-in-law threw me out."

Joyce waited, regarding Marina steadily, but she had to hide her hands in her apron pockets. They were trembling.

Marina ironed another shirt, saying nothing, while Joyce watched her anxiously. Surely Marina was not so small-minded as to reject her for this? If she were, Joyce had badly misread her.

"Why didn't you tell me?" Marina burst out at last, looking up at her indignantly, her face red. "How could you be my closest friend and not tell me such a thing?"

Joyce pulled her hands out of her pockets and stared down at them. She felt more ashamed now than she had even with Sarah and Nicola. "I didn't tell anyone," she said at last. "I was . . . afraid. And in my country these things don't matter so much. It's private what religion you are."

"*Pa pa pa,*" Marina spluttered. "Remind me never to live in such a place. Your religion is private in America but your sex life is out there for all to see, right?"

Joyce smiled, relieved. Marina was back to her old self. "Something like that."

"What do I care if you are a Jew?" Marina went on. "As long as you are not a Turk," she added with a wink. "Come, help me fold these shirts. I must change Yiannis."

Joyce went to work gladly, relief infusing her with affection for Marina. The baby gurgled while Marina changed him on the floor, throwing his soiled diapers into a bucket. "When I am not washing and ironing my father-in-law's shirts, I am washing this little brat's diapers. A laundress for the men in this family, that is what I've become," she grumbled. "So, my wayward friend, is the she-dragon going to forgive you?"

"I don't know. I've never seen her so angry. And she will tell Nikos, then who knows what will happen."

"Nikos doesn't know either? You *are* in trouble, my girl!"

Joyce looked at Marina, who was crouched on the floor powdering the baby's bottom. His nub of a penis jiggled under her ministrations, like a rubber toe. "Do you think Nikos will send me away when he finds out?" she asked.

At this Marina stopped rubbing her baby's legs and looked up at Joyce. "No, I am sure he won't. I have never seen a husband moon over a wife like he does over you. He will forgive you gladly, don't worry."

"But it's not like that anymore, Marina." Joyce ran her hand over a rough, home-woven shirt. "He's angry at me all the time now."

Marina deftly pinned the new diaper onto Yiannis and stood up with him on her hip. "You can win him over. Men are always like this, moody as my Yiannis here. Write to him, tell him while he is still at sea and give him time to digest it before he comes back."

"Marina, you are a good friend. But if Nikos turns against me

I'll have to leave. I love the life here, I'll miss you if I go, but I can't stay without love with my husband."

"Of course you can. Nikos is a sailor. You need only put up with him once every few months. A few days of wifely duty, he's gone, and you are left in peace again. It sounds like a perfect arrangement to me."

Joyce glanced at Marina, not sure whether she was joking. "A life without love? You think that's perfect?"

"Have a baby, then you won't care. The love of a man is nothing to the love of a baby. Have a son and you will never be lonely again." Marina lifted her chubby offspring into the air and kissed his pudgy thighs. "The men can all jump in the sea, as far as I am concerned. Just we women and our little cherubs, that's all we need." She nuzzled Yiannis and laughed.

But that's not true for me, Joyce thought with a shudder. Not for me.

When Alex appeared at Maria's house that afternoon, he was delighted to find Joyce alone.

"Maria had to go to a customer's," she explained with a shy smile. "She won't be back till after siesta."

"And Petros? He's not going to pop in on us, is he?"

Joyce laughed. "Not this time. Though who knows."

Alex took her in his arms. "Thank God," he muttered, burying his face in her hair. "It's so bloody hard to get a moment alone with you. It's killing me."

Upstairs, in the narrow trestle bed that Maria had lent her, Joyce and Alex prepared to make love indoors for the first time. Alex was tentative, for he was not sure how wounded Joyce felt after her illness. He undressed her slowly, undoing her loose shift button by button, slipping it off her shoulders while he kissed her neck, her breasts, and kneeled to kiss her belly. When she was naked on the bed, she watched him strip, too, and commented on the expanded muscles in his arms and shoulders.

"That baker's work suits you," she said, laughing, and touched his newly broadened chest with the tip of her tongue.

"Yes, it's the oar. It's like lifting barbells all day long. I hurt all over."

"They're making a man of you in Greece," she said jokingly.

"That's what my aunt says, too," Alex replied, trying to fit himself on the bed beside her. "I'm not sure it's entirely flattering."

"Be careful," Joyce said to him. "I might still be tender inside." And indeed she was tense as he caressed her. "I think it's the sickness," she whispered. "It's made me scared."

Alex longed to make love to her recklessly the way he had done on the beach, to plunge into her from every side — he had been waiting for her so long. But he felt her wariness and controlled himself. Nevertheless, as he caressed her delicately, patiently, straining to keep his own desire in check, he felt a growing fury at Nikos. When Alex had met Joyce she had been more abandoned and unself-conscious than he'd ever thought possible in a woman. Now she shrank from his caresses as if they were blows. Nikos had polluted her passion.

"Are you ready?" Alex said at last. Joyce nodded uncertainly. "Tell me if it hurts and I'll stop."

It did hurt. Joyce clenched her teeth to prevent herself crying out. It was less a physical pain than the fear of it, as if she expected to be ripped apart. "I can't," she finally gasped, pushing Alex off her. "I can't. I'm sorry." And she covered her face with her hands.

It wasn't that Joyce did not feel desire. Quite the opposite. The sight of Alex's slender body, his waist bending gracefully as he moved, aroused her instantly. But as soon as he touched her, she became afraid. Her body seemed split, the desire and the fear dividing her from herself as if a magician's saw had cut her in two.

Alex lay beside her, thwarted, his lust dissipating as he sensed her anxiety. This is like another test, he thought. I've sneaked into her house disguised, begged at the suitor's table, strung my bow — but I am not accepted yet.

"I'll wait until you're ready," he said at last. "We'll have other chances. We can take it slowly."

She nodded and rested her head on his wide chest. "Let's just talk for a while," she said. "I just want to talk."

So they did. Over the next few days, Alex sneaked away from his aunt's every afternoon during siesta, and both he and Joyce sacrificed sleep in order to be together. They still had to meet in secret because Joyce had no wish to be hauled up before the courts by Dimitra, ostracized even more than she was already, or chased by outraged widows hurling stones. But they could creep off into their dark corners now, hiding like lizards in the cracks between rocks. And if the weather permitted, they could even walk through the sleeping town separately, to meet up in dusty fields or on the rocks leading to Kondias, where they could hold their furtive conversations alone.

The conversations Joyce liked best were about Alex's days at university. When he mentioned the courses he had taken in philosophy and literature, history and political science, she seized on his words and made him describe what he had learned. He would have preferred to talk about her family in Florida and her life among the Ifestian peasants, about love, but she quickly grew impatient with these topics. She wanted to hear about Aristotle and Homer, Plato and Aristophanes, appalled that she had lived all this time in Greece while knowing so little of its past. She was puzzled by Sartre and Wittgenstein, all the rage at university when Alex had been there, for her mind had none of the training one needs to form philosophical arguments. But the books Alex lent her she absorbed quickly and hungrily. She read *The Odyssey* in a week and at last understood Alex's jokes. She read *Madame Bovary* and wept as she recognized the obsessive lusts of a trapped woman. She read books by Emile Zola and George Eliot and Leo Tolstoy. Every one opened a lock within her, and released a hunger for more.

When Joyce was apart from Alex and his books, however, she found herself living in a strange limbo between the housewife she was supposed to be and the hidden mistress she was now. Deprived of selling at the market, which she badly missed, living exiled from her mother-in-law, she felt more the lizard than ever, slinking between the crevices of society, darting into the open only when nothing threatened. Maria was not like that, for as a widow and mother she had respectability, and Petros was discreet. But Joyce, as a still young and childless woman, as a woman whose deceptions had left her alone and reviled, had slipped out of her niche in village life.

She felt this most keenly on market days, a time when the men and women of the village mingled freely and exchanged gossip and news. Other than Marina and one or two of the new brides, most of the housewives had never been overly friendly to Joyce, except when hoping to get a bargain out of her; but now when she arrived, her basket over her arm, they turned their wrapped heads aside and moved away without a word. Joyce knew the news had spread that she was an infidel Jew. That she had been banished by Dimitra for being a bad wife. She only hoped that no one had guessed about Alex. The soldiers, too, were worse than ever, following and taunting her as if they could sense her fallen status. Only the old men were kind. And Marina.

There were also the terrible moments when she caught sight of Dimitra. Her mother-in-law had to do her own selling now, and several times Joyce saw her hobble into town with Phoebus to sell her few extra autumn tomatoes, her squash and eggs and *peponi* melons. Dimitra never acknowledged her, and each time was like a slap. But Joyce noticed that she looked tired and unhappy, her back bent more than usual, her movements slow.

How long can she work like this, all alone? Joyce wondered. How long is she going to hold out against me?

Meanwhile, Joyce continued to try to make money. She took on a few sewing jobs through Maria, once she was good enough, even though they made her fidget agonizingly in her chair, but they paid so little it was hardly worth it. She offered her services to the shopkeepers in town, only to be turned away with a pitying laugh, like a mangy dog. She also tried to find someone to hire her to teach English, but she was a pariah now and nobody wanted her near the village children. Even Marina could not help, except to offer her company. Joyce grew increasingly frustrated. What would she do if nobody let her earn a drachma?

"Don't worry about money," Alex said to her when she complained. "Just leave with me. I'll pay our way to Athens. I have friends there we can stay with for free."

Her answer was always the same. "I have to make it up with Dimitra first. And I want to go on my own money. I'm fed up with depending on other people."

But Joyce had no money. So September grew into October and nothing changed, except the weather.

October was surprisingly harsh to Alex, who had only visited Greece before in the summer, during *kalokeri*, as the Greeks call it, "the good time." The winds could be harsh on Ifestia, especially given its lack of trees, howling around the island like banshees, smashing the fishermen's caïques against the harbor wall. The women struggled through town bent double, their scarves flapping madly at their necks. Goats and sheep huddled together under outcroppings of rock, trying to warm themselves. Alex discovered for the first time just how primitive life on the island could be. No central heating, no electric fires. The peasants warmed themselves with coal and what wood they could find. For him, there was nothing but his aunt's fiery oven and the heat of his own body. He tried for two days at the telephone office before he could get a call through to his mother in England.

"Send me all my jumpers and rain gear," he begged. "I'm freezing my arse off here."

"Isn't it time you came home?" she said, her voice far away and tinny. "The summer holiday is long over now."

"I can't talk anymore, Mum, it's costing me a fortune." And he hung up.

The colder the weather grew, the harder it was to find the privacy to make love to Joyce. Ifestia was an island built for the outdoor life, and without either of them having a home of their own they had no dependable place to go. The beaches were wet and hostile, the rocks slick with rain. Maria stayed home more and more, preventing Alex from visiting. He was growing wild with frustration over this. It made him more eager to leave than ever. But on the few afternoons or evenings he and Joyce did have together, when Maria was visiting customers or celebrating a name day with a relative across town, he felt as if he had entered a dream.

Joyce always greeted him with a special smile when she knew they would be alone. They might eat or drink a little, but they no longer needed wine to dispel any shyness between them. Often, she simply took his hand and led him up the ladder to her room. There, they pulled her heavy stuffed mattress to the floor — they had given up trying to fit him on the bed — and held each other for warmth, undressing slowly as their desire heated them. Sometimes, if they had not been together for a day or two, he still had to move carefully, making sure he was tender and responsive to her mood. At other times she was all passion and impatience, and wouldn't even wait for him to peel off her clothes before she pulled him into her, arching and hissing with pleasure. He sent for more condoms, promising to repay his astonished friend when he returned. "Don't wait," Joyce would gasp, pulling up her dress. "I want you now."

After sessions like these, Alex would stumble back to his

aunt's like a drunk. It's no wonder I can't get off this island, he thought as he returned, dazed, to the bakery. I am bewitched.

Joyce, meanwhile, tried to make herself decide what to do. She, too, was consumed by passion, thinking constantly of Alex, aching for him, wishing she could fall asleep in his arms and not always have to send him home. During the nights, when he could never be with her, she yearned for him, for his smooth skin and scarred forearms, for the assuring board of his chest, just as she had once yearned for Nikos. But at the same time she knew that this could not go on. During those months she had waited for her husband she'd had a purpose, a family, and work that filled her days. Now she was just drifting. Caught in the purgatory of her feud with Dimitra. Working at trivial jobs for Maria. Penniless and, once again, of no use to anybody.

XIV

While Joyce was hiding out at Maria's, Dimitra was growing afraid that she had made a terrible mistake. Such a thought was new to her, for all her life she had been certain of her rectitude, sure that her every decision was upheld and protected by the Holy Virgin herself. Why else would the Virgin have spared her the death and misery most of her friends and sisters had suffered during the wars? Why else had Dimitra never been caught when she fed the starving and slipped comforts to prisoners in the Second World War? When all the men she knew had gone off to fight the Fascists, many never to return, why else had Petros come back without so much as a flesh wound? What could all this luck have been but the Blessed *Panagia's* protection?

Even during the *andartiko* her luck had held. All around her young girls left their villages to become soldiers for the so-called Democratic Army, the royalist forces backed by Britain and the United States to defeat the Communists. Some of these girls went to war voluntarily, but many were dragged from their villages by force and packed off to the mountains to fight. As a childless wife, her husband away in Lesbos, Dimitra was prime recruiting material — but the Virgin saw fit just then to allow her finally to become pregnant. Thus, while two of her nieces and many of her friends went off to find death at the hands of their fellow Greeks, the soldiers permitted Dimitra to stay at home and watch her belly grow.

Nikos was born on December sixth, the day of Saint Nicholas, the saint of children and sailors — was this not also the Virgin's work? It was 1947, in the middle of war, starvation, and a bitter winter, yet the baby was perfect. Dimitra fed him everything she could find to eat, taking only enough for herself to keep standing. Thanks to the milk from the nanny goat she hid in the cellar and the jugs of water she made herself drink every day, she was able to nurse him. Nikos not only survived, constitutionally as strong as his mother, but thrived while other infants starved to death.

By the time Nikos was a year old, the Communists were losing. In revenge, they planted land mines all over the northern regions. The first person Dimitra knew who was killed by one of these was her own niece Savinna, the youngest of all her sister's children. She had gone up the mountain to hunt for dandelion greens to eat. She bent to pluck a flower — who knows what kind — a mountain flower, sweet and delicate, a harbinger of spring. All her fingers were blown off, her head was splattered. Twelve years old.

Dimitra's best friend's daughter lost a hand and half a leg, and so was never marriageable. Three children from Kastron were blown up also, one only a baby. Objects that had once been everyday, ordinary, even friendly — the rock in one's goat pasture, a fig tree providing shade by a stream, an ancient wall that had once held a sheep's pen, a watermelon hidden from the guerrillas under a pile of straw — these became menacing, terrifying. Deadly.

Some of the older men grew so afraid of the mines that they took to making their wives walk in front of them up the mountain paths, instead of the customary twenty paces behind. It was not uncommon then to see a woman teetering under a bundle of wood, her eyes cast modestly to the ground, while her husband lazed slowly behind her on his donkey, waiting to see if she would explode.

Dimitra watched all this as her body ripened into mother-hood. Her black eyes flashed, her broad feet placed themselves firmly along the paths. She scoured the fields despite the mines, hunting for dandelions and wild onions to grind up for Nikos. She planted nasturtiums, knowing that most soldiers didn't realize they were edible and so wouldn't steal them, and slept in the cellar with her goat tethered to her foot. She cultivated hidden patches of spinach and beans, cooked snails and roots into mulch for herself and the baby.

Nothing blew up.

Then the Communists were defeated and Petros returned, speechless, infested, but unscathed. And fell in love with Nikos.

I am blessed, Dimitra decided. I am indeed protected.

How ironic it was, therefore, that now almost thirty years later, with no war threatening, no starvation, and no land mines exploding, she felt weaker than ever before in her life. For the first time since Nikos left home, Dimitra had lost what was most dear to her, as if her own tenacity had turned back on her for revenge. Day after day she wondered what had happened to her special status with the Virgin; why, after protecting her for so long, the Holy One had chosen now to punish her with sorrow and loss. Was it for taking a Jew under her roof? For preferring her infidel daughter-in-law to her own son? Or was it for being unforgiving and cruel?

So, as Dimitra trailed alone about the house doing her chores, nobody to talk to, Petros removed and preoccupied, she blamed herself for the first time for an action of her own. She had driven away the one comfort of her old age, and it made her heart ache unbearably. She missed the soft patience of Joyce's companionship. Her labor, her listening ear. Their giggles, their fights, the sweet obedience that reminded her of little Natalia. She wanted Joyce back so badly she was ready to face ostracism from her neighbors, even to risk the Virgin's further wrath. Above all, Dimitra wanted Joyce back so that, when Nikos returned, he could make her pregnant and give Dimitra a grandson.

But Dimitra was paralyzed by her own stubbornness. She couldn't make a move towards reconciliation without help. She needed Petros to talk her into it, to force her to relent. So she waited and waited for him to make his move.

Petros, however, remained silent on the subject. After that first argument, he no longer tried to persuade Dimitra to take Joyce back, or even to make her admit that her condemnation of Joyce's religion was unjust. Petros knew better than that — he knew an argument would only backfire, force Dimitra further into the murky caverns of her own pride. He knew the best way to wear his wife down was with patience.

Dimitra watched him in puzzlement, unable to understand what he was up to. Finally, too maddened to wait any longer, she tried to prod him into a fight.

"*Barbas*," she said one night as they sat by the fire — she liked to call him "old man" instead of the more respectful "husband." "I have been thinking that we ought to write to our Nikos and tell him the bad news about Joyce. Perhaps he should come back and make her convert, if he still wants her."

Dimitra gazed at Petros expectantly. Several things she had just said were calculated to enrage him.

"He'll find out when he returns," Petros replied with a shrug. "But if he wants to keep her, he will have to accept her as she is."

"But she is a devil! It is wrong to let our son be so deceived."

Petros picked up a poker to resettle a log. "You will have to accept her, too, my wife, if you want her back."

"Never! She must convert!"

"Have it your way." He yawned, and refused to add another word.

After that, Dimitra grew afraid. Petros must have resisted her bait because Joyce did not want to return! That thought was unbearable to her, for if it were so, she would have nobody, nothing anymore. She would be as lonely as she had been before Nikos was born. As devastated as when Natalia died.

So Dimitra plodded about her work, sad and remorseful but too locked in pride and fear to do anything about it. Her back stooped, her lips puckered around her gap-toothed mouth, and she looked more than ever like one of those countless old women of southern Europe, their faces the texture of cracked earth and their bodies encased in shapeless dark dresses, like the shells of black beetles.

When Joyce appeared at the threshold of her in-laws' house on a cold and rainy afternoon in early October, Dimitra was still too ashamed of herself to show any joy. Instead, she narrowed her sunken eyes and filled her mouth as if to spit.

"*Pethera*," Joyce said hastily, stepping out of range. "I'm not here to ask to come back. Only to bring you this." She held out a fresh red mullet she had bought with the few drachmas Petros had smuggled her. It was Dimitra's favorite fish, and although it was wrapped in newspaper, Joyce knew that her mother-in-law was perfectly aware of what it was.

Dimitra remained motionless at her door for some time. Now that Joyce was actually here, her pride paralyzed her. She contemplated the girl suspiciously. Her daughter-in-law looked timid and lumpy in her layers of warm clothes. Her face was pinched — humble. What harm could there be in letting the girl in to dry herself? Dimitra thought of Father Poulianos thundering while he waved his paintbrush about and banished Joyce from her house. What did that silly man know about love, let alone about mothers and daughters? He couldn't even varnish a table properly.

"May I come in *Pethera?*" Joyce asked formally. She understood Dimitra's pride, knew from long practice that she had to pander to it.

Dimitra sniffed. She said nothing but at last stepped outside and went around to the back of the house to fool the evil spirits — the signal for Joyce to do the same. Joyce followed her, closing the door behind them gratefully. The cold had turned her fingers numb.

"Sit." Dimitra grunted, gesturing to the fireplace. "You have grown too skinny. You look like a frozen shish kebab wrapped up like that."

Joyce pulled a chair over to the fire and began to undo her layers. She was bundled up in the jeans Alex had brought back to her, which she now wore every day, a woolen dress which Dimitra had made her, and a sweater, also knitted by Dimitra, the rain beading on the rough wool. She had tied a thick white scarf around her head, and on her feet she had a pair of secondhand men's leather work boots, worn and misshapen but obtained for a good price at the market.

She placed the fish on the table until Dimitra was appeased enough to acknowledge it.

Dimitra stood for a while longer, eyeing Joyce suspiciously. "I teach you to swim and you try to drown me," she muttered. "Why have you taken so long to visit?"

"Mama, it's only been just over two weeks. You banished me yourself, you know." Joyce looked up at her. "You told me never to come to your house again."

"Don't tell me what I said, I know it perfectly well," Dimitra snapped. Finally she pulled up a chair and sat opposite Joyce. Her eyes flickered to Joyce's jeans, but she made no comment.

"So, they tell me you are staying with Widow Kofa," she said at last. "Is she treating you well?"

Joyce glanced at her furtively. It was impossible to tell what Dimitra knew about Maria. Like many Greeks, Dimitra had perfected the art of the stony face. They should speak of Greek inscrutability, she thought, not Oriental.

"Yes, Mama, she is treating me well. She's taught me to sew and embroider. I market for her as well."

Dimitra reached over and pinched Joyce's upper arm, just as she had when they'd first met.

"You are growing flabby. You are not working hard enough." She snorted. "That widow is making you lazy."

"Mama," Joyce said gently. "Are you well? How are you managing without me to help?"

Dimitra turned away, her square, gray-haired head tilted defiantly. "I managed for the first sixty years of my life without you. There is no need to think you are so important. I need no one!" She almost shouted the last phrase and stood abruptly.

But Joyce was not hurt. Dimitra's protest was so transparent that she was only touched by it. So she took a risk. "Mama, I have missed you," she said quietly, looking at Dimitra with serious eyes. And, at that moment, Joyce did need her. She needed the love and shelter of a mother, no matter how cruel.

Dimitra grunted and walked a circle in the room, fighting her longing to hug Joyce. Why was it, she wondered, that her family, her husband, her son, her daughter by default — the very people she loved the most in the world — made her angrier than anybody else? Why couldn't she reserve her anger for her enemies? Love should protect one from the savagery of fury. Instead, it seemed only to inflame it.

At last she turned to Joyce and stared at her, her hooded eyes glittering. This upstart, this foreigner, this American who had fallen into her life like a plummeting star, who had turned everything upside-down, lied to her, displaced her love for her own son, made her criticize him — who was she to ask for forgiveness? Joyce sat there, looking small and frail under her layers of mismatched clothes. Her eyes, dark green in the shadowy room, followed Dimitra pleadingly. The firelight flickered over her skin, making her look smooth and golden like a baby, like Natalia before she was aged by starvation and torture. A great sob rose up through Dimitra. It tore at her heart, her throat. A sob of sorrow and regret, and of terrible, agonizing remorse.

"Come," she croaked at last. "Come, my little one. Give your old mama a hug." She held out her wrinkled arms, encased as they were in scratchy wool. "Come," she commanded.

And Joyce once again walked into the shelter of Dimitra's clumsy, begrudging love.

An hour later, the two women were huddled by the fire, spinning wool, as in the old times. They said little. It was enough to be together again, the mounds of bright wool dwindling on their laps, the spindles swelling in their hands, and to bask in the luxury of a lively fire on a day of rain and wind. In fact, they were far from warm. Their knees were warm, perhaps, their faces too, as long as they leaned forward over their work. But their backs shivered, as if ice were constantly being slipped down their necks. Dimitra complained that her joints ached and creaked like an old door. "Every year it is harder," she said. "It is driving me to my grave."

"Mama, don't say such things," Joyce replied automatically. "You are as strong as a woman half your age. You'll probably outlive me."

Dimitra puffed out her lips to ward off any bad luck Joyce's comment might bring upon her. "From your lips to the ear of God," she muttered. Then she heaved a deep sigh, put her spinning down on her lap, and looked at Joyce intently.

"*Koroulamou*, I have something I wish to tell you. I am getting old — no, it is no use denying it. I have eaten my bread and burned my oil. I wish to be a grandmother before I die, but never mind that now." She crossed herself quickly. "Little one, are you listening?"

Joyce nodded, looking at her in surprise. It wasn't like Dimitra to be so morbid.

"You see my mother's pillows?" Dimitra said, gesturing to the pile of cushions in the corner. They were made of thick, woven wool, dyed with beets until deepened to the color of blood. Their bold brown and green patterns had always reminded

Joyce of the Navajo blankets she used to see in Indian trading post stores at home. "They are all I have left of my mother," Dimitra went on. "I have always refused to throw them out, even thought my neighbors say they reek of Ottoman murder. They were her dowry, did I tell you that?"

Joyce shook her head, wondering where this was leading.

"Yes. They are made of the kilims she wove as a virgin to express her love for her husband to be, my no-good father. Just as we Greeks spend months sewing petticoats and beautiful dresses and linens for our dowry trunks, my mother's people weave carpets. The more a girl loves her fiancé, the bigger and more beautiful she will make her kilim." Dimitra chuckled. "The Turks have a saying: No food for the woman who cannot weave a carpet."

Dimitra sighed and drifted off into a dream, her deep eyes staring at the fire.

"But what is it, Mama?" Joyce said. "What is it about your pillows?"

Dimitra looked at her blankly for a moment, then took a deep breath. "Yes. Listen closely, *koroulamou*. Inside those pillows I have buried the few small treasures I have gathered in my life. Nobody but you knows about this. In the big one there I have sewn the only sovereigns I have managed to save in case my Petros dies, God protect him. In the red-and-blue one is my mother's wedding ring and the silver cross Petros gave to me when Nikos was born. Everything else I owned was stolen, or I had to trade for food in the war. When the Lord chooses to take me to heaven, *pedhi mou*, I want you to bury these pillows with me. Put a gold sovereign on each of my eyes so that I can pass through the gates of death in peace. Lay the cross on my chest, my hands holding it. My mother's ring I want on my finger to help me find her in the next world. Unbraid my hair, little Joyce, and spread it on the smallest pillow, which I want under my head. I tell you these things because Nikos may be away at sea when my time comes, Petros is old himself, and because you are the only daughter I have."

Dimitra stopped talking, as if out of breath, and stared at Joyce expectantly. "Promise me you will do these things?"

Joyce looked away. She wanted to please the old woman, to show that she recognized how much Dimitra had honored her with this request, but what could she say? If she agreed to this she would be promising to live with her again. Could she make such a promise? Yes, she still longed for her old peaceful life in this house. For the warm refuge of her in-laws' affection, and for the absorbing routine of work on their farm. But at the same time the thought of returning here and waiting again for Nikos's mercurial love filled her with dread.

She gazed at the fire, too torn to answer.

Dimitra turned her back, humiliated by Joyce's silence. But she decided to say no more about it. She was too proud to beg.

"I have a letter from Nikos," she said at last, heaving herself to her feet. "It came yesterday. You must read it yourself." Picking up an envelope from the high wooden shelf in the corner, she thrust it at Joyce. "Here. Petros has read it to me. It is important. But little one?"

"Yes, Mama?" Joyce looked at her questioningly.

"Prepare yourself, *koroulamou*. It is not what you expect."

Joyce nodded. Reluctantly, she unfolded the airmail envelope. In badly spelled demotic Greek, Nikos had written:

Send me your blessings, *Mannamou,* for I have made a difficult decision. I have decided to give up the sea. It is not good as a life for a husband. I know now if I had not been away so much, this strangeness between me and Joyce would not have happened. I will come back and work the land with *Papas.* Or maybe take Joyce back to America so she can find me a job there and I can send you good money.

I must finish my contract here first. Then I will return. Tell Joyce I will write to her.

Your loving and obedient son, Nikos.

Joyce lowered the letter to her lap and stared at Dimitra.

"So," Dimitra said warily, "are you not happy? Is this not what you wished for?"

Joyce could say nothing, her whole body stifled by sudden revulsion. She stood, barely knowing what she was doing, and thrust the letter back at her mother-in-law as if it were burning her fingers.

Dimitra took the letter, her hands shaking. "You must convert, little one," she said urgently. "It is the only way to save your marriage. I will help you. Become a good Christian like us. You are already Christian in your soul, I know, *koroulamou*. I can tell. Then you can give me grandchildren before I die."

"But you might never get children from me, Mama," Joyce said, her voice rising. "Perhaps it is best to let Nikos find a new wife. Then she can bury you with your pillows and give you grandchildren. Not me."

"Do not say such things!" Dimitra replied sharply, but at the same time she turned to the shelf and took down another envelope. Her bumpy, twisted fingers fumbling in their eagerness, she pulled out a photograph of Nikos as a baby and handed it to Joyce.

"See how beautiful he was? Maybe your babies will be, too, God willing."

But Joyce was not looking at the picture. She was looking at the high shelf from which Dimitra had taken the envelopes. For there, peeking over its edge, was the red, white, and blue of an American airmail letter.

Joyce jumped to her feet, spilling her wool to the floor. "What's that?"

Dimitra glanced at it, then grew suddenly flustered. "It is nothing. It is part of the envelope Nikos sent his letter in. Come, pick up your spinning."

But Joyce had already stepped across the room, reached up and taken down the letter. "It's from my mother! Why didn't you tell me?"

"How . . . how would I know?" Dimitra replied, throwing up her arms. "I cannot read." But she was stammering, guilt painted all over her usually inscrutable face.

Joyce looked at the postal date. A month earlier. "How long has this letter been sitting here? Why didn't you give it to *Petheros* to take to me?" She was shouting now. "What if I hadn't come by?"

She tore open the letter. Dimitra stepped forward as if to stop her, then hesitated and stepped back again. Her body sagged. She sank into the chair, propped her elbows on her aching knees, and stared down at the cold wooden floor.

Joyce was reading, her eyes wide. Halfway through the letter she groped for her chair and sat, too. Her eyes traveled rapidly over the words, her mouth loose with dismay.

Dear Joyce,

I wonder sometimes why I bother to keep writing you. Perhaps it's a mother's way of sending strings out into the wide world, hoping to touch her daughter. Maybe you'll answer this time if I don't ask you why you haven't. Every time I write you all I get back are these angry postcards once in a while, saying you're happy. I'm glad, sweetie-pie, but why don't you ever answer my questions? Why don't you call us? You needn't explain if you don't want. Just tell me you're okay.

Not much new here to tell you since I last wrote. Ben's baby Emily is doing fine. She's got the family's blond hair. He's working as a manager at the 7-Eleven you used to buy your candy at, remember? Joey got a job working at the garage down the road. He's in love with motorcycles right now. I just hope he doesn't get himself killed.

Joyce, sweetie, I don't have the heart for this. Why didn't you even send baby Emily a present when she was born? Your own niece? I know we were against your marriage, but that was only because you were so young. Are you going to bear a grudge forever? If you're really happy with Nikos, that's all I need to know. He did seem like a nice guy. Maybe we were wrong. Maybe you did know what was right for you. We never wanted you to cut us off.

Call us. I still don't understand how you can live in a house without a phone. Please. We're sick with missing you. Your dad can't sleep, nor can I.

Don't you know that we all love you?

Your loving mother, MOM

Joyce could hardly read the last lines through her tears. But once she had finished the letter, folded it carefully and slid it back into its envelope, her sorrow had turned to fury.

"What did you do with the other letters?" she said between her teeth.

Dimitra said nothing. She only closed her eyes and began to rock in her chair.

Joyce could barely stop herself from seizing her mother-in-law by the arms and shaking her, as Dimitra had done so often to her. Instead she bent down, thrust her face into Dimitra's and shouted, "What did you do with them? I want them now!"

Dimitra shook her head, still rocking. And then, slowly, with a trembling hand, she pointed to the fire.

Joyce was running down the hill. Sliding and falling on the wet rocks, she didn't care. She ran down, scarf blown off her head by the wind, indifferent to her soaked feet and legs. She tore through the village, people staring, and dashed into the bakery.

Alex was there, of course, sweating in front of the oven — probably the only truly warm person in Kastron at that moment. He wore no sweater, only his shirt rolled up at the sleeves, the muscles of his arms straining as he pulled the oar out of the oven.

Joyce burst in with a blast of cold wind, startling him, although he was too practiced by now to tip the bread into the fire. He quickly flipped it to his aunt and stared.

"Alex, I need money," Joyce gasped in English, recklessly, forwardly, in a way she had never behaved in this village before.

"What?" Alex was frightened. She looked wild, her eyes wide, strands of hair sticking to her cheeks. Her face was red from running and the cold. "What's wrong? What's happened?"

"I have to call home. I need money for the phone. Oh, hurry! I'll explain later."

Alex patted his pockets. He had no money. He eyed his aunt's cashbox, but she was right there, staring at Joyce, then at Alex, a new light of grim understanding on her face. *The game's up,* Alex just had time to think. *The whole fucking island will know now. We'll have to get out.*

But Joyce seemed oblivious to this. Joyce, who had always been so cautious! She was hopping in agitation, jumping from foot to foot. "Please," she cried. "Just get me some money!"

"What is the matter with this girl?" Eugenia said severely. "Is it some emergency at home?"

"Yes," Alex said. "She needs to use the telephone to call her family in America. Can I borrow some money for her, Aunt Eugenia, please? I will pay you back tomorrow."

"Hah! What with? Very well, take it, though I don't know why she cannot ask her own family."

"Thank you, *Kyria* Sarafi, thank you!" Joyce said in Greek. Alex and his aunt stared as she dashed out of the bakery.

At the telephone office, Joyce's hands shook as she dialed the overseas operator. At least there was no line for the phone, as there was so often, parents having saved up their precious drachmas to call their emigrant children in London, New York, Chicago, Paris. But it still took the operator twenty minutes to get through. Joyce was sweating with impatience. Her undershirt and dress were sticking to her back. She didn't remember the time difference until the phone at last began to ring. It was the middle of the night in Florida.

Her mother answered, and at the sound of her voice, groggy and irritated, a chill splashed across Joyce's excitement. Just that impatient "Hello?" the voice coarsened by cigarettes and raspy with sleep, was enough to send her spinning back to her former wariness and resentment of her American family.

"Mom, it's Joyce." She did not sound as eager as she'd intended.

A moment's silence. Perhaps her mother was only recouping, registering her surprise, but Joyce suspected that one beat of quiet was long enough for her mother to gather all her reserve, all her coldness, and draw them around her like a skirt.

"Joyce! Why the hell didn't you call before?"

"Because my . . . ." She paused. It was hard to say this. It was hard to betray the mother she adored to the mother she didn't.

"What, sweetie? Why haven't you called us? Why didn't you send anything to Ben's baby?"

"I didn't get any of your letters, Mom. I thought you weren't answering my cards 'cause you were still mad at me. I thought you'd cut me off."

"What? You didn't get my letters?"

"No. My mother-in-law burned them all. I only saw the last one by chance."

The silence this time was different. It was a silence not only of horror but of deep condemnation. It's amazing, Joyce thought, how even over a distance of almost four thousand miles one can read the silences of one's mother.

"Joyce, come home to us. You can't live with people like that. What did that woman think she was doing?"

Joyce could not speak. Her mother's concern touched her deeply. Her throat tightened. All this time she'd thought her family was glad to be rid of her, that they never wanted to see her again. The shock of her mistake made tears gather in her eyes and slip down her cheeks.

"Send me money for a ticket, Mom, " she said when she could speak again. "Send me the money and I'll come home."

"What about Nikos? Will he come too?"

"Nikos?" He seemed so distant now, so irrelevant to all this. "No, Mom. I'll be coming back on my own."

After Joyce had hung up and stood for a time in the telephone booth, staring unseeingly at the dial, she turned to find Alex waiting for her in the vestibule. He had pulled a thick white fisherman's sweater over his baker's apron, which hung below it like a skirt, and his hands and arms were still dusted with flour. He looked, for the moment, like a huge and ungainly nurse.

"Joyce? Is everything all right?" he said, stepping forward.

She gazed at him blankly, her mistakes crowding around her like a threatening mob. I have been running away from nothing. She tried out the thought. Had that been so?

"Joyce?" Alex took her arm, for she looked pale and unsteady. It was the first time he had touched her in public, but she no longer cared. After two years of living in a glass bowl, of dodging and hiding in the shadows, she no longer gave a damn who saw her.

"Let's go back to Maria's," he said, still unable to get her to speak. "You don't look well."

Joyce turned with him, her elbow still in his hand like an old woman's, and they stumbled out of the office and into the street. Rain hit them full in the face, pelting their skin with icy needles, but Joyce felt none of it. Bending forward, they battled their way through it to Maria's door. It was early evening by now and people were out, hurrying to do their errands. Everyone stopped and stared. They tugged at one another's arms. They turned. Gaped. Nikos Koliopoulos's wife with that English boy! With an unmarried man, by herself!

In Maria's house, Alex and Joyce found themselves alone. Maria was out delivering to a customer, although probably not for long. Joyce pulled off her layers of wet wool. I won't have to dress like this anymore, she told herself. Florida is always warm. But she felt no joy at the thought.

She sat in a chair by the fire, still reeling, while Alex stoked the flames. He had tossed off his sweater and apron and looked again the young, strapping man he was. When the glow of the fire began to warm the room, he turned and crouched beside her. "Tell me what's happened," he said again. "You're frightening me being so silent like this."

Joyce shuddered. "God," she said at last. Then she told him.

"She's been burning their letters ever since you came here?"

"Yes. If only I'd tried calling them again. If only I hadn't been so proud." Her arms crept around her ribs, holding in her misery. "I wonder if Petros knew Dimitra was doing this. Oh, Alex, how could she have done that to me?"

Alex put his arms around her. "She was probably afraid you'd go back to them," he said. "Greeks know how strong family ties are. She wouldn't have done it if she hadn't loved you so much."

Joyce closed her eyes, still hugging herself. "I don't care. She's a thief."

She slid off the chair into his arms and they sat by the fire for a while, holding each other and staring into the flames. Joyce was stilled by this for the moment, suspended in his comfort and in the finality she felt settling over her. But Alex's heart was hammering with apprehension.

At last he made himself speak. "Joyce? What are you going to do? You know you can't stay here anymore. The whole village knows about us now."

"I'm going back, of course," she said dully, still staring into the fire. "My mother's going to send me the airfare. I'll fly back as soon as it gets here." She attempted a smile. "At least I won't have to be an Orthodox Christian anymore. No more praying to Saint Dimitrios!"

"But why go back?" Alex said, beginning to panic. "You always said you hated it. You told me your parents don't want you."

"I was wrong. They do. It was me who didn't want them."

"But you don't really want to live with them like a child again, do you?"

"Oh God." Joyce buried her head in her knees.

"Don't go back there, Joyce. You'll hate it. Come with me instead. We'll go wherever you want. Thessaloniki. Athens. London. Come with me."

Joyce raised her head and stared at him. The choices before her were dizzying. And they made her sick with terror.

XV

B y the end of the day, the whole village was talking about Joyce and Alex. Only Maria kept silent. Questioned by her customers all morning, she refused to divulge what had become obvious. However, there were sources enough elsewhere: Christos Zotis from the telephone office, who described the mysterious scene he had witnessed in the vestibule. The two housewives who had seen the couple together in the market. Others who had spotted them in the street that very morning. A fisherman who had watched them meet on the beach. They crept out of the alleyways — the spies, the gossips — and soon Joyce had been dissected and labeled as nothing better than that lowest of the low, an unfaithful wife.

At first Dimitra blamed it all on Petros, more accurately than she knew. "It's because you brought that English boy home, tempting her!" she railed at him. "She could not resist someone of her own tongue!"

Petros was wise enough to say nothing. He could not deny that he had thrown Joyce and Alex together often enough, but he saw no reason to believe the gossip. Nobody had proof that the two youngsters were lovers; all those dirty-minded people could easily be exaggerating, or indulging in that old pastime of small towns and villages — projecting their own sins onto outsiders. What did the stupid old gossips know anyhow?

They had not seen the love and devotion Joyce had given to Nikos over the years, or the bratty contempt he had offered her in return. Anyway, Petros understood only too well Alex's appeal to Joyce. He was from her world, after all, the modern, carefree West. Greece was simply too Eastern for her, too ancient; he could see that now. Even Nikos was steeped in the old ways. Looking back, Petros could see that Joyce had tried to fit herself into a mold too unnatural and confining for a young American like her. She had tried and tried. It wasn't surprising that she needed the occasional escape.

Petros knew better than to say any of these things to Dimitra, however. She would never accept that her way of life could be anything less than perfect. But when she began to curse Joyce, condemning her for being a duplicitous Jew and an infidel whore, he could bear it no longer.

"You burned her letters, Dimitra; you should not have done that," he told her coldly. "If you hadn't cut her off from her family, perhaps she would not have been so lonely."

"Don't try to blame me, old man! She had us, our love, she had Nikos. What did she need another family for?"

"You cannot kidnap a person like that," Petros replied. "You took her past, you took her religion. Nikos took her love. What did you expect?"

"I expected her to do what I have done!" Dimitra shouted back at him. "What all we women have done! To bow to our duty and put our necks in the yoke. And, yes, to leave our mothers for our husbands' families! It is what God has created us for!"

"God has not created us to be slaves," Petros said quietly. "If He had, why would He give us the love of freedom?"

"To torture us!" Dimitra replied fiercely. "Anyway, freedom does not mean becoming a whore." She spat, turned her back, and refused to speak of the matter again.

In the depths of her soul, however, Dimitra knew that she and Joyce were equal partners in their deceptions. Dimitra had burned Joyce's letters, Joyce had betrayed Dimitra's son. Each had done harm to the other, lied and dissembled. They had trampled one another's trust.

Now that Joyce had been labeled an unfaithful wife by the villagers of Kastron, she was in serious danger. Dimitra might have her arrested. She might be dragged before the courts, driven out of town, beaten or stoned. Joyce felt defiant, even scornful about all this, but nevertheless she dared not walk the streets alone. So she hid in Maria's house, thankful that Nikos was far away, and waited for her parent's money.

The only friend who came to see her during this time was Marina. Her face hidden by her scarf, her blond braid tucked out of sight, she knocked furtively on Maria's back door, as if visiting a prisoner. "I cannot stay for long," she said when Joyce let her in. She refused offers of food or a chair but stood, bundled in her shawl, and looked sorrowfully into Joyce's face.

"I have tried in my heart to understand," she said at last, "but it is difficult. You had the most beautiful man in the village. He adored you. Why wasn't that enough?"

Joyce looked down at her fingers. She could not explain, not even to Marina. Anything she said — about her love that had died, about Nikos's unwelcome caresses, about their battle of wills — would only make her sound spoiled, a child. These were the conditions of marriage for almost every Greek woman she knew. Many other women, too; perhaps even her own mother.

"I fell in love with Alex" was all she could think to say. "And Nikos was never here."

Marina tossed her head impatiently. "You are too American for me, my friend. I'm sorry to say it, but your heart is greedy." She leaned forward, her face flushed. "Don't you understand that I would give my right hand for a life like yours? A family that loves you? That treats you like a daughter? The only thing I have that you don't is my Yiannis. What did you need a lover for?"

"For my survival," Joyce replied, and her eyes flashed.

Marina stared, blinking. Then, slowly, she held out her hand. "Come. You are confused and I'm sorry for you, but I do not wish to part enemies. Perhaps one day you will come back a rich tourist and you can look me up in the village. I'll be a toothless old woman then, watching over my grandchildren and weaving my baskets. Perhaps you will buy one to remember your old friend by."

Joyce shook Marina's hand, too agitated to reply. The picture Marina had just drawn was abhorrent to her. A rich tourist! It made Joyce realize, more than anything that had happened yet, just how much of an outsider here she had always been.

"You have been good to me, Marina," she said, when she could speak again. "I longed to tell you everything, but I didn't dare. I never wanted to keep all these secrets from you. Please believe me."

Marina nodded. "*Andheeo,* my friend," she said. "I will pray for you." And she slipped out the door.

Alex, by contrast, hardly suffered at all. The men of the village ribbed him admiringly, chuckling and nudging. The women took to casting him looks of disapproving admiration. He seemed seductive to them now, whereas before he had been merely awkward.

"I was wondering why you weren't visiting the brothel," Stratis the butcher told him when Alex stopped by to pick up some sausages for his aunt. "I was asking myself, is this a man or a pansy? Now I understand. A pretty piece of meat you've sliced for yourself!"

"That's enough, Stratis," Alex said frowning. "It's not what you think."

Stratis shook Alex's hand, beaming. "I will look you up when I get to Chicago, yes? There you will find me lots of pretty *puttanas* like your little American, agreed?"

Alex sighed. "*Ai gamisou* — fuck you — as you like to say, Stratis. I keep telling you, I come from England."

Alex was disgusted by all this snickering praise. He found it so two-faced and sordid that he actually welcomed his aunt's condemnation. "I thought my own nephew would behave better than this," she said severely. "You are a disgrace to your mother. And you have brought a bad name to our family." Finally she uttered words no Greek will say unless driven to extremes: "I think it is time for you to go home."

Alex broke the promise he had made his parents to support himself and cabled them for money to pay for his return, claiming an emergency. When it arrived, he handed over the baker's oar and apron to Eugenia, apologizing, although he was sorry only for leaving her on a bad note, not for what he had done. Then he said farewell to his awestruck cousins and went upstairs to pack and wait for Joyce. She had agreed to travel to Athens with him. From there, she'd said, she would decide what to do next.

Joyce's money order arrived the next day, for six hundred dollars' worth of drachmas. It was more money than Dimitra and Petros saw in two years, sometimes longer, and it made Joyce ashamed. It seemed stained, like ransom money, like hush money. Money sent to save her from her sins.

To turn the money order into cash Joyce had to go to the local bank, and that meant venturing outside. She couldn't ask Maria to walk with her, because, even though Maria had been kind, it was a liability to be seen with Joyce now and she had her own reputation to protect. Alex would have drawn more stares and hostility. So she asked Petros.

Petros had been more attentive than ever since Joyce's exposure. He had assured her that he'd known nothing of the letters Dimitra had burned, and he'd visited her every day, walking with her outside so that she could get fresh air and would not feel too much of a prisoner. He met the eyes of the villagers calmly, staring them down before they turned their backs on Joyce and hurried away. He ushered her into shops and did the marketing for her, because every shopkeeper in town refused to serve her. And he held her elbow protectively as old women and housewives sneered, whispered, and spat on the ground at her feet. He liked his role as her cavalier, walking beside her, his head up high, daring anyone to accost or insult her. He liked showing these old sourpusses that he believed in her faithfulness, even if they didn't. Above all, he liked reminding them what hypocrites they were, especially the men.

Joyce walked beside him, aware of his defiant glares, although her own eyes were fixed to the ground. It was not that she agreed with the village rules or with the laws of Greece. Nor was it that she thought the villagers right, even though she understood how their narrow lives led them to treat her so. It was that she was ashamed of having deceived the people who trusted and loved her, especially Petros. So ashamed she could not bring herself to look at anybody.

When they reached the bank, Petros went to conduct business elsewhere. "Wait for me here after you get your money, *koroulamou*," he said. "Do not go out until I come back."

Joyce agreed and approached a teller, who was half-hidden behind a wooden counter and an old iron grate. She tried to ignore the whispers and stares of the other people in the bank.

"*Kalimera*," she said, and pushed the money order under the bars. "I need this changed into cash, please."

The teller, a skinny boy with boot-polish black hair, scrutinized the paper. Then he slowly shook his head. "*Kyria* Koliopoulou, your husband has not signed the back of this."

"Of course not. It's made out to me. From my parents in America."

"But you have no account here."

Joyce flushed. The married women of Kastron did not have their own bank accounts. As Maria had pointed out, all their money, all their property, belonged to their husbands. If their men were away, they kept their drachmas in pots or dowry trunks, or in the stuffing of their mattresses.

"I do not need an account. It is a money order, not a check. Look. It's as good as cash."

The teller shook his head again, his dark eyebrows drawing together. "I am sorry, *Kyria*. I am not permitted to give you cash without your husband's signature."

"But he's away at sea!" Joyce broke into a sweat. "Let me speak to the manager. You cannot stop me taking money my own parents have sent me!"

The manager, a fat man with a thick mustache, was no more helpful than his subordinate. "I am sorry, *Kyria,* these are the rules," he declared, and Joyce wondered if this was a punishment, like the ostracism that she was suffering in the streets. "You must go home until your husband returns. When he signs the check, we will give him the money."

"But I've told you, it isn't a check!" Joyce shouted, beside herself now. How would she escape if she couldn't get the money?

"Please calm yourself. Move over now, we need to serve the next customer."

Joyce waited miserably in a chair until Petros came back. "What is the matter, little one?" he asked when he saw her face. When she explained, he was enraged.

"What is the meaning of this?" he called to the manager, storming over to the fat man's desk.

"I am sorry, *Kyrie* Koliopoulos," the manager said firmly. "I do not make the bank's rules. We cannot give cash to anyone who does not have an account with us."

Petros glared at him. "You disgust me with this treatment," he said with cold dignity. "I, Petros Koliopoulos, who have known you since you drooled on your mother's tits! You are prepared to insult my family with these idiocies? I will tell your uncles, your father. You will be disgraced!"

The bank manager rubbed his hands anxiously. He glanced

at his other customers. "Please, *Kyrie* Koliopoulos. I mean no insult. It is simply the rules."

"You are filled with as much shit as a baby's diapers," Petros snorted. "I will take responsibility for this money. I am head of the household. It is as good as mine!"

"But your name is not on this check . . ."

"You testicles of a chicken, this is not a check!"

After a long, vicious argument, the manager at last gave in and handed the money over to Petros — not Joyce — in a great wad of worn drachma notes.

"I now give them to my daughter-in-law," Petros said loudly. And, right under the bank manager's nose, he ceremoniously handed them to Joyce.

She stood for a moment, clasping the faded paper notes in her fingers. They were crumpled and thin, as flimsy as a pile of tissue paper. Yet they had the power to rocket her off this island, over land and sea, away from this peasant life forever.

The day she and Alex left was cold and gray. Petros saw them off at the ferry, as did Eugenia, who, now that she had actually driven out her nephew, was full of sorrow at seeing him go. She stood beside Petros, no taller than he, her hard mouth turned down to hide her affection. Alex had been such a sweet boy, and he had worked so hard. He may not have known it, but he'd saved her a fortune in assistant's wages.

Petros said nothing. For the first time in more than two years he hugged Joyce. He had no words for this moment. He knew she had to leave, now that she had been condemned by the village, and he knew it was best for her to go. She needed to find a life where she would be free from Nikos and his arrogant demands, and free from Dimitra, who would crush her if she could, if only with her love. Even so, he adored Joyce, and his tired heart was aching. His rheumy eyes became moist as he hugged her, but his silence remained unbroken. He pressed into her hands all he had to give: his worry beads, brown clay, not even pretty, but worn and shiny from the constant working of his fingers.

Joyce took them and kissed him on his surprisingly soft, crumpled cheeks, then hugged him again, one last time. She felt how bony he was in her arms, like some quick, fragile animal, and suddenly she knew that she would never see Petros again, that he would die soon, worn out by his begrudging patch of land, his troublesome son, even perhaps by his accepting Maria. Worn out, above all, by his unyielding rock of a wife.

"*Andheeo*, my father," she whispered, then turned to step on the boat with Alex.

The last sight Joyce had of her Greek family was Petros, dwindling on the dock until he looked like any small peasant, bundled in shabby layers of clothes, his cloth cap shading his eyes, his face gnarled and tight as a nut. Behind him, the white houses of the village straggled upwards, like so many dice tossed out of a box. They ascended the mountain, gleaming under the gray October sky, up to the bare rocks above. Where, in a small stone house, sat Dimitra, her back turned deliberately to the harbor, her arms clutching her plump belly, locked away in stubborn solitude.

As the ferry chugged towards the mainland, Joyce leaned with Alex against the railing and watched Ifestia slowly shrink to a small bump on the horizon. Already, her Greek life was becoming separate and self-contained, like a glass ornament set upon a shelf. Already, she could sense that her time here would crystallize to a memory, as distant and remote as if it had happened to somebody else. It would become nothing but a story, although a story that had left its scars.

What she could not foresee was whether she would remember her time on Ifestia as an aberration, or whether she would spend the rest of her life longing to recapture it.

She was so full of these thoughts that when Alex tried to talk to her, she didn't hear. She was too dazed, her mind seething and pitching like the waves beneath her feet. Eventually he gave up, took her hand, and pulled her inside. She followed him blindly. Everything she did now was new. Her body felt raw, stripped by it. Holding Alex's hand in front of people. Wearing her jeans, soft now with use, with a shirt instead of hidden beneath a dress. Moving among the men of the crew without raising eyebrows or being pinched. Even the soldiers on the boat acted diffident, taking her for Alex's wife. She felt unbalanced by so much change, like a glider under whose wings the wind had suddenly dropped away.

Once, before they left the deck, she looked down at her wedding ring and began to pull it off. Alex stopped her. "Not yet," he said. "It might help in hotels."

She agreed, but it weighed heavily. The last link in the chain that held her to Nikos. She wanted to throw it overboard.

The boat docked in Kavala, where they caught a slow, rickety bus to Thessaloniki. This at least was familiar to Joyce, the bus full of strong-smelling peasants, the stink of exhaust making her feel queasy as they lurched along the gravelly road. But once they reached Thessaloniki, her giddiness reemerged. She hadn't been in a city this big since she had passed through it with Nikos on her way to Ifestia. She found herself clutching Alex for balance as they crossed streets and lugged their bags on and off buses. Her eyes stung with smog and dirt. The noise made her head ache: the blast of car horns, the screech of brakes, people shouting with no sense of shame or propriety. Nowhere could she hear the lap of waves or the gentle singing of cicadas, the bleat of a goat or the snuffle of a donkey. She fell silent, not wanting to add her own voice to the cacophony.

When Alex said they must find a hotel, she became worried about money. "I have to keep enough to fly home," she said.

Her words pained Alex. But he made himself reply, "Don't worry. We'll find something cheap."

The hotel they found looked decent, but they were alarmed when the proprietor told them that three extra beds were in their room to share with other guests. "No, I wanted a private room, one double bed only," Alex said, but once the man named the price they had to change their minds. Alex slipped him a few extra drachmas. "Keep out any other guests if you can," he said. It would be the first night he and Joyce had ever spent together. He did not want it witnessed by strangers.

The hotel was shabby but tolerably clean. Joyce said it stank, although Alex smelled nothing but the faint odor of feces and ammonia common to so many Greek buildings. The wooden stairs leading up to their room were narrow and painted a dark brown. The room itself was large, papered in faded pink and gold, with a French window, frilly nylon curtains, and a tiny balcony overlooking a side street — it had a sort of decaying grandeur, like the room of a classy call girl past her prime. An oil heater smoked quietly in the corner.

"I better open the window a bit," Alex said, "or we might get poisoned."

He was suddenly shy, as if he had taken Joyce out on a first date.

Joyce sat on the double bed, which creaked on rusted springs and sagged in the middle. She peeled back the cover to check for bugs, but the sheets looked clean, if worn. She, on the other hand, felt filthy, her hair sticky from the sea breeze, her skin layered with grease and exhaust. Above all, she felt disoriented and furtive, a convict on the lam.

Having opened the window a crack and pushed its flimsy curtains aside, Alex sat gingerly beside her. The bed's creaks turned to groans. "I hope this holds us up," he said, grinning awkwardly. "Our own bed, all night, for the first time," he added, looking at her.

Joyce gazed at his face, eager and bright under his shaggy hair, barely listening. The finality of what she had done was still dawning upon her. She had cut all her ties: No husband. No in-laws. No work. Far away, over seas and oceans, lay one place she could go, but her childhood home seemed as foreign to her now as someone else's dream. Before her sat Alex, offering to take her to other places even more foreign. All the possibilities unfolded before her: Her deadening family in Florida. The unknowns of Athens or London. Or none of those, just flight, somewhere, anywhere, by herself. None of these choices seemed more compelling than any other. They seemed equally attractive and repellent, feasible and impossible.

That night she and Alex ate in a dark taverna, a cheap place with only two dishes on display in the kitchen. If it hadn't been so cold they would have contented themselves with *souvlaki* eaten on a bench, but the wind was too bitter to allow them to sit outside. They chose roast chicken, heavily spiced with oregano and chopped up in odd, haphazard shapes, the likes of which no American butcher would have recognized; then they took a table by the window, the only people in the room. Joyce was silent, withdrawn, still trying to hold together the threads of her unraveling life. Alex watched her, concerned. He had hoped she would be jubilant by now, or at least in a romantic mood. Instead she seemed more troubled than ever.

"Are you all right?" he asked her at last, pouring them each a warming glass of red wine.

Joyce stared down at her plate. The chicken was tough, the rice heavy. She had forgotten how bad restaurant food could be compared to Dimitra's cooking.

"I don't know," she said. The wine was loosening her hold on herself, letting her emotions leak. Her throat ached. She took Petro's worry beads from her pocket. "I'll never see Petros or Dimitra again," she said, quietly fingering them. "I feel like I've lost everything."

Alex reached across the grease-stained tablecloth for her hand. He had been worried that she might seem diminished away from the romance of her captivity, that she might begin to seem like an ordinary woman. But her silence, her preoccupation, only stirred his love more deeply. It was he who felt diminished, he realized, for he seemed to have become irrelevant to her, a presence she could barely hear or see.

"Joyce, don't say that. You haven't lost everything. You've only freed yourself."

"I've failed, Alex. I wanted to make a life here and I've failed."

"Don't look at it like that. It wasn't a life, it was a dream. It would never have worked. And you're not alone, don't forget that. You've got me."

Joyce frowned at him, the candlelight dancing over her cheeks, the shadows of her eyelashes stretching across them like tribal marks. "I can't run from man to man, Alex," she said quietly. "I've got to figure things our for myself."

But that night, in bed, she belied her own words. She was still too frightened to be that independent. She clung to Alex, her body tense and closed down. "I can't," she whispered when he tried to make love to her. She was feeling too dismantled to open herself physically, her emotions like a jigsaw puzzle that had been strewn across a floor. She needed to gather each piece of herself close and hold it tight.

For a long time that night, Joyce lay awake. She had never slept next to any man but Nikos before, and she felt tense, invasive and lonely, as if she had sneaked into the bed of a stranger. Alex seemed to be asleep, but she dared not move. She didn't want him to wake up and ask her what was wrong; she didn't want to be forced to explain. What am I doing in this stinky hotel in a city I don't even know? she caught herself thinking. She felt more alone than ever, more alone than even during her first weeks in Dimitra's house, when Nikos had sailed away over the sea.

On the train to Athens the next day, as it chugged south through the scrubby countryside, the Aegean a brilliant turquoise strip in the distance, Alex told Joyce about his friends in Athens. He had a whole group of them from his years of studying there every summer since he was thirteen. "I can't wait for you to meet them," he said, his blue eyes alight with anticipation. "They're amazing blokes, all of them, 'specially Dimitrios. He got his skull broken demonstrating against the Colonels in 'seventy-two, did I tell you?" Joyce could hear a note of wistfulness in Alex's voice. "You'll like him. He's fantastic."

Alex was eager for Joyce to like not only his friends but Athens itself. Others complained of its dirt and noise and the cheap, modern ugliness that was swallowing up the ancient beauty of the city, but Alex thought it the most vital place he had been in his life. He loved the rough manners of Athenians, shouting and bargaining and honking at one another in their cars. The outdoor restaurants tucked down side streets, covered with lush vine arbors to shelter them from smog and sun. He loved in particular the juxtaposition of the majesty of the Parthenon, shining in the sun like polished bones upon its hill, with the dirt and rubble of the streets below — humanity, as he saw it, at its greatest and its worst. He wanted Joyce to fall in love with Athens, as he had.

When they arrived at the end of the day, Alex telephoned Dimitrios from the station and asked for a bed. Joyce would have preferred to avoid strangers — she felt vulnerable and shy after her village life — but they had to save money and she was curious to meet Alex's hero. So she tried to smile when he told her that they were welcome.

"Come on," he said enthusiastically, grabbing her suitcase. "Let's go to his place for tonight, then tomorrow I'll take you out to see the sights."

Alex's plan was to keep Joyce so busy that she had no time to think herself away from him. He hoped to seduce her with Athens, overwhelm her with excitement until she was in such a whirl that she would follow him anywhere.

Dimitrios turned out to be a swarthy young man with a large, square head, dark eyes, and a black mustache. His torso

was long and supple, but Joyce was surprised by the short-
ness of his legs. "Alexandros, where were you all summer?" he
shouted when he opened the door. He wrapped his arms
around Alex, not unlike a boy hugging a tree. "We have missed
you so much! A summer without Alexandros is empty and
sad!"

Alex blushed. "It's all her fault." He turned to Joyce proudly.
"Dimitrios, meet Joyce . . ." He hesitated, suddenly embarrassed. He could not bear to use her married name. "Perlman,"
he added awkwardly.

Dimitrios shook Joyce's hand, looking her up and down as if
she were a cut of beef, then immediately lost interest. "Come
in," he said jovially to Alex. "I have a corner you can sleep in
and an extra mattress to put on the floor. I am sure you are hungry, yes? Alexandros, wait till you see who I have lined up to go
out with us tonight!"

The next five days passed in a blur for Joyce. In the mornings, Alex took her to see the city. They climbed the Acropolis.
Strolled down streets rich and poor. Drifted through museums,
talking about what they saw, about Alex's Athenian friends —
about everything but what mattered most to them both, their
future. Joyce let Alex take her hand as they walked, listening as
he explained paintings and sculptures to her, knowledge he
had picked up from his mother as much as from his studies.
Joyce gazed at the stark white statues, the intricate figures on
vases and plates, the Minoan, the Mycenaean, the Classical
Greek artifacts, and fell into a humbled silence. Alex was her
own age, but he knew so much more than she. The world was
full of beauty, history, stories and myths, none of which she
knew anything about. At first she was awed by all she saw. But
as the days wore on, she began to feel suffocated by it, op-
pressed by her own ignorance.

The nights were no better. They spent every evening with
Dimitrios and Alex's other friends, getting drunk and arguing

about matters such as the latest crisis in Cyprus and whether the United States and England were Greece's allies or foes. All night long, it seemed to Joyce, she was dragged from restaurant to *kaphenio,* taverna to somebody's home, the outside air dark and cold, the indoor air hot and smoky. She worried about the money they were spending, although it was all Alex's — he had grown reckless in his excitement, as if, she sometimes suspected, he wanted to strand himself in Athens. Yet he was gentle, too, attentive, except when distracted by his friends. He talked to her quietly and comfortably during their days alone, and coaxed her to love every night. She knew she was lucky. Still, she felt increasingly groggy and hungover, sleeping badly on Dimitrios's lumpy mattress when she did sleep, staggering through the days, then returning to the smoke and booze every night. She felt as if she'd been kidnapped. Drugged and kidnapped.

Alex's friends were a tight group of men who were opinionated, loud, and madly in love with one another's company. Like Dimitrios, they had all demonstrated against the Colonel's regime as students and still liked to boast of their exploits, to argue and drape their arms over one another's shoulders. Often they grew angry, swearing never to speak to one or another of the company again, leaping to their feet, threatening, swinging their arms. But it never seemed to make any difference. The next night they were at it again, as intoxicated with each other as ever.

Joyce sat on the periphery of all this, the lone woman, ignored by everyone but Alex. He tried to draw her into the discussions, but she resisted, too intimidated by her outsider's status and her own uncertainties. It was not that she had nothing to say. Her mind was full of retorts and questions as she listened to the men, but she was too unsure of herself to speak them aloud. She listened to them argue about dictatorship and remembered Maria's words about freedom. She watched them puff themselves up as they traded stories of being clubbed by the police or dragged off to jail, and thought of the women of the Resistance, whose heroism nobody boasted of in bars.

The men formed a circle that shrank tighter and tighter, totally absorbed in one another, placing her aside like an emptied pot of soup.

"Why don't you join in?" Alex asked her one evening while his friends were discussing the Junta. "You have plenty to say about this. I've heard you."

Joyce shook her head. "I can't," she said hastily. "Your friends make me feel dumb."

Nevertheless, she envied these fellows. She envied the confidence with which they proclaimed their opinions, made jokes, interrupted, and insisted. She also envied their courage, the fact that every one of them — like Maria, Dimitra, and Petros — had risked his life for a cause. She knew this confidence came from experience, education, and the certainty of their political beliefs. If only she were able to be like them, instead of sitting there tongue-tied like some idiot child. If only she were able to feel the ease she could hear in their voices, the power she could see in the tilt of their heads. Soon her mind began to fill with the same dreams she'd had at Maria's. As she sat pushed outside the men's circle, her chair behind theirs, their backs locked against her — even Alex was guilty of this sometimes — she began to play a game to entertain herself. She pictured herself sitting at the head of the table in the place of one of these men. She saw an audience hanging on her every phrase, their eyes ablaze with inspiration. She imagined herself uttering words of wisdom and revolution.

On the outside she might be nothing but an attachment to Alex, a decoration, a tagalong. But on the inside she longed to be somebody worth listening to.

Then, one evening, as she listened to Alex argue about the origins of democracy, a favorite subject among Greeks, Joyce found herself watching him as if from a great distance. His face was absorbed and flushed with fervor. His lean body was tilted over the table, lithe and strong, capable of anything. His words were eloquent, decisive. Confidence radiated from the set of his shoulders to the steadiness of his long hands.

Alex is wonderful, she realized. He is everything a person should be. I want to be like him.

"Joyce, isn't this an amazing city?" he said to her the next day as they climbed Lykavittos Hill to see the view. He was still full of the previous night's conversation, giddy with it, fueled by the thrill of argument and triumph. He swept his arms over the scenery, a mass of concrete and cars. "Isn't it just packed with life?" He turned to her, his face glowing. "Isn't it exciting?"

Joyce squinted through the smog. Below her lay a jumble of gray houses, some light, some dark, many of them dusty and dilapidated. The roads were crammed with cars weaving in every direction, their exhaust visibly pulsating into the thick, yellow air. Here and there in the rubble she could see a pool of stillness. Pale grass. A patch of orange earth. Marble ruins. A splash of dark cypresses. But her main impression was of clutter and desperation. She knew that Alex was in his element here, that he loved the noise and bustle, even the dirt — but it was not for her. After her island life she could no longer tolerate the viciousness of cities, of people piled on top of one another, scrabbling for a living. It made her feel choked.

"The people are exciting, yes," she said at last.

Alex's eager smile faded. "You don't really like it here, do you?" He stared into the distance a moment. "Look, we don't have to stay if you don't want. Not now. I don't mind going home for a while. We could go to London and get a flat. You might like London, Joyce. It's much calmer than Athens, at least most of it is. It has beautiful parks and — "

"No," she said firmly. "I don't think that's going to work. I'm sorry."

He turned to her, his face pale. "What do you mean? Are you saying you want to go home?"

She shrugged. "I don't know what home is anymore. But I want to go back to América, yes."

She lifted her eyes to him. They shone a dense green under the bright gray of the sky. "I have to start all over again. Find some other way to be. I can't be a peasant anymore."

Alex's jaw tightened. But he recovered himself quickly and began talking again, faster than ever. "You could find something here, Joyce. Or we could go to Brighton, where I went to university. You would like it there. It's a seaside town, more like what you're used to. Brighton has piles of language schools where I could teach. I'd support you, I would."

His last words were pleading, urgent, but they already trembled with the underlying presentiment of defeat.

Joyce reached over to take his wrist. "No. Can't you see?" She paused. "America isn't the end of the world," she added quietly. "You've never been there, have you? You could visit me."

Alex pressed his lips together. He looked at her for a moment, then down at his wrist, which she was holding in both hands, as if to make him understand.

That night, Joyce and Alex made love quietly on the floor of Dimitrios's living room. Alex ran his hands lingeringly over her body, trying to memorize it. The modest breasts he loved, the flare of her ribs, the sinewy muscles of her arms and legs. He kissed each part of her, this body he had wooed so passionately. Smoothed his hands over her like a blind man trying to read the future. Swore to himself with every touch that he would find her again.

Joyce, in turn, held him tenderly, inhaling the musty smell of his cheeks and the unshaven stubble on his neck. Alex might be the kindest man she would ever meet. Perhaps no one again would love her the way he did. She stroked his smooth hair, the vulnerable point of his nose, the sharp edges of his shoulder

blades. Who knew what would happen? But she was too un-
finished to settle for him or any man now. She could not, would
not, wrap her life soley around love again.

When at last she fell asleep, Joyce found herself back in a
Florida supermarket, just as she had in her dreams of long ago.
She was standing in an aisle that reached so high above her
head it curved over her like the dome of the Kastron church.
Before her were rows and rows of brightly colored objects. Plastic bottles of detergent glowed in neon reds and greens. Jewels
dangled beside toilet brushes. Snowy white gowns lay in feathery puffs next to dog bowls and tins of cat food. Joyce was
searching frantically, trying to find something for Dimitra,
something that Dimitra desperately needed. She saw lipsticks
glittering in serried rows of golden tubes, promising glamour
and late nights of wine and candlelight. She saw bottles of per-
fume, saucepans, scrubbing brushes, hair ribbons dotted with
diamonds. She saw sacks of kitty litter, barbecue bricks, cans of
roach spray, popcorn pans, silk stockings, and phosphorescent
pink ostrich feathers. She searched more and more wildly, high
on the top shelves, low among boxes and bottles and cans and
tubs, blues, oranges, pinks, yellows — among all the gaudy
colors of plastic and paint. Nothing was right. Dimitra needed
nothing here. Nothing in this place could be of the slightest use
to her.

When Alex awakened her, Joyce was still searching.